Too Much Happiness

**Center Point
Large Print**

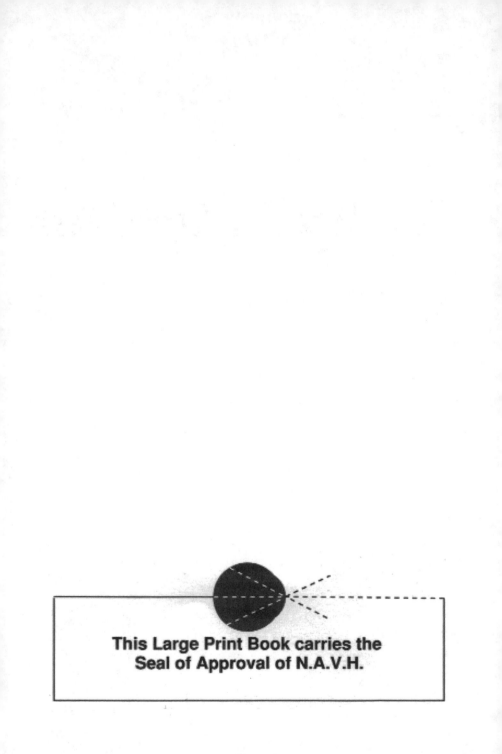

**This Large Print Book carries the
Seal of Approval of N.A.V.H.**

Too Much Happiness

Alice Munro

CENTER POINT PUBLISHING
THORNDIKE, MAINE

This Center Point Large Print edition
is published in the year 2010 by arrangement with
Alfred A. Knopf, a division of Random House, Inc.

Grateful acknowledgment is made to
The Society of Authors for permission to reprint
"Away" from *The Complete Poems of Walter de la Mare*
(London: Faber, 1969).
Reprinted by permission of The Society of Authors.
This is a work of fiction. Any resemblance to actual
persons, living or dead, events,
or locales is entirely coincidental.
The text of this Large Print edition is unabridged.
In other aspects, this book may vary
from the original edition.
Printed in the United States of America
on permanent paper.
Set in 16-point Times New Roman type.

ISBN: 978-1-60285-646-2

Library of Congress Cataloging-in-Publication Data

Munro, Alice.
  Too much happiness / Alice Munro.
     p. cm.
  ISBN 978-1-60285-646-2 (library binding : alk. paper)
  1. Large type books. I. Title.

PR9199.3.M8A6 2009b
813'.54--dc22

2009032766

To David Connelly

Contents

Dimensions

Doree had to take three buses—one to Kincardine, where she waited for the one to London, where she waited again for the city bus out to the facility. She started the trip on a Sunday at nine in the morning. Because of the waiting times between buses, it took her till about two in the afternoon to travel the hundred-odd miles. All that sitting, either on the buses or in the depots, was not a thing she should have minded. Her daily work was not of the sitting-down kind.

She was a chambermaid at the Blue Spruce Inn. She scrubbed bathrooms and stripped and made beds and vacuumed rugs and wiped mirrors. She liked the work—it occupied her thoughts to a certain extent and tired her out so that she could sleep at night. She was seldom faced with a really bad mess, though some of the women she worked with could tell stories to make your hair curl. These women were older than she was, and they all thought she should try to work her way up. They told her she should get trained for a job behind the desk while she was still young and decent looking. But she was content to do what she did. She didn't want to have to talk to people.

None of the people she worked with knew what had happened. Or, if they did, they didn't let on. Her picture had been in the paper—they'd used the picture he took of her and the three kids, the new baby, Dimitri, in her arms, and Barbara Ann and Sasha on either side, looking on. Her hair had been long and wavy and brown then, natural in curl and color, as he liked it, and her face bashful and soft—a reflection less of the way she was than of the way he wanted to see her.

Since then, she had cut her hair short and bleached and spiked it, and she had lost a lot of weight. And she went by her second name now: Fleur. Also, the job they had found for her was in a town a good distance away from where she used to live.

This was the third time she had made the trip. The first two times he had refused to see her. If he did that again she would just quit trying. Even if he did see her, she might not come again for a while. She was not going to go overboard. As a matter of fact, she didn't really know what she was going to do.

On the first bus she was not too troubled. Just riding along and looking at the scenery. She had grown up on the coast, where there was such a thing as spring, but here winter jumped almost directly into summer. A month ago there had been snow, and now it was hot enough to go bare armed. Dazzling patches of water lay in the fields, and the sunlight was pouring down through the naked branches.

On the second bus she began to feel jittery, and

she couldn't help trying to guess which of the women around her might be bound for the same place. They were women alone, usually dressed with some care, maybe to make themselves look as if they were going to church. The older ones looked like they belonged to strict old-fashioned churches where you had to wear a skirt and stockings and some sort of hat, while the younger ones might have been part of a livelier congregation which accepted pantsuits, bright scarves, earrings, and puffy hairdos.

Dorcc didn't fit into either category. In the whole year and a half she had been working she had not bought herself a single new piece of clothing. She wore her uniforms at work and her jeans everywhere else. She had got out of the way of wearing makeup because he hadn't allowed it, and now, though she could have, she didn't. Her spikes of corn-colored hair didn't suit her bony bare face, but it didn't matter.

On the third bus she got a seat by the window and tried to keep herself calm by reading the signs—both the advertising and street signs. There was a certain trick she had picked up to keep her mind occupied. She took the letters of whatever words her eyes lit on, and she tried to see how many new words she could make out of them. "Coffee," for instance, would give you "fee," and then "foe," and "off" and "of," and "shop" would provide "hop" and "sop" and "so" and—wait a minute—"posh." Words were more than plentiful on the way out of the city, as they passed billboards, monster stores, car lots, even balloons moored on roofs to advertise sales.

Doree had not told Mrs. Sands about her last two attempts, and probably wouldn't tell her about this one either. Mrs. Sands, whom she saw on Monday afternoons, spoke of moving on, though she always said that it would take time, that things should not be hurried. She told Doree that she was doing fine, that she was gradually discovering her own strength.

"I know those words have been done to death," she said. "But they're still true."

She blushed at what she heard herself say— "death"—but did not make it worse by apologizing.

When Doree was sixteen—that was seven years ago—she'd gone to visit her mother in the hospital every day after school. Her mother was recovering from an operation on her back, which was said to be serious but not dangerous. Lloyd was an orderly. He and Doree's mother had in common the fact that they both were old hippies—though Lloyd was actually a few years the younger—and whenever he had time he'd come in and chat with her about the concerts and protest marches they'd both attended, the outrageous people they'd known, drug trips that had knocked them out, that sort of thing.

Lloyd was popular with the patients because of his jokes and his sure, strong touch. He was stocky and broad shouldered and authoritative enough to be sometimes taken for a doctor. (Not that he was pleased by that—he held the opinion that a lot of medicine was a fraud and a lot of doctors were jerks.) He had sensitive reddish skin and light hair and bold eyes.

He kissed Doree in the elevator and told her she was a flower in the desert. Then he laughed at himself and said, "How original can you get?"

"You're a poet and don't know it," she said, to be kind.

One night her mother died suddenly, of an embolism. Doree's mother had a lot of women friends who would have taken Doree in—and she stayed with one of them for a time—but the new friend Lloyd was the one Doree preferred. By her next birthday she was pregnant, then married. Lloyd had never been married before, though he had at least two children whose whereabouts he was not certain of. They would have been grown up by then, anyway. His philosophy of life had changed as he got older—he believed now in marriage, constancy, and no birth control. And he found the Sechelt Peninsula, where he and Doree lived, too full of people these days—old friends, old ways of life, old lovers. Soon he and Doree moved across the country to a town they picked from a name on the map: Mildmay. They didn't live in town; they rented a place in the country. Lloyd got a job in an ice-cream factory. They planted a garden. Lloyd knew a lot about gardening, just as he did about house carpentry, managing a woodstove, and keeping an old car running.

Sasha was born.

"Perfectly natural," Mrs. Sands said.

Doree said, "Is it?"

Doree always sat on a straight-backed chair in front of a desk, not on the sofa, which had a flowery pattern and cushions. Mrs. Sands moved her own chair to the side of the desk, so they could talk without any kind of barrier between them.

"I've sort've been expecting you would," she said. "I think it's what I might have done in your place."

Mrs. Sands would not have said that in the beginning. A year ago, even, she'd have been more cautious, knowing how Doree would have revolted, then, at the idea that anybody, any living soul, could be in her place. Now she knew that Doree would just take it as a way, even a humble way, of trying to understand.

Mrs. Sands was not like some of them. She was not brisk, not thin, not pretty. Not too old either. She was about the age that Doree's mother would have been, though she did not look as if she'd ever been a hippie. Her graying hair was cut short and she had a mole riding on one cheekbone. She wore flat shoes and loose pants and flowered tops. Even when they were of a raspberry or turquoise color these tops did not make her look as if she really cared what she put on—it was more as if somebody had told her she needed to smarten herself up and she had obediently gone shopping for something she thought might do that. Her large, kind, impersonal sobriety drained all assaulting cheerfulness, all insult, out of those clothes.

"Well the first two times I never saw him," Doree said. "He wouldn't come out."

"But this time he did? He did come out?"

"Yes, he did. But I wouldn't hardly have known him."

"He'd aged?"

"I guess so. I guess he's lost some weight. And those clothes. Uniforms. I never saw him in anything like that."

"He looked to you like a different person?"

"No." Doree caught at her upper lip, trying to think what the difference was. He'd been so still. She had never seen him so still. He hadn't even seemed to know that he would sit down opposite her. Her first words to him had been "Aren't you going to sit down?" And he had said, "Is it all right?"

"He looked sort of vacant," she said. "I wondered if they had him on drugs?"

"Maybe something to keep him on an even keel. Mind you, I don't know. Did you have a conversation?"

Doree wondered if it could be called that. She had asked him some stupid, ordinary questions. How was he feeling? (Okay.) Did he get enough to eat? (He thought so.) Was there anyplace where he could walk if he wanted to? (Under supervision, yes. He guessed you could call it a place. He guessed you could call it walking.)

She'd said, "You have to get fresh air."

He'd said, "That's true."

She nearly asked him if he had made any friends. The way you ask your kid about school. The way, if your kids went to school, you would ask them.

"Yes, yes," Mrs. Sands said, nudging the ready box of Kleenex forward. Doree didn't need it; her eyes were dry. The trouble was in the bottom of her stomach. The heaves.

Mrs. Sands just waited, knowing enough to keep her hands off.

And, as if he'd detected what she was on the verge of saying, Lloyd had told her that there was a psychiatrist who came and talked to him every so often.

"I tell him he's wasting his time," Lloyd said. "I know as much as he does."

That was the only time he had sounded to Doree anything like himself.

All through the visit her heart had kept thumping. She'd thought she might faint or die. It costs her such an effort to look at him, to get him into her vision as this thin and gray, diffident yet cold, mechanically moving yet uncoordinated man.

She had not said any of this to Mrs. Sands. Mrs. Sands might have asked—tactfully—who she was afraid of. Herself or him?

But she wasn't *afraid*.

When Sasha was one and a half, Barbara Ann was born, and, when Barbara Ann was two, they had Dimitri. They had named Sasha together, and they made a pact after that that he would name the boys and she would name the girls.

Dimitri was the first one to be colicky. Doree thought that he was maybe not getting enough milk, or that her milk was not rich enough. Or too rich? Not right, anyway. Lloyd had a lady from the La Leche League come and talk to her. Whatever you do, the lady said, you must not put him on a supplementary bottle. That would be the thin edge of the wedge, she said, and pretty soon you would have him rejecting the breast altogether.

Little did she know that Doree had been giving him a supplement already. And it seemed to be true that he preferred that—he fussed more and more at the breast. By three months he was

17

entirely bottle-fed, and then there was no way to keep it from Lloyd. She told him that her milk had dried up, and she'd had to start supplementing. Lloyd squeezed one breast after the other with frantic determination and succeeded in getting a couple of drops of miserable-looking milk out. He called her a liar. They fought. He said that she was a whore like her mother.

All those hippies were whores, he said.

Soon they made up. But whenever Dimitri was fretful, whenever he had a cold, or was afraid of Sasha's pet rabbit, or still hung on to chairs at the age when his brother and sister had been walking unsupported, the failure to breast-feed was recalled.

The first time Doree had gone to Mrs. Sands's office, one of the other women there had given her a pamphlet. On the front of it was a gold cross and words made up of gold and purple letters. "When Your Loss Seems Unbearable . . ." Inside there was a softly colored picture of Jesus and some finer print Doree did not read.

In her chair in front of the desk, still clutching the pamphlet, Doree began to shake. Mrs. Sands had to pry it out of her hand.

"Did somebody give you this?" Mrs. Sands said.

Doree said, "Her," and jerked her head at the closed door.

"You don't want it?"

"When you're down is when they'll try to get at you," Doree said, and then realized this was something her mother had said when some ladies with a similar message came to visit her in the hospital. "They think you'll fall on your knees and then it will be all right."

Mrs. Sands sighed.

"Well," she said, "it's certainly not that simple."

"Not even possible," Doree said.

"Maybe not."

They never spoke of Lloyd in those days. Doree never thought of him if she could help it, and then only as if he were some terrible accident of nature.

"Even if I believed in that stuff," she said, meaning what was in the pamphlet, "it would be only so that . . ." She meant to say that such a belief would be convenient because she could then think of Lloyd burning in hell, or something of that sort, but she was unable to go on, because it was too stupid to talk about. And because of the familiar impediment, that was like a hammer hitting her in the belly.

Lloyd thought that their children should be educated at home. This was not for religious reasons—going against dinosaurs and cavemen and monkeys and all that—but because he wanted them to be close to their parents and to be introduced to the world carefully and gradually, rather than thrown into it all at once. "I just happen to think they are my kids," he said. "I mean, they are our kids, not the Department of Education's kids."

Doree was not sure that she could handle this, but it turned out that the Department of Education had guidelines, and lesson plans that you could get from your local school. Sasha was a bright boy who practically taught himself to read, and the other two were still too little to learn much yet. In evenings and on weekends Lloyd taught Sasha about geography and the solar system and the hibernation of animals and how a car runs, covering each subject as the questions came up. Pretty soon Sasha was ahead of the school plans, but Doree picked them up anyway and put him through the exercises right on time so that the law would be satisfied.

There was another mother in the district doing homeschooling. Her name was Maggie, and she had a minivan. Lloyd needed his car to get to work, and Doree had not learned to drive, so she was glad when Maggie offered her a ride to the school once a week to turn in the finished exercises and pick up the new ones. Of course they took all the children along. Maggie had two boys. The older one had so many allergies that she had to keep a strict eye on everything he ate—that was why she taught him at home. And then it seemed that she might as well keep the younger one there as well. He wanted to stay with his brother and he had a problem with asthma, anyway.

How grateful Doree was then, comparing her healthy three. Lloyd said it was because she'd had all her children when she was still young, while Maggie had waited until she was on the verge of the menopause. He was exaggerating how old Maggie was, but it was true that she had waited. She was an optometrist. She and her husband had been partners, and they hadn't started their family until she could leave the practice and they had a house in the country.

Maggie's hair was pepper-and-salt, cropped close to her head. She was tall, flat-chested, cheerful, and opinionated. Lloyd called her the Lezzie. Only behind her back, of course. He kidded with her on the phone but mouthed at Doree, "It's the Lezzie." That didn't really bother Doree—he called lots of women Lezzies. But she was afraid that the kidding would seem overly friendly to Maggie, an intrusion, or at least a waste of time.

"You want to speak to the ole lady? Yeah. I got her right here. Workin at the scrub board. Yeah, I'm a real slave driver. She tell you that?"

Doree and Maggie got into the habit of shopping for groceries together after they'd picked up the papers at the school. Then sometimes they'd get takeout coffees at Tim Hortons and drive the children to Riverside Park. They sat on a bench while Sasha and Maggie's boys raced around or hung from the climbing contraptions, and Barbara Ann pumped on the swing and Dimitri played in the sandbox. Or they sat in the mini, if it was cold. They talked mostly about the children and things they cooked, but somehow Doree found out how Maggie had trekked around Europe before training as an optometrist, and Maggie found out how young Doree had been when she got married. Also about how easily she had become pregnant at first, and how she didn't so easily anymore, and how that made Lloyd suspicious, so that he went through her dresser drawers looking for birth-control pills—thinking she must be taking them on the sly.

"And are you?" Maggie asked.

Doree was shocked. She said she wouldn't dare.

"I mean, I'd think that was awful to do, without telling him. It's just kind of a joke when he goes looking for them."

"Oh," Maggie said.

And one time Maggie said, "Is everything all right with you? I mean in your marriage? You're happy?"

Doree said yes, without hesitation. After that she was more careful about what she said. She saw that there were things that she was used to that another person might not understand. Lloyd had a certain way of looking at things: that was

22

just how he was. Even when she'd first met him, in the hospital, he'd been like that. The head nurse was a starchy sort of person, so he'd call her Mrs. Bitch-out-of-Hell, instead of her name, which was Mrs. Mitchell. He said it so fast that you could barely catch on. He'd thought that she picked favorites, and he wasn't one of them. Now there was someone he detested at the ice-cream factory, somebody he called Suck-Stick Louie. Doree didn't know the man's real name. But at least that proved that it wasn't only women who provoked him.

Doree was pretty sure that these people weren't as bad as Lloyd thought, but it was no use contradicting him. Perhaps men just had to have enemies, the way they had to have their jokes. And sometimes Lloyd did make the enemies into jokes, just as if he was laughing at himself. She was even allowed to laugh with him, as long as she wasn't the one who started the laughing.

She hoped he wouldn't get that way about Maggie. At times she was afraid she saw something of the sort coming. If he prevented her from riding to the school and the grocery store with Maggie it would be a big inconvenience. But worse would be the shame. She would have to make up some stupid lie to explain things. But Maggie would know—at least she would know that Doree was lying, and she would interpret that probably as meaning that Doree was in a worse

23

situation than she really was. Maggie had her own sharp way of looking at things.

Then Doree asked herself why she should care what Maggie might think. Maggie was an outsider, not even somebody Doree felt comfortable with. It was Lloyd said that, and he was right. The truth of things between them, the bond, was not something that anybody else could understand and it was not anybody else's business. If Doree could watch her own loyalty it would be all right.

It got worse, gradually. No direct forbidding, but more criticism. Lloyd coming up with the theory that Maggie's boys' allergies and asthma might be Maggie's fault. The reason was often the mother, he said. He used to see it at the hospital all the time. The overcontrolling, usually overeducated mother.

"Some of the time kids are just born with something," Doree said, unwisely. "You can't say it's the mother every time."

"Oh. Why can't I?"

"I didn't mean *you*. I didn't mean you can't. I mean, couldn't they be born with things?"

"Since when are you such a medical authority?"

"I didn't say I was."

"No. And you're not."

Bad to worse. He wanted to know what they talked about, she and Maggie.

"I don't know. Nothing really."

"That's funny. Two women riding in a car. First I heard of it. Two women talking about nothing. She is out to break us up."

"Who is? *Maggie?*"

"I've got experience of her kind of woman."

"What kind?"

"Her kind."

"Don't be silly."

"Careful. Don't call me silly."

"What would she want to do that for?"

"How am I supposed to know? She just wants to do it. You wait. You'll see. She'll get you over there bawling and whining about what a bastard I am. One of these days."

And in fact it turned out as he had said. At least it would certainly have looked that way, to Lloyd. She did find herself at around ten o'clock one night in Maggie's kitchen, sniffling back her tears and drinking herbal tea. Maggie's husband had said, "What the hell?" when she knocked—she heard him through the door. He hadn't known who she was. She'd said, "I'm really sorry to bother you—" while he stared at her with lifted eyebrows and a tight mouth. And then Maggie had come.

Doree had walked all the way there in the dark, first along the gravel road that she and Lloyd lived on, and then on the highway. She headed for the ditch every time a car came, and that slowed her down considerably. She did take a look at the cars that passed, thinking that one of them might be Lloyd. She didn't want him to find her, not yet, not till he was scared out of his craziness. Other times she had been able to scare him out of it herself, by weeping and howling and even banging her head on the floor, chanting, "It's not true, it's not true, it's not true" over and over. Finally he would back down. He would say, "Okay, okay. I'll believe you. Honey, be quiet. Think of the kids. I'll believe you, honest. Just stop."

But tonight she had pulled herself together just as she was about to start that performance. She had put on her coat and walked out the door, with him calling after her, "Don't do this. I warn you!"

Maggie's husband had gone to bed, not looking any better pleased about things, while Doree kept saying, "I'm sorry. I'm so sorry, barging in on you at this time of night."

"Oh, shut up," Maggie said, kind and businesslike. "Do you want a glass of wine?"

"I don't drink."

"Then you'd better not start now. I'll get you some tea. It's very soothing. Raspberry-chamomile. It's not the kids, is it?"

"No."

Maggie took her coat and handed her a wad of Kleenex for her eyes and nose. "Don't tell me anything yet. We'll soon get you settled down."

Even when she was partly settled down, Doree didn't want to blurt out the whole truth and let

Maggie know that she herself was at the heart of the problem. More than that, she didn't want to have to explain Lloyd. No matter how worn out she got with him, he was still the closest person in the world to her, and she felt that everything would collapse if she were to bring herself to tell someone exactly how he was, if she were to be entirely disloyal.

She said that she and Lloyd had got into an old argument and she was so sick and tired of it that all she'd wanted was to get out. But she would get over it, she said. They would.

"Happens to every couple sometime," Maggie said.

The phone rang then, and Maggie answered.

"Yes. She's okay. She just needed to walk something out of her system. Fine. Okay then, I'll deliver her home in the morning. No trouble. Okay. Good night.

"That was him," she said. "I guess you heard."

"How did he sound? Did he sound normal?"

Maggie laughed. "Well, I don't know how he sounds when he's normal, do I? He didn't sound drunk."

"He doesn't drink either. We don't even have coffee in the house."

"Want some toast?"

In the morning, early, Maggie drove her home. Maggie's husband hadn't left for work yet, and he stayed with the boys.

Maggie was in a hurry to get back, so she just said, "Bye-bye. Phone me if you need to talk," as she turned the minivan around in the yard.

It was a cold morning in early spring, snow still on the ground, but there was Lloyd sitting on the steps without a jacket on.

"Good morning," he said, in a loud, sarcastically polite voice. And she said good morning, in a voice that pretended not to notice his.

He did not move aside to let her up the steps.

"You can't go in there," he said.

She decided to take this lightly.

"Not even if I say please? Please."

He looked at her but did not answer. He smiled with his lips held together.

"Lloyd?" she said. "Lloyd?"

"You better not go in."

"I didn't tell her anything, Lloyd. I'm sorry I walked out. I just needed a breathing space, I guess."

"Better not go in."

"What's the matter with you? Where are the kids?"

He shook his head, as he did when she said something he didn't like to hear. Something mildly rude, like "holy shit."

"*Lloyd.* Where are the kids?"

He shifted just a little, so that she could pass if she liked.

Dimitri still in his crib, lying sideways. Barbara

Ann on the floor beside her bed, as if she'd got out or been pulled out. Sasha by the kitchen door—he had tried to get away. He was the only one with bruises on his throat. The pillow had done for the others.

"When I phoned last night?" Lloyd said. "When I phoned, it had already happened.

"You brought it all on yourself," he said.

The verdict was that he was insane, he couldn't be tried. He was criminally insane—he had to be put in a secure institution.

Doree had run out of the house and was stumbling around the yard, holding her arms tight across her stomach as if she had been sliced open and was trying to keep herself together. This was the scene that Maggie saw, when she came back. She had had a premonition, and had turned the van around in the road. Her first thought was that Doree had been hit or kicked in the stomach by her husband. She could understand nothing of the noises Doree was making. But Lloyd, who was still sitting on the steps, moved aside courteously for her, without a word, and she went into the house and found what she was now expecting to find. She phoned the police.

For some time Doree kept stuffing whatever she could grab into her mouth. After the dirt and grass it was sheets or towels or her own clothing. As if she were trying to stifle not just the howls that

29

rose up but the scene in her head. She was given a shot of something, regularly, to quiet her down, and this worked. In fact she became very quiet, though not catatonic. She was said to be stabilized. When she got out of the hospital and the social worker brought her to this new place, Mrs. Sands took over, found her somewhere to live, found her a job, established the routine of talking with her once a week. Maggie would have come to see her, but she was the one person Doree could not stand to see. Mrs. Sands said that that feeling was natural—it was the association. She said that Maggie would understand.

Mrs. Sands said that whether or not Doree continued to visit Lloyd was up to her. "I'm not here to approve or disapprove, you know. Did it make you feel good to see him? Or bad?"

"I don't know."

Doree could not explain that it had not really seemed to be him she was seeing. It was almost like seeing a ghost. So pale. Pale loose clothes on him, shoes that didn't make any noise—probably slippers—on his feet. She had the impression that some of his hair had fallen out. His thick and wavy, honey-colored hair. There seemed to be no breadth to his shoulders, no hollow in his collarbone where she used to rest her head.

What he had said, afterwards, to the police—and it was quoted in the newspapers—was "I did it to save them the misery."

What misery?

"The misery of knowing that their mother had walked out on them," he said.

That was burned into Doree's brain, and maybe when she decided to try to see him it had been with the idea of making him take it back. Making him see, and admit, how things had really gone.

"You told me to stop contradicting you or get out of the house. So I got out of the house.

"I only went to Maggie's for one night. I fully intended to come back. I wasn't walking out on anybody."

She remembered perfectly how the argument had started. She had bought a tin of spaghetti that had a very slight dent in it. Because of that it had been on sale, and she had been pleased with her thriftiness. She had thought she was doing something smart. But she didn't tell him that, once he had begun questioning her about it. For some reason she'd thought it better to pretend she hadn't noticed.

Anybody would notice, he said. We could have all been poisoned. What was the matter with her? Or was that what she had in mind? Was she planning to try it out on the kids or on him?

She told him not to be crazy.

He had said it wasn't him who was crazy. Who but a crazy woman would buy poison for her family?

The children had been watching from the

31

doorway of the front room. That was the last time she'd seen them alive.

So was that what she had been thinking—that she could make him see, finally, who it was who was crazy?

When she realized what was in her head, she should have got off the bus. She could have got off even at the gates, with the few other women who plodded up the drive. She could have crossed the road and waited for the bus back to the city. Probably some people did that. They were going to make a visit and then decided not to. People probably did that all the time.

But maybe it was better that she had gone on, and seen him so strange and wasted. Not a person worth blaming for anything. Not a person. He was like a character in a dream.

She had dreams. In one dream she had run out of the house after finding them, and Lloyd had started to laugh in his old easy way, and then she had heard Sasha laughing behind her and it had dawned on her, wonderfully, that they were all playing a joke.

"You asked me if it made me feel good or bad when I saw him? Last time you asked me?"

"Yes, I did," Mrs. Sands said.

"I had to think about it."

"Yes."

"I decided it made me feel bad. So I haven't gone again."

It was hard to tell with Mrs. Sands, but the nod she gave seemed to show some satisfaction or approval.

So when Doree decided that she would go again, after all, she thought it was better not to mention it. And since it was hard not to mention whatever happened to her—there being so little, most of the time—she phoned and cancelled her appointment. She said that she was going on a holiday. They were getting into summer, when holidays were the usual thing. With a friend, she said.

"You aren't wearing the jacket you had on last week."

"That wasn't last week."

"Wasn't it?"

"It was three weeks ago. The weather's hot now. This is lighter, but I don't really need it. You don't need a jacket at all."

He asked about her trip, what buses she'd had to take from Mildmay.

She told him that she wasn't living there anymore. She told him where she lived, and about the three buses.

"That's quite a trek for you. Do you like living in a bigger place?"

"It's easier to get work there."

"So you work?"

She had told him last time about where she lived, the buses, where she worked.

"I clean rooms in a motel," she said. "I told you."

"Yes, yes. I forgot. I'm sorry. Do you ever think of going back to school? Night school?"

She said she did think about it but never seriously enough to do anything. She said she didn't mind the cleaning work.

Then it seemed as if they could not think of anything more to say.

He sighed. He said, "Sorry. Sorry. I guess I'm not used to conversation."

"So what do you do all the time?"

"I guess I read quite a bit. Kind of meditate. Informally."

"Oh."

"I appreciate your coming here. It means a lot to me. But don't think you have to keep it up. I mean, just when you want to. If something comes up, or if you feel like it—what I'm trying to say is, just the fact that you could come at all, that you even came once, that's a bonus for me. Do you get what I mean?"

She said yes, she thought so.

He said that he didn't want to interfere with her life.

"You're not," she said.

"Was that what you were going to say? I thought you were going to say something else."

In fact, she had almost said, What life?

No, she said, not really, nothing else.

"Good."

Three more weeks and she got a phone call. It was Mrs. Sands herself on the line, not one of the women in the office.

"Oh, Doree. I thought you might not be back yet. From your holiday. So you are back?"

"Yes," Doree said, trying to think where she could say she had been.

"But you hadn't got around to arranging another appointment?"

"No. Not yet."

"That's okay. I was just checking. You are all right?"

"I'm all right."

"Fine. Fine. You know where I am if you ever need me. Ever just want to have a talk."

"Yes."

"So take care."

She hadn't mentioned Lloyd, hadn't asked if the visits had continued. Well, of course, Doree had said that they weren't going to. But Mrs. Sands was pretty good, usually, about sensing what was going on. Pretty good at holding off, too, when she understood that a question might not get her anywhere. Doree didn't know what she would have said, if asked—whether she would have backtracked and told a lie or come out with the

35

truth. She had gone back, in fact, the very next Sunday after he more or less told her it didn't matter whether she came or not.

He had a cold. He didn't know how he got it.

Maybe he had been coming down with it, he said, the last time he saw her, and that was why he'd been so morose.

"Morose." She seldom had anything to do, nowadays, with anyone who used a word like that, and it sounded strange to her. But he had always had a habit of using such words, and of course at one time they hadn't struck her as they did now.

"Do I seem like a different person to you?" he asked.

"Well, you look different," she said cautiously. "Don't I?"

"You look beautiful," he said sadly.

Something softened in her. But she fought against it.

"Do you feel different?" he asked. "Do you feel like a different person?"

She said she didn't know. "Do you?"

He said, "Altogether."

Later in the week a large envelope was given to her at work. It had been addressed to her care of the motel. It contained several sheets of paper, with writing on both sides. She didn't think at first of its being from him—she somehow had the

36

idea that people in prison were not allowed to write letters. But, of course, he was a different sort of prisoner. He was not a criminal; he was only criminally insane.

There was no date on the document and not even a "Dear Doree." It just started talking to her in such a way that she thought it had to be some sort of religious invitation:

People are looking all over for the solution. Their minds are sore (from looking). So many things jostling around and hurting them. You can see in their faces all their bruises and pains. They are troubled. They rush around. They have to shop and go to the laundromat and get their hair cut and earn a living or pick up their welfare checks. The poor ones have to do that and the rich ones have to look hard for the best ways to spend their money. That is work too. They have to build the best houses with gold faucets for their hot and cold water. And their Audis and magical toothbrushes and all possible contraptions and then burglar alarms to protect against slaughter and all (neigh) neither rich nor poor have any peace in their souls. I was going to write "neighbor" instead of "neither," why was that? I have not got any neighbor here. Where I am at least people have got beyond a lot of confusion. They know what their possessions are and always will be and they don't even have to buy or cook their own food. Or choose it. Choices are eliminated.

All we that are here can get is what we can get out of our own minds.

At the beginning all in my head was purturbation (Sp?). There was everlasting storm, and I would knock my head against cement in the hope of getting rid of it. Stopping my agony and my life. So punishments were meted. I got hosed down and tied up and drugs introduced in my bloodstream. I am not complaining either, because I had to learn there is no profit in that. Nor is it any different from the so-called real world, in which people drink and carry on and commit crimes to eliminate their thoughts which are painful. And often they get hauled off and incarcerated but it is not long enough for them to come out on the other side. And what is that? It is either total insanity or peace.

Peace. I arrived at peace and am still sane. I imagine reading this now you are thinking I am going to say something about God Jesus or at any rate Buddha as if I had arrived at a religious conversion. No. I do not close my eyes and get lifted up by any specific Higher Power. I do not really know what is meant by any of that. What I do is Know Myself. Know Thyself is some kind of Commandment from somewhere, probably the Bible so at least in that I have followed Christianity. Also, To Thy Own Self Be True—I have attempted that if is it in the Bible also. It does not say which parts—the bad or the good—to be true to so it is not intended as a guide to morality. Also Know Thyself does not relate to morality as we know it in Behavior. But Behavior is not really my concern because I have been judged quite correctly as a person who cannot be trusted to judge how he should behave and that is the reason I am here.

Back to the Know part of Know Thyself. I can say perfectly soberly that I know myself and I know the worst I am capable of and I know that I have done it. I am judged by the World as a Monster and I have no quarrel with that, even though I might say in passing that people who rain down bombs or burn cities or starve and murder hundreds of thousands of people are not generally considered Monsters but are showered with medals and honors, only acts against small numbers being considered shocking and evil. This being not meant as an excuse but just observation.

What I Know in Myself is my own Evil. That is the secret of my comfort. I mean I know my Worst. It may be worse than other people's worst but in fact I do not have to think or worry about that. No excuses. I am at peace. Am I a

Monster? The World says so and if it is said so then I agree. But then I say, the World does not have any real meaning for me. I am my Self and have no chance to be any other Self. I could say that I was crazy then but what does that mean? Crazy. Sane. I am I. I could not change my I then and I cannot change it now.

Doree, if you have read this far, there is one special thing I want to tell you about but cannot write it down. If you ever think of coming back here then maybe I can tell you. Do not think I am heartless. It isn't that I wouldn't change things if I could, but I can't.

I am sending this to your place of work which I remember and the name of the town so my brain is working fine in some respects.

She thought that they would have to discuss this piece of writing at their next meeting and she read it over several times, but she could not think of anything to say. What she really wanted to talk about was whatever he had said was impossible to put in writing. But when she saw him again he behaved as if he had never written to her at all. She searched for a topic and told him about a once-famous folksinger who had stayed at the motel that week. To her surprise he knew more than she did about the singer's career. It turned out that he had a television, or at least access to one, and watched some shows and, of course, the news, regularly. That gave them a bit more to talk about, until she could not help herself.

"What was the thing you couldn't tell me except in person?"

He said he wished she hadn't asked him. He didn't know if they were ready to discuss it.

Then she was afraid that it would be something she really could not handle, something unbearable, such as that he still loved her. "Love" was a word she could not stand to hear.

"Okay," she said. "Maybe we're not."

Then she said, "Still, you better tell me. If I walked out of here and was struck down by a car, then I would never know, and you would never have the chance to tell me again."

"True," he said.

"So what is it?"

"Next time. Next time. Sometimes I can't talk anymore. I want to but I just dry up, talking."

I have been thinking of you Doree ever since you left and regret I disappointed you. When you are sitting opposite me I tend to get more emotional than perhaps I show. It is not my right to go emotional in front of you, since you certainly have the right more than me and you are always very controlled. So I am going to reverse what I said before because I have come to the conclusion I can write to you after all better than I can talk.

Now where do I start.

Heaven exists.

That is one way but not right because I never believed in Heaven and Hell, etc. As far as I was concerned that was always a pile of crap. So it must sound pretty weird of me to bring up the subject now.

I will just say then: I have seen the children.

I have seen and talked to them.

There. What are you thinking at the moment? You are thinking well, now he is really round the bend. Or, it's a dream and he can't distinguish a dream, he doesn't know the difference between a dream and awake. But I want to tell you I do know the difference and what I know is, they exist. I say they exist, not they are alive, because alive means in our particular Dimension, and I am not saying that is where they are. In fact I think they are not. But they do exist and it must be that there is another Dimension or maybe innumerable Dimensions, but what I know is that I have got across to whatever one they are in. Possibly I got hold of this from being so much on my own and having to think and think and with such as I have to think about. So after such suffering and solitude there is a Grace that has seen the way to giving me this reward. Me the very one that deserves it the least to the world's way of thinking.

Well if you have kept reading this far and not torn this to pieces you must want to know something. Such as how they are.

They are fine. Really happy and smart. They don't seem to have any memory of anything bad. They are maybe a little older than they were but that is hard to say. They seem to understand at different levels. Yes. You can notice with Dimitri he has learned to talk which he was not able to do. They are in a room I can partly recognize. It's like our house but more spacious and nice. I asked them how they were being looked after and they just laughed at me and said something like they were able to look after themselves. I think Sasha was the one who said that. Sometimes they talk separately or at least I can't separate their voices but their identities are quite clear and, I must say, joyful.

Please don't conclude that I am crazy. That is the fear that made me not want to tell you about this. I was crazy at one time but believe me I have shed all my old craziness like the bear that sheds his coat. Or maybe I should say the snake that sheds his skin. I know that if I had not done that I would never have been given this ability to reconnect with Sasha and Barbara Ann and Dimitri. Now I wish that you could be granted this chance as well because if it is a matter of deserving, then you are way ahead of me. It may be harder for you to do because you live in the world so much more than I do but at least I can give you this information—the Truth—and in telling you I have seen them, I hope that it will make your heart lighter.

Doree wondered what Mrs. Sands would say or think if she read this letter. Mrs. Sands would be careful, of course. She would be careful not to pass an outright verdict of craziness, but she would carefully, kindly, steer Doree around in that direction.

Or you might say she wouldn't steer—she would just pull the confusion away so that Doree would have to face what would seem to have been her own conclusion all along. She would have to put the whole dangerous nonsense—this was Mrs. Sands speaking—out of her mind.

That was why Doree was not going anywhere near her.

Doree did think that he was crazy. And in what he had written there seemed to be some trace of the old bragging. She didn't write back. Days went by. Weeks. She didn't alter her opinion, but she still held on to what he'd written, like a secret. And from time to time, when she was in the middle of spraying a bathroom mirror or tightening a sheet, a feeling came over her. For almost two years she had not taken any notice of the things that generally made people happy, such as nice weather or flowers in bloom or the smell of a bakery. She still did not have that spontaneous sense of happiness, exactly, but she had a reminder of what it was like. It had nothing to do with the weather or flowers. It was the idea that the children were in what he had called their Dimension that came sneaking up on her in this way, and for the first time brought a light feeling to her, not pain.

In all the time since what had happened, any thought of the children had been something she had to get rid of, pull out immediately like a knife in her throat. She could not think their names, and if she heard a name that sounded like one of theirs she had to pull that out too. Even children's voices, their shrieks and slapping feet as they ran to and from the motel swimming pool, had to be banished by a sort of gate that she could slam down behind her ears. What was different now was that she had a refuge she could go to as soon as such dangers arose anywhere around her.

And who had given it to her? Not Mrs. Sands— that was for sure. Not in all those hours sitting by the desk with the Kleenex discreetly handy.

Lloyd had given it to her. Lloyd, that terrible person, that isolated and insane person.

Insane if you wanted to call it that. But wasn't it possible that what he said was true—that he had come out on the other side? And who was to say that the visions of a person who had done such a thing and made such a journey might not mean something?

This notion wormed its way into her head and stayed there.

Along with the thought that Lloyd, of all people, might be the person she should be with now. What other use could she be in the world—she seemed to be saying this to somebody, probably to Mrs. Sands—what was she here for if not at least to listen to him?

I didn't say "forgive," she said to Mrs. Sands in her head. I would never say that. I would never do it.

But think. Aren't I just as cut off by what happened as he is? Nobody who knew about it would want me around. All I can do is remind people of what nobody can stand to be reminded of.

Disguise wasn't possible, not really. That crown of yellow spikes was pathetic.

So she found herself travelling on the bus again, heading down the highway. She remembered those nights right after her mother had died, when she would sneak out to meet Lloyd, lying to her mother's friend, the woman she was staying with, about where she was going. She remembered the friend's name, her mother's friend's name. Laurie.

Who but Lloyd would remember the children's

names now, or the color of their eyes. Mrs. Sands, when she had to mention them, did not even call them children but "your family," putting them in one clump together.

Going to meet Lloyd in those days, lying to Laurie, she had felt no guilt, only a sense of destiny, submission. She had felt that she was put on earth for no reason other than to be with him and to try to understand him.

Well, it wasn't like that now. It was not the same.

She was sitting in the front seat across from the driver. She had a clear view through the windshield. And that was why she was the only passenger on the bus, the only person other than the driver, to see a pickup truck pull out from a side road without even slowing down, to see it rock across the empty Sunday-morning highway in front of them and plunge into the ditch. And to see something even stranger: the driver of the truck flying through the air in a manner that seemed both swift and slow, absurd and graceful. He landed in the gravel at the edge of the pavement.

The other passengers didn't know why the driver had put on the brakes and brought them to a sudden uncomfortable stop. And at first all that Doree thought was, How did he get out? The young man or boy, who must have fallen asleep at the wheel. How did he fly out of the truck and launch himself so elegantly into the air?

"Fellow right in front of us," the driver said to the passengers. He was trying to speak loudly and calmly, but there was a tremor of amazement, something like awe, in his voice. "Just plowed across the road and into the ditch. We'll be on our way again as soon as we can, and in the meantime please don't get out of the bus."

As if she had not heard that, or had some special right to be useful, Doree got out behind him. He did not reprimand her.

"Goddamn asshole," he said as they crossed the road, and there was nothing in his voice now but anger and exasperation. "Goddamn asshole kid, can you believe it?"

The boy was lying on his back, arms and legs flung out, like somebody making an angel in the snow. Only there was gravel around him, not snow. His eyes were not quite closed. He was so young, a boy who had shot up tall before he even needed to shave. Possibly without a driver's license.

The driver was talking on his phone.

"Mile or so south of Bayfield, on Twenty-one, east side of the road."

A trickle of pink foam came out from under the boy's head, near the ear. It did not look like blood at all, but like the stuff you skim off from strawberries when you're making jam.

Doree crouched down beside him. She laid a hand on his chest. It was still. She bent her ear close. Somebody had ironed his shirt recently—it had that smell.

No breathing.

But her fingers on his smooth neck found a pulse.

She remembered something she'd been told. It was Lloyd who had told her, in case one of the children had an accident and he wasn't there. The tongue. The tongue can block the breathing, if it has fallen into the back of the throat. She laid the fingers of one hand on the boy's forehead and two fingers of the other hand under his chin. Press down on the forehead, press up the chin, to clear the airway. A slight but firm tilt.

If he still didn't breathe she would have to breathe into him.

She pinches the nostrils, takes a deep breath, seals his mouth with her lips, and breathes. Two breaths and check. Two breaths and check.

Another male voice, not the driver's. A motorist must have stopped. "You want this blanket under his head?" She shook her head slightly. She had remembered something else, about not moving the victim, so that you do not injure the spinal cord. She enveloped his mouth. She pressed his warm fresh skin. She breathed and waited. She breathed and waited again. And a faint moisture seemed to rise against her face.

The driver said something but she could not look up. Then she felt it for sure. A breath out of the boy's mouth. She spread her hand on the skin of his chest and at first she could not tell if it was rising and falling because of her own trembling.

Yes. Yes.

It was a true breath. The airway was open. He was breathing on his own. He was breathing.

"Just lay it over him," she said to the man with the blanket. "To keep him warm."

"Is he alive?" the driver said, bending over her.

She nodded. Her fingers found the pulse again. The horrible pink stuff had not continued to flow. Maybe it was nothing important. Not from his brain.

"I can't hold the bus for you," the driver said. "We're behind schedule as it is."

The motorist said, "That's okay. I can take over."

Be quiet, be quiet, she wanted to tell them. It seemed to her that silence was necessary, that everything in the world outside the boy's body had to concentrate, help it not to lose track of its duty to breathe.

Shy but steady whiffs now, a sweet obedience in the chest. Keep on, keep on.

"You hear that? This guy says he'll stay and watch out for him," the driver said. "Ambulance is coming as fast as they can."

"Go on," Doree said. "I'll hitch a ride to town with them and catch you on your way back tonight."

He had to bend to hear her. She spoke dismissively, without raising her head, as if she were the one whose breath was precious.

"You sure?" he said.

Sure.

"You don't have to get to London?"

No.

Fiction

I

The best thing in winter was driving home, after her day teaching music in the Rough River schools. It would already be dark, and on the upper streets of the town snow might be falling, while rain lashed the car on the coastal highway. Joyce drove beyond the limits of the town into the forest, and though it was a real forest with great Douglas firs and cedar trees, there were people living in it every quarter mile or so. There were some people who had market gardens, a few who had some sheep or riding horses, and there were enterprises like Jon's—he restored and made furniture. Also the services advertised beside the road, and more particular to this part of the world—tarot readings, herbal massage, conflict resolution. Some people lived in trailers; others had built their own houses, incorporating thatched roofs and log ends, and still others, like Jon and Joyce, were renovating old farmhouses.

There was the one special thing Joyce loved to see as she was driving home and turning in to their own property. At this time many people, even some of the thatched-roof people, were putting in what were called patio doors—even if like Jon and Joyce they had no patio. These were usually left uncurtained, and the two oblongs of light seemed to be a sign or pledge of comfort, of safety and replenishment. Why this should be so, more than with ordinary windows, Joyce could not say. Perhaps it was that most were meant not just to look out on but to open directly into the forest darkness, and that they displayed the haven of home so artlessly. Full-length people cooking or watching television—scenes which beguiled her, even if she knew things would not be so special inside.

What she saw when she turned in to her own unpaved puddled driveway was the set of these doors put in by Jon, framing the gutted glowing interior of their house. The stepladder, the unfinished kitchen shelves, exposed stairs, warm wood lit up by the lightbulb that Jon positioned to shine wherever he wanted it, wherever he was working. He worked all day in his shed, and then when it began to get dark he sent his apprentice home and started working on the house. Hearing her car, he would turn his head in Joyce's direction just for a moment, in greeting. Usually his hands would be too busy to wave. Sitting there, with the car lights off, gathering up whatever groceries or mail she had to take into the house, Joyce was happy even to have that last dash to the door, through the dark and the wind and the cold rain. She felt herself shedding the day's work, which was harried and uncertain, filled with the dispensing of music to the indifferent as well as the responsive. How much better to work with wood and by yourself— she did not count the apprentice—than with the unpredictable human young.

She didn't say any of that to Jon. He disliked hearing people talk about how basic and fine and honorable it was to work with wood. What integrity that had, what dignity.

He would say, Crap.

Jon and Joyce had met at an urban high school in a factory city in Ontario. Joyce had the second-highest IQ in their class, and Jon had the highest IQ in the school and probably in that city. She was expected to turn into a fine performer on the violin—that was before she gave it up for the cello—and he was to become some daunting sort of scientist whose labors were beyond description in the ordinary world.

In their first year at college they dropped out of their classes and ran away together. They got jobs here and there, travelled by bus across the continent, lived for a year on the Oregon coast, were reconciled, at a distance, with their parents, for whom a light had gone out in the world. It was getting rather late in the day for them to be called hippies, but that was what their parents called them. They never thought of themselves that way. They did not do drugs, they dressed conservatively though rather shabbily, and Jon made a point of shaving and getting Joyce to cut his hair.

They tired of their temporary minimum-wage jobs after a while and borrowed from their disappointed families so that they could qualify to make a better living. Jon learned carpentry and woodworking, and Joyce got a degree that made her eligible to teach music in the schools.

The job she got was in Rough River. They bought this tumbledown house for almost nothing and settled into a new phase in their lives. They planted a garden, got to know their neighbors—some of whom were still real hippies, tending small grow operations deep in the bush and making bead necklaces and herb sachets to sell.

Their neighbors liked Jon. He was still skinny and bright eyed, egotistical but ready to listen. And it was a time when most people were just getting used to computers, which he understood and could patiently explain. Joyce was less popular. Her methods of teaching music were thought to be too formalized.

Joyce and Jon cooked supper together and drank some of their homemade wine. (Jon's method of winemaking was strict and successful.) Joyce talked about the frustrations and comedy of her day. Jon did not talk much—he was, for one thing, more involved in the cooking. But when they got around to eating he might tell her about some customer who had come in, or about his apprentice, Edie. They would laugh about something Edie had said. But not in a disparaging way—Edie was like a pet, Joyce sometimes thought. Or like a child. Though if she had been a child, their child, and had been the way she was, they might have been too puzzled and perhaps too concerned to laugh.

Why? What way? She wasn't stupid. Jon said she was no genius when it came to woodworking, but she learned and remembered what she was taught. And the important thing was that she wasn't garrulous. That was what he had been most afraid of when the business of hiring an apprentice had come up. A government program had been started—he was to be paid a certain amount for teaching the person, and whoever it was would be paid enough to live on while learning. At first he hadn't been willing, but Joyce had talked him into it. She believed they had an obligation to society.

Edie might not have talked a lot, but when she did talk it was forceful.

"I abstain from all drugs and alcohol" was what she told them at her first interview. "I belong to AA and I am a recovering alcoholic. We never say we are recovered, because we never are. You never are as long as you live. I have a nine-year-old daughter and she was born without a father so she is my total responsibility and I mean to bring her up right. My ambition is to learn wood-working so I can provide for myself and my child."

While delivering this speech she sat staring at them, one after the other, across their kitchen table. She was a short sturdy young woman who did not look old enough or damaged enough to have much of a career of dissipation behind her. Broad shoulders, thick bangs, tight ponytail, no possibility of a smile.

"And one more thing," she said. She unbuttoned and removed her long-sleeved blouse. She was wearing an undershirt. Both arms, her upper chest, and—when she turned around—her upper back were decorated with tattoos. It was as if her skin had become a garment, or perhaps a comic book of faces both leering and tender, beset by dragons, whales, flames, too intricate or maybe too horrid to be comprehended.

The first thing you had to wonder was whether her whole body had been transformed in the same way.

"How amazing," said Joyce, as neutrally as possible.

"Well, I don't know how amazing it is, but it would have cost a pile of money if I'd had to pay for it," Edie said. "That's what I was into at one time. What I'm showing it to you for is that some people would object to it. Like supposing I got hot in the shed and had to work in my shirt."

"Not us," said Joyce, and looked at Jon. He shrugged.

She asked Edie if she would like a cup of coffee.

"No, thank you." Edie was putting her shirt back on. "A lot of people at AA, they just seem like they live on coffee. What I say to them, I say, Why are you changing one bad habit for another?"

"Extraordinary," Joyce said later. "You feel that no matter what you said she might give you a lecture. I didn't dare inquire about the virgin birth."

Jon said, "She's strong. That's the main thing. I took a look at her arms."

When Jon says "strong" he means just what the word used to mean. He means she could carry a beam.

While Jon works he listens to CBC Radio. Music, but also news, commentaries, phone-ins. He sometimes reports Edie's opinions on what they have listened to.

Edie does not believe in evolution.

(There had been a phone-in program in which some people objected to what was being taught in the schools.)

Why not?

"Well, it's because in those Bible countries," Jon said, and then he switched into his firm monotonous Edie voice, "in those Bible countries they have a lot of monkeys and the monkeys were always swinging down from the trees and that's how people got the idea that monkeys just swung down and turned into people."

"But in the first place—" said Joyce.

"Never mind. Don't even try. Don't you know

the first rule about arguing with Edie? Never mind and shut up."

Edie also believed that big medical companies knew the cure for cancer, but they had a bargain with doctors to keep the information quiet because of the money they and the doctors made.

When "Ode to Joy" was played on the radio she had Jon shut it off because it was so awful, like a funeral.

Also, she thought Jon and Joyce—well, really Joyce—should not leave wine bottles with wine in them right out in sight on the kitchen table.

"That's her business?" said Joyce.

"Apparently she thinks so."

"When does she get to examine our kitchen table?"

"She has to go through to the toilet. She can't be expected to piss in the bush."

"I really don't see what business—"

"And sometimes she comes in and makes a couple of sandwiches for us—"

"So? It's my kitchen. Ours."

"It's just that she feels so threatened by the booze. She's still pretty fragile. It's a thing you and I can't understand."

Threatened. Booze. Fragile.

What words were these for Jon to use?

She should have understood, and at that moment, even if he himself was nowhere close to knowing. He was falling in love.

Falling. That suggests some time span, a slipping under. But you can think of it as a speeding up, a moment or a second when you fall. Now Jon is not in love with Edie. Tick. Now he is. No way this could be seen as probable or possible, unless you think of a blow between the eyes, a sudden calamity. The stroke of fate that leaves a man a cripple, the wicked joke that turns clear eyes into blind stones.

Joyce set about convincing him that he was mistaken. He had so little experience of women. None, except for her. They had always thought that experimenting with various partners was childish, adultery was messy and destructive. Now she wondered, Should he have played around more?

And he had spent the dark winter months shut up in his workshop, exposed to the confident emanations of Edie. It was comparable to getting sick from bad ventilation.

Edie would drive him crazy, if he went ahead and took her seriously.

"I've thought of that," he said. "Maybe she already has."

Joyce said that was stupid adolescent talk, making himself out to be dumbstruck, helpless.

"What do you think you are, some knight of the Round Table? Somebody slipped you a potion?"

Then she said she was sorry. The only thing to do, she said, was to take this up as a shared program. Valley of the shadow. To be seen someday as a mere glitch in the course of their marriage.

"We will ride this out," she said.

Jon looked at her distantly, even kindly.

"There is no 'we,'" he said.

How could this have happened? Joyce asks it of Jon and of herself and then of others. A heavy-striding heavy-witted carpenter's apprentice in baggy pants and flannel shirts and—as long as the winter lasted—a dull thick sweater flecked with sawdust. A mind that plods inexorably from one cliché or foolishness to the next and proclaims every step of the journey to be the law of the land. Such a person has eclipsed Joyce with her long legs and slim waist and long silky braid of dark hair. Her wit and her music and the second-highest IQ.

"I'll tell you what I think it was," says Joyce. This is later on, when the days have lengthened and the dandles of swamp lilies flame in the ditches. When she went to teach music wearing tinted glasses to hide eyes that were swollen from weeping and drinking, and instead of driving home after work drove to Willingdon Park where she hoped Jon would come looking for her, fearing suicide. (He did that, but only once.)

"I think it was that she'd been on the streets," she said. "Prostitutes get themselves tattooed for business reasons, and men are aroused by that sort of thing. I don't mean the tattoos—well that too, of course, they're aroused by that too—I mean the fact of having been for sale. All that availability and experience. And now reformed. It's your fucking Mary Magdalene, that's what it is. And he's such an infant sexually, it all makes you sick."

She has friends now to whom she can talk like this. They all have stories. Some of them she knew before, but not as she knows them now. They confide and drink and laugh till they cry. They say they can't believe it. Men. What they do. It's so sick and stupid. You can't believe it.

That's why it's true.

In the midst of this talk Joyce feels all right. Really all right. She says that she is actually having moments in which she feels grateful to Jon, because she feels more alive now than ever before. It is terrible but wonderful. A new beginning. Naked truth. Naked life.

But when she woke up at three or four in the morning she wondered where she was. Not in their house anymore. Edie was in that house now. Edie and her child and Jon. This was a switch that Joyce herself had favored, thinking it might bring Jon to his senses. She moved to an apartment in town. It belonged to a teacher who was on a sabbatical. She woke in the night with the vibrating pink lights of the restaurant sign across the street flashing through her window, illuminating the other teacher's Mexican doodads. Pots of cacti, dangling cat's eyes, blankets with stripes the color of dried blood. All that drunken insight, that exhilaration, cast out of her like vomit. Aside from that, she was not hungover. She could wallow in lakes of alcohol, it seemed, and wake up dry as cardboard, flattened.

Her life gone. A commonplace calamity.

The truth was that she was still drunk, though feeling dead sober. She was in danger of getting into her car and driving out to the house. Not of driving into a ditch, because her driving at such times became very slow and sedate, but of parking in the yard outside the dark windows and crying out to Jon that they simply must stop this.

Stop this. This is not right. Tell her to go away.

Remember we slept in the field and woke up and the cows were munching all around us and we hadn't known they were there the night before. Remember washing in the ice-cold creek. We were picking mushrooms up on Vancouver Island and flying back to Ontario and selling them to pay for the trip when your mother was sick and we thought she was dying. And we said, What a joke, we're not even druggies, we're on an errand of filial piety.

The sun came up and the Mexican colors began to blare at her in their enhanced hideousness, and after a while she got up and washed and slashed her cheeks with rouge and drank coffee that she made strong as mud and put on some of her new clothes. She had bought new flimsy tops and fluttering skirts and earrings decked with rainbow feathers. She went out to teach music in the schools, looking like a Gypsy dancer or a cocktail waitress. She laughed at everything and flirted with everybody. With the man who cooked her breakfast in the diner downstairs and the boy who put gas in her car and the clerk who sold her stamps in the post office. She had some idea that Jon would hear about how pretty she looked, how sexy and happy, how she was simply bowling over all the men. As soon as she went out of the apartment she was on a stage, and Jon was the essential, if secondhand, spectator. Although Jon had never been taken in by showy looks or flirty behavior, had never thought that was what made her attractive. When they travelled they had often made do with a common wardrobe. Heavy socks, jeans, dark shirts, Windbreakers.

Another change.

Even with the youngest or the dullest children she taught, her tone had become caressing, full of mischievous laughter, her encouragement irresistible. She was preparing her pupils for the recital held at the conclusion of the school year. She had not previously been enthusiastic about this evening of public performance—she had felt that it interfered with the progress of those students who had ability, it shoved them into a situation they were not ready for. All that effort and tension could only create false values. But this year she was throwing herself into every aspect of the show. The program, the lighting, the introductions, and of course the performances. This ought to be fun, she proclaimed. Fun for the students, fun for the audience.

Of course she counted on Jon's being there. Edie's daughter was one of the performers, so Edie would have to be there. Jon would have to accompany Edie.

Jon and Edie's first appearance as a couple before the town. Their declaration. They could not avoid it. Such switches as theirs were not unheard of, particularly among the people who lived south of town. But they were not exactly commonplace. The fact that rearrangements were not scandalous didn't mean they didn't get attention. There was a necessary period of interest before things settled down and people got used to the new alliance. As they did, and the newly aligned partners would be seen chatting with, or at least saying hello to, the castoffs in the grocery store.

But this was not the role Joyce saw herself playing, watched by Jon and Edie—well, really by Jon—on the evening of the recital.

What did she see? God knows. She did not, in any sane moment, think of impressing Jon so favorably that he would come to his senses when she appeared to take the applause of the audience at the end of the show. She did not think his heart would break for his folly, once he saw her happy and glamorous and in command rather than moping and suicidal. But something not far off from that—something she couldn't define but couldn't stop herself hoping for.

It was the best recital ever. Everybody said so. They said there was more verve. More gaiety, yet more intensity. The children costumed in harmony with the music they performed. Their faces made up so they did not seem so scared and sacrificial.

When Joyce came out at the end she wore a long black silk skirt that shone with silver as she moved. Also silver bangles and glitter in her loose hair. Some whistles mingled with the applause.

Jon and Edie were not in the audience.

II

Joyce and Matt are giving a party at their house in North Vancouver. This is to celebrate Matt's sixty-fifth birthday. Matt is a neuropsychologist who is also a good amateur violinist. That is how he met Joyce, now a professional cellist and his third wife.

"Look at all the people here," Joyce keeps saying. "It's positively a life story."

She is a lean eager-looking woman with a mop

67

of pewter-colored hair and a slight stoop which may come from coddling her large instrument, or simply from the habit of being an obliging listener and a ready talker.

There are Matt's colleagues, of course, from the college; the ones he considers his personal friends. He is a generous but outspoken man so it stands to reason not all colleagues fall into that category. There is his first wife, Sally, accompanied by her caregiver. Sally's brain was damaged when she was in a car accident at the age of twenty-nine, so it is unlikely that she knows who Matt is, or who her three grown sons are, or that this is the house she lived in as a young wife. But her pleasant manners are intact, and she is delighted to meet people, even if she has met them already, fifteen minutes before. Her caregiver is a tidy little Scotswoman who explains often that she is not used to big noisy parties like this and that she doesn't drink while on duty.

Matt's second wife, Doris, lived with him for less than a year, though she was married to him for three. She is here with her much younger partner, Louise, and their baby daughter, whom Louise bore a few months ago. Doris has stayed friends with Matt and especially with Matt and Sally's youngest son, Tommy, who was small enough to be in her care when she was married to his father. Matt's two older sons are present with their children and the children's mothers, though one of the mothers is no longer married to that father. He is accompanied by his current partner and her son, who has got into a fight with one of the bloodline children over turns on the swing.

Tommy has brought along for the first time his lover named Jay, who has not yet said anything. Tommy has said to Joyce that Jay is not used to families.

"I feel for him," says Joyce. "There was actually a time when I wasn't either." She is laughing—she has hardly stopped laughing as she explains the status of the official and outlying members of what Matt calls the clan. She herself has no children, though she does have an ex-husband, Jon, who lives up the coast in a mill town that has fallen on evil days. She invited him to come down for the party, but he could not come. His third wife's grandchild was being christened on that day. Of course Joyce had invited the wife too—her name is Charlene and she runs a bakeshop. She had written the nice note about the christening, causing Joyce to say to Matt that she can't believe Jon could have got religion.

"I do wish they could have come," she says, explaining all this to a neighbor. (Neighbors have been invited, so there won't be any fuss about the noise.) "Then I could have had my share in the complications. There was a second wife, but I have no idea where she has got to and I don't believe he has either."

There is lots of food that Matt and Joyce have made and that people have brought, and lots of wine and children's fruit punch and a real punch that Matt has concocted for the occasion—in honor of the good old days, he says, when people really knew how to drink. He says he would have made it in a scrubbed-out garbage can, the way they did then, but nowadays everybody would be too squeamish to drink that. Most of the young adults leave it alone, anyway.

The grounds are large. There is croquet, if people want to play, and the disputed swing from Matt's own childhood that he got out of the garage. Most of the children have seen only park swings and plastic play units in the backyard. Matt is surely one of the last people in Vancouver to have a childhood swing handy and to be living in the house he grew up in, a house on Windsor Road on the slope of Grouse Mountain on what used to be the edge of the forest. Now houses keep climbing above it, most of them castle affairs with massive garages. One of these days this place will have to go, Matt says. The taxes are monstrous. It will have to go, and a couple of hideosities will replace it.

Joyce cannot think of her life with Matt happening anywhere else. There's always so much going on here. People coming and going and leaving things behind and picking them up later (including children). Matt's string quartet in the study on Sunday afternoons, the Unitarian Fellowship meeting in the living room on Sunday evenings, Green Party strategy being planned in the kitchen. The play-reading group emoting in the front of the house while somebody spills out the details of real-life drama in the kitchen (Joyce's presence required in both locations). Matt and some faculty colleague hammering out strategy in the study with the door closed.

She often remarks that she and Matt are seldom alone together except in bed.

"And then he'll be reading something important."

While she is reading something unimportant.

Never mind. There is some large conviviality and appetite he carries with him that she may need. Even at the college—where he is involved with graduate students, collaborators, possible enemies, and detractors—he seems to move in a barely managed whirlwind. All this once seemed to her so comforting. And probably it still would, if she had time to look at it from outside. She would probably envy herself, from outside. People may envy her, or at least admire her—thinking she matched him so well, with all her friends and duties and activities and of course her own career as well. You would never look at her now and think that when she had first come down to Vancouver she was so lonely that she had agreed to go out with the boy from the dry cleaner who was a decade too young for her. And then he had stood her up.

71

Now she is walking across the grass with a shawl over her arm for old Mrs. Fowler, the mother of Doris the second wife and late-blooming lesbian. Mrs. Fowler can't sit in the sun, but she gets shivers in the shade. And in the other hand she carries a glass of freshly made lemonade for Mrs. Gowan, the on-duty companion of Sally. Mrs. Gowan has found the children's punch too sweet. She does not allow Sally to have anything to drink—she might spill it on her pretty dress or throw it at somebody in a fit of playfulness. Sally does not seem to mind the deprivation.

On the journey across the lawn Joyce skirts a group of young people sitting in a circle. Tommy and his new friend and other friends she has often seen in the house and others she does not believe she has ever seen at all.

She hears Tommy say, "No, I am not Isadora Duncan."

They all laugh.

She realizes that they must be playing that difficult and snobby game that was popular years ago. What was it called? She thinks the name started with a *B*. She would have thought they were too anti-elitist nowadays for any such pastime.

Buxtehude. She has said it out loud.

"You're playing Buxtehude."

"You got the *B* right anyway," says Tommy, laughing at her so that the others can laugh.

"See," he says. "My *belle mère,* she ain't so

dumb. But she's a musician. Wasn't Buxtahoody a musician?"

"Buxtehude walked fifty miles to hear Bach play the organ," says Joyce in a mild huff. "Yes. A musician."

Tommy says, "Hot damn."

A girl in the circle gets up, and Tommy calls to her.

"Hey Christie. Christie. Aren't you playing anymore?"

"I'll be back. I'm just going to hide in the bushes with my filthy cigarette."

This girl is wearing a short frilly black dress that makes you think of a piece of lingerie or a nightie, and a severe but low-necked little black jacket. Wispy pale hair, evasive pale face, invisible eyebrows. Joyce has taken an instant dislike to her. The sort of girl, she thinks, whose mission in life is to make people feel uncomfortable. Tagging along—Joyce thinks she must have tagged along—to a party at the home of people she doesn't know but feels a right to despise. Because of their easy (shallow?) cheer and their bourgeois hospitality. (Do people say "bourgeois" anymore?)

It's not as if a guest couldn't smoke anywhere she wants to. There aren't any of those fussy little signs around, even in the house. Joyce feels a lot of her cheer drained away.

"Tommy," she says abruptly. "Tommy, would

you mind taking this shawl to Grandma Fowler? Apparently she's feeling chilly. And the lemonade is for Mrs. Gowan. You know. The person with your mother."

No harm in reminding him of certain relationships and responsibilities.

Tommy is quickly and gracefully on his feet.

"Botticelli," he says, relieving her of the shawl and the glass.

"I'm sorry. I didn't mean to spoil your game."

"We're no good anyway," says a boy she knows. Justin. "We're not as smart as you guys used to be."

"Used to be is right," says Joyce. At a loss, for a moment, as to what to do or where to go next.

They are washing the dishes in the kitchen. Joyce and Tommy and the new friend, Jay. The party is over. People have departed with hugs and kisses and hearty cries, some bearing platters of food that Joyce has no room for in the refrigerator. Wilted salads and cream tarts and devilled eggs have been thrown out. Few of the devilled eggs were eaten anyway. Old-fashioned. Too much cholesterol.

"Too bad, they were a lot of work. They probably reminded people of church suppers," says Joyce, tipping a platterful into the garbage.

"My granma used to make them," says Jay. These are the first words he has addressed to Joyce, and she sees Tommy looking grateful. She feels grateful herself, even if she has been put in the category of his grandmother.

"We ate several and they were good," says Tommy. He and Jay have worked for at least half an hour alongside her, gathering glasses and plates and cutlery that were scattered all over the lawn and verandah and throughout the house, even in the most curious places such as flowerpots and under sofa cushions.

The boys—she thinks of them as boys—have stacked the dishwasher more skillfully than she in her worn-out state could ever manage, and prepared the hot soapy water and cool rinse water in the sinks for the glasses.

"We could just save them for the next load in the dishwasher," Joyce has said, but Tommy has said no.

"You wouldn't think of putting them in the dishwater if you weren't out of your right mind with all you had to do today."

Jay washes and Joyce dries and Tommy puts away. He still remembers where everything goes in this house. Out on the porch Matt is having a strenuous conversation with a man from the department. Apparently he's not so drunk as the plentiful hugs and prolonged farewells of a short time ago would indicate.

"Quite possibly I am not in my right mind," says Joyce. "At the moment my gut feeling is to pitch these all out and buy plastic."

"Postparty syndrome," says Tommy. "We know all about it."

"So who was that girl in the black dress?" says Joyce. "The one who walked out on the game?"

"Christie? You must mean Christie. Christie O'Dell. She's Justin's wife, but she has her own name. You know Justin."

"Of course I know Justin. I just didn't know he was married."

"Ah, how they all grow up," says Tommy, teasing.

"Justin's thirty," he adds. "She's possibly older."

Jay says, "Definitely older."

"She's an interesting-looking girl," says Joyce. "What's she like?"

"She's a writer. She's okay."

Jay, bending over the sink, makes a noise that Joyce cannot interpret.

"Inclined to be rather aloof," Tommy says. He speaks to Jay. "Am I right? Would you say that?"

"She thinks she's hot shit," Jay says distinctly.

"Well, she's just got her first book published," Tommy says. "I forget what it's called. Some title like a how-to book, I don't think it's a good title. You get your first book out, I guess you are hot shit for a while."

Passing a bookstore on Lonsdale a few days later, Joyce sees the girl's face on a poster. And there is her name, Christie O'Dell. She is wearing a black hat and the same little black jacket she wore to the party. Tailored, severe, very low in the neck. Though she has practically nothing there to show off. She stares straight into the camera, with her somber, wounded, distantly accusing look.

Where has Joyce seen her before? At the party, of course. But even then, in the midst of her probably unwarranted dislike, she felt she had seen that face before.

A student? She'd had so many students in her time.

She goes into the store and buys a copy of the book. *How Are We to Live*. No question mark. The woman who sold it to her says, "And you know if you bring it back Friday afternoon between two and four, the author will be here to sign it for you.

"Just don't tear the little gold sticker off so it shows you bought it here."

Joyce has never understood this business of lining up to get a glimpse of the author and then going away with a stranger's name written in your book. So she murmurs politely, indicating neither yes nor no.

She doesn't even know if she will read the book. She has a couple of good biographies on the go at the moment that she is sure are more to her taste than this will be.

How Are We to Live is a collection of short stories, not a novel. This in itself is a disappointment. It seems to diminish the book's authority, making the author seem like somebody who is just hanging on to the gates of Literature, rather than safely settled inside.

Nevertheless Joyce takes the book to bed with her that night and turns dutifully to the table of contents. About halfway down the list a title catches her eye.

"Kindertotenlieder."

Mahler. Familiar territory. Reassured, she turns to the page indicated. Somebody, probably the author herself, has had the sense to supply a translation.

"Songs on the Death of Children."

Beside her, Matt gives a snort.

She knows that he has disagreed with something he is reading and would like her to ask what it is. So she does.

"Christ. This idiot."

She puts *How Are We to Live* facedown on her chest, making sounds to show that she is listening to him.

On the back cover of the book there is the same author's photo, without the hat this time. Unsmiling still, and sulky, but a bit less pretentious. While Matt talks, Joyce shifts her knees so that she can position the book against them and read the few sentences of the cover biography.

Christie O'Dell grew up in Rough River, a small town on the coast of British Columbia. She is a graduate of the UBC Creative Writing

Program. She lives in Vancouver, British Columbia, with her husband, Justin, and her cat, Tiberius.

When he has explained to her what the idiocy in his book is all about, Matt lifts his eyes from his book to look at her book and says, "There's that girl that was at our party."

"Yes. Her name's Christie O'Dell. She's Justin's wife."

"She's written a book then? What is it?"

"Fiction."

"Oh."

He has resumed his reading but in a moment asks her, with a hint of contrition, "Is it any good?"

"I don't know yet."

"She lived with her mother," she reads, "in a house between the mountains and the sea—"

As soon as she has read those words Joyce feels too uncomfortable to continue reading. Or to continue reading with her husband beside her. She closes the book and says, "I think I'll go downstairs for a little."

"Is the light bothering you? I'm about to turn it off."

"No. I think I want some tea. See you in a while."

"I'll probably be asleep."

"Good night then."

"Good night."

She kisses him and takes the book with her.

She lived with her mother in a house between the mountains and the sea. Before that she had lived with Mrs. Noland who took in foster children. The number of children in Mrs. Noland's house varied from time to time but there were always too many. The little ones slept in a bed in the middle of the room and the bigger ones slept in cots on either side of the bed so the little ones wouldn't roll off. A bell rang to get you up in the morning. Mrs. Noland stood in the doorway ringing the bell. When she rang the next bell you were supposed to have been to pee and got yourself washed and dressed and be ready for breakfast. Big ones were supposed to help the little ones then make the beds. Sometimes the little ones in the middle had wet the bed because it was hard for them to crawl out in time over the big ones. Some big ones would tell on them but other big ones were nicer and they just pulled up the covers and let it dry and sometimes when you got back in bed at night it was not quite dried. That was most of what she remembered about Mrs. Noland's.

Then she went to live with her mother and every night her mother would take her to the AA meeting. She had to take her because there wasn't anybody to leave her with. At the AA there was a box of Legos for kids to play with but she didn't like Legos very much. After she started learning the violin at school she took her child's violin with her to AA. She couldn't play it there, but she had to hang on to it all the time because it belonged to the school. If people got talking very loudly she could practice a little softly.

The violin lessons were given at the school. If you didn't want to play an instrument you could just play the triangles, but the teacher liked it better if you played something harder. The teacher was a tall woman with brown hair that she wore usually in a long braid down her back. She smelled different from the other teachers. Some of them had perfume on, but she never did. She smelled of wood or a stove or trees. Later the child would believe the smell was crushed cedar. After the child's mother went to work for the teacher's husband she smelled the same way but not quite the same. The difference seemed to be that her mother smelled of wood, but the teacher smelled of wood in music.

The child was not very talented, but she worked hard. She didn't do that because she loved music. She did it for love of the teacher, nothing else.

Joyce puts the book down on the kitchen table and looks again at the picture of the author. Is there anything of Edie in that face? Nothing. Nothing in the shape or the expression.

She gets up and fetches the brandy, puts a little of it in her tea. She searches her mind for the name of Edie's child. Surely not Christie. She could not remember any time when Edie had brought her to the house. At the school there had been several children learning the violin.

The child could not have been entirely without ability, or Joyce would have steered her to something less difficult than the violin. But she couldn't have been gifted—well, she had as much as said she wasn't gifted—or her name would have stuck.

A blank face. A blob of female childishness. Though there had been something that Joyce recognized in the face of the girl, the woman, grown up.

Could she not have come to the house if Edie was helping Jon on a Saturday? Or even on those days when Edie just turned up as some sort of visitor, not to work but just to see how work was coming along, lend a hand if needed. Plunk herself down to watch whatever Jon was doing and get in the way of any conversation he might have with Joyce on her precious day off.

Christine. Of course. That was it. Translated easily into Christie.

Christine must have been privy in some way to the courtship, Jon must have dropped in at the apartment, just as Edie had dropped in at the house. Edie might have sounded the child out.

How do you like Jon?

How do you like Jon's house?

Wouldn't it be nice to go and live in Jon's house?

Mommy and Jon like each other very much and when people like each other very much they want to live in the same house. Your music teacher and Jon don't like each other as much as Mommy and Jon do so you and Mommy and Jon are going to live in Jon's house and your music teacher is going to go and live in an apartment.

That was all wrong; Edie would never spout such blather, give her credit.

Joyce thinks she knows the turn the story will take. The child all mixed up in the adults' dealings and delusions, pulled about hither and yon. But when she picks up the book again she finds the switch of dwelling places hardly mentioned.

Everything is hinged on the child's love for the teacher.

Thursday, the day of the music lesson, is the momentous day of the week, its happiness or unhappiness depending on the success or failure of the child's performance, and the teacher's notice of that performance. Both are nearly unbearable. The teacher's voice could be controlled, kind, making jokes to cover its weariness and disappointment. The child is wretched. Or the teacher is suddenly lighthearted and merry.

"Good for you. Good for you. You've really

made the grade today." And the child is so happy she has cramps in her stomach.

Then there is the Thursday when the child has tripped on the playground and has a scratched knee. The teacher cleaning the injury with a warmed wet cloth, her suddenly soft voice claiming that this calls for a treat, as she reaches for the bowl of Smarties she uses to encourage the youngest children.

"Which is your favorite?"

The child overcome, saying, "Any."

Is this the beginning of a change? Is it because of spring, the preparations for the recital?

The child feels herself singled out. She is to be a soloist. This means she must stay after school on Thursdays to practice, and so she misses her ride out of town on the school bus, to the house where she and her mother are now living. The teacher will drive her. On the way she asks if the child is nervous about the recital.

Sort of.

Well then, the teacher says, she must train herself to think of something really nice. Such as a bird flying across the sky. What is her favorite bird?

Favorites again. The child can't think, can't think of a single bird. Then, "A crow?"

The teacher laughs. "Okay. Okay. Think of a crow. Just before you begin to play, think of a crow."

Then perhaps to make up for laughing, sensing

the child's humiliation, the teacher suggests they go down to Willingdon Park and see if the ice-cream stand has opened for the summer.

"Do they worry if you don't come straight home?"

"They know I'm with you."

The ice-cream stand is open though the selection is limited. They haven't got the more exciting flavors in yet. The child picks strawberry, this time making sure to be ready, in the middle of her bliss and agitation. The teacher picks vanilla, as many adults do. Though she jokes with the attendant, telling him to hurry up and get rum raisin or she won't like him anymore.

Maybe that is when there is another change. Hearing the teacher speak in that way, in a saucy voice almost the way big girls speak, the child relaxes. From then on she is less stricken with adoration, though entirely happy. They drive down to the dock to look at the moored boats, and the teacher says she has always wanted to live on a houseboat. Wouldn't it be fun, she says, and the child of course agrees. They pick the one they'd choose. It is homemade and painted a light blue, with a row of little windows in which there are potted geraniums.

This leads to a conversation about the house the child lives in now, the house where the teacher used to live. And somehow after that, on their drives, they often come back to that subject. The child reports that she likes having her own bed-room but doesn't like how dark it is outside. Sometimes she thinks she can hear wild animals outside her window.

What wild animals?

Bears, cougars. Her mother says those are in the bush and never to go there.

"Do you run and get into your mother's bed when you hear them?"

"I'm not supposed to."

"Goodness, why not?"

"Jon's there."

"What does Jon think about the bears and cougars?"

"He thinks it's just deer."

"Was he mad at your mother for what she'd told you?"

"No."

"I guess he's never mad."

"He was sort of mad one time. When me and my mother poured all his wine down the sink."

The teacher says it is a pity to be scared of the woods all the time. There are walks you can take there, she says, where wild animals won't bother you, especially if you make a noise and usually you do. She knows the safe paths and she knows the names of all the wildflowers that will be coming out about now. Dogtooth violets. Trilliums. Wake-robins. Purple violets and columbines. Chocolate lilies.

"I think there is another proper name for them, but I like to call them chocolate lilies. It sounds so delicious. Of course, it isn't anything about the way they taste but the way they look. They look just like chocolate with a bit of purple like crushed berries. They're rare but I know where there are some."

Joyce puts the book down again. Now, now, she really has caught the drift, she can feel the horror coming. The innocent child, the sick and sneaking adult, that seduction. She should have known. All so in fashion these days, practically obligatory. The woods, the spring flowers. Here was where the writer would graft her ugly invention onto the people and the situation she had got out of real life, being too lazy to invent but not to malign.

For some of it was true, certainly. She does remember things she had forgotten. Driving Christine home, and never thinking of her as Christine but always as Edie's child. She remembers how she could not drive into the yard to turn around but always let the child off by the side of the road, then drove another half mile or so to get a place to turn. She does not remember anything about the ice cream. But there used to be a houseboat exactly like that moored down at the dock. Even the flowers, and the sly horrible questioning of the child—that could be true.

She has to continue. She would like to pour more brandy, but she has a rehearsal at nine o'clock in the morning.

Nothing of the sort. She has made another mistake. The woods and the chocolate lilies drop out of the story, the recital is almost passed over. School has just ended. And on the Sunday morning after the final week the child is wakened early. She hears the teacher's voice in the yard and she goes to her window. There is the teacher in her car with the window down, talking to Jon. A small U-Haul is attached to the car. Jon is in his bare feet, bare chested, wearing only his jeans. He calls to the child's mother and she comes to the kitchen door and walks a few steps into the yard but does not go up to the car. She is wearing a shirt of Jon's which she uses as a dressing gown. She always wears long sleeves to hide her tattoos.

The conversation is about something in the apartment which Jon promises to pick up. The teacher tosses him the keys. Then he and the child's mother, talking over each other, urge her to take some other things. But the teacher laughs unpleasantly and says, "All yours." Soon Jon says, "Okay. See you," and the teacher echoes "See you," and the child's mother doesn't say anything you can hear. The teacher laughs in the same way she did before and Jon gives her directions about how to turn the car and the U-Haul around in the yard. By this time the child is running downstairs in her pajamas, though she knows the teacher is not in the right mood to talk to her.

"You just missed her," the child's mother says. "She had to catch the ferry."

There is a honk of the horn; Jon raises one hand. Then he comes across the yard and says to the child's mother, "That's that."

The child asks if the teacher is going to come back and he says, "Not likely."

What takes up another half page is the child's increasing understanding of what has been going on. As she grows older she recalls certain questions, the seemingly haphazard probing there had been. Information—quite useless really—about Jon (whom she does not call Jon) and her mother. When did they get up in the morning? What did they like to eat and did they cook together? What did they listen to on the radio? (Nothing—they had bought a television.)

What was the teacher after? Did she hope to hear bad things? Or was she just hungry to hear anything, to be in contact with somebody who slept under the same roof, ate at the same table, was close to those two people daily?

That is what the child can never know. What she can know is how little she herself counted for, how her infatuation was manipulated, what a poor little fool she was. And this fills her with bitterness, certainly it does. Bitterness and pride. She thinks of herself as a person never to be fooled again.

But something happens. And here is the surprise ending. Her feelings about the teacher and that period in her childhood one day change. She doesn't know how or when, but she realizes that she no longer thinks of that time as a cheat. She thinks of the music she painfully learned to play (she gave it up, of course, before she was even in her teens). The buoyancy of her hopes, the streaks of happiness, the curious and delightful names of the forest flowers that she never got to see.

Love. She was glad of it. It almost seemed as if there must be some random and of course unfair thrift in the emotional housekeeping of the world, if the great happiness—however temporary, however flimsy—of one person could come out of the great unhappiness of another.

Why yes, Joyce thinks. Yes.

On Friday afternoon she goes to the bookstore. She brings her book to be signed, as well as a small box from Le Bon Chocolatier. She joins a lineup. She is slightly surprised to see how many people have come. Women of her own age, women older and younger. A few men who are all younger, some accompanying their girlfriends.

The woman who sold Joyce the book recognizes her.

"Good to see you back," she says. "Did you read the review in the *Globe*? Wow."

Joyce is bewildered, actually trembling a little. She finds it hard to speak.

The woman passes along the lineup, explaining that only books bought in this store can be autographed here and that a certain anthology in which one of Christie O'Dell's stories appears is not acceptable, she is sorry.

The woman in front of Joyce is both tall and broad, so she does not get a look at Christie O'Dell until this woman bends forward to place her book on the autographing table. Then she sees a young woman altogether different from the girl on the poster and the girl at the party. The black outfit is gone, also the black hat. Christie O'Dell wears a jacket of rosy-red silk brocade, with tiny gold beads sewn to its lapels. A delicate pink camisole is worn underneath. There is a fresh gold rinse in her hair, gold rings in her ears, and a gold chain fine as a hair around her neck. Her lips glisten like flower petals and her eyelids are shaded with umber.

Well—who wants to buy a book written by a grouch or a loser?

Joyce has not thought out what she will say. She expects it to come to her.

Now the saleswoman is speaking again.

"Have you opened your book to the page where you wish it to be signed?"

Joyce has to set her box down to do that. She can actually feel a flutter in her throat.

Christie O'Dell looks up at her, smiles at her—a smile of polished cordiality, professional disengagement.

"Your name?"

"Just Joyce will be fine."

Her time is passing so quickly.

"You were born in Rough River?"

"No," says Christie O'Dell with some slight displeasure, or at least some diminishing of cheer. "I did live there for a time. Shall I put the date?"

Joyce retrieves her box. At Le Bon Chocolatier they did sell chocolate flowers, but not lilies. Only roses and tulips. So she had bought tulips, which were not actually unlike lilies. Both bulbs.

"I want to thank you for *'Kindertotenlieder,'*" she says so hastily that she almost swallows the long word. "It means a great deal to me. I brought you a present."

"Isn't that a wonderful story." The saleswoman takes the box. "I'll just hang on to this."

"It isn't a bomb," says Joyce with a laugh. "It's chocolate lilies. Actually tulips. They didn't have lilies so I got tulips, I thought they were the next best thing."

She notices that the saleswoman is not smiling now but taking a hard look at her. Christie O'Dell says, "Thank you."

There is not a scrap of recognition in the girl's

face. She doesn't know Joyce from years ago in Rough River or two weeks ago at the party. You couldn't even be sure that she had recognized the title of her own story. You would think she had nothing to do with it. As if it was just something she wriggled out of and left on the grass.

Christie O'Dell sits there and writes her name as if that is all the writing she could be responsible for in this world.

"It's been a pleasure to chat with you," says the saleswoman, still looking at the box which the girl at Le Bon Chocolatier has fixed with a curly yellow ribbon.

Christie O'Dell has raised her eyes to greet the next person in line, and Joyce at last has the sense to move on, before she becomes an object of general amusement and her box, God knows, possibly an object of interest to the police.

Walking up Lonsdale Avenue, walking uphill, she feels flattened, but gradually regains her composure. This might even turn into a funny story that she would tell someday. She wouldn't be surprised.

Wenlock Edge

My mother had a bachelor cousin who used to visit us on the farm once a summer. He brought along his mother, Aunt Nell Botts. His own name was Ernie Botts. He was a tall florid man with a good-natured expression, a big square face, and fair curly hair springing straight up from his forehead. His hands, his fingernails, were as clean as soap, and his hips were a little plump. My name for him—when he was not around—was Earnest Bottom. I had a mean tongue.

But I believed I meant no harm. Hardly any harm. After Aunt Nell Botts died he did not come anymore, but sent a Christmas card.

When I went to college in London—that is, in London, Ontario—where he lived, he started a custom of taking me out to dinner every other Sunday evening. It seemed to me that this was the sort of thing he would do because I was a relative—he would not even have to consider whether we were suited to spending time together. He always took me to the same place, a restaurant called the Old Chelsea, which was upstairs, looking down on Dundas Street. It had velvet curtains, white tablecloths, little rose-shaded lamps on the tables. It probably cost more than he could afford, but I did not think of that, having a country girl's notion that all men who lived in cities, wore a suit every day, and sported such clean finger-nails had reached a level of prosperity where indulgences like this were the usual thing.

I had the most exotic offering on the menu, such as chicken *vol au vent* or duck *à l'orange,* while he always ate roast beef. Desserts were wheeled up to the table on a dinner wagon. There was usually a tall coconut cake, custard tarts topped with out-of-season strawberries, chocolate-coated pastry horns full of whipped cream. I took a long time to decide, like a five-year-old with flavors of ice cream, and then on Monday I had to fast all day, to make up for such gorging.

Ernie looked a little too young to be my father. I hoped that nobody from the college would see us and think he was my boyfriend.

He inquired about my courses, and nodded seriously when I told him, or reminded him, that I was in Honors English and Philosophy. He didn't roll up his eyes at the information, the way people at home did. He told me that he had a great respect for education and regretted that he did not have the means to continue his own after high school. Instead, he had got a job working for the Canadian National railways, as a ticket salesman. Now he was a supervisor.

He liked serious reading, but it was not a substitute for a college education.

I was pretty sure that his idea of serious reading would be the Condensed Books of the Reader's

Digest, and to get him off the subject of my studies I told him about my rooming house. In those days the college had no dormitories—we all lived in rooming houses or cheap apartments or fraternity or sorority houses. My room was the attic of an old house, with a large floor space and not much headroom. But being the former maid's quarters, it had its own bathroom. On the second floor were the rooms occupied by two other scholarship students, who were in their final year in Modern Languages. Their names were Kay and Beverly. In the high-ceilinged but chopped-up rooms downstairs lived a medical student, who was hardly ever home, and his wife, Beth, who was home all the time, because she had two very young children. Beth was the house manager and rent collector, and there was often a feud going on between her and the second-floor girls about how they washed their clothes in the bathroom and hung them there to dry. When the medical student was home he sometimes had to use that bathroom because of the baby stuff in the one downstairs, and Beth said he shouldn't have to cope with stockings in his face and a bunch of intimate doo-dads. Kay and Beverly retorted that use of their own bathroom had been promised when they moved in.

This was the sort of thing I chose to tell to Ernie, who flushed and said that they should have got it in writing.

Kay and Beverly were a disappointment to me. They worked hard at Modern Languages, but their conversation and preoccupations seemed hardly different from those of girls who might work in banks or offices. They did their hair up in pin curls and painted their fingernails on Saturdays, because that was the night they had dates with their boyfriends. On Sundays they had to soothe their faces with lotion because of the whisker-burns the boyfriends had inflicted on them. I didn't find either boyfriend in the least desirable, and I wondered how they could.

They said that they had once had some crazy idea of being translators at the United Nations, but now they figured they would teach high school, and with any luck get married.

They gave me unwelcome advice.

I had got a job in the college cafeteria. I pushed a cart around collecting dirty dishes off the tables and wiped the tables clean when they were empty. And I set out food to be picked up from the shelves.

They said that this job was not a good idea.

"Boys won't ask you out if they see you at a job like that."

I told Ernie this, and he said, "So, what did you say?"

I told him that I had said I would not want to go out with anybody who would make such a judgment, so what was the problem?

98

Now I'd hit the right note. Ernie glowed; he chopped his hands up and down in the air.

"Absolutely right," he said. "That is absolutely the attitude to take. Honest work. Never listen to anybody who wants to put you down for doing honest work. Just go right ahead and ignore them. Keep your pride. Anybody that doesn't like it, you tell them they can lump it."

This speech of his, the righteousness and approval lighting his large face, the jerky enthusiasm of his movements, roused the first doubts in me, the first gloomy suspicion that the warning, after all, might have some weight to it.

There was a note under my door saying that Beth wanted to talk to me. I was afraid it would be about my coat hung over the bannister to dry, or my feet making too much noise on the stairs when her husband Blake (sometimes) and the babies (always) had to sleep in the daytime.

The door opened on the scene of misery and confusion in which it seemed that all Beth's days were passed. Wet laundry—diapers and smelly baby woolens—was hanging from some ceiling racks, bottles in a sterilizer bubbled and rattled on the stove. The windows were steamed up, and soggy cloths or soiled stuffed toys were thrown on the chairs. The big baby was hanging on to the rungs of the playpen and letting out an accusing howl—Beth had obviously just set him in there—

and the smaller baby was in the high chair, with some mushy pumpkin-colored food spread like a rash across his mouth and chin.

Beth peered out from all this with a tight expression of superiority on her small flat face, as if to say that not many people could put up with such a nightmare as well as she could, even if the world was too ungenerous to give her the least credit.

"You know when you moved in," she said, then raised her voice to compete with the big baby, "when you moved in I mentioned to you that there was enough space up there for two?"

Not in the matter of headroom, I was about to say, but she continued right on, informing me that there was another girl moving in. She was going to be there from Tuesdays to Fridays. She would be auditing some courses at the college.

"Blake will get the daybed in tonight. She won't take up much room. I don't imagine she'll bring many clothes—she lives in town. You've had it all to yourself for six weeks now, and you'll still have it that way on weekends."

No mention of any reduction in the rent.

Nina actually did not take up much room. She was small, and thoughtful in her movements—she never bumped her head against the rafters, as I did. She spent a lot of her time sitting cross-legged on the daybed, her brownish-blond hair falling over her face, a Japanese kimono loose

over her childish white underwear. She had beautiful clothes—a camel's hair coat, cashmere
sweaters, a pleated tartan skirt with a large silver
pin. Just the sort of clothes you would see in a
magazine layout, with the heading: "Outfitting
Your Junior Miss for Her New Life on Campus."
But the moment she got back from the college she
discarded her costume for the kimono. She usually didn't bother hanging anything up. I followed
the same routine of getting out of my school
clothes, but in my case it was to keep the press in
my skirt and preserve a reasonable freshness in
the blouse or sweater, so I hung everything up
carefully. In the evenings I wore a woolly
bathrobe. I had eaten an early supper at the college as part of my wages, and Nina too seemed to
have eaten, though I didn't know where. Perhaps
her supper was just what she ate all evening—
almonds and oranges and a supply of little chocolate kisses wrapped in red or gold or purple foil.

I asked her if she didn't get cold, in that light
kimono.

"Unh-unh," she said. She grabbed my hand and
pressed it to her neck. "I'm permanently warm,"
she said, and in fact she was. Her skin even
looked warm, though she said that was just her
tan, and it was fading. And connected with this
skin warmth was a particular odor which was
nutty or spicy, not displeasing but not the odor of
a body that was constantly bathed and showered.

(Nor was I entirely fresh myself, due to Beth's rule of one bath a week. Many people then bathed no more than once a week, and I have an idea that there was more human smell around, in spite of talcum and the gritty paste deodorants.)

I usually read some book until late at night. I had thought it might be harder to read with someone else in the room, but Nina was an easy presence. She peeled her oranges and chocolates, she laid out games of patience. When she had to stretch to move a card she would sometimes make a little noise, a groan or grunt, as if she complained of this slight adjustment of her body, but took pleasure in it, all the same. Otherwise she was content, and curled up to sleep with the light on anytime she was ready. And because there was no demand or special need for talk we soon began to talk, and tell about our lives.

Nina was twenty-two years old and this was what had happened to her since she was fifteen:

First, she had gotten herself pregnant (that was how she put it) and married the father, who wasn't much older than she was. This was in a town somewhere out from Chicago. The name of the town was Laneyville, and the only jobs were at the grain elevator or fixing machinery, for the boys, and working in stores for the girls. Nina's ambition was to be a hairdresser, but you had to go away and train for that. Laneyville wasn't where she had always lived, it was where her

grandmother lived, and she lived with her grandmother because her father had died and her
mother got married again and her stepfather had
kicked her out.

She had a second baby, another boy, and her
husband was supposed to have a job promised in
another town, so he went off there. He was going
to send for her, but he never did. She left both the
children with her grandmother and took the bus to
Chicago.

On the bus she met a girl named Marcy who
like her was headed for Chicago. Marcy knew a
man there who owned a restaurant and would
give them jobs. But when they got to Chicago
and located the restaurant it turned out he didn't
own it but had only worked there and he had quit
some time before. The man who did own it had
an empty room upstairs and he let them stay there
in return for cleaning the place up every night.
They had to use the ladies' in the restaurant but
weren't supposed to spend much time there in the
daytime because it was for customers. They had
to wash any clothes that needed it after closing
time.

They didn't sleep hardly at all. They made
friends with a barman—he was a queer but nice—
in a place across the street and he let them drink
ginger ale for free. They met a man there who
invited them to a party and from that they got
asked to other parties and it was during this time

that Nina met Mr. Purvis. It was he in fact who gave her the name Nina. Before that she had been June. She went to live in Mr. Purvis's place in Chicago.

She was waiting till the right time to bring up the subject of her boys. There was so much room in Mr. Purvis's house that she was thinking they could live with her there. But when she mentioned it Mr. Purvis told her he despised children. He did not want her to get pregnant, ever. But somehow she did, and she and Mr. Purvis went to Japan to get her an abortion.

Up until the last minute that was what she thought she would do, and then she decided, no. She would go ahead and have the baby.

All right, he said. He would pay her way back to Chicago, and from then on, she was on her own.

She knew her way around a bit by this time, and she went to a place where they looked after you till the baby was born, and you could have it adopted. It was born and it was a girl and Nina named her Gemma and made up her mind to keep her.

She knew another girl who had had a baby in this place and kept it, and she and this girl made an arrangement that they would work shifts and live together and raise their babies. They got an apartment that they could afford and they got jobs—Nina's in a cocktail lounge—and everything was all right. Then Nina came home just before Christmas—Gemma was then eight months old—and found the other mother half drunk and fooling around with a man and the baby, Gemma, burning up with fever and too sick to even cry.

Nina wrapped her up and got a cab and took her to the hospital. The traffic was all snarled up because of Christmas, and when they finally got there they told her it was the wrong hospital for some reason and sent her off to another hospital, and on the way there Gemma had a convulsion and died.

She wanted to have a real burial for Gemma, not just have her put in with some old pauper who had died (that was what she heard happened with a baby's body when you didn't have any money), so she went to Mr. Purvis. He was nicer to her than she had expected, and he paid for the casket and everything and the gravestone with Gemma's name, and after it was all over he took Nina back. They went on a long trip to London and Paris and a lot of other places to cheer her up. When they got back he shut up the house in Chicago and moved here. He owned some property near here, out in the country, he owned racehorses.

He asked her if she would like to get an education, and she said she would. He said she should just sit in on some courses to see what she would like to study. She told him that she would like to live part of the time just the way ordinary students lived, and dress like them and study like them, and he said he thought that could be managed.

Her life made me feel like a simpleton.

I asked her what was Mr. Purvis's first name.

"Arthur."

"Why don't you call him that?"

"It wouldn't sound natural."

Nina was not supposed to go out at night, except to the college for certain specified events, such as a play or a concert or a lecture. She was supposed to eat dinner and lunch at the college. Though as I said, I don't know whether she ever did. Breakfast was Nescafé in our room, and day-old doughnuts I got to take home from the cafeteria. Mr. Purvis did not like the sound of this but accepted it as part of Nina's imitation of a college student's life. As long as she ate a good hot meal once a day and a sandwich and soup at another meal he was satisfied, and this was what he thought she did. She checked what the cafeteria was offering, so she could tell him that she'd had the sausages or the Salisbury steak, and the salmon or the egg salad sandwich.

"So how would he know if you did go out?"

Nina got to her feet, with that little personal sound of complaint or pleasure, and padded to the attic window.

"Come over here," she said. "And stay behind the curtain. See?"

A black car, parked not right across the street, but a few doors down. A streetlight caught the white hair of the driver.

"Mrs. Winner," said Nina. "She'll be there till midnight. Or later, I don't know. If I went out she'd follow me and hang around wherever I went and follow me back."

"What if she went to sleep?"

"Not her. Or if she did and I tried anything she'd be awake like a shot."

Just to give Mrs. Winner some practice, as Nina said, we left the house one evening and took a bus to the city library. From the bus window we watched the long black car having to slow and dawdle at every bus stop, then speed up and stay with us. We had to walk a block to the library, and Mrs. Winner passed us and parked beyond the front entrance, and watched us—we believed—in her rearview mirror.

I wanted to see if I could check out a copy of *The Scarlet Letter,* which was required for one of my courses. I could not afford to buy one, and the copies from the college library were all out. Also I had an idea of getting a book out for Nina—the sort of book that showed simplified charts of history.

Nina had bought the textbooks for the courses she was auditing. She had bought notebooks and pens—the best fountain pens of that time—in matching colors. Red for Middle-American Pre-

Columbian Civilizations, blue for the Romantic Poets, green for Victorian and Georgian English Novelists, yellow for Fairy Tales from Perrault to Andersen. She went to every lecture, sitting in the back row because she thought that was the proper place for her. She spoke as if she enjoyed walking through the Arts building with the throng of other students, finding her seat, opening her textbook at the page specified, taking out her pen. But her notebooks remained empty.

The trouble was, as I saw it, that she had no pegs to hang anything on. She did not know what Victorian meant, or Romantic, or Pre-Columbian. She had been to Japan, and Barbados, and many of the countries in Europe, but she could never have found those places on a map. She wouldn't have known whether or not the French Revolution came before the First World War.

I wondered how these courses had been chosen for her. Did she like the sound of them, had Mr. Purvis thought she could master them, or had he perhaps chosen them cynically, so that she would soon get her fill of being a student?

When I was looking for the book I wanted, I caught sight of Ernie Botts. He had an armful of mysteries, which he had picked up for an old friend of his mother's. He had told me how he always did that, just as he always played checkers on Saturday mornings with a crony of his father's out in the War Veterans' Home.

I introduced him to Nina. I had told him about her moving in, but nothing, of course, about her former or even her present life.

He shook Nina's hand and said he was pleased to meet her and asked at once if he could give us a ride home.

I was about to say no thanks, we'd get a ride on the bus, when Nina asked him where his car was parked.

"In the back," he said.

"Is there a back door?"

"Yes, yes. It's a sedan."

"No, I didn't mean that," said Nina nicely. "I meant in the library. In the building."

"Yes. Yes, there is," said Ernie in a fluster. "I'm sorry, I thought you meant the car. Yes. A back door in the library. I came in that way myself. I'm sorry." Now he was blushing, and he would have gone on apologizing if Nina had not broken in with a kind, even flattering, laugh.

"Well then," she said. "We can go out the back door. So that's settled. Thanks."

Ernie drove us home. He asked if we would like to detour by his place, for a cup of coffee or a hot chocolate.

"Sorry, we're sort of in a rush," said Nina. "But thanks for asking."

"I guess you've got homework."

"Homework, yes," she said. "We sure do."

I was thinking that he had never once asked me

109

to his house. Propriety. One girl, no. Two girls, okay.

No black car across the street when we said our thanks and good nights. No black car when we looked through the attic window. In a short time the phone rang, for Nina, and I heard her saying, on the landing, "Oh no, we just went in the library and got a book and came straight home on the bus. There was one right away, yes. I'm fine. Absolutely. Night-night."

She came swaying and smiling up the stairs.

"Mrs. Winner's got herself in hot water tonight."

Then she made a little leap and started to tickle me, as she did every once in a while, without the least warning, having discovered that I was extraordinarily ticklish.

One morning Nina did not get out of bed. She said she had a sore throat, a fever.

"Touch me."

"You always feel hot to me."

"Today I'm hotter."

It was a Friday. She asked me to call Mr. Purvis, to tell him she wanted to stay here for the weekend.

"He'll let me—he can't stand anybody being sick around him. He's a nut that way."

Mr. Purvis wondered if he should send a doctor. Nina had foreseen that, and told me to say she just needed to rest, and she'd phone him, or I would, if she got any worse. Well then, tell her to take care, he said, and thanked me for phoning, and for being a good friend to Nina. And then, having started to say good-bye, he asked me if I would care to join him for Saturday night's dinner. He said he found it boring to eat alone.

Nina had thought of that too.

"If he asks you to go and eat with him tomorrow night, why don't you go? There's always something good to eat on Saturday nights, it's special."

On Saturdays the cafeteria was closed. The possibility of meeting Mr. Purvis disturbed and interested me.

"Should I really? If he asks?"

So I went upstairs, having agreed to dine with Mr. Purvis—he had actually said "dine"—and asked Nina what I should wear.

"Why worry now? It's not till tomorrow night."

Why worry indeed? I had only one good dress, the turquoise crepe that I had bought with some of my scholarship money, to wear when I gave the valedictory address at the high school commencement exercises.

"And anyway it doesn't matter," said Nina. "He'll never notice."

Mrs. Winner came to get me. Her hair was not white, but platinum blond, a color that to me certified a hard heart, immoral dealings, a long bumpy ride through the sordid back alleys of life. Nevertheless I pressed down on the handle of the front door to ride beside her, because I thought that was the decent and democratic thing to do. She let me do this, standing beside her, then briskly opened the back door.

I had thought that Mr. Purvis must live in one of the stodgy mansions surrounded by acres of lawns and unfarmed fields north of the city. It was probably the racehorses that had made me think so. Instead, we travelled east through prosperous but not lordly streets, past brick and mock-Tudor houses with their lights on in the early dark and their Christmas lights blinking already out of the snow-capped shrubbery. We turned in at a narrow driveway between high hedges and parked in front of a house that I recognized as *modern* because of its flat roof and long wall of windows and the fact that the building material appeared to be cement. No Christmas lights here, no lights of any kind.

No sign of Mr. Purvis either. The car slid into a basement cavern, we rode in an elevator up one floor and came out in a hall dimly lit and furnished like a living room with upholstered hard chairs and little polished tables, and mirrors and rugs. Mrs. Winner waved me ahead of her through one of the doors that opened off this hall, into a windowless room with a bench and hooks around the walls. It was just like a school cloakroom except for the polish on the wood and carpet on the floor.

"Here is where you leave your clothes," Mrs. Winner said.

I removed my boots, I stuffed my mittens into my coat pockets, I hung my coat up. Mrs. Winner stayed with me. I supposed she had to, to show me which way to take next. There was a comb in my pocket and I wanted to fix my hair, but not with her watching. And I did not see a mirror.

"Now the rest."

She looked straight at me to see if I understood, and when I appeared not to (though in a sense I did, I understood but hoped to have made a mistake) she said, "Don't worry, you won't be cold. The house is well heated throughout."

I did not yet move to obey, and she spoke to me casually, as if she could not be bothered with contempt.

"I hope you're not a baby."

I could have reached for my coat, at that point. I could have demanded to be driven back to the rooming house. If that was refused, I could have walked back on my own. I remembered the way we had come and though it would have been cold to walk, it would have taken me less than an hour.

I don't suppose that the outside door would have been locked, or that there would have been any effort to bring me back.

"Oh no," said Mrs. Winner, seeing I still did not make a move. "Do you think you're made any different from the rest of us? You think I haven't seen all you got before now?"

It was partly her contempt that made me stay. Partly. That and my pride.

I sat down. I removed my shoes. I unfastened and peeled down my stockings. I stood up and unzipped then yanked off the dress in which I had delivered the valedictory address with its final words of Latin. *Ave atque vale.*

Still reasonably covered by my slip, I reached back and unhooked the fastenings of my brassiere, then somehow hauled the whole thing free of my arms and around to the front, to be discarded in one movement. Next came my garter belt, then my panties—when they were off I balled them up and hid them under the brassiere. I put my feet back into my shoes.

"Bare feet," said Mrs. Winner, sighing. It seemed the slip was too tiresome for her to mention, but after I had again taken my shoes off she said, "Bare. Do you know the meaning of the word? Bare."

I pulled the slip over my head and she handed me a bottle of lotion and said, "Rub yourself with this."

It smelled like Nina. I rubbed some on my arms and shoulders, the only parts of myself that I could touch with Mrs. Winner standing there watching, and then we went out into the hall, my eyes avoiding the mirrors, and she opened another door and I went into the next room alone.

It had never occurred to me that Mr. Purvis might be waiting in the same naked condition as myself, and he was not. He wore a dark blue blazer, a white shirt, an ascot scarf (I did not know it was called that), and gray slacks. He was hardly taller than I was, and he was thin and old, mostly bald, and with wrinkles in his forehead when he smiled.

It had not occurred to me either that the undressing might be a prelude to rape, or to any ceremony but supper. (And indeed it was not to be, to judge by the appetizing smells in the room and the silver-lidded dishes on the sideboard.) Why had I not thought of such a thing? Why was I not more apprehensive? It had something to do with my ideas about old men. I thought that they were not only incapable but too worn down, made too dignified—or depressed—by various trials and experiences and their own unsavory physical decline to have any interest left. I wasn't stupid enough to think that my being undressed had nothing to do with the sexual uses of my body, but I took it more as a dare than as a preliminary to further trespass, and my going along with it had more to do with the folly of pride, as I have said, more to do with some shaky recklessness than with anything else.

Here I am, I might have wished to say, in the skin of my body which does not shame me any more than the bareness of my teeth. Of course that was not true and in fact I had broken out in a sweat, although not for fear of any violation.

Mr. Purvis shook hands with me, making no sign of awareness that I lacked clothing. He said it was a pleasure for him to meet Nina's friend. Just as if I was somebody Nina had brought home from school.

Which in a way was true.

An inspiration to Nina, he said I was.

"She admires you very much. Now, you must be hungry. Shall we see what they've provided for us?"

He lifted the lids and set about serving me. Cornish hens, which I took to be pygmy chickens, saffron rice with raisins, various finely cut vegetables fanned out at an angle and preserving their color more faithfully than the vegetables that I regularly saw. A dish of muddy green pickles and a dish of dark red preserve.

"Not too much of these," Mr. Purvis said of the pickles and the preserve. "A bit hot to start with."

He ushered me back to the table, turned again to the sideboard and served himself sparingly, and sat down.

There was a pitcher of water on the table, and a bottle of wine. I got the water. Serving me wine in his house, he said, would probably be classed as a capital offense. I was a little disappointed as I had never had a chance to drink wine. When we went to the Old Chelsea, Ernie always expressed his

116

satisfaction that no wine or liquor was served on Sundays. Not only did he refuse to drink, on Sundays or any other day, but he disliked seeing others do it.

"Now Nina tells me," said Mr. Purvis, "Nina tells me that you are studying English philosophy, but I think it must be English *and* philosophy, am I right? Because surely there is not so great a supply of English philosophers?"

In spite of his warning, I had taken a dollop of green pickle on my tongue and was too stunned to reply. He waited courteously while I gulped down water.

"We start with Greeks. It's a survey course," I said, when I could speak.

"Oh yes. Greece. Well as far as you've got with the Greeks, who is your favorite—oh, no, just a minute. It will fall apart more easily like this."

There followed a demonstration of separating and removing the meat from the bones of a Cornish hen—nicely done, and without condescension, rather as if it was a joke we might share.

"Your favorite?"

"We haven't got to him yet, we're doing the pre-Socratics," I said. "But Plato."

"Plato is your favorite. So you read ahead, you don't just stay where you're supposed to? Plato. Yes, I could have guessed that. You like the cave?"

"Yes."

"Yes of course. The cave. It's beautiful, isn't it?"

When I was sitting down, the most flagrant part of me was out of sight. If my breasts had been tiny and ornamental, like Nina's, instead of full and large nippled and bluntly serviceable, I could have been almost at ease. I tried to look at him when I spoke, but against my will I would suffer waves of flushing. When this happened I thought his voice changed slightly, becoming soothing and politely satisfied. Just as if he'd made a winning move in a game. But he went on talking nimbly and entertainingly, telling me about a trip he had made to Greece. Delphi, the Acropolis, the famous light that you believed couldn't be true but was true, the bare bones of the Peloponnesus.

"And then to Crete—do you know about the Minoan civilization?"

"Yes."

"Of course you do. Of course. And you know the way the Minoan ladies dressed?"

"Yes."

I looked into his face this time, his eyes. I was determined not to squirm away, not even when I felt the heat on my throat.

"Very nice, that style," he said almost sadly. "Very nice. It's odd the different things that are hidden in different eras. And the things that are displayed."

Dessert was vanilla custard and whipped cream,

with bits of cake in it, and raspberries. He ate only a few bites of his. But after failing to settle down enough to enjoy the first course, I was determined not to miss out on anything rich and sweet, and I fixed my appetite and attention on every spoonful.

He poured coffee into small cups and said that we would drink it in the library.

My buttocks made a slapping noise, as I loosened myself from the sleek upholstery of the dining room chair. But this was almost covered up by the clatter of the delicate coffee cups on the tray in his shaky old grasp.

Libraries in a house were known to me only from books. This one was entered through a panel in the dining room wall. The panel swung open without a sound, at a touch of his raised foot. He apologized for going ahead of me, as he had to do since he carried the coffee. To me it was a relief. I thought that our backsides—not just mine but everybody's—were the most beastly part of the body.

When I was seated in the chair he indicated, he gave me my coffee. It was not so easy to sit here, out in the open, as it had been at the dining room table. That chair had been covered with smooth striped silk, but this one was upholstered in some dark plush material, which prickled me. An intimate agitation was set up.

The light in this room was brighter than it had

been in the dining room, and the books lining the walls had an expression more disturbing and reproving than the look of the dim dining room with its landscape pictures and light-absorbing panels.

For a moment, as we left one room for the other, I had had some notion of a story—the sort of story I had heard of but that few people then got the chance to read—in which the room referred to as a library would turn out to be a bedroom, with soft lights and puffy cushions and all manner of downy coverings. I did not have time to figure out what I would do in such circumstances, because the room we were in was plainly nothing but a library. The reading lights, the books on the shelves, the invigorating smell of coffee. Mr. Purvis pulling out a book, riffling through its leaves, finding what he wanted.

"It would be very kind if you would read to me. My eyes are tired in the evenings. You know this book?"

A Shropshire Lad.

I knew it. In fact I knew many of the poems by heart.

I said that I would read.

"And may I ask you please—may I ask you please—not to cross your legs?"

My hands were trembling when I took the book from him.

"Yes," he said. "Yes."

He chose a chair in front of the bookcase, facing me.

"Now—"

"On Wenlock Edge the wood's in trouble—"

Familiar words and rhythms calmed me down. They took me over. Gradually I began to feel more at peace.

> *The gale, it plies the saplings double,*
> *It blows so hard, 'twill soon be gone:*
> *To-day the Roman and his trouble*
> *Are ashes under Uricon.*

Where is Uricon? Who knows?

It wasn't really that I forgot where I was or who I was with or in what condition I sat there. But I had come to feel somewhat remote and philosophical. The notion came to me that everybody in the world was naked, in a way. Mr. Purvis was naked, though he wore clothes. We were all sad, bare, forked creatures. Shame receded. I just kept turning the pages, reading one poem and then another, then another. Liking the sound of my voice. Until to my surprise and almost to my disappointment—there were still famous lines to come—Mr. Purvis interrupted me. He stood up, he sighed.

"Enough, enough," he said. "That was very nice. Thank you. Your country accent is quite suitable. Now it's my bedtime."

I let the book go. He replaced it on the shelves

and closed the glass doors. The country accent was news to me.

"And I'm afraid it's time to send you home."

He opened another door, into the hall I had seen so long ago, at the beginning of the evening, and I passed in front of him and the door was closed behind me. I may have said good night. It is even possible that I thanked him for dinner, and that he spoke to me in a few dry words (not at all, thank you for your company, it was very kind of you, thank you for reading Housman) in a suddenly tired, old, crumpled, and indifferent voice. He did not lay a hand on me.

The same dimly lit cloakroom. My same clothes. The turquoise dress, my stockings, my slip. Mrs. Winner appeared while I was fastening my stockings. She said only one thing to me, as I was ready to leave.

"You forgot your scarf."

And there indeed was the scarf I had knit in Home Economics class, the only thing I would ever knit in my life. I had come close to abandoning it, in this place.

As I got out of the car Mrs. Winner said, "Mr. Purvis would like to speak to Nina before he goes to bed. If you would remind her."

But there was no Nina waiting to receive this message. Her bed was made up. Her coat and

122

boots were gone. A few of her other clothes were still hanging in the closet.

Beverly and Kay had both gone home for the weekend, so I ran downstairs to see if Beth had any information.

"I'm sorry," said Beth, whom I never saw sorry about anything. "I can't keep track of all your comings and goings."

Then as I turned away, "I've asked you several times not to thump so much on the stairs. I just got Sally-Lou to sleep."

I had not made up my mind, when I got home, what I would say to Nina. Would I ask her if she was required to be naked, in that house, if she had known perfectly well what sort of an evening was waiting for me? Or would I say nothing much, waiting for her to ask me? And even then, I could say innocently that I'd eaten Cornish hen and yellow rice, and that it was very good. That I'd read from *A Shropshire Lad*.

I could just let her wonder.

Now that she was gone, none of this mattered. The focus was shifted. Mrs. Winner phoned after ten o'clock—breaking another of Beth's rules—and when I told her that Nina was not there she said, "Are you sure of that?"

The same when I told her that I had no idea where Nina had gone. "Are you sure?"

I asked her not to phone again till morning, because of Beth's rules and the babies' sleep, and she said, "Well. I don't know. This is serious."

When I got up in the morning the car was parked across the street. Later, Mrs. Winner rang the bell and told Beth that she had been sent to check Nina's room. Even Beth was quelled by Mrs. Winner, who then came up the stairs without a reproach or a warning being uttered. After she looked all around our room she looked in the bathroom and the closet, even shaking out a couple of blankets that were folded on the closet floor.

I was still in my pajamas, writing an essay on *Sir Gawain and the Green Knight,* and drinking Nescafé.

Mrs. Winner said that she had had to phone the hospitals, to see if Nina had been taken ill, and that Mr. Purvis had gone out himself to check on several other places where she might be.

"If you know anything it would be better to tell us," she said. "Anything at all."

Then as she started down the stairs she turned and said in a voice that was less menacing, "Is there anybody at the college she was friendly with. Anybody you know?"

I said that I didn't think so.

I had seen Nina only a couple of times at the college. Once she was walking down the lower corridor of the Arts Building in the crush between classes. Once she was in the cafeteria. Both times she was alone. It was not particularly unusual to be alone when you were hurrying from one class to another, but it was a little strange to sit alone in the cafeteria with a cup of coffee at around a quarter to four in the afternoon when that space was practically deserted. She sat with a smile on her face, as if to say how pleased, how privileged, she felt to be there, how alert and ready to respond to the demands of this life she was, once she understood what they were.

In the afternoon it began to snow. The car across the street had to depart to make way for the snowplow. When I went into the bathroom and caught the flutter of her kimono on its hook, I felt what I had been suppressing—a true fear for Nina. I had a picture of her, disoriented, weeping into her loose hair, wandering around in the snow in her white underwear instead of her camel's hair coat, though I knew perfectly well that she had taken the coat with her.

The phone rang just as I was about to leave for my first class on Monday morning.

"It's me," said Nina, in a rushed warning, but with something like triumph in her voice. "Listen. Please. Could you please do me a favor?"

"Where are you? They're looking for you."

"Who is?"

"Mr. Purvis. Mrs. Winner."

"Well, you're not to tell them. Don't tell them anything. I'm here."

"Where?"

"Ernest's."

"Ernest's?" I said. *"Ernie's?"*

"Sshh. Did anybody there hear you?"

"No."

"Listen, could you please, please get on a bus and bring me the rest of my stuff? I need my shampoo. I need my kimono. I'm going around in Ernest's bathrobe. You should see me, I look like an old woolly brown dog. Is the car still outside?"

I went and looked.

"Yes."

"Okay then, you should get on the bus and ride up to the college just like you normally do. And then catch the bus downtown. You know where to get off. Campbell and Howe. Then walk over here. Carlisle Street. Three sixty-three. You know it, don't you?"

"Is Ernie there?"

"No, dum-dum. He's at work. He's got to support us, doesn't he?"

Us? Was Ernie to support Nina and me?

No. Ernie and Nina. *Ernie and Nina.*

Nina said, "Oh, please. You're the only person I've got."

I did as directed. I caught the college bus, then the downtown bus. I got off at Campbell and Howe and walked west to Carlisle Street. The snowstorm was over; the sky was clear; it was a bright, windless, deep-frozen day. The light hurt

126

my eyes and the fresh snow squeaked under my feet.

Now half a block north, on Carlisle Street, to the house where Ernie had lived with his mother and father and then with his mother and then alone. And now—how was it possible?—with Nina.

The house looked just as it had when I had come here once or twice with my mother. A brick bungalow with a tiny front yard, an arched living room window with an upper pane of colored glass. Cramped and genteel.

Nina was wrapped, just as she had described herself, in a man's brown woolly tasselled dressing gown, with its manly but innocent Ernie-smell of shaving lather and Lifebuoy soap.

She grabbed my hands, which were stiff with cold inside my gloves. Each of them had been holding on to the handle of a shopping bag.

"Frozen," she said. "Come on, we'll get them into some warm water."

"They are not *frozen*," I said. "Just frozen."

But she went ahead and helped me off with my things, and took me into the kitchen and ran a bowlful of water, and then as the blood returned painfully to my fingers she told me how Ernest (Ernie) had come to the rooming house on Saturday night. He was bringing a magazine that had a lot of pictures of old ruins and castles and things that he thought might interest me. She got herself out of bed and came downstairs, because of course he could not go upstairs, and when he saw how sick she was he said she had to come home with him so he could look after her. Which he had done so well that her sore throat was practically gone and her fever completely gone. And then they had decided that she would stay here. She would just stay with him and never go back to where she was before.

She seemed unwilling even to mention Mr. Purvis's name.

"But it has to be a huge big secret," she said. "You are the only one to know. Because you're our friend and you are the reason we met."

She was making coffee. "Look up there," she said, waving at the open cupboard. "Look at the way he keeps things. Mugs here. Cups and saucers here. Every cup has got its own hook. Isn't it tidy? The house is just like that all over. I love it.

"You are the reason we met," she repeated. "If we have a baby and it's a girl, we could name it after you."

I held my hands round the mug, still feeling a throb in my fingers. There were African violets on the windowsill over the sink. His mother's order in the cupboards, his mother's houseplants. The big fern was probably still in front of the living room window, and the doilies on the armchairs. What she had said, in regard to herself and Ernie, seemed brazen and—especially when I thought of the Ernie part of it—abundantly distasteful.

"You're going to get married?"

"Well."

"You said if you have a baby."

"Well, you never know, we might have started that without being married," said Nina, ducking her head mischievously.

"With Ernie?" I said. "With *Ernie*?"

"Well, why not? Ernie's nice," she said. "And anyway I'm calling him Ernest." She hugged the bathrobe around herself.

"What about Mr. Purvis?"

"What about him?"

"Well, if it's something happening already, couldn't it be his?"

Everything changed about Nina. Her face turned mean and sour. *"Him,"* she said with contempt. "What do you want to talk about him for? He never had it in him."

"Oh?" I said, and was going to ask what about Gemma, but she interrupted.

"What do you want to talk about the past for? Don't make me sick. That's all dead and gone. It doesn't matter to me and Ernest. We're together now. We're in love now."

In love. With Ernie. Ernest. Now.

"Okay," I said.

"Sorry I yelled at you. Did I yell? I'm sorry. You're our friend and you brought me my things and I appreciate it. You're Ernest's cousin and you're our family."

She slipped behind me and her fingers darted into my armpits and she began to tickle me, at first lazily and then furiously, saying, "Aren't you? Aren't you?"

I tried to get free, but I couldn't. I went into spasms of suffering laughter and wriggled and cried out and begged her to stop. Which she did, when she had me quite helpless, and both of us were out of breath.

"You're the ticklishest person I ever met."

I had to wait a long time for the bus, stamping my feet on the pavement. When I got to the college I had missed my second as well as my first class, and I was late for my work in the cafeteria. I changed into my green cotton uniform in the broom closet and pushed my mop of black hair (the worst hair in the world for showing up in food, as the manager had warned me) under a cotton snood.

I was supposed to get the sandwiches and salads out on the shelves before the doors opened for lunch, but now I had to do it with an impatient lineup watching me, and that made me feel clumsy. I was so much more noticeable now than when I pushed the cart among the tables to collect the dirty dishes. People were concentrating then on their food and conversation. Now they were just looking at me.

I thought of what Beverly and Kay had said about spoiling my chances, marking myself off in the wrong way. It seemed now it could be right.

After I finished cleaning up the cafeteria tables, I changed back into my ordinary clothes and went to the college library to work on my essay. It was my afternoon free of classes.

An underground tunnel led from the Arts Building to the library, and around the entrance to this tunnel were posted advertisements for movies and restaurants and used bicycles and typewriters, as well as notices for plays and concerts. The Music Department announced that a free recital of songs composed to fit the poems of English Country Poets would be presented on a date that had now passed. I had seen this notice before, and did not have to look at it to be reminded of the names Herrick, Housman, Tennyson. And a few steps into the tunnel the lines began to assault me.

On Wenlock Edge the wood's in trouble

I would never think of those lines again without feeling the prickles of the upholstery on my bare haunches. The sticky prickly shame. A far greater shame it seemed now, than at the time. He had done something to me, after all.

From far, from eve and morning
And yon twelve-winded sky,
The stuff of life to knit me
Blew hither—here am I.

No.

What are those blue remembered hills,
What spires, what farms are those?

No, never.

White in the moon the long road lies
That leads me from my love.

No. No. No.

I would always be reminded of what I had
agreed to do. Not been forced, not ordered, not
even persuaded. Agreed to do.

Nina would know. She had been too preoccupied with Ernie to say anything that morning, but
there would come a time when she would laugh
about it. Not cruelly, but just the way she
laughed at so many things. And she might even
tease me about it. Her teasing would have in it
something like her tickling, something insistent,
obscene.

Nina and Ernie. In my life from now on.

The college library was a high beautiful space,
designed and built and paid for by people who
believed that those who sat at the long tables
before open books—even those who were hungover, sleepy, resentful, and uncomprehending—
should have space above them, panels of dark

gleaming wood around them, high windows bordered with Latin admonitions, through which to look at the sky. For a few years before they went into schoolteaching or business or began to rear children, they should have that. And now it was my turn and I should have it too.

Sir Gawain and the Green Knight.

I was writing a good essay. I would probably get an A. I would go on writing essays and getting A's because that was what I could do. The people who awarded scholarships, who built universities and libraries, would continue to dribble out money so that I could do it.

But that was not what mattered. That was not going to keep you from damage.

Nina did not stay with Ernie even for one week. One day very soon he would come home and find her gone. Gone her coat and boots, her lovely clothes and the kimono that I had brought over. Gone her taffy hair and her tickling habits and the extra warmth of her skin and the little *un-unh*s as she moved. All gone with no explanation, not a word on paper. Not a word.

Ernie was not one, however, to shut himself up and mourn. He said so, when he phoned to tell me the news and check on my availability for Sunday dinner. We climbed the stairs to the Old Chelsea and he commented on the fact that this was our last dinner before the Christmas holidays. He helped me off with my coat and I smelled Nina's smell. Could it still be on his skin?

No. The source was revealed when he passed something to me. Something like a large handkerchief.

"Just put it in your coat pocket," he said.

Not a handkerchief. The texture was sturdier, with a slight ribbing. An undershirt.

"I don't want it around," he said, and by his voice you might have thought that it was just underwear itself he did not want around, never mind that it was Nina's and smelled of Nina.

He ordered the roast beef, and cut and chewed it with his normal efficiency and polite appetite. I gave him the news from home, which as usual at this time of year consisted of the size of snow-drifts, the number of blocked roads, the winter havoc which gave us distinction.

After some time Ernie said, "I went round to his house. There was nobody in it."

Whose house?

Her uncle's, he said. He knew which house because he and Nina had driven past it, after dark. There was nobody there now, he said, they had packed up and gone. Her choice, after all.

"It's a woman's privilege," he said. "Like they say, it's a woman's privilege to change her mind."

His eyes, now that I looked into them, had a dry famished look, and the skin around them was dark and wrinkled. He pursed his mouth, controlling a tremor, then talked on, with an air of trying to see all sides, trying to understand.

"She couldn't leave her old uncle," he said. "She didn't have the heart to run out on him. I said we could take him in with us, because I was used to old people, but she said she would sooner make a break. Then I guess she didn't have the heart to after all."

"Better not to expect too much. Some things I guess you're just not meant to have."

When I went past the coats on my way to the washroom I got the shirt out of my pocket. I stuffed it in with the used towels.

That day in the library I had been unable to go on with Sir Gawain. I had torn a page from my notebook and picked up my pen and walked out. On the landing outside the library doors there was a pay phone, and beside that hung a phone book. I looked through the phone book and on the piece of paper I had brought I wrote two numbers. They were not phone numbers but addresses.

1648 Henfryn Street.

The other number, which I needed only to check, having seen it both recently and on Christmas card envelopes, was 363 Carlisle.

I walked back through the tunnel to the Arts Building and entered the little shop across from the Common Room. I had enough change in my pocket to buy an envelope and a stamp. I tore off the paper with the Carlisle Street address on it and put that scrap into the envelope. I sealed the envelope and on the front of it I wrote the other, longer number with the name of Mr. Purvis and the address on Henfryn Street. All in block capitals. Then I licked and fixed the stamp. I think that in those days it would have been a four-cent stamp.

Just outside the shop was a mail chute. I slipped the envelope into it, there in the wide lower corridor of the Arts Building with people passing me on the way to classes, on the way to have a smoke and maybe a game of bridge in the Common Room. On their way to deeds they didn't know they had in them.

Deep-Holes

Sally packed devilled eggs—something she hated to take on a picnic, because they were so messy. Ham sandwiches, crab salad, lemon tarts—also a packing problem. Kool-Aid for the children, a half-size Mumm's for herself and Alex. She would have just a sip, because she was still nursing. She had bought plastic champagne glasses for this occasion, but when Alex spotted her handling them he got the real ones—a wedding present—out of the china cabinet. She protested, but he insisted, and took charge of them himself, the wrapping and packing.

"Dad is really a sort of bourgeois *gentilhomme*," Kent was to say to Sally some years later when he was in his teens and acing everything at school. So sure of becoming some sort of scientist that he could get away with spouting French around the house.

"Don't make fun of your father," said Sally mechanically.

"I'm not. It's just that most geologists seem so grubby."

The picnic was in honor of Alex's publishing his first solo article in *Zeitschrift für Geomorphology*. They were going to Osler Bluff because it figured largely in the article, and because Sally and the children had never been there.

They drove a couple of miles down a rough country road—having turned off a decent unpaved country road—and there was a place for cars to park, with no cars in it at present. The sign was roughly painted on a board and needed retouching.

CAUTION. DEEP-HOLES.

Why the hyphen? Sally thought. But who cares?

The entrance to the woods looked quite ordinary and unthreatening. Sally understood, of course, that these woods were on top of a high bluff, and she expected a daunting lookout somewhere. She did not expect to find what had to be skirted almost immediately in front of them.

Deep chambers, really, some as big as a coffin, some much bigger than that, like rooms cut out of the rocks. Corridors zigzagging between them and ferns and mosses growing out of their sides. Not enough greenery, however, to make any sort of cushion over the rubble that seemed so far below. The path went meandering amongst them, over hard earth or shelves of not-quite-level rock.

"Ooee," came the call of the boys, Kent and Peter, nine and six years old, running ahead.

"No tearing around in here," called Alex. "No stupid showing off, you hear me? You understand? Answer me."

They called okay, and he proceeded, carrying the picnic basket and apparently believing that no further fatherly warning was necessary. Sally stumbled along faster than was easy for her, with the diaper bag and the baby Savanna. She couldn't slow down till she had her sons in sight, saw them trotting along taking sidelong looks into the black chambers, still making exaggerated but discreet noises of horror. She was nearly crying with exhaustion and alarm and some familiar sort of seeping rage.

The outlook did not appear until they had gone along these dirt and rock paths for what seemed to her like half a mile, and was probably a quarter mile. Then there was a brightening, an intrusion of sky, and a halt of her husband ahead. He gave a cry of arrival and display, and the boys hooted with true astonishment. Sally, emerging from the woods, found them lined up on an outcrop above the treetops—above several levels of treetops, as it turned out—with the summer fields spread far below in a shimmer of green and yellow.

As soon as she was put down on her blanket Savanna began to cry.

"Hungry," said Sally.

Alex said, "I thought she got her lunch in the car."

"She did. But she's hungry again."

She got Savanna latched onto one side and with her free hand unfastened the picnic basket. This was not of course how Alex had planned things. But he gave a good-humored sigh and retrieved the champagne glasses from their wrappings in his pockets, placing them on their sides on a patch of grass.

"Glug-glug I'm thirsty too," said Kent, and Peter immediately imitated him.

"Glug-glug me too glug-glug."

"Shut up," said Alex.

Kent said, "Shut up, Peter."

Alex said to Sally, "What did you bring for them to drink?"

"Kool-Aid in the blue jug. And the plastic glasses in a napkin underneath."

Of course Alex believed that Kent had started that nonsense not because he was really thirsty but because he was crudely excited by the sight of Sally's breast. He thought it was high time Savanna was transferred to the bottle—she was nearly six months old. And he thought Sally was far too casual about the whole procedure, sometimes going around the kitchen doing things with one hand while the infant guzzled. With Kent sneaking peeks and Peter referring to Mommy's milk jugs. That came from Kent, Alex said. Kent was a sneak and a troublemaker and the possessor of a dirty mind.

"Well, I have to keep doing those things," said Sally.

"Nursing's not one of the things you have to do. You could have her on the bottle tomorrow."

"I will soon. Not quite tomorrow, but soon."

But here she is, still letting Savanna and the milk jugs dominate the picnic.

The Kool-Aid is poured, then the champagne.

Sally and Alex touch glasses, with Savanna in their way. Sally has her sip and wishes she could have more. She smiles at Alex to communicate this wish, and maybe the wish that it would be nice to be alone with him. He drinks his champagne, and as if her sip and smile had been enough to soothe him, he starts in on the picnic. She instructs him as to which sandwiches have the mustard he likes and which have the mustard she and Peter like and which are for Kent who likes no mustard at all.

While this is going on, Kent manages to slip in behind her and finish up her champagne. Peter must have seen him do this, but for some peculiar reason he does not tell on him. Sally discovers what has happened sometime later and Alex never knows about it at all, because he soon forgets there was anything left in her glass and packs it neatly away with his own, while telling the boys about dolomite. They listen, presumably, while they gobble up the sandwiches and ignore the devilled eggs and crab salad and grab the tarts.

Dolomite, Alex says. That is the thick caprock they see. Underneath it is shale, clay turned into rock, very fine, fine grained. Water works through the dolomite and when it gets to the shale it just lies there, it can't get through the thin layers, the fine grain. So the erosion—that's the destruction of the dolomite—works and works its way back to the source, eats a channel back, and the caprock

141

develops vertical joints; do they know what vertical means?

"Up and down," says Kent lackadaisically.

"Weak vertical joints, and they get to lean out and then they leave crevasses behind them and after millions of years they break off altogether and go tumbling down the slope."

"I have to go," says Kent.

"Go where?"

"I have to go pee."

"Oh for God's sake, go."

"Me too," says Peter.

Sally clamps her mouth down on the automatic injunction to be careful. Alex looks at her and approves of the clamping down. They smile faintly at each other.

Savanna has fallen asleep, her lips slack around the nipple. With the boys out of the way, it's easier to detach her. Sally can burp her, settle her on her blanket, without worrying about an exposed breast. If Alex finds the sight distasteful—she knows he does, he dislikes the whole conjunction of sex and nourishment, his wife's breast turned into udders—he can look away, and he does.

As she buttons herself up there comes a cry, not sharp but lost, diminishing, and Alex is on his feet before she is, running along the path. Then a louder cry getting closer. It's Peter.

"Kent fell in. Kent fell in."

His father yells, "I'm coming."

Sally will always believe that she knew at once, even before she heard Peter's voice she knew what had happened. If any accident happened it would not be to her six-year-old who was brave but not inventive, not a show-off. It would be to Kent. She could see exactly how. Peeing into the hole, balancing on the rim, teasing Peter, teasing himself.

He was alive. He was lying far down in the rubble at the bottom of the crevasse, but he was moving his arms, struggling to push himself up. Struggling so feebly. One leg caught under him, the other oddly bent.

"Can you carry the baby?" she said to Peter. "Go back to the picnic and put her down and watch her. That's my good boy. My good strong boy."

Alex was getting down into the hole, scrambling down, telling Kent to stay still. Getting down in one piece was just possible. It would be getting Kent out that was hard.

Should she run to the car and see if there was a rope? Tie the rope around a tree trunk. Maybe tie it around Kent's body so she could lift him when Alex raised him up to her.

There wouldn't be a rope. Why should there be a rope?

Alex had reached him. He bent and lifted him. Kent gave a beseeching scream of pain. Alex draped him around his shoulders, head hanging down on one side and useless legs—one so oddly protruding—on the other. He rose, stumbled a couple of steps, and while still hanging on to Kent dropped onto his knees. He had decided to crawl, and was making his way—Sally could understand this now—to the rubble which partly filled the far end of the crevasse. He shouted some order to her without raising his head, and though she could not make out a single word she understood. She got up off her knees—why was she on her knees?—and pushed through some saplings to the rim where the rubble came to within perhaps three feet of the surface. Alex was crawling along with Kent dangling from him like a shot deer.

She called, "I'm here. I'm here."

Kent would have to be raised up by his father, pulled to the solid shelf of rock by his mother. He was a skinny boy who had not yet reached his first spurt of growth, but he seemed heavy as a bag of cement. Sally's arms could not do it on the first try. She shifted her position, crouching instead of lying flat on her stomach, and with the whole power of her shoulders and chest and with Alex supporting and shoving Kent's body from behind they heaved him over. Sally fell back with him in her arms and saw his eyes open, roll back in his head as he fainted again.

When Alex had clawed and heaved his way out they collected the other children and drove to the

Collingwood Hospital. There seemed to be no internal injury. Both legs were broken. One break was clean, as the doctor put it; the other leg was shattered.

"Kids have to be watched every minute in there," he said to Sally, who had gone in with Kent while Alex managed the other children. "Haven't they got any warning signs up?"

With Alex, she thought, he would have spoken differently. That's the way boys are. Turn your back and they're tearing around where they shouldn't be. "Boys will be boys."

Her gratitude—to God, whom she did not believe in, and Alex, whom she did—was so immense that she resented nothing.

It was necessary for Kent to spend the next half year out of school, strung up for the first while in a rented hospital bed. Sally picked up and took back his school assignments, which he completed in no time. Then he was encouraged to go ahead with Extra Projects. One of these was Travels and Explorations—Choose Your Country.

"I want to pick what nobody else would pick," he said.

Now Sally told him something she had not told to another soul. She told him how she was attracted to remote islands. Not to the Hawaiian Islands or the Canaries or the Hebrides or the Isles of Greece, where everybody wanted to go, but to small or obscure islands nobody talked about and which were seldom if ever visited. Ascension, Tristan da Cunha, Chatham Islands, and Christmas Island and Desolation Island and the Faeroes. She and Kent began to collect every scrap of information they could find about these places, not allowing themselves to make anything up. And never telling Alex what they were doing.

"He would think we were off our heads," said Sally.

Desolation Island's main boast was of a vegetable of great antiquity, a unique cabbage. They imagined worship ceremonies for it, costumes, cabbage parades in its honor.

And before he was born, Sally told her son, she had seen on television the inhabitants of Tristan da Cunha disembarking at Heathrow Airport, having all been evacuated due to a great earthquake on their island. How strange they looked, docile and dignified, like human creatures from another century. They must have adjusted to London, more or less, but when the volcano quieted down they wanted to go home.

When Kent could go back to school things changed, of course, but he still seemed old for his age, patient with Savanna who had grown venturesome and stubborn, and with Peter who always burst into the house as if on a gale of calamity. And he was especially courteous to his father, bringing him the paper that had been res-

146

cued from Savanna and carefully refolded, pulling out his chair at dinnertime.

"Honor to the man who saved my life," he might say, or, "Home is the hero."

He said this rather dramatically though not at all sarcastically. Yet it got on Alex's nerves. Kent got on his nerves, had done so even before the deep-hole drama happened.

"Cut that out," he said, and complained privately to Sally.

"He's saying you must have loved him, because you rescued him."

"Christ, I'd have rescued anybody."

"Don't say that in front of him. Please."

When Kent got to high school things improved with his father. He chose to study science. He picked the hard sciences, not the soft earth sciences, and even this roused no opposition in Alex. The harder the better.

But after six months at college Kent disappeared. People who knew him a little—there did not seem to be anyone claiming to be a friend—said that he had talked of going to the West Coast. And a letter came, just as his parents were deciding to go to the police. He was working in a Canadian Tire store in a suburb just north of Toronto. Alex went to see him there, to order him back to his education. But Kent refused, said he was very happy with the job he had now, and was making good money, or soon would be, as he got promoted. Then Sally went to see him, without telling Alex, and found him jolly and ten pounds heavier. He said it was the beer. He had friends now.

"It's a phase," she said to Alex when she confessed the visit. "He wants to get a taste of independence."

"He can get a bellyful of it as far as I'm concerned."

Kent had not told her where he was living, but it did not matter, because when she made her next visit she was told that he had quit. She was embarrassed—she thought she caught a smirk on the face of the employee who told her that—and she did not ask where Kent had gone. She thought he would get in touch, anyway, as soon as he had settled again.

He did that, three years later. His letter was mailed in Needles, California, but he told them not to take the trouble to trace him there—he was only passing through. Like Blanche, he said, and Alex said, Who the hell is Blanche?

"Just a joke," said Sally. "It doesn't matter."

Kent did not say what he was working at or where he had been or whether he had formed any connections. He did not apologize for leaving them so long without any information or ask how they were, or how his brother and sister were. Instead he wrote pages about his own life. Not the practical side of his life but what he believed he should be doing—what he was doing—with it.

"It seems so ridiculous to me," he said, "that a person should be expected to lock themselves into a suit of clothes. I mean like the suit of clothes of an engineer or a doctor or a geologist and then the skin grows over it, over the clothes, I mean, and that person can't ever get them off. When we are given a chance to explore the whole world of inner and outer reality and to live in a way that takes in the spiritual and the physical and the whole range of the beautiful and the terrible available to mankind, that is pain as well as joy and turmoil. This way of expressing myself may seem overblown to you, but one thing I have learned to give up is intellectual pridefulness—"

"He's on drugs," said Alex. "You can tell a mile off. His brain's rotted with drugs."

In the middle of the night he said, "Sex."

Sally was lying beside him wide awake.

"What about sex?"

"That's what makes you get into that state he's talking about. Become a something-or-other so you can earn a living. So you can pay for your steady sex and the consequences. That's not a consideration for him."

Sally said, "My, how romantic."

"Getting down to basics is never very romantic. He's not normal, is all I'm trying to say."

Further on in the letter—or the rampage, as Alex called it—Kent had said that he had been luckier than most people in having what he called his near-death experience, which had given him an extra awareness, and for this he must be forever grateful to his father who had lifted him back into the world and his mother who had lovingly received him there.

"Perhaps in those moments I was reborn."

Alex had groaned.

"No. I won't say it."

"Don't," said Sally. "You don't mean it."

"I don't know whether I do or not."

That letter, signed with love, was the last they had heard from him.

Peter went into medicine, Savanna into law.

Sally became interested in geology, to her own surprise. One time, in a trusting mood after sex, she told Alex about the islands—though not about her fantasy that Kent was now living on one or another of them. She said that she had forgotten many of the details she used to know, and that she should look all these places up in the encyclopedia where she had first got her information. Alex said that everything she wanted to know could probably be found on the Internet. Surely not something so obscure, she said, and he got her out of bed and downstairs and there in no time before her eyes was Tristan da Cunha, a green plate in the South Atlantic Ocean, with information galore. She was shocked and turned away, and Alex who was disappointed in her—no wonder—asked why.

"I don't know. I feel now as if I'd lost it."

He said that this was no good, she needed something real to do. He had just retired from his teaching at this time and was planning to write a book. He needed an assistant and he could not call on the graduate students now as he could when he was still on the faculty. (She didn't know if this was true or not.) She reminded him that she knew nothing about rocks, and he said never mind that, he could use her for scale, in the photographs.

So she became the small figure in black or bright clothing, contrasting with the ribbons of Silurian or Devonian rock. Or with the gneiss formed by intense compression, folded and deformed by clashes of the American and Pacific plates to make the present continent. Gradually she learned to use her eyes and apply new knowledge, till she could stand in an empty suburban street and realize that far beneath her shoes was a crater filled with rubble never to be seen, that never had been seen, because there were no eyes to see it at its creation or throughout the long history of its being made and filled and hidden and lost. Alex did such things the honor of knowing about them, the very best he could, and she admired him for that, although she knew enough not to say so. They were good friends in these last years, which she did not know were their last years, though maybe he did. He went into the hospital for an operation, taking his charts and photographs with him, and on the day he was supposed to come home he died.

This was in the summer, and that fall there was a dramatic fire in Toronto. Sally sat in front of her television watching the fire for a while. It was in a district that she knew, or used to know, in the days when it was inhabited by hippies with their tarot cards and beads and paper flowers the size of pumpkins. And for a while after that when the vegetarian restaurants were being transformed into expensive bistros and boutiques. Now a block of those nineteenth-century buildings was being wiped out, and the newsman was bemoaning this, speaking of the people who had lived above the shops in old-fashioned apartments and who had now lost their homes, and were being dragged out of harm's way onto the street.

Not mentioning the landlords of such buildings, thought Sally, who were probably getting away with substandard wiring as well as epidemics of cockroaches and bedbugs, not to be complained about by the deluded or fearful poor.

She sometimes felt Alex talking in her head these days, and that was surely what was happening now. She turned off the fire.

No more than ten minutes later the phone rang. It was Savanna.

"Mom. Have you got your TV on? Did you see?"

"You mean the fire? I did have it on but I turned it off."

"No. Did you see—I'm looking for him right now—I saw him not five minutes ago. Mom, it's Kent. Now I can't find him. But I saw him."

"Is he hurt? I'm turning it on now. Was he hurt?"

"No, he was helping. He was carrying one end of a stretcher, there was a body on it, I don't know if it was dead or just hurt. But Kent. It was him. You could even see him limping. Have you got it on now?"

"Yes."

"Okay, I'll calm down. I bet he went back in the building."

"But surely they wouldn't allow—"

"He could be a doctor for all we know. Oh fuck, now they're doing that same old guy they talked to before, his family owned some business for a hundred years—let's hang up and just keep our eyes on the screen. He's sure to come in range again."

He didn't. The shots became repetitive.

Savanna phoned back.

"I'm going to get to the bottom of this. I know a guy that works on the news. I can get to see that shot again, we have to find out."

Savanna had never known her brother very well—what was all the fuss about? Did her father's death make her feel the need of family? She should marry, soon; she should have children. But she had such a stubborn streak when she set her mind on something—was it possible she would find Kent? Her father had told her when she was about ten years old that she could gnaw an idea to the bone, she ought to be a lawyer. And from then on, that was what she said she would be.

Sally was overcome by a trembling, a longing, a weariness.

It was Kent, and within a week Savanna had found out all about him. No. Change that to found out all he meant to tell her. He had been living in Toronto for years. He had often passed the building Savanna worked in and had spotted her a couple of times on the street. Once they were nearly face-to-face at an intersection. Of course she wouldn't have recognized him because he was wearing a kind of robe.

"A Hare Krishna?" said Sally.

"Oh, Mom, if you're a monk it doesn't mean you're a Hare Krishna. Anyway he's not that now."

"So what is he?"

"He says he lives in the present. So I said well don't we all, nowadays, and he said no, he meant in the real present."

Where they were now, he had said, and Savanna had said, "You mean in this dump?" Because it was, the coffee shop he had asked her to meet him in was a dump.

"I see it differently," he said, but then he said he had no objection to her way of seeing it, or anybody's.

"Well, that's big of you," said Savanna, but she made a joke of it and he sort of laughed.

He said that he had seen Alex's obituary in the paper and thought it was well done. He thought Alex would have liked the geological references. He had wondered if his own name would appear, included in the family, and he was rather surprised that it was there. He wondered, had his father told them what names he wanted listed, before he died?

Savanna said no, he wasn't planning on dying anything like so soon. It was the rest of the family who had a conference and decided Kent's name should be there.

"Not Dad," Kent said. "Well no."

Then he asked about Sally.

Sally felt a kind of inflated balloon in her chest. "What did you say?"

"I said you were okay, maybe at loose ends a little, you and Dad being so close and not much time yet to get used to being alone. Then he said tell her she can come to see me if she wants to and I said I would ask you."

Sally didn't reply.

"You there, Mom?"

"Did he say when or where?"

"No. I'm supposed to meet him in a week in the same place and tell him. I think he sort of enjoys calling the shots. I thought you'd agree right away."

"Of course I agree."

"You aren't alarmed at coming in by yourself?"

"Don't be silly. Was he really the man you saw in the fire?"

"He wouldn't say yes or no. But my information is yes. He's quite well known as it turns out in certain parts of town and by certain people."

✦ Sally receives a note. This in itself was special, since most people she knew used e-mail or the phone. She was glad it wasn't the phone. She did not trust herself to hear his voice yet. The note instructed her to leave her car in the subway parking lot at the end of the line and take the subway to a specified station where she should get off and he would meet her.

She expected to see him on the other side of the turnstile, but he was not there. Probably he meant that he would meet her outside. She climbed the steps and emerged into the sunlight and paused, with all sorts of people hurrying and pushing past her. She had a feeling of dismay and embarrassment. Dismay because of Kent's apparent

156

absence, and embarrassment because she was feeling just what people from her part of the country often seemed to feel, though she would never say what they said. You'd think you were in the Congo or India or Vietnam, they would say. Anyplace but Ontario. Turbans and saris and dashikis were much in evidence, and Sally was all in favor of their swish and bright colors. But they weren't being worn as foreign costumes. The wearers hadn't just arrived here; they had got past the moving-in phase. She was in their way.

On the steps of an old bank building just beyond the subway entrance, several men were sitting or lounging or sleeping. This was no longer a bank, of course, though its name was cut in stone. She looked at the name rather than the men, whose slouching or reclining or passed-out postures were such a contrast to the old purpose of the building, and the hurry of the crowd coming out of the subway.

"Mom."

One of the men on the steps came towards her in no hurry, with a slight drag of one foot, and she realized that it was Kent and waited for him.

She would almost as soon have run away. But then she saw that not all the men were filthy or hopeless looking, and that some looked at her without menace or contempt and even with a friendly amusement now that she was identified as Kent's mother.

Kent didn't wear a robe. He wore gray pants that were too big for him, belted in, and a T-shirt with no message on it and a very worn jacket. His hair was cut so short you could hardly see the curl. He was quite gray, with a seamed face, some missing teeth, and a very thin body that made him look older than he was.

He did not embrace her—indeed she did not expect him to—but put his hand just lightly on her back to steer her in the direction they were supposed to go.

"Do you still smoke your pipe?" she said, sniffing the air and remembering how he had taken up pipe smoking in high school.

"Pipe? Oh. No. It's the smoke from the fire you smell. We don't notice it anymore. I'm afraid it'll get stronger, in the direction we're walking."

"Are we going to go through where it was?"

"No, no. We couldn't, even if we wanted to. They've got it all blocked off. Too dangerous. Some buildings will have to be taken down. Don't worry, it's okay where we are. A good block and a half away from the mess."

"Your apartment building?" she said, alert to the "we."

"Sort of. Yes. You'll see."

He spoke gently, readily, yet with an effort, like someone speaking, as a courtesy, in a foreign language. And he stooped a little, to make sure she heard him. The special effort, the slight labor involved in speaking to her, as if making a scrupulous translation, seemed something she was meant to notice.

The cost.

As they stepped off a curb he brushed her arm—perhaps he had stumbled a little—and he said, "Excuse me." And she thought he gave the least shiver.

AIDS. Why had that never occurred to her before?

"No," he said, though she had certainly not spoken aloud. "I'm quite well at present. I'm not HIV positive or anything like that. I contracted malaria years ago, but it's under control. I may be a bit run-down at present but nothing to worry about. We turn here, we're right in this block."

"We" again.

"I'm not psychic," he said. "I just figured out something that Savanna was trying to get at and I thought I'd put you at rest. Here we are then."

It was one of those houses whose front doors open only a few steps from the sidewalk.

"I'm celibate, actually," he said, holding open the door.

A piece of cardboard was tacked up where one of its panes should be.

The floorboards were bare and creaked underfoot. The smell was complicated, all-pervasive. The street smell of smoke had got in here, of course, but it was mixed with smells of ancient cooking, burnt coffee, toilets, sickness, decay.

"Though 'celibate' might be the wrong word. That sounds as if there's something to do with willpower. I guess I should have said 'neuter.' I don't think of it as an achievement. It isn't."

He was leading her around the stairs and into the kitchen. And there a gigantic woman stood with her back to them, stirring something on the stove.

Kent said, "Hi, Marnie. This is my mom. Can you say hello to my mom?"

Sally noticed a change in his voice. A relaxation, honesty, perhaps a respect, different from the forced lightness he managed with her.

She said, "Hello, Marnie," and the woman half turned, showing a squeezed doll's face in a loaf of flesh but not focusing her eyes.

"Marnie is our cook this week," said Kent. "Smells okay, Marnie."

To his mother he said, "We'll go and sit in my sanctum, shall we?" and led the way down a couple of steps and along a back hall. It was hard to move there because of the stacks of newspapers, flyers, magazines neatly tied.

"Got to get these out of here," Kent said. "I told Steve this morning. Fire hazard. Jeez, I used to just say that. Now I know what it means."

Jeez. She had been wondering if he belonged to some plainclothes religious order, but if he did, he surely wouldn't say that, would he? Of course it could be an order of some faith other than Christian.

His room was down some further steps, actually in the cellar. There was a cot, a battered old-fashioned desk with cubbyholes, a couple of straight-backed chairs with rungs missing.

"The chairs are perfectly safe," he said. "Nearly all our stuff is scavenged from somewhere, but I draw the line at chairs you can't sit on."

Sally seated herself with a feeling of exhaustion.

"What are you?" she said. "What is it you do? Is this one of those halfway houses or something like that?"

"No. Not even quarter way. We take in anybody that comes."

"Even me."

"Even you," he said without smiling. "We aren't supported by anybody but ourselves. We do some recycling with stuff we pick up. Those newspapers. Bottles. We make a bit here and there. And we take turns soliciting the public."

"Asking for charity?"

"Begging," he said.

"On the street?"

"What better place for it? On the street. And we go in some pubs that we have an understanding with, though it is against the law."

"You do that too?"

"I could hardly ask them to do it if I wouldn't. That's something I had to overcome. Just about all of us have something to overcome. It can be shame. Or it can be the concept of 'mine.' When somebody drops in a ten-dollar bill or even a loonie, that's when the private ownership kicks in. Whose is it, huh? Mine or—skip a beat—ours? If the answer comes mine it usually gets spent right away and we have the person coming back smelling of booze and saying, I don't know what's the matter with me today, I couldn't get a bite. Then they might start to feel bad later and confess. Or not confess, never mind. We see them disappear for days—weeks—then show up back here when the going gets too rough. And sometimes you'll see them working the street on their own, never letting on they recognize you. Never come back. And that's all right. They're our graduates, you could say. If you believe in the system."

"Kent—"

"Around here I'm Jonah."

"Jonah?"

"I just chose it. I thought of Lazarus, but it's too self-dramatizing. You can call me Kent if you like."

"I want to know what's happened in your life. I mean not so much these people—"

"These people are my life."

"I knew you'd say that."

"Okay, it was kind of smart-arse. But this—this is what I've been doing for—seven years? Nine years. Nine years."

She persisted. "Before that?"

"What do I know? Before that? Before that. Man's days are like grass, eh? Cut down and put into the oven. Listen to me. Soon as I meet you again I start the showing off. Cut down and put in the oven—I'm not interested in that. I live each day as it happens. Really. You wouldn't understand that. I'm not in your world, you're not in mine—you know why I wanted to meet you here today?"

"No. I didn't think of it. I mean, I thought naturally maybe the time had come—"

"Naturally. When I saw about my father's death in the paper I naturally thought, Well, where is the money? I thought, Well, she can tell me."

"It went to me," said Sally, with flat disappointment but great self-control. "For the time being. The house as well, if you're interested."

"I thought likely that was it. That's okay."

"When I die, to Peter and his boys and Savanna."

"Very nice."

"He didn't know if you were alive or dead—"

"You think I'm asking for myself? You think I'm that much of an idiot to want the money for myself? But I did make a mistake thinking how I could use it. Thinking family money, sure, I can use that. That's the temptation. Now I'm glad, I'm glad I can't have it."

"I could let—"

"The thing is, though, this place is con-demned—"

"I could let you borrow."

"Borrow? We don't borrow around here. We don't use the borrow system around here. Excuse me, I've got to go get hold of my mood. Are you hungry? Would you like some soup?"

"No thanks."

When he was gone she thought of running away. If she could locate a back door, a route that didn't go through the kitchen. But she could not do it, because it would mean she would never see him again. And the backyard of a house like this, built before the days of automobiles, would have no access to the street.

It was maybe half an hour before he came back. She had not worn her watch. Thinking maybe a watch was out of favor in the life he lived and being right, it seemed. Right at least about that.

He seemed a little surprised or bewildered to find her still there.

"Sorry. I had to settle some business. And then I talked to Marnie, she always calms me down."

"You wrote a letter to us?" Sally said. "It was the last we heard from you."

"Oh, don't remind me."

"No, it was a good letter. It was a good attempt to explain what you were thinking."

"Please. Don't remind me."

"You were trying to figure out your life—"

"My life, my life, my progress, what all I could discover about my stinking self. Purpose of me. My crap. My spirituality. My intellectuality. There isn't any inside stuff, Sally. You don't mind if I call you Sally? It just comes out easier. There is only outside, what you do, every moment of your life. Since I realized this I've been happy."

"You are? Happy?"

"Sure. I've let go of that stupid self stuff. I think, How can I help? And that's all the thinking that I allow myself."

"Living in the present?"

"I don't care if you think I'm banal. I don't care if you laugh at me."

"I'm not—"

"I don't care. Listen. If you think I'm after your money, fine. I am after your money. Also I am after you. Don't you want a different life? I'm not saying I love you, I don't use stupid language. Or, I want to save you. You know you can only save yourself. So what is the point? I don't usually try to get anywhere talking to people. I usually try to avoid personal relationships. I mean I do. I do avoid them."

Relationships.

"Why are you trying not to smile?" he said. "Because I said 'relationships'? That's a cant word? I don't fuss about my words."

Sally said, "I was thinking of Jesus. 'Woman, what have I to do with thee?'"

The look that leapt to his face was almost savage.

"Don't you get tired, Sally? Don't you get tired being clever? I can't go on talking this way, I'm sorry. I've got things to do."

"So have I," said Sally. It was a complete lie. "We'll be—"

"Don't say it. Don't say, 'We'll be in touch.' "

"Maybe we'll be in touch. Is that any better?"

Sally gets lost, then finds her way. The bank building again, the same or possibly a whole new regiment of loiterers. The subway ride, the parking lot, the keys, the highway, the traffic. Then the lesser highway, the early sunset, no snow yet, the bare trees, and the darkening fields.

She loves this countryside, this time of year. Must she now think herself unworthy?

The cat is glad to see her. There are a couple of messages from friends on her machine. She heats up the single serving of lasagna. She buys these separated precooked and frozen portions now. They are quite good and not too expensive when you think of no waste. She sips from a glass of wine during the seven-minute wait.

Jonah.

She is shaking with anger. What is she supposed to do, go back to the condemned house and scrub the rotten linoleum and cook up the chicken parts that were thrown out because they're past the best-before date? And be reminded every day how she falls short of Marnie or any other afflicted creature? All for the privilege of being useful in the life somebody else—Kent—has chosen.

He's sick. He's wearing himself out, maybe he's dying. He wouldn't thank her for clean sheets and fresh food. Oh no. He'd rather die on that cot under the blanket with the burned hole in it.

But a check, she can write some sort of check, not an absurd one. Not too big or too small. He'll not help himself with it, of course. He'll not stop despising her, of course.

Despising. No. Not the point. Nothing personal.

There is something, anyway, in having got through the day without its being an absolute disaster. It wasn't, was it? She had said maybe. He hadn't corrected her.

Free Radicals

At first people were phoning to make sure that Nita was not too depressed, not too lonely, not eating too little or drinking too much. (She had been such a diligent wine drinker that many forgot she was now forbidden to drink at all.) She held them off, without sounding nobly grief stricken or unnaturally cheerful or absentminded or confused. She said she didn't need groceries, she was working through what she had on hand. She had enough of her prescription pills and enough stamps for her thank-you notes.

Her better friends probably suspected the truth—that she was not bothering to eat much and that she threw out any sympathy note she happened to get. She had not even written to people at a distance, to elicit such notes. Not even to Rich's former wife in Arizona or his semi-estranged brother in Nova Scotia, though they might understand, perhaps better than the people near at hand, why she had proceeded with the non-funeral as she had done.

Rich had called to her that he was going to the village, to the hardware store. It was around ten o'clock in the morning—he had started to paint the railing of the deck. That is, he was scraping it to prepare for the painting, and the old scraper had come apart in his hand.

She did not have time to wonder about his being late. He died bent over the sidewalk sign that stood out in front of the hardware store, offering a discount on lawn mowers. He had not even had time to get into the store. He was eighty-one years old and in fine health, aside from some deafness in his right ear. He had been checked over by his doctor only the week before. Nita was to learn that the recent checkup, the clean bill of health, cropped up in a surprising number of the sudden-death stories that she was now presented with. You would almost think such visits ought to be avoided, she said.

She should have spoken like this only to her close and bad-mouthing friends, Virgie and Carol, women close to her own age, which was sixty-two. Younger people found this sort of talk unseemly and evasive. At first they were ready to crowd in on Nita. They did not actually speak of the grieving process, but she was afraid that at any moment they might start.

As soon as she got on with the arrangements, of course, all but the tried and true fell away. The cheapest box, into the ground immediately, no ceremony of any kind. The undertaker suggested that this might be against the law, but she and Rich had their facts straight. They had got their information almost a year ago, when her diagnosis became final.

"How was I to know he'd steal my thunder?"

People had not expected a traditional service, but they had looked forward to some kind of contemporary affair. Celebrating the life. Playing his favorite music, holding hands all together, telling stories that praised Rich while touching humorously on his quirks and forgivable faults.

The sort of thing that Rich had said made him puke.

So it was dealt with immediately, and the stir, the widespread warmth around Nita, melted away, though some people, she supposed, would still be saying they were concerned about her. Virgie and Carol didn't say that. They said only that she was a selfish bloody bitch if she was thinking of conking out now, any sooner than necessary. They would come round, they said, and revive her with Grey Goose.

She said she wasn't, though she could see a certain logic.

Her cancer was at present in remission—whatever that really meant. It did not mean "in retreat." Not for good, anyway. Her liver is the main theater of operations and as long as she sticks to nibbles it is not complaining. It would only depress her friends to remind them that she can't have wine. Or vodka.

The radiation last spring had done her some good after all. Here it is midsummer. She thinks she doesn't look so jaundiced now—but maybe that only means she has got used to it.

She gets out of bed early and washes herself and dresses in anything that comes to hand. But she does dress, and wash, and she brushes her teeth and combs out her hair, which has grown back decently, gray around her face and dark at the back, the way it was before. She puts on lipstick and darkens her eyebrows, which are now very scanty, and out of a lifelong respect for a narrow waist and moderate hips, she checks on the achievements she has made in that direction, though she knows the proper word for all parts of her now might be "scrawny."

She sits in her usual ample armchair, with piles of books and unopened magazines around her. She sips cautiously from the mug of weak herb tea which is now her substitute for coffee. At one time she thought that she could not live without coffee, but it turned out that it is really the warm large mug she wants in her hands, that is the aid to thought or whatever it is she practices through the procession of hours, or of days.

This was Rich's house. He bought it when he was with his wife Bett. It was to be nothing but a weekend place, closed up for the winter. Two tiny bedrooms, a lean-to kitchen, half a mile from the village. But soon he was working on it, learning carpentry, building a wing for two bedrooms and bathrooms, another wing for his study, turning the original house into an open-plan living room/ dining room/kitchen. Bett became interested—

she had said in the beginning that she could not understand why he had bought such a dump, but practical improvements always engaged her, and she bought matching carpenter's aprons. She needed something to become involved in, having finished and published the cookbook that had occupied her for several years. They had no children.

And at the same time that Bett was telling people how she had found her role in life becoming a carpenter's helper, and how it had brought her and Rich much closer than before, Rich was falling in love with Nita. She worked in the Registrar's Office of the university where he taught Medieval Literature. The first time they had made love was amid the shavings and sawn wood of what would become the central room with its arched ceiling. Nita left her sunglasses behind—not on purpose, though Bett who never left anything behind could not believe that. The usual ruckus followed, trite and painful, and ended with Bett going off to California, then Arizona, Nita quitting her job at the suggestion of the registrar, and Rich missing out on becoming dean of arts. He took early retirement, sold the city house. Nita did not inherit the smaller carpenter's apron but read her books cheerfully in the midst of disorder, made rudimentary dinners on a hot plate, went for long exploratory walks and came back with ragged bouquets of tiger lilies and wild carrot, which she stuffed into empty paint cans. Later, when she and Rich had settled down, she became somewhat embarrassed to think how readily she had played the younger woman, the happy home wrecker, the lissome, laughing, tripping ingenue. She was really a rather serious, physically awkward, self-conscious woman—hardly a girl—who could recite all the queens, not just the kings but the queens, of England, and knew the Thirty Years' War backwards, but was shy about dancing in front of people and was never going to learn, as Bett had, to get up on a stepladder.

Their house has a row of cedars on one side, and a railway embankment on the other. The railway traffic has never amounted to much, and by now there might be only a couple of trains a month. Weeds were lavish between the tracks. One time, when she was on the verge of menopause, Nita had teased Rich into making love up there—not on the ties of course but on the narrow grass verge beside them, and they had climbed down inordinately pleased with themselves.

She thought carefully, every morning when she first took her seat, of the places where Rich was not. He was not in the smaller bathroom where his shaving things still were, and the prescription pills for various troublesome but not serious ailments that he refused to throw out. Nor was he in the bedroom which she had just tidied and left.

Not in the larger bathroom which he had entered only to take tub baths. Or in the kitchen that had become mostly his domain in the last year. He was of course not out on the half-scraped deck, ready to peer jokingly in the window—through which she might, in earlier days, have pretended to be starting a striptease.

Or in the study. That was where of all places his absence had to be most firmly established. At first she had found it necessary to go to the door and open it and stand there, surveying the piles of paper, moribund computer, spilling files, books lying open or facedown as well as crowded on the shelves. Now she could manage just by picturing things.

One of these days she would have to enter. She thought of it as invading. She would have to invade her husband's dead mind. This was one thing that she had never considered. Rich had seemed to her such a tower of efficiency and competence, so vigorous and firm a presence, that she had always believed, quite unreasonably, in his surviving her. Then in the last year this had become not a foolish belief at all, but in both their minds, as she thought, a certainty.

She would do the cellar first. It really was a cellar, not a basement. Planks made walkways over the dirt floor, and the small high windows were hung with dirty cobwebs. Nothing was down there that she ever needed. Just Rich's half-filled paint tins, boards of various lengths that might have come in handy someday, tools that might be usable or ready to be discarded. She had opened the door and gone down the steps just once, to see that no lights had been left on, and to assure herself that the switches were there, with labels written beside them to tell her which controlled what. When she came up she bolted the door as usual, on the kitchen side. Rich used to laugh about that habit of hers, asking what she thought could get in, through the stone walls and elf-sized windows, to menace them.

Nevertheless the cellar would be easier to start on; it would be a hundred times easier than the study.

She did make up the bed and tidy her own little mess in the kitchen or bathroom, but in general the impulse to manage any wholesale sweep of housecleaning was beyond her. She could barely throw out a twisted paper clip or a fridge magnet that had lost its attraction, let alone the dish of Irish coins that she and Rich had brought home from a trip fifteen years ago. Everything seemed to have acquired its own peculiar heft and strangeness.

Carol or Virgie phoned every day, usually towards suppertime, when they must have thought her solitude might be least bearable. She said she was okay, she would come out of her lair soon, she just needed this time, she was just thinking and reading. And eating okay, and sleeping.

That was true too, except for the reading. She sat in the chair surrounded by her books without opening one of them. She had always been such a reader—that was one reason Rich said she was the right woman for him, she could sit and read and let him alone—and now she couldn't stick it for even half a page.

She hadn't been just a once-through reader either. *Brothers Karamazov, Mill on the Floss, Wings of the Dove, Magic Mountain,* over and over again. She would pick one up, thinking that she would just read that special bit—and find herself unable to stop until the whole thing was redigested. She read modern fiction too. Always fiction. She hated to hear the word "escape" used about fiction. She might have argued, not just playfully, that it was real life that was the escape. But this was too important to argue about.

And now, most strangely, all that was gone. Not just with Rich's death but with her own immersion in illness. Then she had thought the change was temporary and the magic would reappear once she was off certain drugs and exhausting treatments.

Apparently not.

Sometimes she tried to explain why, to an imaginary inquisitor.

"I got too busy."

"So everybody says. Doing what?"

"Too busy paying attention."

"To what?"

"I mean thinking."

"What about?"

"Never mind."

One morning after sitting for a while she decided that it was a very hot day. She should get up and turn on the fans. Or she could, with more environmental responsibility, try opening the front and back doors and let the breeze, if there was any, blow through the screen and through the house.

She unlocked the front door first. And even before she had allowed half an inch of morning light to show itself, she was aware of a dark stripe cutting that light off.

There was a young man standing outside the screen door, which was hooked.

"Didn't mean to startle you," he said. "I was looking for a doorbell or something. I gave a little knock on the frame here, but I guess you didn't hear me."

"Sorry," she said.

"I'm supposed to look at your fuse box. If you could tell me where it is."

She stepped aside to let him in. She took a moment to remember.

"Yes. In the cellar," she said. "I'll turn the light on. You'll see it."

He shut the door behind him and bent to take off his shoes.

"That's all right," she said. "It's not as if it's raining."

"Might as well, though. I make it a habit. Could leave you dust tracks insteada mud."

She went into the kitchen, not able to sit down again until he left the house.

She opened the door for him as he came up the steps.

"Okay?" she said. "You found it okay?"

"Fine."

She was leading him towards the front door, then realized there were no steps behind her. She turned and saw him standing in the kitchen.

"You don't happen to have anything you could fix up for me to eat, do you?"

There was a change in his voice—a crack in it, a rising pitch, that made her think of a television comedian doing a rural whine. Under the kitchen skylight she saw that he wasn't so young. When she opened the door she had just been aware of a skinny body, a face dark against the morning glare. The body, as she saw it now, was certainly skinny, but more wasted than boyish, affecting a genial slouch. His face was long and rubbery, with prominent light blue eyes. A jokey look, but a persistence, as if he generally got his way.

"See, I happen to be a diabetic," he said. "I don't know if you know any diabetics, but the fact

179

is when you get hungry you got to eat, otherwise your system all goes weird. I should have ate before I came in here, but I let myself get in a hurry. You don't mind if I sit down?"

He was already sitting down at the kitchen table.

"You got any coffee?"

"I have tea. Herbal tea, if you'd like that."

"Sure. Sure."

She measured tea into a cup, plugged in the kettle, and opened the refrigerator.

"I don't have much on hand," she said. "I have some eggs. Sometimes I scramble an egg and put ketchup on it. Would you like that? I have some English muffins I could toast."

"English, Irish, Yukoranian, I don't care."

She cracked a couple of eggs into the pan, broke up the yolks, and stirred them all together with a cooking fork, then sliced a muffin and put it into the toaster. She got a plate from the cupboard, set it down in front of him. Then a knife and fork from the cutlery drawer.

"Pretty plate," he said, holding it up as if to see his face in it. Just as she turned her attention to the eggs she heard it smash on the floor.

"Oh mercy me," he said in a new voice, a squeaky and definitely nasty voice. "Look what I gone and done now."

"It's all right," she said, knowing now that nothing was.

"Musta slipped through my fingers."

She got down another plate, set it on the counter until she was ready to put the toasted muffin halves and then eggs smeared with ketchup on top of it.

He had stooped down, meanwhile, to gather up the pieces of broken china. He held up one piece that had broken so that it had a sharp point to it. As she set his meal down on the table he scraped the point lightly down his bare forearm. Tiny beads of blood appeared, at first separate, then joining to form a string.

"It's okay," he said. "It's just a joke. I know how to do it for a joke. If I'd of wanted to be serious we wouldn't of needed no ketchup, eh?"

There were still some pieces on the floor that he had missed. She turned away, thinking to get the broom, which was in a closet near the back door. He caught her arm in a flash.

"You sit down. You sit right here while I'm eating." He lifted the bloodied arm to show it to her again. Then he made an eggburger out of the muffin and the eggs and ate it in a very few bites. He chewed with his mouth open. The kettle was boiling. "Tea bag in the cup?" he said.

"Yes. It's loose tea actually."

"Don't you move. I don't want you near that kettle, do I?"

He poured boiling water into the cup.

"Looks like hay. Is that all you got?"

"I'm sorry. Yes."

"Don't go on saying you're sorry. If it's all you got it's all you got. You never did think I come here to look at the fuse box, did you?"

"Well yes," Nita said. "I did."

"You don't now."

"No."

"You scared?"

She chose to consider this not as a taunt but as a serious question.

"I don't know. I'm more startled than scared, I guess. I don't know."

"One thing. One thing you don't need to be scared of. I'm not going to rape you."

"I hardly thought so."

"You can't never be too sure." He took a sip of the tea and made a face. "Just because you're an old lady. There's all kinds out there, they'll do it to anything. Babies or dogs and cats or old ladies. Old men. They're not fussy. Well I am. I'm not interested in getting it any way but normal and with some nice lady I like and what likes me. So rest assured."

Nita said, "I am. But thank you for telling me."

He shrugged, but seemed pleased with himself.

"That your car out front?"

"My husband's car."

"Husband? Where's he?"

"He's dead. I don't drive. I mean to sell it, but I haven't yet."

What a fool, what a fool she was to tell him that.

"Two thousand four?"

"I think so. Yes."

"For a minute I thought you were going to trick me with the husband stuff. Wouldn't of worked, though. I can smell it if a woman's on her own. I know it the minute I walk in a house. Minute she opens the door. Instinct. So it runs okay? You know the last day he drove it?"

"The seventeenth of June. The day he died."

"Got any gas in it?"

"I would think so."

"Nice if he filled it up right before. You got the keys?"

"Not on me. I know where they are."

"Okay." He pushed his chair back, hitting one of the pieces of crockery. He stood up, shook his head in some kind of surprise, sat down again.

"I'm wiped. Gotta sit a minute. I thought it'd be better when I'd ate. I was just making that up about being a diabetic."

She pushed her chair and he jumped.

"You stay where you are. I'm not that wiped I couldn't grab you. It's only I walked all night."

"I was just going to get the keys."

"You wait till I say. I walked the railway track. Never seen a train. I walked all the way to here and never seen a train."

"There's hardly ever a train."

"Yeah. Good. I went down in the ditch going round some of them half-assed little towns. Then it come daylight I was still okay except where it crossed the road and I took a run for it. Then I looked down here and seen the house and the car and I said to myself, That's it. I could have took my old man's car, but I got some brains left in my head."

She knew he wanted her to ask what had he done. She was also sure that the less she knew the better for her.

Then for the first time since he entered the house she thought of her cancer. She thought of how it freed her, put her out of danger.

"What are you smiling about?"

"I don't know. Was I smiling?"

"I guess you like listening to stories. Want me to tell you a story?"

"Maybe I'd rather you'd leave."

"I will leave. First I'll tell you a story."

He put his hand in a back pocket. "Here. Want to see a picture? Here."

It was a photograph of three people, taken in a living room with closed floral curtains as a backdrop. An old man—not really old, maybe in his sixties—and a woman of about the same age were sitting on a couch. A very large younger woman was sitting in a wheelchair drawn up close to one end of the couch and a little in front of it. The old man was heavy and gray haired, with eyes narrowed and mouth slightly open, as if he might suffer some chest wheezing, but he was smiling as well as he could. The old woman was much smaller, with dark dyed hair and lipstick, wearing what used to be called a peasant blouse, with little red bows at the wrists and neck. She smiled determinedly, even a bit frantically, lips stretched over perhaps bad teeth.

But it was the younger woman who monopolized the picture. Distinct and monstrous in her bright muumuu, dark hair done up in a row of little curls along her forehead, cheeks sloping into her neck. And in spite of all that bulge of flesh an expression of some satisfaction and cunning.

"That's my mother and that's my dad. And that's my sister Madelaine. In the wheelchair.

"She was born funny. Nothing no doctor or anybody could do for her. And ate like a pig. There was bad blood between her and me since ever I remember. She was five years older than I was and she just set out to torment me. Throwing anything at me she could get her hands on and knockin me down and tryin to run over me with her fuckin wheelchair. Pardon my French."

"It must have been hard for you. And hard for your parents."

"Huh. They just rolled over and took it. They went to this church, see, and this preacher told them, she's a gift from God. They took her with them to church and she'd fuckin howl like a fuckin cat in the backyard and they'd say oh, she's tryin to make music, oh God fuckin bless her. Excuse me again.

"So I never bothered much with sticking around home, you know, I went and got my own life. That's all right, I says, I'm not hanging around for this crap. I got my own life. I got work. I nearly always got work. I never sat around on my ass drunk on government money. On my rear end, I mean. I never asked my old man for a penny. I'd get up and tar a roof in the ninety-degree heat or I'd mop the floors in some stinkin old restaurant or go grease-monkey for some rotten cheatin garage. I'd do it. But I wasn't always up for taking their shit so I wasn't lasting too long. That shit people are always handing people like me and I couldn't take it. I come from a decent home. My dad worked till he got too sick, he worked on the buses. I wasn't brought up to take shit. Okay though—never mind that. What my parents always told me was, the house is yours. The house is all paid up and it's in good shape and it's yours. That's what they told me. We know you had a hard time here when you were young and if you hadn't had such a hard time you could of got an education, so we want to make it up to you how we can. So then not long ago I'm talking to my dad on the phone and he says, Of course you understand the deal. So I'm what deal? He says, It's only a deal if you sign the papers you will take care of your sister as long as she lives. It's only your home if it's her home too, he says.

"Jesus. I never heard that before. I never heard

186

that was the deal before. I always thought the deal was, when they died she'd go into a Home. And it wasn't going to be my home.

"So I told my old man that wasn't the way I understood it and he says it's all sewed up for you to sign and if you don't want to sign it you don't have to. Your aunt Rennie will be around to keep an eye on you too so when we're gone you see you stick to the arrangements.

"Yeah, my aunt Rennie. She's my mom's youngest sister and she is one prize bitch.

"Anyway he says your aunt Rennie will be keeping an eye on you and suddenly I just switched. I said, Well, I guess that's the way it is and I guess it is only fair. Okay. Okay, is it all right if I come over and eat dinner with you this Sunday.

"Sure, he says. Glad you have come to look at it the right way. You always fire off too quick, he says, at your age you ought to have some sense.

"Funny you should say that, I says to myself.

"So over I go, and Mom has cooked chicken. Nice smell when I first go into the house. Then I get the smell of Madelaine, just her same old awful smell I don't know what it is but even if Mom washes her every day it's there. But I acted very nice. I said, This is an occasion, I should take a picture. I told them I had this wonderful new camera that developed right away and they could see the picture. Right off the bat you can see yourself, what do you think of that? And I got them all sitting in the front room just the way I showed you. Mom she says, Hurry up I have to get back in my kitchen. Do it in no time, I says. So I take their picture and she says, Come on now, let's see how we look, and I say, Hang on, just be patient, it'll only take a minute. And while they're waiting to see how they look I take out my nice little gun and bin-bang-bam I shoot the works of them. Then I take another picture and I went out to the kitchen and ate up some of the chicken and didn't look at them no more. I kind of had expected Aunt Rennie to be there too but Mom had said she had some church thing. I would of shot her too just as easy. So lookie here. Before and after."

The old man's head was fallen sideways, the old woman's backwards. Their expressions were blown away. The sister had fallen forward so there was no face to be seen, just her great flowery swathed knees and dark head with its elaborate and outdated coiffure.

"I could of just sat there feelin good for a week. I felt so relaxed. But I didn't stay past dark. I made sure I was all cleaned up and I finished off the chicken and I knew I better get out. I was pre-pared for Aunt Rennie walkin in but I got out of the mood I had been in and I knew I'd have to work myself up to do her. I just didn't feel like it anymore. One thing my stomach was so full, it was a big chicken. I had ate it all instead of packin it with me because I was scared the dogs would smell it and cut up a fuss when I went by the back lanes like I figured to do. I thought that chicken inside of me would do me for a week. Yet look how hungry I was when I got to you."

He looked around the kitchen. "I don't suppose you got anything to drink here, have you? That tea was awful."

"There might be some wine," she said. "I don't know, I don't drink anymore—"

"You AA?"

"No. It just doesn't agree with me."

She got up and found her legs were shaking. Of course.

"I fixed up the phone line before I come in here," he said. "Just thought you ought to know."

Would he get careless and more easygoing as he drank, or would he get meaner and wilder? How could she tell? She found the wine without having to leave the kitchen. She and Rich used to drink red wine every day in reasonable quantities because it was supposed to be good for your heart. Or bad for something that was not good for your heart. In her fright and confusion she was not able to think what that was called.

Because she was frightened. Certainly. The fact of her cancer was not going to be any help to her at the present moment, none at all. The fact that she was going to die within a year refused to cancel out the fact that she might die now.

He said, "Hey, this is the good stuff. No screw top. Haven't you got no corkscrew?"

She moved towards a drawer, but he jumped up and put her aside, not too roughly.

"Unh-unh, I get it. You stay away from this drawer. Oh my, lots of good stuff in here."

He put the knives on the seat of his chair where she would never be able to grab them and used the corkscrew. She did not fail to see what a wicked instrument it could be in his hand but there was not the least possibility that she herself would ever be able to use it.

"I'm just getting up for glasses," she said, but he said no. No glass, he said, you got any plastic?

"No."

"Cups then. I can see you."

She set down the two cups and said, "Just a very little for me."

"And me," he said, businesslike. "I gotta drive." But he filled his cup to the brim. "I don't want no cop stickin his head in to see how I am."

"Free radicals," she said.

"What's that supposed to mean?"

"It's something about red wine. It either destroys them because they're bad or builds them up because they're good, I can't remember."

She drank a sip of the wine and it didn't make her feel sick, as she had expected. He drank, still standing. She said, "Watch for those knives when you sit down."

"Don't start kidding with me."

He gathered the knives and put them back in the drawer, and sat.

"You think I'm dumb? You think I'm nervous?"

She took a big chance. She said, "I just think you haven't ever done anything like this before."

"Course I haven't. You think I'm a murderer? Yeah, I killed them but I'm not a murderer."

"There's a difference," she said.

"You bet."

"I know what it's like. I know what it's like to get rid of somebody who has injured you."

"Yeah?"

"I have done the same thing you did."

"You never." He pushed back his chair but did not stand.

"Don't believe me if you don't want to," she said. "But I did it."

"Hell you did. How'd you do it then?"

"Poison."

"What are you talkin about? You make them drink some of this fuckin tea or what?"

"It wasn't a them, it was a her. There's nothing wrong with the tea. It's supposed to prolong your life."

"Don't want my life prolonged if it means drinkin junk like that. They can find out poison in a body when it's dead anyway."

"I'm not sure that's true of vegetable poisons. Anyway nobody would think to look. She was one of those girls who had rheumatic fever as a child and coasted along on it, can't play sports or do anything much, always having to sit down and have a rest. Her dying would not be any big surprise."

"What she ever done to you?"

"She was the girl my husband was in love with. He was going to leave me and marry her. He had told me. I had done everything for him. He and I were working on this house together, he was everything I had. We had not had any children because he didn't want them. I learned carpentry and I was frightened to get up on ladders but I did it. He was my whole life. Then he was going to kick me out for this useless whiner who worked in the registrar's office. The whole life we'd worked for was to go to her. Was that fair?"

"How would a person get poison?"

"I didn't have to get it. It was right in the back garden. Here. There was a rhubarb patch from years back. There's a perfectly adequate poison in the veins of rhubarb leaves. Not the stalks. The stalks are what we eat. They're fine. But the thin little red veins in the big rhubarb leaves, they're poisonous. I knew about this, but I have to confess I didn't know exactly what it would take to be effective so what I did was more in the nature of an experiment. Various things were lucky for me. First, my husband was away at a symposium in Minneapolis. He might have taken her along, of course, but it was summer holidays and she was the junior who had to keep the office going. Another thing, though, she might not have been absolutely on her own, there might have been another person around. And moreover, she might have been suspicious of me. I had to assume that she did not know I knew, and would still think of me as a friend. She had been entertained at my house, we were friendly. I had to count on my husband's being the kind of person who delays everything and who would tell me to see how I took it but not yet tell her he had done so. So then you say, Why get rid of her? He might still have been thinking both ways?

"No. He would have kept her on somehow. And even if he didn't our life was poisoned by her. She poisoned my life so I had to poison hers.

"I baked two tarts. One had the poison veins in it and one didn't. Of course I marked the one that didn't. I drove down to the university and got two cups of coffee and went to her office. Nobody there but her. I told her I'd had to come into town and as I was passing the university grounds I saw this nice little bakery my husband was always praising for their coffee and their baked goods, so I dropped in and bought a couple of tarts and two cups of coffee. Thinking of her all alone when the rest of them got to go on their holidays and me all alone with my husband gone to Minneapolis. She was sweet and grateful. She said it was very boring for her there and the cafeteria was closed so you had to go over to the science building for coffee and they put hydrochloric acid in it. Ha-ha. So we had our little party."

"I hate rhubarb," he said. "It wouldn't of worked with me."

"It did with her. I had to take a chance that it would work fast, before she realized what was wrong and had her stomach pumped. But not so fast she would associate it with me. I had to be out of the way and so I was. The building was deserted and so far as I know to this day nobody saw me arrive or leave. Of course I knew some back ways."

"You think you're smart. You got away scot-free."

"But so have you."

"What I done wasn't so underhanded as what you done."

"It was necessary to you."

"You bet it was."

"Mine was necessary to me. I kept my marriage. He came to see that she wouldn't have been any good anyway. She'd have got sick on him, almost certainly. She was just the type. She'd have been nothing but a burden to him. He saw that."

"You better not of put nothing in them eggs," he said. "You did you'll be sorry."

"Of course I didn't. I wouldn't want to. It's not something you'd go around doing regularly. I don't actually know anything about poison, it was just by chance I had that one little piece of information."

He stood up so suddenly that he knocked over the chair he'd been sitting on. She noticed there was not much wine left in the bottle.

"I need the keys to the car."

She couldn't think for a moment.

"Keys to the car. Where'd you put them?"

It could happen. As soon as she gave him the keys it could happen. Would it help her to tell him she was dying of cancer? How stupid. It wouldn't help at all. Cancer death in the future would not keep her from talking today.

"Nobody knows what I've told you," she said. "You are the only person I've told."

A fat lot of good all that might do. The whole advantage she had presented to him had probably gone right over his head.

"Nobody knows yet," he said, and she thought, Thank God. He's on the right track. He does realize. Does he realize?

Thank God maybe.

"The keys are in the blue teapot."

"Where? What the fuck blue teapot?"

"At the end of the counter—the lid got broken, so we used it to just throw things in—"

"Shut up. Shut up or I'll shut you up for good." He tried to stick his fist in the blue teapot but it would not go in. "Fuck, fuck, fuck," he cried, and he turned the teapot over, and banged it on the counter so that not only the car keys and house keys and various coins and a wad of old Canadian Tire money fell out on the floor, but pieces of blue pottery hit the boards.

"With the red string on them," she said faintly.

He kicked things about for a moment before he picked the proper keys up.

"So what are you going to say about the car?" he said. "You sold it to a stranger. Right?"

The import of this did not come to her for a moment. When it did, the room quivered. "Thank you," she said, but her mouth was so dry she was not sure any sound came out. It must have, though, for he said, "Don't thank me yet.

"I got a good memory," he said. "Good long memory. You make that stranger look nothin like me. You don't want them goin into graveyards diggin up dead bodies. You just remember, a word outta you and there'll be a word outta me."

She kept looking down. Not stirring or speaking, just looking at the mess on the floor.

Gone. The door closed. Still she didn't move. She wanted to lock the door but she couldn't move. She heard the engine starting, then die. What now? He was so jumpy, he'd do everything wrong. Then again, starting, starting, turning over. The tires on the gravel. She walked trembling to the phone and found that he had told the truth; it was dead.

Beside the phone was one of their many book-cases. This one held mostly old books, books that had not been opened for years. There was *The Proud Tower.* Albert Speer. Rich's books.

A Celebration of Familiar Fruits and Vegetables: Hearty and Elegant Dishes and Fresh Surprises, assembled, tested, and created by Bett Underhill.

Once they had got the kitchen finished Nita had made the mistake for a while of trying to cook like Bett. For a rather short while, because it turned out that Rich did not want to be reminded of all that fuss, and she herself had not enough patience for so much chopping and simmering. But she had learned a few things that surprised her. Such as the poisonous aspects of certain familiar and generally benign plants.

She should write to Bett.

Dear Bett, Rich is dead and I have saved my life by becoming you.

What does Bett care that her life was saved? There's only one person really worth telling.

Rich. Rich. Now she knows what it is to really miss him. Like the air sucked out of the sky.

She should walk down to the village. There was a police office in the back of the Township Hall.

She should get a cell phone.

She was so shaken, so deeply tired, she could hardly stir a foot. She had first of all to rest.

She was wakened by a knocking on her still unlocked door. It was a policeman, not the one from the village but one of the provincial traffic police. He asked if she knew where her car was.

She looked at the patch of gravel where it had been parked.

"It's gone," she said. "That's where it was."

"You didn't know it was stolen? When did you last look out and see it?"

"It must have been last night."

"The keys were left in it?"

"I suppose they must have been."

"I have to tell you it's been in a bad accident. A one-car accident just this side of Wallenstein. The driver rolled it down into the culvert and totalled it. And that's not all. He's wanted for a triple murder. That's the latest we heard, anyway. Murder in Mitchellston. You were lucky you didn't run into him."

"Was he hurt?"

"Killed. Instantly. Serves him right."

There followed a kindly stern lecture. Leaving keys in the car. Woman living alone. These days you never know.

Never know.

Face

I am convinced that my father looked at me, stared at me, saw me, only once. After that, he could take for granted what was there.

In those days they didn't let fathers into the glare of the theater where babies were born, or into the room where the women about to give birth were stifling their cries or suffering aloud. Fathers laid eyes on the mothers only after they were cleaned up and conscious and tucked up under pastel blankets in the ward, or in the semi-private or private rooms. My mother had a private room, as became her status in the town, and just as well, actually, seeing the way things turned out.

I don't know whether it was before or after his first look at my mother that my father stood outside the window of the nursery for his first glimpse of me. I rather think it was after, and that when she heard his steps outside her door and crossing her room, she heard the anger in them but did not know yet what had caused it. After all, she had borne him a son, which was presumably what all men wanted.

I know what he said. Or what she told me he said.

"What a chunk of chopped liver."

Then, "You don't need to think you're going to bring that into the house."

One side of my face was—is—normal. And my entire body was normal from toes to shoulders. Twenty-one inches was my length, eight pounds five ounces my weight. A strapping male infant, fair skinned though probably still red from my unremarkable recent journey.

My birthmark not red, but purple. Dark in my infancy and early childhood, fading somewhat as I got older, but never fading to a state of inconsequence, never ceasing to be the first thing you notice about me, head-on, or are shocked to see if you have come at me from the left, or clean, side. It looks as if someone has dumped grape juice or paint on me, a big serious splash that does not turn to driblets till it reaches my neck. Though it does skirt my nose pretty well, after dousing one eyelid.

"It makes the white of that eye look so lovely and clear" was one of the idiotic though pardonable things my mother would say, in the hope of making me admire myself. And an odd thing happened. Sheltered as I was, I almost believed her.

Of course my father could not do anything to prevent my coming home. And of course my presence, my existence, made a monstrous rift between my father and mother. Though it is hard for me to believe there had not always been some rift, some incomprehension at least, or chilly disappointment.

My father was the son of an uneducated man

who owned a tannery and then a glove factory. Prosperity was ebbing as the twentieth century progressed, but the big house was still there, the cook and the gardener. My father went to college, joined a fraternity, had what was referred to as a high old time, entered the insurance business when the glove factory went under. He was as popular around our town as he had been at college. A good golfer, an excellent sailor. (I have not mentioned that we lived on the cliffs above Lake Huron, in the Victorian house my grandfather had built facing the sunset.)

At home my father's most vivid quality was a capacity for hating and despising. In fact those two verbs often went together. He hated and despised certain foods, makes of automobile, music, manners of speech and modes of dress, radio comedians and later on television personalities, as well as the usual assortment of races and classes it was customary to hate and despise (though perhaps not so thoroughly as he did) in his day. In fact most of his opinions would have found no argument outside our house, in our town, with his sailing companions, or his old fraternity brothers. It was his vehemence, I think, that brought out an uneasiness that could also amount to admiration.

Calls a spade a spade. That was what was said of him.

Of course a production like myself was an

insult he had to face every time he opened his own door. He took breakfast alone and did not come home for lunch. My mother ate those meals with me and part of her dinner also, the rest of dinner with him. Then I think there was some sort of row about this, and she sat through my meal with me but ate with him.

It can be seen that I could not contribute to a comfortable marriage.

But how had they ever come together? She had not gone to college, she had to borrow money to attend a school where teachers were trained in her day. She was frightened of sailing, clumsy at golf, and if she was beautiful, as some people have told me (it is hard to make that judgment of your own mother), her looks cannot have been of the kind my father admired. He spoke of certain women as stunners, or, later in his life, as dolls. My mother did not wear lipstick, her brassieres were unassertive, her hair was done in a tight crown of braids that emphasized her wide white forehead. Her clothes lagged behind the style, being somewhat shapeless and regal—she was the sort of woman you could imagine wearing a rope of fine pearls, though I don't think she ever did.

What I seem to be saying, I guess, is that I may have been a pretext, a blessing even, in that I furnished them with a ready-made quarrel, an insoluble problem which threw them back on their natural differences where they may in fact have been more comfortable. In all my years in the town, I encountered no one who was divorced, and so it may be taken for granted that there were other couples living separate lives in one house, other men and women who had accepted the fact that there were differences never to be mended, a word or an act never to be forgiven, a barrier never to be washed away.

It follows, unsurprisingly in such a story, that my father smoked and drank too much—though most of his friends did too, whatever their situations. He had a stroke while still in his fifties, and died after several months in bed. And it was not a surprise that my mother nursed him all that time, kept him at home, where instead of becoming tender and appreciative he called her quite foul names, thickened by his misfortune but always decipherable to her, and to him, it seemed, quite gratifying.

At the funeral a woman said to me, "Your mother is a saint." I remember this woman's appearance quite well, though not her name. White curls, rouged cheeks, dainty features. A tearful whisper. I disliked her instantly. I scowled. I was at that time in my second year at college. I had not joined, or been invited to join, my father's fraternity. I hung around with people who were planning to be writers and actors and were at present wits, dedicated time wasters, savage social critics, newborn atheists. I had no respect for people who behaved like saints. And to be truthful, that was not what my mother aimed for. She was far enough from pious notions that she had never asked me, on any of my trips home, to go into my father's room, to try for a word of reconciliation with him. And I had never gone. There was no notion of a reconciliation, or any blessing. My mother was no fool.

She had been devoted to me—not the word either of us would have used, but I think the right one—till I was nine years old. She taught me herself. Then she sent me away to school. This sounds like a recipe for disaster. The mother-coddled purple-faced lad, thrown suddenly amongst the taunts, the ruthless assaults of young savages. But I didn't have a bad time, and to this day I'm not sure why not. I was tall and strong for my age, and that might have helped. I think, though, that the atmosphere in our house, that climate of ill temper and ferocity and disgust— even coming from an often unseen father—may have made any other place seem reasonable, almost accepting, though in a negative not a positive way. It was not a question of anybody making an effort, being nice to me. There was a name for me—it was Grape-Nuts. But almost everybody had a derogatory nickname. A boy with particularly smelly feet that did not seem to benefit from daily showers cheerfully put up with the name of Stink. I got along. I wrote my mother comical letters, and she replied somewhat in kind, taking a mildly satirical tone about events in town and in church—I remember her describing a row about the right way to cut sandwiches for a ladies' tea—and even managing to be humorous but not bitter about my father, whom she referred to as His Grace.

I have made my father the beast in my account so far, and my mother the rescuer and protector, and I believe this to be true. But they are not the only people in my story, and the atmosphere in the house was not the only one I knew. (I am speaking now of the time even before I went to school.) What I have come to think of as the Great Drama of my life had already occurred outside that house.

Great Drama. It embarrasses me to have written that. I wonder if it sounds cheaply satirical or tiresome. But then I think, Isn't it quite natural for me to see my life that way, talk about it that way, when you consider how I made my living?

I became an actor. Surprising? Of course in college I hung around with people active in the theater, and in my final year I directed a play. There was a standing joke, originating with myself, about how I would manage a role by keeping my unmarked profile always to the audience and walking backwards across the stage when necessary. But no such drastic maneuvers were necessary.

At that time there were regular dramas on national radio. A particularly ambitious program on Sunday evenings. Adaptations of novels. Shakespeare. Ibsen. My voice was naturally adaptable and with a bit of training it improved. I was taken on. Small parts at first. But by the time television put the whole business to rest I was on almost every week and my name was known to a certain faithful if never large audience. There were letters objecting to bad language or mention of incest (we did some of the Greek plays as well). But on the whole, not so much rebuke raining down on me as my mother was afraid of, when she settled in her chair by the radio, faithful and apprehensive, every Sunday evening.

Then television, and acting was over, certainly for me. But my voice stood me in good stead, and I was able to get a job as an announcer, first in Winnipeg, then back in Toronto. And for the last twenty years of my working life I was host of an eclectic musical show presented on weekday afternoons. I did not choose the selections, as people often thought. I have a limited appreciation of music. But I had crafted an agreeable, slightly quirky, durable radio personality. The program received many letters. We heard from old people's homes and homes for the blind, from people regularly driving long or monotonous distances on business, from housewives alone in the middle of the day with the baking and ironing, and farmers in tractor cabs plowing or harrowing some sweeping acreage. All over the country.

A flattering outpouring when I at last retired. People wrote that they were bereft, they felt as if they had lost a close friend or member of the family. What they meant was that a certain amount of time had been filled for them five days a week. Time had been filled, reliably, agreeably, they had not been left adrift, and for this they were truly embarrassingly grateful. And surprisingly, I shared in their emotion. I would have to be careful of my voice, so that I would not choke up as I read some of their letters on the air.

And yet memory of the program, and of myself, faded rapidly. New allegiances were formed. I had made a complete break, refusing to chair charity auctions or give nostalgic speeches. My mother had died after living to a great age, but I had not sold the house, only rented it. Now I prepared to sell it, and gave the tenants notice. I meant to live there myself for the time it took to get the place—particularly the garden—into shape.

I had not been lonely in these years. Aside from my audience I had friends. I had women too. Some women of course specialize in those men they imagine in need of bucking up—they are eager to sport you around as a sign of their own munificence. I was on the watch for them. The woman I was closest to in those years was a receptionist at the station, a nice sensible person, left on her own with four children. There was some feeling that we would move in together once the youngest was off her hands. But the youngest was a daughter, who managed to have a child of her own without ever leaving home, and somehow our expectation, our affair, dwindled. We kept in touch by e-mail after I retired and came back to my old home. I invited her to come to see me. Then there was a sudden announcement that she was getting married and going to live in Ireland. I was too surprised and perhaps too much knocked off my perch to ask whether the daughter and the baby were going too.

The garden is in a great mess. But I feel more at ease there than in the house, which looks the same on the outside but is drastically altered on the inside. My mother had the back parlor made into a bedroom, and the pantry into a full bathroom, and later on the ceilings were lowered, cheap doors hung, garish geometric wallpaper pasted on, to accommodate tenants. In the garden there were no such alterations, merely neglect on a grand scale. Old perennials still straggle up among the weeds, ragged leaves larger than umbrellas mark the place of a sixty- or seventy-year-old rhubarb bed, and a half-dozen apple trees remain, bearing little wormy apples of some variety whose name I don't remember. The patches I clear look minute, yet the piles of weeds and brush I have collected seem mountainous. They must be hauled away, furthermore, at my expense. The town no longer allows bonfires.

All this used to be looked after by a gardener named Pete. I have forgotten his last name. He dragged one leg after him and carried his head always bent to one side. I don't know if he had had an accident or suffered a stroke. He worked slowly but diligently and was more or less always in a bad temper. My mother spoke to him with soft-voiced respect, but she proposed—and got—certain changes in the flower beds which he did not think much of. And he disliked me because I was constantly riding my tricycle where I shouldn't be and making hideouts under the apple trees and because he probably knew that I called him Sneaky Pete under my breath. I don't know where I got that. Was it from a comic strip?

Another reason for his growling dislike has just occurred to me, and it's odd I didn't think of it before. We were both flawed, obvious victims of physical misfortune. You would think such people would make common cause, but it could just as often happen that they don't. Each may be reminded by the other of something sooner forgotten.

But I'm not sure of this. My mother had arranged things so that most of the time I seem to have been quite unaware of my condition. She claimed that she was teaching me at home because of a bronchial ailment and the need to protect me from the onslaught of germs that occurs in the first couple of years at school. Whether anybody believed her I don't know. And as to my father's hostility, that had spread so wide in our house that I really don't believe I felt singled out by it.

And here at the cost of repeating myself I must say that I think my mother did right. The emphasis on one notable flaw, the goading and ganging up, would have caught me too young and with nowhere to hide. Things are different now, and the danger to a child afflicted as I was would be of too much fuss and showy kindness, not of taunts and isolation. Or so it seems to me. The life of those times took much of its liveliness, its wit and folklore, as my mother may have known, from pure viciousness.

Until a couple of decades ago—maybe more— there was another building on our property. I knew it as a small barn or large wooden shed where Pete stored his tools and where various things once of use to us were put out of the way until there was some decision about what to do with them. It was torn down shortly after Pete was replaced by an energetic young couple, Ginny and Franz, who brought their own up-to-date equipment in their own truck. Later they were not available, having gone into market gardening, but by that time they were able to supply their teenage children to cut the grass, and my mother had lost interest in doing anything else.

"I've just let it go," she said. "It's surprising how easy it is, just to let things go."

To get back to the building—how I circle and dither around this subject—there was a time, before it became just a storage shed, when people lived in it. There was a couple named the Bells, who were cook-housekeeper and gardener-chauffeur to my grandparents. My grandfather owned a Packard which he never learned to drive. Both the Bells and the Packard were gone in my time, but the place was still referred to as Bells' Cottage.

For a few years in my childhood Bells' Cottage was rented to a woman named Sharon Suttles. She lived there with her daughter, Nancy. She had come to town with her husband, a doctor who was setting up his first practice, and within a year or so he died, of blood poisoning. She remained in town with her baby, having no money and, as was said, no people. This must have meant no people who could help her or who had offered to take her in. At some time she got a job in my father's insurance office, and came to live in Bells' Cottage. I am not certain about when all this happened. I have no memory of them moving in, or of the cottage when it was empty. It was painted, at that time, a dusty pink, and I always thought of that as Mrs. Suttles's choice, as if she could not have lived in a house of any other color.

I called her Mrs. Suttles, of course. But I was aware of her first name, as I seldom was of any other grown-up woman's. Sharon was an unusual name in those days. And it had a connection with a hymn I knew from Sunday school, which my mother allowed me to attend because there was close monitoring and no recess. We sang hymns whose words were flashed on a screen, and I think that most of us even before we learned to read got some idea of the verses from their shape in front of us.

> *By cool Siloam's shady rill*
> *How sweet the lily grows.*
> *How sweet the breath, beneath the hill,*
> *Of Sharon's dewy rose.*

I can't believe that there was actually a rose in a corner of the screen and yet I saw one, I see one, of a faded pink, whose aura was transferred to the name Sharon.

I don't mean to say that I fell in love with Sharon Suttles. I had been in love, when barely out of my infancy, with a tomboyish young maid named Bessie, who took me out on jaunts in my stroller and swung me so high on the park swings that I nearly went over the top. And some time later with a friend of my mother's, who had a velvet collar on her coat and a voice that seemed somehow to be related to it. Sharon Suttles was not for falling in love with in that way. She was not velvet voiced and she had no interest in showing me a good time. She was tall and very thin to be anybody's mother—there were no slopes on her. Her hair was the color of toffee, brown with golden edges, and in the time of the Second World War she was still wearing it bobbed. Her lipstick was bright red and thick looking, like the mouths of movie stars I had seen on posters, and around her house she usually wore a kimono, on which I believe there were some pale birds—storks?—whose legs reminded me of hers. She spent a lot of her time lying on the couch, smoking, and sometimes, to amuse us or herself, she would kick those legs straight up in the air, one after the other, and send a feathery slipper flying. When she was not mad at us her voice would be throaty and exasperated, not unfriendly, but in no way wise or tender or reproving, with the full tones, the suggestion of sadness, that I expected in a mother.

You dumb twerps, she called us.

"Get out of here and let me have some peace, you dumb twerps."

She would already be lying on the couch with an ashtray on her stomach while we scooted Nancy's toy cars across the floor. How much peace did she want?

She and Nancy ate peculiar foods at irregular hours, and when she went into the kitchen to fix herself a snack, she never came back with cocoa or graham crackers for us. On the other hand, Nancy was never forbidden to spoon vegetable soup, thick as pudding, out of the can, or to grab handfuls of Rice Krispies straight from the box.

Was Sharon Suttles my father's mistress? Her job provided for her, and the pink cottage rent free?

My mother spoke of her kindly, not infrequently mentioning the tragedy that had befallen her, with the death of the young husband. Whatever maid we had at the time would be sent over with presents of raspberries or new potatoes or shelled fresh peas from our garden. I remember the peas particularly. I remember Sharon Suttles—still lying on the couch—flipping them into thc air with her forefinger, saying, "What am I supposed to do with these?"

"You cook them on the stove with water," I said helpfully.

"No kidding?"

As for my father, I never saw him with her. He left for work rather late and knocked off early, to keep up with his various sporting activities. There were weekends when Sharon caught the train to Toronto, but she always had Nancy with her. And Nancy would come back full of the adventures she had had and the spectacles she had seen, such as the Santa Claus Parade.

There were certainly times when Nancy's

mother was not at home, not in her kimono on the couch, and it could be presumed that at those times she was not smoking or relaxing but doing regular work in my father's office, that legendary place that I had never seen and where I would certainly not be welcome.

At such times—when Nancy's mother had to be at work and Nancy had to be at home—a grouchy person named Mrs. Codd sat listening to radio soap operas, ready to chase us out of the kitchen where she herself was eating anything on hand. It never occurred to me that since we usually spent all our time together, my mother could have offered to keep an eye on Nancy as well as me, or ask our maid to do so, to save the hiring of Mrs. Codd.

It does seem to me now that we played together all our waking hours. This would be from the time I was about five years old until I was around eight and a half, Nancy being half a year younger. We played mostly outdoors—those must have been rainy days, because of my memory of us in Nancy's cottage annoying Nancy's mother. We had to keep out of the vegetable garden and try not to knock down the flowers, but we were constantly in and out of the berry patches and under the apple trees and in the absolutely wild trashy area beyond the cottage, which was where we constructed our air-raid shelters and hideouts from the Germans.

There was actually a training base to the north of our town, and real planes were constantly flying over us. Once there was a crash, but to our disappointment the plane that was out of control went into the lake. And because of all this reference to the war we were able to make of Pete not just a local enemy but a Nazi, and of his lawn mower a tank. Sometimes we lobbed apples at him from the crab-apple tree that sheltered our bivouac. Once he complained to my mother and it cost us a trip to the beach.

She often took Nancy along on trips to the beach. Not to the one with the water slide, just down the cliff from our house, but to a smaller one you had to drive to, where there were no rowdy swimmers. In fact she taught us both to swim. Nancy was more fearless and reckless than I was, which annoyed me, so once I pulled her under an incoming wave and sat on her head. She kicked and held her breath and fought her way free.

"Nancy is a little girl," my mother scolded. "She is a little girl and you should treat her like a little sister."

Which was exactly what I was doing. I did not think of her as weaker than me. Smaller, yes, but sometimes that was an advantage. When we climbed trees she could hang like a monkey from branches that would not support me. And once in a fight—I can't recall what any of our fights were about—she bit me on my restraining arm and drew blood. That time we were separated, supposedly for a week, but our glowering from windows soon turned to longing and pleading, so the ban was lifted.

In winter we were allowed the whole property, where we built snow forts furnished with sticks of firewood and provided with arsenals of snowballs to fling at anyone who came along. Which few did, this being a dead-end street. We had to make a snowman, so that we could pummel him.

If a major storm kept us inside, at my house, my mother presided. We had to be kept quiet if my father was home in bed with a headache, so she would read us stories. *Alice in Wonderland,* I remember. We were both upset when Alice drinks the potion that makes her grow so large she gets stuck in the rabbit hole.

What about sex games, you may wonder. And yes, we had those too. I recall our hiding, one extremely hot day, in a tent that had been pitched—I have no idea why—behind the cottage. We had crawled in there on purpose to explore each other. The canvas had a certain erotic but infantile smell, like the underclothes that we removed. Various ticklings excited but shortly made us cross, and we were drenched in sweat, itchy, and soon ashamed. When we got ourselves out of there we felt more separate than usual and oddly wary of each other. I don't remember if the same thing happened again with the same result, but I would not be surprised if it did.

I cannot bring Nancy's face to mind so clearly as I can her mother's. I think her coloring was, or would in time be, much the same. Fair hair naturally going brown, but now bleached by so much time in the sun. Very rosy, even reddish skin. Yes. I see her cheeks red, almost as if crayoned. That too owing to so much time outdoors in summer, and such decisive energy.

In my house, it goes without saying, all rooms except those specified to us were forbidden. We would not dream of going upstairs or down into the cellar or into the front parlor or the dining room. But in the cottage everywhere was allowed, except wherever Nancy's mother was trying to get some peace or Mrs. Codd was glued to the radio. The cellar was a good place to go when even we tired of the heat in the afternoons. There was no railing alongside the steps and we could take more and more and more daring jumps to land on the hard dirt floor. And when we tired of that we could climb onto an old cot and bounce up and down, whipping an imaginary horse. Once we tried to smoke a cigarette filched from Nancy's mother's pack. (We would not have dared take more than one.) Nancy managed better with it than I did, having had more practice.

There was also in the cellar an old wooden dresser, on which sat several tins of mostly dried-up paint and varnish, an assortment of stiffened paintbrushes, stirring sticks, and boards on which colors had been tried or brushes wiped. A few tins had their lids still on tight, and these we pried open with some difficulty and discovered paint that could be stirred to an active thickness. Then we spent time trying to loosen up the brushes by pushing them down into the paint and then hitting them against the boards of the dresser, making a mess but not getting much of a result. One of the tins, however, proved to contain turpentine, which worked much better. Now we began to paint with those bristles that had become usable. I could read and spell to some extent, thanks to my mother, and Nancy could too, because she had finished the second grade.

"Don't look till I'm finished," I said to her, and pushed her slightly out of the way. I had thought of something to paint. She was busy anyway, smashing her own brush around in a can of red paint.

I wrote NAZI WAS IN THIS SELLER.

"Now look," I said.

She had turned her back on me but was wielding the paintbrush on herself.

She said, "I'm busy."

When she turned her face to me it was generously smeared all over with red paint.

"Now I look like you," she said, drawing the brush down on her neck. "Now I look like you."

She sounded very excited and I thought she was taunting me, but in fact her voice was bursting with satisfaction, as if this was what she had been aiming for her whole life.

Now I must try to explain what happened in the next several minutes.

In the first place, I thought she looked horrible.

I did not believe that any part of my face was red. And in fact it wasn't. The half of it that was colored was the usual mulberry birthmark color, which, as I believe I have said, has faded somewhat as I have aged.

But this was not how I saw it in my mind. I believed my birthmark to be a soft brown color, like the fur of a mouse.

My mother had not done anything so foolish, so dramatic, as to ban mirrors from our house. But mirrors can be hung too high for a young child to see himself in them. That was certainly so in the bathroom. The only one in which I saw my reflection readily hung in the front hall, which was dim in the daytime and weakly lit at night. That must have been where I got the idea that half my face was this dull mild sort of color, a furry shadow.

This was the idea I had got used to, and that made Nancy's paint such an insult, a leering joke. I pushed her against the dresser as hard as I could and ran away from her, up the stairs. I think I was running to find a mirror, or even a person who could tell me that she was in the wrong. And once that was confirmed I could sink my teeth into pure hatred of her. I would punish her. I had no time at the moment to think how.

I ran through the cottage—Nancy's mother was not anywhere to be seen, though it was Saturday—and I slammed its screened door. I ran on the gravel, then on the flagstone path between stalwart rows of gladioli. I saw my mother rise from the wicker chair where she sat reading, on our back verandah.

"Not red," I shouted with gulps of angry tears. "I'm not red." She came down the steps with a shocked face but so far no understanding. Then Nancy ran out of the cottage behind me all amazed, with her garish face.

My mother understood.

"You nasty little beast," she cried at Nancy, in a voice that I had never heard. A loud, wild, shaking voice.

"Don't you come near us. Don't you dare. You are a bad bad girl. You have no decent human kindness in you, do you? You never have been taught—"

Nancy's mother came out of the cottage, with streaming wet hair in her eyes. She was holding a towel.

"Jeez can't I even wash my hair around here—"

My mother screamed at her too.

"Don't you dare use that language in front of my son and me—"

"Oh blah blah," said Nancy's mother immediately. "Just listen to you yelling your head off—"

My mother took a deep breath.

"I am—not—yelling—my—head off. I just want to tell your cruel child she will never be welcome in our house again. She is a cruel spiteful child to mock my little boy for what he cannot help. You have never taught her anything, any manners, she did not even know enough to thank me when I took her with us to the beach, doesn't even know how to say please and thank you, no wonder with a mother flaunting around in her wrapper—"

All this poured out of my mother as if there was a torrent of rage, of pain, of absurdity in her that would never stop. Even though by now I was pulling at her dress and saying, "Don't, don't."

Then things got even worse as tears rose and swallowed her words and she choked and shook.

Nancy's mother had pushed the wet hair out of her eyes and stood there observing.

"I'll tell you one thing," she said. "You carry on like this and they're going to take you to the loony bin. Can I help it if your husband hates you and you got a kid with a messed-up face?"

My mother held her head in both hands. She cried, "Oh—oh," as if pains were devouring her. The woman who worked for us at that time—Velma—had come out on the verandah and was saying, "Missus. Come on, missus." Then she raised her voice and called to Nancy's mother.

"You go on. You go in your house. You scat."

"Oh I will. Don't worry, I will. Who do you think you are telling me what to do? And how do you like working for an ole witch with bats in the belfry?" Then she turned on Nancy.

"How in Jesus' name am I ever going to get you cleaned up?"

After that she raised her voice again to make sure I could hear her.

"He's a suck. Look at him hangin' on to his ole lady. You're not ever going to play with him again. Ole lady's suck."

Velma on one side and I on the other, we tried to ease my mother back to the house. She had stopped the noise she was making. She straightened herself and spoke in an unnaturally cheerful voice that could carry as far as the cottage.

"Fetch me my garden shears, would you Velma? While I'm out here I might as well trim the glads. Some of them are downright wilted."

But by the time she was finished they were all over the path, not one standing, wilted or blooming.

All this must have happened on a Saturday, as I said, because Nancy's mother was home and Velma was there, who did not come on Sundays. By Monday, or maybe sooner, I am sure the cottage was empty. Perhaps Velma got hold of my father in the clubhouse or on the greens or wher-

223

ever he was, and he came home, impatient and rude but soon compliant. Compliant, that is, about Nancy and her mother getting out. I had no idea where they went. Maybe he put them up in a hotel till he could find another place for them. I don't think Nancy's mother would have made any fuss about leaving.

The fact that I would never see Nancy again dawned on me slowly. At first I was angry at her and did not care. Then when I inquired about her, my mother must have put me off with some vague reply, not wanting to recall the anguished scene to me or herself. It was surely at that time that she became serious about sending me away to school. In fact I think that I was installed at Lakefield that very autumn. She probably suspected that once I got used to being at a boys' school the memory of having had a female playmate would grow dim and seem unworthy, even ridiculous.

On the day after my father's funeral my mother surprised me by asking if I would take her out to dinner (of course it would be a case of her taking me) at a restaurant some miles along the lakeshore, where she hoped there would be nobody we knew.

"I just feel I've been penned up in this house forever," she said. "I need some air."

In the restaurant she looked around discreetly and announced that there was nobody she knew.

"Will you join me in a glass of wine?"

Had we driven all this way so that she could drink wine in public?

When the wine had come, and we had ordered, she said, "There is something I think you ought to know."

These may be among the most unpleasant words that a person ever has to hear. There is a pretty good chance that whatever you ought to know will be burdensome, and that there will be a suggestion that other people have had to bear the burden, while you have been let off lightly, all this while.

"My father isn't my real father?" I said. "Goody."

"Don't be silly. You remember your little friend Nancy?"

I actually did not remember, for a moment. Then I said, "Vaguely."

At this time all my conversations with my mother seemed to call for strategy. I must keep myself lighthearted, jokey, unmoved. In her voice and face was a lurking sorrow. She never complained about her own plight, but there were so many innocent and ill-used people in the stories she told me, there were so many outrages, that I was surely meant, at the very least, to go off to my friends and my lucky life with a heavier heart.

I would not cooperate. All she wanted, possibly, was some sign of sympathy, or maybe of physical tenderness. I would not grant that. She was a fastidious woman not yet contaminated by age, but I backed off from her as if there was some danger of insistent dreariness, a contagious mold. I particularly backed off from any reference to my affliction, which it seemed to me she especially cherished—the shackle I could not loosen, that I had to admit to, that bound me to her from the womb.

"You would probably have known about it if you were around home much," she said. "But it happened shortly before we sent you off to school."

Nancy and her mother had gone to live in an apartment that belonged to my father, on the Square. There in the bright early fall morning Nancy's mother had come upon her daughter, in the bathroom, using a razor blade to slice into her cheek. There was blood on the floor and in the sink and here and there on Nancy. But she had not given up on her purpose or made a sound of pain.

How did my mother know all this? I can only suppose it was a town drama, supposed to be hushed up but too gory—and that in the literal sense of the word—not to be related in detail.

Nancy's mother wrapped a towel around her and somehow got her to the hospital. There was no ambulance at that time. She probably flagged a car on the Square. Why did she not phone my father? No matter—she didn't. The cuts were not deep and the blood loss was not so great in spite of the splatters—there was no cut to any major blood vessel. Nancy's mother kept berating the child that whole time and asking was she right in the head.

"You're just my luck," she kept saying. "A kid like you."

"If there had been social workers around at that time," said my mother, "no doubt that poor little thing would have been made a ward of the Children's Aid.

"It was the same cheek," she said. "Like yours."

I tried to keep silent, pretending not to know what she was talking about. But I had to speak.

"The paint was over her whole face," I said.

"Yes. But she was doing it more carefully this time, she cut open just that one cheek, trying the best she could to make herself look like you."

This time I did manage to keep quiet.

"If she had been a boy it would have been different. But what an awful thing for a girl."

"Plastic surgeons can do remarkable things nowadays."

"Oh, maybe they can."

After a moment she said, "Such deep feelings. Children have."

"They get over that."

She said she did not know what had become of them, the child or her mother. She said she was glad I had never asked, because she would have hated to tell me anything so distressing, when I was still young.

・ ・ ・

I don't know what bearing it has on anything, but I have to say that my mother changed completely in extreme old age, becoming ribald and fanciful. She claimed that my father had been a magnificent lover and that she herself had been "a pretty bad girl." She announced that I should have married "that girl who sliced up her face" because neither one of us would be able to crow over the other about doing a good deed. One of us, she cackled, would be just as much a mess as the other.

I agreed. I liked her then quite a bit.

A few days ago I was stung by a wasp while clearing out some rotten apples under one of the old trees. The sting was on my eyelid, which rapidly closed. I drove myself to the hospital, using the other eye (the swollen one was on the "good" side of my face), and was surprised to be told I must stay overnight. The reason was that once I was given an injection, both eyes had to be bandaged, thus avoiding strain on the one that could see. I had what they call a restless night, waking often. Of course it is never really quiet in a hospital, and just in that short time without my sight it seemed that my hearing grew more acute. When certain footsteps came into my room I knew that they were those of a woman, and I had the feeling that she was not a nurse.

But when she said, "Good. You're awake. I'm your reader," I thought that I must have been mistaken, she was a nurse after all. I stretched out an arm, believing she had come to read what are known as the vital signs.

"No, no," she said, in her small persistent voice. "I've come to read to you, if that's what you would like. Sometimes people like it; they get bored lying there with their eyes closed."

"Do they choose, or do you?"

"They do, but sometimes I sort of remind them. Sometimes I try and remind them of some Bible story, some part of the Bible they remember. Or a story from when they were children. I carry a whole batch of things around with me."

"I like poetry," I said.

"You don't sound very enthusiastic."

I realized that this was true, and I knew why. I have some experience of reading poetry aloud, over the radio, and of listening to other trained voices read, and there are some styles of reading I find comfortable, and some I abhor.

"Then we could have a game," she said, just as if I had explained this, when I hadn't. "I could read you a line or two, then I stop and see if you can do the next line. Okay?"

It struck me that she might be quite a young person, anxious to get some takers, to be a success on this job.

I said okay. But nothing in Old English, I told her.

" 'The king sat in Dunfermline town—' " she began in a questioning voice.

" 'Drinking the blood-red wine—' " I chimed in, and we proceeded in good humor. She read well enough, though at a rather childlike, show-off speed. I began to like the sound of my own voice, now and then falling into a bit of an actorly flourish.

"That's nice," she said.

" 'And show you where the lilies grow, / On the banks of Italie—' "

"Is it 'grow' or 'blow'?" she said. "I don't actually have a book with that in it. I should remember, though. Never mind, it's lovely. I always liked your voice on the radio."

"Really? Did you listen?"

"Of course. Lots of people did."

She stopped feeding me lines and just let me go ahead. You can imagine. "Dover Beach" and "Kubla Khan" and "West Wind" and "Wild Swans" and "Doomed Youth." Well, maybe not all of them, and maybe not right through to the end.

"You're getting short of breath," she said. Her little quick hand was laid on my mouth. And then her face or the side of her face, laid on mine. "I have to go. Here's another just before I go. I'll make it harder because I won't start at the beginning.

" 'None will long mourn for you, / Pray for you, miss you / Your place left vacant—' "

"I've never heard that," I said.

"Sure?"

"Sure. You win."

By now I suspected something. She seemed distracted, slightly cross. I heard the geese calling as they flew over the hospital. They take practice runs at this time of year, and then the runs get longer and one day they're gone. I was waking up, in that state of surprise, indignation, that follows a convincing dream. I wanted to go back and have her lay her face on mine. Her cheek, on mine. But dreams are not so obliging.

When I got my eyesight back, and was at home, I looked for those lines she had left me with in my dream. I went through a couple of anthologies and did not find them there. I began to suspect that the lines did not belong to a real poem at all, but had just been devised in the dream, to confound me.

Devised by whom?

But later in the fall, when I was getting some old books ready to donate to a charity bazaar, a piece of brownish paper fell out, with lines on it written in pencil. It was not my mother's writing, and I can hardly think it would be my father's. Whose, then? Whoever it was had written the author's name at the end. Walter de la Mare. No title. Not a writer whose works I have any particular knowledge of. But I must have seen the poem at some time, maybe not in this copy, maybe in a textbook. I must have buried the words in a deep cubbyhole of my mind. And why? Just so that I could be teased by them, or teased by a determined girl-child phantom, in a dream?

There is no sorrow
Time heals never;
No loss, betrayal,
Beyond repair.
Balm for the soul, then,
Though grave shall sever
Lover from loved
And all they share.
See the sweet sun shines
The shower is over;
Flowers preen their beauty,
The day how fair!
Brood not too closely
On love, on duty;
Friends long forgotten
May wait you where
Life with death
Brings all to an issue;
None will long mourn for you,
Pray for you, miss you,
Your place left vacant,
You not there.

The poem didn't depress me. In some peculiar way it seemed to back up the decision I had made by that time, not to sell the property, but to stay.

Something happened here. In your life there are a few places, or maybe only the one place, where something happened, and then there are all the other places.

Of course I know that if I had spotted Nancy—on the subway, for instance, in Toronto—both of us bearing our recognizable marks, we would in all probability have managed only one of those embarrassed and meaningless conversations, hurriedly listing useless autobiographical facts. I would have noted the mended nearly normal cheek or the still obvious wound, but it would probably not have come into the conversation. Children might have been mentioned. Not that unlikely, whether she was mended or not. Grandchildren. Jobs. I might not have had to tell her mine. We would have been shocked, hearty, dying to get away.

You think that would have changed things?

The answer is of course, and for a while, and never.

Some Women

I am amazed sometimes to think how old I am. I can remember when the streets of the town I lived in were sprinkled with water to lay the dust in summer, and when girls wore waist cinches and crinolines that could stand up by themselves, and when there was nothing much to be done about things like polio and leukemia. Some people who got polio got better, crippled or not, but people with leukemia went to bed, and after some weeks' or months' decline in a tragic atmosphere, they died.

It was because of such a case that I got my first job, in the summer holidays when I was thirteen. Young Mr. Crozier (Bruce) had come safely home from the war, where he had been a fighter pilot, had gone to college and studied history, and graduated, and got married, and now he had leukemia. He and his wife had come back to stay with his stepmother, Old Mrs. Crozier. Young Mrs. Crozier (Sylvia) was going off two afternoons a week to teach summer school at that same college where they had met, about forty miles away. I was hired to look after Young Mr. Crozier while she was away. He was in bed in the front corner bedroom upstairs, and he could still get to the bathroom by himself. All I had to do was to bring him fresh water and pull the shades up or down and see what he wanted when he rang the little bell on his bedside table.

Usually what he wanted was to have the fan moved. He liked the breeze it created but he was disturbed by the noise. So he wanted the fan in the room for a while and then he wanted it out in the hall, but close to his open door.

When my mother heard about this she wondered why they hadn't put him in a bed downstairs, where they surely had high ceilings and he would be cooler.

I told her that they did not have any bedrooms downstairs.

"Well, my heavens, couldn't they fix one up? Temporarily?"

That showed how little she knew about the Crozier household or the rule of Old Mrs. Crozier. Old Mrs. Crozier walked with a cane. She made one ominous-sounding progress up the stairs to see her stepson on the afternoons I was there, and I suppose no more than that on the afternoons when I was not there. Then another, as necessary, when she went to bed. But the idea of a bedroom downstairs would have outraged her as much as the notion of a toilet in the parlor. Fortunately there was already a toilet downstairs, behind the kitchen, but I was sure that if the only one had been upstairs she would have made the climb as often and as laboriously as necessary, rather than see a change so radical and unnerving.

My mother had an idea of going into the antique business, so she was very interested in the inside of that house. She did get in, once, during my very first afternoon. I was in the kitchen, and I stood petrified, hearing her "yoo-hoo" and my own merrily called name. Then her perfunctory knock, her steps on the kitchen stairs. And Old Mrs. Crozier stumping out from the sunroom.

My mother said that she had just dropped in to see how her daughter was getting along.

"She's all right," said Old Mrs. Crozier, who stood in the hall doorway, blocking the view of antiques.

My mother made a few more mortifying remarks and took herself off. That night she said that Old Mrs. Crozier had no manners because she was only a second wife picked up on a business trip to Detroit, which was why she smoked and dyed her hair black as tar and put on lipstick like a smear of jam. She was not even the mother of the invalid upstairs. She did not have the brains to be.

(We were having one of our fights then, this one relating to her visit, but that is neither here nor there.)

The way Old Mrs. Crozier saw it, I must have seemed just as intrusive as my mother, just as cheerily self-regarding. On my very first afternoon I had gone into the back parlor and opened the bookcase and stood there taking stock of the

Harvard Classics set out in their perfect row. Most of them discouraged me, but I took one out that might be fiction, in spite of its title in a foreign language, *I Promessi Sposi*. It appeared to be fiction all right, and it was in English.

I must have had the idea then that all books came free, wherever you found them. Like water from a public tap.

When Old Mrs. Crozier saw me with the book she asked where I had got it and what I was doing with it. From the bookcase, I said, and I had brought it upstairs to read. The thing that most perplexed her seemed to be that I had got it downstairs, but brought it upstairs. The reading part she appeared to let go, as if such an activity was too foreign for her contemplation. Finally she said that if I wanted a book I should bring one from home.

I Promessi Sposi was heavy going anyway. I did not mind putting it back in the bookcase.

Of course there were books in the sickroom. Reading seemed to be acceptable there. But they were mostly open and facedown, as if Mr. Crozier just read a little here and there and put them aside. And their titles did not tempt me. *Civilization on Trial. The Great Conspiracy Against Russia.*

And my grandmother had warned me that if I could help it I should not touch anything the patient had touched, because of germs, and I should always keep a cloth between my fingers and his water glass.

My mother said leukemia did not come from germs.

"So what does it come from?" said my grandmother.

"The medical men don't know."

"Hunh."

It was Young Mrs. Crozier who picked me up and drove me home, though the distance was no more than from one side of the town to the other. She was a tall, thin, fair-haired woman with a variable complexion. Sometimes there were patches of red on her cheeks as if she had scratched them. Word had been passed that she was older than her husband, that he had been her student at college. My mother said that nobody seemed to have got around to figuring out that since he was a war veteran, he could easily have been her student without that making her older. People were just down on her because she had got an education.

Another thing they said was that she could have stayed home and looked after him now, as promised in the marriage ceremony, instead of going out to teach. My mother again defended her, saying it was only two afternoons a week and she had to keep up her profession, seeing she would be on her own soon enough. And if she didn't get out of the old lady's way once in a while, wouldn't you think she'd go crazy? My mother always defended women who were working on their own, and my grandmother always got after her for it.

One day I tried a conversation with Young Mrs. Crozier, or Sylvia. She was the only college graduate I knew, let alone being a teacher. Except for her husband, of course, and he had stopped counting.

"Did Toynbee write history books?"

"Beg pardon? Oh. Yes."

None of us mattered to her, not me, or her critics or defenders. No more than bugs on a lampshade.

What Old Mrs. Crozier cared about really was her flower garden. She had a man who came and helped her, someone about as old but more limber than she was. He lived on our street and in fact it was through him that she heard about me as a possible employee. At home he only gossiped and grew weeds, but here he plucked and mulched and fussed, while she followed him around, leaning on her stick and shaded by her big straw hat. Sometimes she sat on her bench, still commenting and giving orders, and smoking a cigarette. Early on, I dared to go between the perfect hedges to ask if she or her helper would like a glass of water, and she cried out, "Mind my borders," before saying no.

There were no flowers brought into the house. Some poppies had escaped and were growing wild beyond the hedge, almost on the road, so I asked if I could pick a bouquet to brighten the sickroom.

"They'd only die," she said, not seeming to realize that this remark had a double edge to it, in the circumstances.

Certain suggestions, or notions, would make the muscles of her lean spotty face quiver, her eyes go sharp and black, and her mouth work as if there was a despicable taste in it. She could stop you in your tracks then, like a savage thornbush.

The two days I worked were not consecutive. Let us say they were Tuesdays and Thursdays. The first day I was alone with the sick man and Old Mrs. Crozier. The second day somebody arrived whom I had not been told about. I heard the car in the driveway, and some brisk running up the back steps and a person entering the kitchen without knocking. Then somebody called "Dorothy," which I had not known was Old Mrs. Crozier's name. The voice was a woman's or girl's, and it was bold and teasing all at once, so that you could almost feel this person was tickling you.

I ran down the back stairs saying, "I think she's in the sunroom."

"Holy Toledo. Who are you?"

I told her who I was and what I was doing there, and this young woman said her name was Roxanne.

"I'm the masseuse."

I didn't like being caught by a word I didn't know. I didn't say anything but she saw how things were.

"Got you stumped, eh? I give massages. You ever heard of that?"

Now she was unpacking the bag she had with her. Various pads and cloths and flat velour-covered brushes appeared.

"I'll need some hot water to warm these up," she said. "You can heat me some in the kettle."

This was a grand house, but there was only cold water on tap, as in my house.

She had sized me up, apparently, as somebody who was willing to take orders—especially, perhaps, orders given in such a coaxing voice. And she was right, though maybe she didn't guess that my willingness had more to do with my own curiosity than her charm.

She was tanned this early in the summer, and her pageboy hair had a copper sheen—something you could get easily nowadays from a bottle, but that was unusual and enviable then. Brown eyes, a dimple in one cheek, such smiling and teasing that you never got a good-enough look at her to say whether she was really pretty, or how old she was.

Her rump curved out handsomely to the back instead of spreading to the sides.

I learned right away that she was new in town, married to the mechanic at the Esso station, and that she had two little boys, one four years old and one three. "It took me a while to find out what was causing them," she said with one of her conspiratorial twinkles.

She had trained to be a masseuse in Hamilton where they used to live and it turned out to be just the sort of thing she had always had a knack for.

"Dor-thee?"

"She's in the sunroom," I told her again.

"I know, I'm just kidding her. Now maybe you don't know about getting a massage, but when you get one, you got to take off all your clothes. Not such a problem when you're young, but when you're older, you know, you can get all embarrassed."

She was wrong about one thing, at least as far as I was concerned. About it not being a problem to take off all your clothes when you're young.

"So maybe you should skedaddle."

This time I took the front staircase while she was busy with the hot water. That way I got a glance in through the open door of the sunroom—which was not much of a sunroom at all, having its windows on three sides all filled up with the fat leaves of catalpa trees.

There I saw Old Mrs. Crozier stretched out on a daybed, on her stomach, head turned away from me, absolutely naked. A skinny streak of pale flesh. It didn't look so old as the parts of her that were daily exposed—her brown-freckled dark-veined hands and forearms, her brown-blotched cheeks. This usually covered length of her body was yellow-white, like wood freshly stripped of its bark.

I sat on the top step and listened to the sounds of the massage. Thumps and grunts. Roxanne's voice bossy now, cheerful but full of exhortation.

"Stiff knot here. Oh brother. I'm going to have to whack you one. Just kidding. Aw, come on, just loosen up for me. You know you got a nice skin here. Small of your back, what do they say? It's like a baby's bum. Now I gotta bear down a bit, you're going to feel it here. Take away the tension. Goody girl."

Old Mrs. Crozier was making little yelps. Sounds of complaint and gratitude. It went on for quite a while and I got bored. I went back to reading some old *Canadian Home Journal*s that I had found in a hall cupboard. I read recipes and checked on old-time fashions till I heard Roxanne say, "Now I'll just clean this stuff up and we'll go upstairs like you decided."

Upstairs. I slid the magazines back into their place in the cupboard that would have been coveted by my mother and went into Mr. Crozier's room. He was asleep, or at least he had his eyes closed. I moved the fan a few inches and smoothed his cover and went and stood by the window twiddling with the blind.

Sure enough there came a noise on the back stairs, Old Mrs. Crozier with her slow and threatening cane steps, Roxanne running ahead, and calling, "Look out, look out, wherever you are. We're coming to get you wherever you are."

Mr. Crozier had his eyes open now. Beyond his usual weariness was a faint expression of alarm. But before he could pretend to be asleep again Roxanne burst into the room.

"So here's where you're hiding. I just told your stepmom I thought it was about time I got introduced to you."

Mr. Crozier said, "How do you do, Roxanne."

"How did you know my name?"

"Word gets around."

"Fresh fellow you got here," said Roxanne to Old Mrs. Crozier, who now came stumping into the room.

"Stop fooling around with that blind," Old Mrs. Crozier said to me. "Go and fetch me a drink of cool water if you want something to do. Not cold—just cool."

"You're a mess," said Roxanne to Mr. Crozier. "Who gave you that shave and when was it?"

"Yesterday," he said. "I handle it myself as well as I can."

"That's what I thought," said Roxanne. And to me, "When you're getting her water, how'd you like to heat some up for me and I'll undertake to give him a decent shave?"

That was how Roxanne took on this other job, once a week, following the massage. She told Mr. Crozier on that first day not to worry.

"I'm not going to pound on you like you must have heard me doing to Dorothy-doodle downstairs. Before I got my massage training I used to be a nurse. Well, a nurse's aide. One of the ones do all the work and the nurses come around and boss you. Anyway, I learned how to make people comfortable."

Dorothy-doodle? Mr. Crozier grinned. But the odd thing was that Old Mrs. Crozier just grinned too.

Roxanne shaved him deftly. She sponged his face and neck and torso and arms and hands. She pulled his sheets around, somehow managing not to disturb him, and she pounded and rearranged his pillows. Talking all the time, pure teasing and nonsense.

"Dorothy, you're a liar. You said you had a sick man upstairs and I walk in here and I think, Where's the sick man? I don't see a sick man round here. Do I?"

Mr. Crozier said, "What would you say I am then?"

"Recovering. That's what I would say. I don't say you should be up and running around, I'm not so stupid as all that. I know you need your bed rest. But I say recovering. Nobody sick like you

246

are supposed to be ever looked as good as what you do."

I thought this flirtatious prattle insulting. Mr. Crozier looked terrible. A tall man whose ribs had shown like those of somebody fresh from a famine when she sponged him, whose head was bald and whose skin looked as if it had the texture of a plucked chicken's, his neck corded like an old man's. Whenever I had waited on him in any way I had avoided looking at him. And this was not really because he was sick and ugly. It was because he was dying. I would have felt something of the same reticence even if he had looked angelically handsome. I was aware of an atmosphere of death in the house, growing thicker as you approached this room, and he was at the center of it, like the host the Catholics kept in the box so powerfully called the tabernacle. He was the one stricken, marked out from everybody else, and here was Roxanne trespassing on his ground with her jokes and her swagger and notions of entertainment.

Inquiring, for instance, as to whether there was a game in the house called Chinese checkers.

This was perhaps on her second visit, when she asked him what he did all day.

"Read sometimes. Sleep."

And how did he sleep at night?

"If I can't sleep I lie awake. Think. Sometimes read."

"Doesn't that disturb your wife?"

"She sleeps in the back bedroom."

"Un-huh. You need some entertainment."

"Are you going to sing and dance for me?"

I saw Old Mrs. Crozier look aside with her odd involuntary grin.

"Don't you get cheeky," said Roxanne. "Are you up to cards?"

"I hate cards."

"Well, have you got Chinese checkers in the house?"

Roxanne directed this question at Old Mrs. Crozier, who first said she had no idea, then wondered if there might be a board in a drawer of the dining room buffet.

So I was sent down to look and came back with the board and the jar of marbles.

Roxanne set the board up over Mr. Crozier's legs, and she and I and Mr. Crozier played, Old Mrs. Crozier saying she had never understood the game or been able to keep her marbles straight. (To my surprise she seemed to offer this as a joke.) Roxanne might squeal when she made a move or groan whenever somebody jumped over one of her marbles, but she was careful never to disturb the patient. She held her body still and set her marbles down like feathers. I tried to learn to do the same, because she would widen her eyes warningly at me if I didn't. All without losing her dimple.

I remembered Young Mrs. Crozier, Sylvia, saying to me in the car that her husband did not welcome conversation. It tired him out, she said, and when he was tired he could become irritable. So I thought, If ever there was a time for him to become irritable, it is now. Being forced to play a silly game on his deathbed, when you could feel his fever in the sheets.

But Sylvia must have been wrong. He had developed greater patience and courtesy than she was perhaps aware of. With inferior people— Roxanne was surely an inferior person—he had made himself tolerant, gentle. When all he must want to do was lie there and meditate on the pathways of his life and gear up for his future.

Roxanne patted sweat off his forehead, saying, "Don't get excited, you haven't won yet."

"Roxanne," he said. "Roxanne. Do you know whose name that was, Roxanne?"

"Hmm?" she said, and I broke in. I couldn't help it.

"It was Alexander the Great's wife's name."

My head was a magpie's nest lined with such bright scraps of information.

"Is that so?" said Roxanne. "And who was that supposed to be? Great Alexander?"

I realized something when I looked at Mr. Crozier at that moment. Something shocking, saddening.

He liked her not knowing. I could tell. He liked

her not knowing. Her ignorance woke a pleasure that melted on his tongue, like a lick of toffee.

On the first day she had worn shorts, as I did, but the next time and always after that Roxanne wore a dress of some stiff and shiny light green material. You could hear it rustle as she ran up the stairs. She brought a fleecy pad for Mr. Crozier, so he would not develop bedsores. She was dissatisfied with the arrangement of his bedclothes, always, had to put them to rights. But however she scolded, her movements never irritated him, and she made him admit to feeling more comfortable afterwards.

She was never at a loss. Sometimes she came equipped with riddles. Or jokes. Some of the jokes were what my mother would call smutty and would not allow around our house, except when they came from certain of my father's relatives who had practically no other kind of conversation.

These jokes usually started off with serious-sounding but absurd questions.

Did you hear about the nun who went shopping for a meat grinder?

Did you hear what the bride and groom went and ordered for dessert on their wedding night?

The answers always coming with a double meaning, so that whoever told the joke could pretend to be shocked and accuse the audience of having dirty minds.

And after she had got everybody used to her telling these jokes Roxanne went on to the sort of jokes I didn't believe my mother knew existed, often involving sex with sheep or hens or milking machines.

"Isn't that awful?" she always said at the finish. She said she wouldn't know this stuff if her husband didn't bring it home from the garage.

The fact that Old Mrs. Crozier snickered shocked me as much as the jokes themselves. I thought that she maybe didn't get the point but simply enjoyed listening to whatever Roxanne said. She sat with that chewed-in yet absent-minded smile on her face as if she'd been given a present she knew she would like, even if she hadn't got the wrapping off it yet.

Mr. Crozier didn't laugh, but he never laughed, really. He raised his eyebrows, pretending to scold, to find Roxanne outrageous but endearing all the same. This could have been good manners, or gratitude for all her efforts, whatever they might be.

I myself made sure to laugh, so that Roxanne would not put me down as being full of priggish innocence.

The other thing she did, to keep things lively, was tell about her life. Coming down from some lost little town in northern Ontario to Toronto to visit her older sister, then getting a job at Eaton's, first cleaning things up in the cafeteria, then being noticed by one of the managers because she worked fast and was always cheerful, and suddenly finding herself a salesgirl in the glove department. (I thought she made this sound something like being discovered by Warner Brothers.) And who should come in one day but Barbara Ann Scott, the skating star, who bought a pair of elbow-length white kid gloves.

Meanwhile Roxanne's sister had so many boyfriends that she would flip a coin to see who she would go out with almost every night, and she employed Roxanne to meet the rejects regretfully at the front door of the rooming house, while she herself and her pick sneaked out the back. Roxanne said maybe that was how she had developed such a gift of the gab. And pretty soon some of the boys she met this way were taking her out on her own, instead of her sister. They did not know her real age.

"I had me a ball," she said.

I began to understand that there were certain talkers—certain girls—whom people liked to listen to, not because of what they, the girls, had to say, but because of the delight they took in saying it. A delight in themselves, a shine on their faces, a conviction that whatever they were telling about was remarkable and that they themselves could not help but give pleasure. There might be other people—people like me—who didn't concede this, but that was their loss. And people like me would never be the audience these girls were after, anyway.

Mr. Crozier sat propped up on his pillows and looked for all the world as if he was happy. Happy just to close his eyes and let her talk, then open his eyes and find her there, like a chocolate bunny on Easter morning. And then with his eyes open follow every twitch of her candy lips and sway of her sumptuous bottom.

Old Mrs. Crozier would rock slightly back and forth in her curious state of satisfaction.

The time Roxanne spent upstairs was as long as she spent downstairs, giving the massage. I wondered if she was being paid. If she wasn't, how could she afford to take the time? And who could be paying her but Old Mrs. Crozier?

Why?

To keep her stepson happy and comfortable? I doubted it.

To keep herself entertained in a curious way?

One afternoon when Roxanne had left his room, Mr. Crozier said he felt thirstier than usual. I went downstairs to get him some water from the pitcher that was always in the refrigerator. Roxanne was packing up to go home.

"I never meant to stay so late," she said. "I wouldn't want to run into that schoolteacher."

I didn't understand for a moment.

"You know. Syl-vi-a. She's not crazy about me

either, is she? She ever mention me when she drives you home?"

I said that Sylvia had never mentioned Roxanne's name to me, during any of our drives. But why should she?

"Dorothy says she doesn't know how to handle him. She says I make him a lot happier than what she does. Dorothy says that. I wouldn't be surprised she even told her that to her face."

I thought of how Sylvia ran upstairs into her husband's room every afternoon when she got home, before she even spoke to me or her mother-in-law, her face flushed with eagerness and desperation. I wanted to say something about that—I wanted somehow to defend her, but I didn't know how. And people as confident as Roxanne often seemed to get the better of me, even if it was only by not listening.

"You sure she never says anything about me?"

I said again that no, she didn't. "She's tired when she gets home."

"Yeah. Everybody's tired. Some just learn to act like they aren't."

I did say something then, to balk her. "I quite like her."

"You qwat like her?" mocked Roxanne.

Playfully, sharply, she jerked at a strand of the bangs I had recently cut for myself.

"You ought to do something decent with your hair."

Dorothy says.

If Roxanne wanted admiration, which was her nature, what was it Dorothy wanted? I had a feeling there was mischief stirring, but I could not pin it down. Maybe it was just a desire to have Roxanne in the house, her liveliness in the house, double time.

Midsummer passed. Water was low in the wells. The sprinkler truck stopped coming and some stores had put up sheets of what looked like yellow cellophane in their windows to keep their goods from fading. Leaves were spotty, grass dry.

Old Mrs. Crozier kept her garden man hoeing, day after day. That's what you do in the dry weather, hoe and hoe to bring up any moisture that you can find in the ground underneath.

Summer school at the college would end after the second week of August, and then Sylvia Crozier would be home every day.

Mr. Crozier was still glad to see Roxanne, but he often fell asleep. He could fall asleep without letting his head fall back, during one of her jokes or anecdotes. Then after a moment he would be awake, he would ask where he was.

"Right here, you sleepy noodle. You're supposed to be paying attention to me. I should bat you one. Or how 'bout I try tickling you instead?"

Anybody could see how he was failing. There were hollows in his cheeks like an old man's and the light shone through the tops of his ears as if they were not flesh but plastic. (Though we didn't say "plastic" then; we said "celluloid.")

The last day of my working there, Sylvia's last day of teaching, was a massage day. Sylvia had to leave early for the college, because of some ceremony, so I walked across town, arriving when Roxanne was already there. Old Mrs. Crozier was also in the kitchen, and they both looked at me as if they had forgotten I was coming, as if I had interrupted them.

"I ordered them specially," said Old Mrs. Crozier.

She must have meant the macaroons sitting in the baker's box on the table.

"Yeah, but I told you," said Roxanne. "I can't eat that stuff. Not no way no how."

"I sent Hervey down to the bakeshop to get them."

Hervey was the name of our neighbor, her garden man.

"Okay let Hervey eat them. I'm not kidding, I break out something awful."

"I thought we'd have a treat, like something special," said Old Mrs. Crozier. "Seeing it's the last day we've got before—"

"Last day before she parks her butt here permanently, yeah, I know. Doesn't help me breaking out like a spotted hyena."

Who was it whose butt was parked permanently? Sylvia's. Sylvia.

Old Mrs. Crozier was wearing a beautiful black silk wrapper, with water lilies and geese on it. She said, "No chance of having anything special with her around. You'll see."

"So let's get going and get some time today. Don't bother about this stuff, it's not your fault. I know you got it to be nice."

"I know you got it to be nice," imitated Old Mrs. Crozier in a mean mincing voice, and then they both looked at me, and Roxanne said, "Pitcher's where it always is."

I took Mr. Crozier's pitcher of water out of the fridge. It occurred to me that they could offer me a golden macaroon out of those sitting in the box, but apparently it did not occur to them.

I expected him to be lying back on the pillows with his eyes closed, but Mr. Crozier was wide awake.

"I've been waiting," he said, and took a breath. "For you to get here," he said. "I want to ask you—do something for me. Will you?"

I said sure.

"Keep it a secret?"

I had been worried that he might ask me to help him to the commode that had recently appeared in his room, but surely that would not have to be a secret.

Yes.

He told me to go to the bureau across from his bed and open the left-hand little drawer, and see if I could find a key there.

I did so. I found a large heavy old-fashioned key.

He wanted me to go out of this room and shut the door and lock it. Then hide the key in a safe place, perhaps in the pocket of my shorts.

I was not to tell anybody what I had done.

I was not to let anybody know I had the key until his wife came home, and then I was to give it to her. Did I understand?

Okay.

He thanked me.

Okay.

All the time he was talking to me there was a film of sweat on his face and his eyes were bright as if he had a fever.

"Nobody is to get in."

"Nobody to get in," I repeated.

"Not my stepmother or—Roxanne. Just my wife."

I locked the door from the outside and put the key in the pocket of my shorts. But then I was afraid it could be seen through the light cotton material, so I went downstairs and into the back parlor and hid it between the pages of *I Promessi Sposi*. I knew that Roxanne and Old Mrs. Crozier would not hear me because the massage was going on, and Roxanne was using her professional voice.

"I got my work cut out for me getting these knots out of you today."

And I heard Old Mrs. Crozier's voice, full of her new displeasure.

". . . punching harder than you normally do."

"Well I gotta."

I was headed upstairs when some further thoughts came to me.

If he and not I had locked the door—which was evidently what he wanted the others to think—and I had been sitting on the top step as usual, I would certainly have heard him and called out and roused the others in the house. So I went back down and sat on the bottom step of the front stairs, a place from which it could have been possible for me not to hear a thing.

The massage seemed to be brisk and businesslike today; they were evidently not teasing and making jokes. Pretty soon I could hear Roxanne running up the back stairs.

She stopped. She said, "Hey. Bruce."

Bruce.

She rattled the knob of the door.

"Bruce."

Then she must have put her mouth to the keyhole, hoping he could hear but nobody else could. I could not make out exactly what she was saying, but I could tell she was pleading. First teasing, then pleading. In a while she sounded as if she was saying her prayers.

When she gave that up she started pounding up and down on the door with her fists, not too hard but urgently.

After a while she stopped that too.

"Come on," she said in a firmer voice. "If you got to the door to lock it you can get there to open it up."

Nothing happened. She came and looked over the bannister and saw me.

"Did you take Mr. Crozier's water into his room?"

I said yes.

"So his door wasn't locked or anything then?"

No.

"Did he say anything to you?"

"He just said thanks."

"Well, he's got his door locked and I can't get him to answer."

I heard Old Mrs. Crozier's stick pounding to the top of the back stairs.

"What's the commotion up here?"

"He's locked hisself in and I can't get him to answer me."

"What do you mean locked himself in? Likely the door's stuck. Wind blew it shut and it stuck."

There was no wind that day.

"Try it yourself," said Roxanne. "It's locked."

"I wasn't aware there was a key to this door,"

said Old Mrs. Crozier, as if her not being aware could negate the fact. Then, perfunctorily, she tried the knob and said, "Well. It'd appear to be locked."

He had counted on this, I thought. That they would not suspect me, thinking of his being in charge. And in fact he was.

"We have to get in," said Roxanne. She gave a kick to the door.

"Stop that," said Old Mrs. Crozier. "Do you want to wreck the door? You couldn't get through it anyway; it's solid oak. Every door in this house is solid oak."

"Then we have to get the police."

There was a pause.

"They could get up to the window," said Roxanne.

Old Mrs. Crozier drew in her breath and spoke decisively.

"You do not know what you are saying. I won't have the police in this house. I won't have them climbing all over my walls like caterpillars."

"We don't know what he could be doing in there."

"Well, then, that's up to him. Isn't it?"

Another pause.

Now steps—Roxanne's—retreating to the back staircase.

"Yes, you better," said Mrs. Crozier. "You better just take yourself away before you forget whose house this is."

Roxanne was going down the stairs. A couple of stomps of the stick went after her but did not continue down.

"And don't get the idea you'll go to the constable behind my back. He's not going to take his orders from you. Who gives the orders around here anyway? It's certainly not you. You hear me?"

Very soon I heard the kitchen door slam shut. And then Roxanne's car start.

I was no more worried about the police than Old Mrs. Crozier was. The police in our town meant Constable McClarty who came to the school to warn us about sledding on the streets in the winter and swimming in the millrace in summer, both of which we continued to do. It was ridiculous to think of him climbing up on a ladder or lecturing Mr. Crozier through a locked door.

He would tell Roxanne to mind her own business and let the Croziers mind theirs.

It was not ridiculous, however, to think of Old Mrs. Crozier giving orders, and I thought she might do so now that Roxanne—whom she apparently did not like anymore—was gone. She might turn on me and demand to know if I had anything to do with this.

But she did not even rattle the knob. She just stood at the locked door and said one thing.

"Stronger than you'd think," she muttered.

Then made her way downstairs. The usual punishing noises with her steady stick.

I waited awhile and then I went out to the kitchen. Old Mrs. Crozier wasn't there. She wasn't in either parlor or in the dining room or the sunroom. I got up my nerve and knocked on the toilet door, then opened it, and she was not there either. Then I looked out the window over the kitchen sink and I saw her straw hat moving along slowly above the cedar hedge. She was out in the garden in the heat, stumping along between her flower beds.

I was not worried by the thought that had troubled Roxanne. I did not stop to consider it, because I believed that it would be quite absurd for a person with only a short time to live to commit suicide. It could not happen.

All the same, I was nervous. I ate two of the macaroons that were still sitting on the kitchen table. I ate them hoping that pleasure would bring back normalcy, but I barely tasted them. Then I shoved the box into the refrigerator so I would not hope to turn the trick by eating more.

Old Mrs. Crozier was still outside when Sylvia got home. And she didn't come in then.

I got the key from between the pages of the book as soon as I heard the car and I gave it to Sylvia as soon as she was in the house. I just told her quickly what had happened, leaving out most of the fuss. She would not have waited to listen to that, anyway. She went running upstairs.

I stood at the bottom of the stairs to hear what I could hear.

Nothing. Nothing.

Then Sylvia's voice, surprised and upset but in no way desperate, and too low for me to make out what she was saying. Within about five minutes she was downstairs, saying it was time to get me home. She was flushed as if the spots in her cheeks had spread all over her face, and she looked shocked but unable to resist her happiness.

Then, "Oh. Where is Mother Crozier?"

"In the flower garden, I think."

"Well, I suppose I better speak to her, just for a moment."

After she had done that, she no longer looked quite so happy.

"I suppose you know," she said as she backed out the car, "I suppose you can imagine Mother Crozier is upset. Not that I am blaming you. It was very good and loyal of you. Doing what Mr. Crozier asked you to do. You weren't scared of anything happening? With Mr. Crozier? Were you?"

I said no.

Then I said, "I think Roxanne was."

"Mrs. Hoy? Yes. That's too bad."

As we were driving down what was known as Croziers' Hill she said, "I don't think he wanted to be mean and frighten them. You know when you're sick, sick for a long time, you can get not to appreciate other people's feelings. You can get turned against people even when they're so good and doing what they can to help you. Mrs. Crozier and Mrs. Hoy were certainly trying their best, but Mr. Crozier just didn't feel that he wanted them around anymore. He'd just had enough of them. You understand?"

She did not seem to know she was smiling when she said this.

Mrs. Hoy.

Had I ever heard that name before?

And spoken so gently and respectfully, yet with light-years' condescension.

Did I believe what Sylvia had said?

I believed it was what he had told her.

I did see Roxanne again that day. I saw her at the very time that Sylvia was talking to me and introducing to me this new name. Mrs. Hoy.

She—Roxanne—was in her car and she had stopped at the first cross street at the bottom of Croziers' Hill to watch us drive by. I didn't turn to look at her because it was all too confusing, with Sylvia talking to me.

Of course Sylvia would not know whose car that was. She wouldn't know that Roxanne must have come back to get an idea of what was going on. Or that maybe she had kept driving around the block—could she have done that?—all the time since she had left the Croziers' house.

Roxanne would recognize Sylvia's car, probably. She would notice me. She would know that things must be all right, from the kindly, serious, faintly smiling way that Sylvia was talking to me.

She didn't turn the corner and drive back up the hill to the Croziers' house. Oh no. She drove across the street—I watched in the rearview mirror—towards the east part of town where the wartime houses had been put up. That was where she lived.

"Feel the breeze," said Sylvia. "Maybe those clouds are going to bring us rain."

The clouds were high and white, glaring; they looked nothing like rain clouds; and the breeze was because we were in a moving car with the windows rolled down.

I understood pretty well the winning and losing that had taken place, between Sylvia and Roxanne, but it was strange to think of the almost obliterated prize, Mr. Crozier—and to think that he could have had the will to make a decision, even to deprive himself, so late in his life. The carnality at death's door—or the true love, for that matter—were things I had to shake off with shivers down my spine.

Sylvia took Mr. Crozier away to a rented cottage on the lake, where he died sometime before the leaves were off.

The Hoy family moved on, as mechanics' families often did.

My mother struggled with a crippling disease, which put an end to all her moneymaking dreams.

Dorothy Crozier had a stroke, but recovered, and famously bought Halloween candy for the children whose older brothers and sisters she had ordered from her door.

I grew up, and old.

Child's Play

I suppose there was talk in our house, afterwards.

How sad, how *awful*. (My mother.)

There should have been supervision. Where were the counsellors? (My father.)

It is possible that if we ever passed the yellow house my mother said, "Remember? Remember you used to be so scared of her? The poor thing."

My mother had a habit of hanging on to—even treasuring—the foibles of my distant infantile state.

Every year, when you're a child, you become a different person. Generally it's in the fall, when you reenter school, take your place in a higher grade, leave behind the muddle and lethargy of the summer vacation. That's when you register the change most sharply. Afterwards you are not sure of the month or year but the changes go on, just the same. For a long while the past drops away from you easily and it would seem automatically, properly. Its scenes don't vanish so much as become irrelevant. And then there's a switchback, what's been all over and done with sprouting up fresh, wanting attention, even wanting you to do something about it, though it's plain there is not on this earth a thing to be done.

Marlene and Charlene. People thought we must be twins. There was a fashion in those days for naming twins in rhyme. Bonnie and Connie. Ronald and Donald. And then of course we— Charlene and I—had matching hats. Coolie hats, they were called, wide shallow cones of woven straw with some sort of tie or elastic under the chin. They became familiar later on in the century, from television shots of the war in Vietnam. Men on bicycles riding along a street in Saigon would be wearing them, or women walking in the road against the background of a bombed village.

It was possible at that time—I mean the time when Charlene and I were at camp—to say *coolie,* without a thought of offense. Or *darkie,* or to talk about *jewing* a price down. I was in my teens, I think, before I ever related that verb to the noun.

So we had those names and those hats, and at the first roll call the counsellor—the jolly one we liked, Mavis, though we didn't like her as well as the pretty one, Pauline—pointed at us and called out, "Hey. Twins," and went on calling out other names before we had time to deny it.

Even before that we must have noticed the hats and approved of each other. Otherwise one or both of us would have pulled off those brand-new articles, and been ready to shove them under our cots, declaring that our mothers had made us wear them and we hated them, and so on.

I may have approved of Charlene, but I was not sure how to make friends with her. Girls nine or ten years old—that was the general range of this crop, though there were a few a bit older—do not pick friends or pair off as easily as girls do at six or seven. I simply followed some other girls from my town—none of them my particular friends— to one of the cabins where there were some unclaimed cots, and dumped my things on top of the brown blanket. Then I heard a voice behind me say, "Could I please be next to my twin sister?"

It was Charlene, speaking to somebody I didn't know. The dormitory cabin held perhaps two dozen girls. The girl she had spoken to said, "Sure," and moved along.

Charlene had used a special voice. Ingratiating, teasing, self-mocking, and with a seductive merriment in it, like a trill of bells. It was evident right away that she had more confidence than I did. And not simply confidence that the other girl would move, and not say sturdily, "I got here first." (Or—if she was a roughly brought-up sort of girl—and some were, having their way paid by the Lions Club or the church and not by their parents—she might have said, "Go poop your pants, I'm not moving.") No. Charlene had confidence that anybody would *want* to do as she asked, not just agree to do it. With me too she had taken a chance, for could I not have said, "I don't want to be twins," and turned back to sort my things. But of course I didn't. I felt flattered, as she had expected, and I watched her dump out the contents of her suitcase with such an air of celebration that some things fell on the floor.

All I could think of to say was, "You got a tan already."

"I always tan easy," she said.

The first of our differences. We applied ourselves to learning them. She tanned, I freckled. We both had brown hair but hers was darker. Hers was wavy, mine bushy. I was half an inch taller, she had thicker wrists and ankles. Her eyes had more green in them, mine more blue. We did not grow tired of inspecting and tabulating even the moles or notable freckles on our backs, length of our second toes (mine longer than the first toe, hers shorter). Or of recounting all the illnesses or accidents that had befallen us so far, as well as the repairs or removals performed on our bodies. Both of us had had our tonsils out—a usual precaution in those days—and both of us had had measles and whooping cough but not mumps. I had had an eyetooth pulled because it was growing in over my other teeth and she had a thumbnail with an imperfect half-moon, because her thumb had been slammed under a window.

And once we had the peculiarities and history of our bodies in place we went on to the stories—the dramas or near dramas or distinctions—of our families. She was the youngest and the only girl in her family and I was an only child. I had an aunt who had died of polio in high school and she—Charlene—had an older brother who was in the Navy. For it was wartime, and at the campfire sing-song we would choose "There'll Always Be an England" and "Hearts of Oak," and "Rule Britannia," and sometimes "The Maple Leaf Forever." Bombing raids and battles and sinking ships were the constant, though distant, backdrop of our lives. And once in a while there was a near strike, frightening but solemn and exhilarating, as when a boy from our town or our street would be killed, and the house where he had lived, without having any special wreath or black drapery on it, seemed nevertheless to have a special weight inside it, a destiny fulfilled and dragging it down. Though there was nothing special inside it at all, maybe just a car that didn't belong there parked at the curb, showing that some relatives or a minister had come to sit with the bereaved family.

One of the camp counsellors had lost her fiancé in the war and wore his watch—we believed it was his watch—pinned to her blouse. We would like to have felt for her a mournful interest and concern, but she was sharp voiced and bossy, and she even had an unpleasant name. Arva.

The other backdrop of our lives, which was supposed to be emphasized at camp, was religion. But since the United Church of Canada was offi-

273

cially in charge there was not so much harping on that subject as there would have been with the Baptists or the Bible Christians, or so much formal acknowledgment as the Roman Catholics or even the Anglicans would have provided. Most of us had parents who belonged to the United Church (though some of the girls who were having their way paid for them might not have belonged to any church at all), and being used to its hearty secular style, we did not even realize that we were getting off easy with just evening prayers and grace sung at meals and the half-hour special talk—it was called a Chat—after breakfast. Even the Chat was relatively free of references to God or Jesus and was more about honesty and loving-kindness and clean thoughts in our daily lives, and promising never to drink or smoke when we grew up. Nobody had any objection to this sort of thing or tried to get out of attending, because it was what we were used to and because it was pleasant to sit on the beach in the warming sun and a little too cold yet for us to long to jump into the water.

Grown-up women do the same sort of thing that Charlene and I did. Not counting the moles on each other's backs and comparing toe lengths, maybe. But when they meet and feel a particular sympathy with each other they also feel a need to set out the important information, the big events whether public or secret, and then go ahead to fill in all the blanks between. If they feel this warmth and eagerness it is quite impossible for them to bore each other. They will laugh at the very triviality and silliness of what they're telling, or at the revelation of some appalling selfishness, deception, meanness, sheer badness.

There has to be great trust, of course, but that trust can be established at once, in an instant.

I've observed this. It's supposed to have begun in those long periods of sitting around the campfire stirring the manioc porridge or whatever while the men were out in the bush deprived of conversation because it would warn off the wild animals. (I am an anthropologist by training though a rather slack one.) I've observed but never taken part in these female exchanges. Not truly. Sometimes I've pretended because it seemed to be required, but the woman I was supposed to be making friends with always got wind of my pretense and became confused and cautious.

As a rule, I've felt less wary with men. They don't expect such transactions and are seldom really interested.

This intimacy I'm talking about—with women—is not erotic, or pre-erotic. I've experienced that as well, before puberty. Then too there would be confidences, probably lies, maybe leading to games. A certain hot temporary excitement, with or without genital teasing. Followed by ill feeling, denial, disgust.

Charlene did tell me about her brother, but with true repugnance. This was the brother now in the Navy. She went into his room looking for her cat and there he was doing it to his girlfriend. They never knew she saw them.

She said they slapped as he went up and down.

You mean they slapped on the bed, I said.

No, she said. It was his thing slapped when it was going in and out. It was gross. Sickening.

And his bare white bum had pimples on it. Sickening.

I told her about Verna.

Up until the time I was seven years old my parents had lived in what was called a double house. The word "duplex" was perhaps not in use at that time, and anyway the house was not evenly divided. Verna's grandmother rented the rooms at the back and we rented the rooms at the front. The house was tall and bare and ugly, painted yellow. The town we lived in was too small to have residential divisions that amounted to anything, but I suppose that as far as there were divisions, that house was right on the boundary between decent and fairly dilapidated. I am speaking of the way things were just before the Second World War, at the end of the Depression. (That word, I believe, was unknown to us.)

My father being a teacher had a regular job but little money. The street petered out beyond us between the houses of those who had neither. Verna's grandmother must have had a little money because she spoke contemptuously of people who were On Relief. I believe my mother argued with her, unsuccessfully, that it was Not Their Fault. The two women were not particular friends but they were cordial about clothesline arrangements.

The grandmother's name was Mrs. Home. A man came to see her occasionally. My mother spoke of him as Mrs. Home's friend.

You are not to speak to Mrs. Home's friend.

In fact I was not even allowed to play outside when he came, so there was not much chance of my speaking to him. I don't even remember what he looked like, though I remember his car, which was dark blue, a Ford V-8. I took a special interest in cars, probably because we didn't have one.

Then Verna came.

Mrs. Home spoke of her as her granddaughter and there is no reason to suppose that not to be true, but there was never any sign of a connecting generation. I don't know if Mrs. Home went away and came back with her, or if she was delivered by the friend with the V-8. She appeared in the summer before I was to start school. I can't remember her telling me her name—she was not communicative in the ordinary way and I don't believe I would have asked her. From the very beginning I had an aversion to her unlike anything I had felt up to that time for any other person. I said that I hated her, and my mother said, How can you, what has she ever done to you?

The poor thing.

Children use that word "hate" to mean various things. It may mean that they are frightened. Not that they feel in danger of being attacked—the way I did, for instance, by certain big boys on bicycles who liked to cut in front of you, yelling fearsomely, as you walked on the sidewalk. It is not physical harm that is feared—or that I feared in Verna's case—so much as some spell, or dark intention. It is a feeling you can have when you are very young even about certain house faces, or tree trunks, or very much about moldy cellars or deep closets.

She was a good deal taller than I was and I don't know how much older—two years, three years? She was skinny, indeed so narrowly built and with such a small head that she made me think of a snake. Fine black hair lay flat on this head, and fell over her forehead. The skin of her face seemed dull to me as the flap of our old canvas tent, and her cheeks puffed out the way the flap of that tent puffed in a wind. Her eyes were always squinting.

But I believe there was nothing remarkably unpleasant about her looks, as other people saw her. Indeed my mother spoke of her as pretty, or almost pretty (as in, *isn't it too bad, she could be pretty*). Nothing to object to either, as far as my mother could see, in her behavior. *She is young for her age.* A roundabout and inadequate way of saying that Verna had not learned to read or write or skip or play ball, and that her voice was hoarse and unmodulated, her words oddly separated, as if they were chunks of language caught in her throat.

Her way of interfering with me, spoiling my solitary games, was that of an older not a younger girl. But of an older girl who had no skill or rights, nothing but a strenuous determination and an inability to understand that she wasn't wanted.

Children of course are monstrously conventional, repelled at once by whatever is off-center, out of whack, unmanageable. And being an only child I had been coddled a good deal (also scolded). I was awkward, precocious, timid, full of my private rituals and aversions. I hated even the celluloid barrette that kept slipping out of Verna's hair, and the peppermints with red or green stripes on them that she kept offering to me. In fact she did more than offer; she would try to catch me and push these candies into my mouth, chuckling all the time in her disconnected way. I dislike peppermint flavoring to this day. And the name Verna—I dislike that. It doesn't sound like spring to me, or like green grass or garlands of flowers or girls in flimsy dresses. It sounds more like a trail of obstinate peppermint, green slime.

I didn't believe my mother really liked Verna either. But because of some hypocrisy in her nature, as I saw it, because of a decision she had made, as it seemed to spite me, she pretended to be sorry for her. She told me to be kind. At first, she said that Verna would not be staying long and at the end of the summer holidays would go back to wherever she had been before. Then, when it became clear that there was nowhere for Verna to go back to, the placating message was that we ourselves would be moving soon. I had only to be kind for a little while longer. (As a matter of fact it was a whole year before we moved.) Finally, out of patience, she said that I was a disappointment to her and that she would never have thought I had so mean a nature.

"How can you blame a person for the way she was born? How is it her fault?"

That made no sense to me. If I had been more skilled at arguing I might have said that I didn't blame Verna, I just did not want her to come near me. But I certainly did blame her. I did not question that it was somehow her fault. And in this, whatever my mother might say, I was in tune to some degree with an unspoken verdict of the time and place I lived in. Even grown-ups smiled in a certain way, there was some irrepressible gratification and taken-for-granted superiority that I could see in the way they mentioned people who were *simple* or *a few bricks short of a load*. And I believed my mother must be really like this, underneath.

I started to school. Verna started to school. She was put into a special class in a special building in a corner of the school grounds. This was actually the original school building in the town, but nobody had any time for local history then, and a few years later it was pulled down. There was a fenced-off corner in which pupils housed in that building spent recess. They went to school a half hour later than we did in the morning and got out a half hour earlier in the afternoon. Nobody was supposed to harass them at recess but since they usually hung on the fence watching whatever went on in the regular school grounds there would be occasions when there was a rush, a whooping and brandishing of sticks, to scare them. I never went near that corner, hardly ever saw Verna. It was at home I still had to deal with her.

First she would stand at the corner of the yellow house, watching me, and I would pretend that I didn't know she was there. Then she would wander into the front yard, taking up a position on the front steps of the part of the house that was mine. If I wanted to go inside to the bathroom or because I was cold, I would have to go so close as to touch her and to risk her touching me.

She could stay in one place longer than anybody I ever knew, staring at just one thing. Usually me.

I had a swing hung from a maple tree, so that I either faced the house or the street. That is, I either had to face her or to know that she was staring at my back, and might come up to give me a push. After a while she would decide to do that. She always pushed me crooked, but that was not the worst thing. The worst was that her fingers had pressed my back. Through my coat, through my other clothing, her fingers like so many cold snouts. Another activity of mine was to build a leaf house. I raked up and carried armloads of leaves fallen from the maple tree that held the swing, and I dumped and arranged these leaves into a house plan. Here was the living room, here was the kitchen, here was a big soft pile for the bed in the bedroom, and so on. I had not invented this occupation—leaf houses of a more expansive sort were laid out in, and even in a way furnished, every recess in the girls' playground at school, until the janitor finally raked up all the leaves and burned them.

At first Verna just watched what I was doing, with her squinty-eyed expression of what seemed to me superior (how could she think herself superior?) puzzlement. Then the time came when she moved closer, lifted an armful of leaves which dripped all over because of her uncertainty or clumsiness. And these came not from the pile of spare leaves but from the very wall of my house. She picked them up and carried them a short distance and let them fall—dumped them—in the middle of one of my tidy rooms.

I yelled at her to stop, but she bent to pick up

282

her scattered load again, and was unable to hang on to them, so she just flung them about and when they were all on the ground began to kick them foolishly here and there. I was still yelling at her to stop, but this had no effect, or else she took it for encouragement. So I lowered my head and ran at her and butted her in the stomach. I was not wearing a cap, so the hairs of my head came in contact with the woolly coat or jacket she had on, and it seemed to me that I had actually touched bristling hairs on the skin of a gross hard belly. I ran hollering with complaint up the steps of the house and when my mother heard the story she further maddened me by saying, "She only wants to play. She doesn't know how to *play.*"

By the next fall we were in a new bungalow and I never had to go past the yellow house which reminded me so much of Verna, as if it had positively taken on her narrow slyness, her threatening squint. The yellow paint seemed to be the very color of insult, and the front door, being off center, added a touch of deformity.

The bungalow was only three blocks away from that house, close to the school. But my idea of the town's size and complexity was still such that it seemed I was escaping Verna altogether. I realized that this was not true, not altogether true, when a schoolmate and I came face-to-face with her one day on the main street. We must have been sent on some errand by one of our mothers. I did not look up but I believed I heard a chuckle of greeting or recognition as we passed.

The other girl said a horrifying thing to me.

She said, "I used to think that was your sister."

"What?"

"Well, I knew you lived in the same house so I thought you must be related. Like cousins, anyway. Aren't you? Cousins?"

"No."

The old building where the Special Classes had been held was condemned, and its pupils were transferred to the Bible Chapel, now rented on weekdays by the town. The Bible Chapel happened to be across the street and around a corner from the bungalow where my mother and father and I now lived. There were a couple of ways that Verna could have walked to school, but the way she chose was past our house. And our house was only a few feet from the sidewalk, so this meant that her shadow could practically fall across our steps. If she wished she could kick pebbles onto our grass, and unless we kept the blinds down she could peer into our hall and front room.

The hours of the Special Classes had been changed to coincide with ordinary school hours, at least in the morning—the Specials still went home earlier in the afternoon. Once they were in the Bible Chapel it must have been felt that there was no need to keep them free of the rest of us on the way to school. This meant, now, that I had a chance of running into Verna on the sidewalk. I would always look in the direction from which she might be coming, and if I saw her I would duck back into the house with the excuse that I had forgotten something, or that one of my shoes was rubbing my heel and needed a plaster, or a ribbon was coming loose in my hair. I would never have been so foolish now as to mention Verna, and hear my mother say, "What's the problem, what are you afraid of, do you think she's going to eat you?"

What was the problem? Contamination, infection? Verna was decently clean and healthy. And it was hardly likely that she was going to attack and pummel me or pull out my hair. But only adults would be so stupid as to believe she had no power. A power, moreover, that was specifically directed at me. I was the one she had her eye on. Or so I believed. As if we had an understanding between us that could not be described and was not to be disposed of. Something that clings, in the way of love, though on my side it felt absolutely like hate.

I suppose I hated her as some people hate snakes or caterpillars or mice or slugs. For no decent reason. Not for any certain harm she could do but for the way she could disturb your innards and make you sick of your life.

When I told Charlene about her we had got into the deeper reaches of our conversation—that conversation which seems to have been broken only when we swam or slept. Verna was not so solid an offering, not so vividly repulsive, as Charlene's brother's pumping pimpled bum, and I remember saying that she was awful in a way that I could not describe. But then I did describe her, and my feelings about her, and I must have done not too bad a job because one day towards the end of our two-week stay at camp Charlene came rushing into the dining hall at midday, her face lit up with horror and strange delight.

"She's here. She's here. That girl. That awful girl. Verna. She's *here*."

Lunch was over. We were in the process of tidying up, putting our plates and mugs on the kitchen shelf to be grabbed away and washed by the girls on kitchen duty that day. Then we would line up to go to the Tuck Shop, which opened every day at one o'clock. Charlene had just run back to the dormitory to get some money. Being rich, with a father who was an undertaker, she was rather careless, keeping money in her pillowcase. Except when swimming I always had mine on my person. All of us who could in any way afford to went to the Tuck Shop after lunch, to get something to take away the taste of the desserts we hated but always tried, just to see if they were as disgusting as we expected. Tapioca pudding, mushy baked apples, slimy custard. When I first saw the look on Charlene's face I thought that her money had been stolen. But then I thought that such a calamity would not have made her look so transformed, the shock on her face so joyful.

Verna? How could Verna be here? Some mistake.

This must have been a Friday. Two more days at camp, two more days to go. And it turned out that a contingent of Specials—here too they were called Specials—had been brought in to enjoy with us the final weekend. Not many of them— maybe twenty altogether—and not all from my town but from other towns nearby. In fact as Charlene was trying to get the news through to me a whistle was being blown, and Counsellor Arva had jumped up on a bench to address us.

She said that she knew we would all do our best to make these visitors—these new campers—welcome, and that they had brought their own tents and their own counsellor with them. But they would eat and swim and play games and attend the Morning Chat with the rest of us. She was sure, she said, with that familiar warning or upbraiding note in her voice, that we would all treat this as an opportunity to make new friends.

It took some time to get the tents up and these newcomers and their possessions settled. Some apparently took no interest and wandered off and had to be yelled at and fetched back. Since it was our free time, or rest hour, we got our chocolate bars or licorice whips or sponge toffee from the Tuck Shop and went to lie on our bunks and enjoy them.

Charlene kept saying, "Imagine. Imagine. She's here. I can't believe it. Do you think she followed you?"

"Probably," I said.

"Do you think I can always hide you like that?"

When we were in the Tuck Shop lineup I had ducked my head and made Charlene get between me and the Specials as they were being herded by. I had taken one peek and recognized Verna from behind. Her drooping snaky head.

"We should think of some way to disguise you."

From what I had said, Charlene seemed to have got the idea that Verna had actively harassed me. And I believed that was true, except that the harassment had been more subtle, more secret, than I had been able to describe. Now I let Charlene think as she liked because it was more exciting that way.

Verna did not spot me immediately, because of the elaborate dodges Charlene and I kept making, and perhaps because she was rather dazed, as most of the Specials appeared to be, trying to figure out what they were doing here. They were soon taken off to their own swimming class, at the far end of the beach.

At the supper table they were marched in while we sang.

The more we get together, together, together,
The more we get together,
The happier we'll be.

They were then deliberately separated, and distributed amongst the rest of us. They all wore name tags. Across from me there was one named Mary Ellen something, not from my town. But I had hardly time to be glad of that when I saw Verna at the next table, taller than those around her but thank God facing the same way I was so she could not see me during the meal.

She was the tallest of them, and yet not so tall, not so notable a presence, as I remembered her. The reason was probably that I had had a growing spurt during the last year, while she had perhaps stopped her growing altogether.

After the meal, when we stood up and collected our dishes, I kept my head bowed, I never looked in her direction, and yet I knew when her eyes rested on me, when she recognized me, when she smiled her sagging little smile or made that odd chuckle in her throat.

"She's seen you," said Charlene. "Don't look. Don't look. I'll get between you and her. Move. Keep moving."

"Is she coming this way?"

"No. She's just standing there. She's just looking at you."

"Smiling?"

"Sort of."

"I can't look at her. I'd be sick."

How much did she persecute me in the remaining day and a half? Charlene and I used that word constantly, though in fact Verna never got near us. *Persecute.* It had an adult, legal sound. We were always on the lookout, as if we were being stalked, or I was. We tried to keep track of Verna's whereabouts, and Charlene reported on her attitude or expression. I did risk looking at her a couple of times, when Charlene had said, "Okay. She won't notice now."

At those times Verna appeared slightly downcast, or sullen, or bewildered, as if, like most of the Specials, she had been set adrift and did not completely understand where she was or what she was doing there. Some of them—though not she—had caused a commotion by wandering away into the pine and cedar and poplar woods on the bluff behind the beach, or along the sandy road that led to the highway. After that a meeting was called, and we were all asked to watch out for our new friends, who were not so familiar with the place as we were. Charlene poked me in the ribs at that. She of course was not aware of any change, any falling away of confidence or even a diminishing of physical size, in this Verna, and she continually reported on her sly and evil expression, her look of menace. And maybe she was right—maybe Verna saw in Charlene, this new friend or bodyguard of mine, this stranger, some sign of how everything was changed and uncertain here, and that made her scowl, though I didn't see it.

"You never told me about her hands," said Charlene.

"What about them?"

"She's got the longest fingers I have ever seen. She could just twist them round your neck and strangle you. She could. Wouldn't it be awful to be in a tent with her at night?"

I said that it would be. Awful.

"But those others in her tent are too idiotic to notice."

There was a change, that last weekend, a whole different feeling in the camp. Nothing drastic. The meals were announced by the dining room gong at the regular times, and the food served did not improve or deteriorate. Rest time arrived, game time and swimming time. The Tuck Shop operated as usual, and we were drawn together as always for the Chat. But there was an air of growing restlessness and inattention. You could detect it even in the counsellors, who might not have the same reprimands or words of encouragement on the tip of their tongues and would look at you for a second as if trying to recall what it was they usually said. And all this seemed to have begun with the arrival of the Specials. Their presence had changed the camp. There had been a real camp before, with all its rules and deprivations and enjoyments set up, inevitable as school or any part of a child's life, and then it had begun to crumple at the edges, to reveal itself as something provisional. Playacting.

Was it because we could look at the Specials and think that if they could be campers, then there was no such thing as real campers? Partly it was that. But it was partly that the time was coming very soon when all this would be over, the routines would be broken up, and we would be fetched by our parents to resume our old lives, and the counsellors would go back to being ordinary people, not even teachers. We were living in a stage set about to be dismantled, and with it all the friendships, enmities, rivalries that had flourished in the last two weeks. Who could believe it had been only two weeks?

Nobody knew how to speak of this, but a lassitude spread amongst us, a bored ill temper, and even the weather reflected this feeling. It was probably not true that every day during the past two weeks had been hot and sunny, but most of us would certainly go away with that impression. And now, on Sunday morning, there was a change. While we were having the Outdoor Devotions (that was what we had on Sundays instead of the Chat) the clouds darkened. There was no change in temperature—if anything, the heat of the day increased—but there was in the air what some people called the smell of a storm. And yet such stillness. The counsellors and even the minister, who drove out on Sundays from the nearest town, looked up occasionally and warily at the sky.

A few drops did fall, but no more. The service came to its end and no storm had broken. The clouds grew somewhat lighter, not so much as to promise sunshine, but enough so that our last swim would not have to be cancelled. After that there would be no lunch; the kitchen had been closed down after breakfast. The shutters on the Tuck Shop would not be opened. Our parents would begin arriving shortly after noon to take us home, and the bus would come for the Specials. Most of our things were already packed, the sheets were stripped, and the rough brown blankets, that always felt clammy, were folded across the foot of each cot.

Even when it was full of us, chattering and changing into our bathing suits, the inside of the dormitory cabin revealed itself as makeshift and gloomy.

It was the same with the beach. There appeared to be less sand than usual, more stones. And what sand there was seemed gray. The water looked as if it might be cold, though in fact it was quite warm. Nevertheless our enthusiasm for swimming had waned and most of us were wading about aimlessly. The swimming counsellors—

Pauline and the middle-aged woman in charge of the Specials—had to clap their hands at us.

"Hurry up, what are you waiting for? Last chance this summer."

There were good swimmers among us who usually struck out at once for the raft. And all who were even passably good swimmers—that included Charlene and me—were supposed to swim out to the raft at least once and turn around and swim back in order to prove that we could swim at least a couple of yards in water over our heads. Pauline would usually swim out there right away, and stay in the deeper water to watch out for anybody who got into trouble and also to make sure that everybody who was supposed to do the swim had done it. On this day, however, fewer swimmers than usual seemed to be going out there as they were supposed to, and Pauline herself after her first cries of encouragement or exasperation—required simply to get everybody into the water—was just bobbing around the raft, laughing and teasing with the faithful expert swimmers. Most of us were still paddling around in the shallows, swimming a few feet or yards, then standing on the bottom and splashing one another or turning over and doing the dead man's float, as if swimming was something hardly anybody could be bothered with anymore. The woman in charge of the Specials was standing where the water came barely up to her waist—

most of the Specials themselves went no farther than where the water came up to their knees—and the top part of her flowered, skirted bathing suit had not even got wet. She was bending over and making little hand splashes at her charges, laughing and telling them, Isn't this fun.

The water Charlene and I were in was probably up to our chests and no more. We were in the ranks of the silly swimmers, doing the dead man's, and flopping about backstroking or breaststroking, with nobody telling us to stop fooling around. We were trying to see how long we could keep our eyes open underwater, we were sneaking up and jumping on one another's backs. All around us were plenty of others yelling and screeching with laughter as they did the same things.

During this swim some parents or collectors of campers had arrived early and let it be known they had no time to waste, so the campers who belonged to them were being summoned from the water. This made for some extra calling and confusion.

"Look. Look," said Charlene. Or sputtered, in fact, because I had pushed her underwater and she had just come up soaked and spitting.

I looked, and there was Verna making her way towards us, wearing a pale blue rubber bathing cap, slapping at the water with her long hands and smiling, as if her rights over me had suddenly been restored.

I have not kept up with Charlene. I don't even remember how we said good-bye. If we said good-bye. I have a notion that both sets of parents arrived at around the same time and that we scrambled into separate cars and gave ourselves over—what else could we do?—to our old lives. Charlene's parents would certainly have had a car not so shabby and noisy and unreliable as the one my parents now owned, but even if that had not been so we would never have thought of making the two sets of relatives acquainted with each other. Everybody, and we ourselves, would have been in a hurry to get off, to leave behind the pockets of uproar about lost property or who had or had not met their relatives or boarded the bus.

By chance, years later, I did see Charlene's wedding picture. This was at a time when wedding pictures were still published in the newspapers, not just in small towns but in the city papers as well. I saw it in a Toronto paper which I was looking through while I waited for a friend in a café on Bloor Street.

The wedding had taken place in Guelph. The groom was a native of Toronto and a graduate of Osgoode Hall. He was quite tall—or else Charlene had turned out to be quite short. She barely came up to his shoulder, even with her hair done up in the dense, polished helmet-style of the day. The hair made her face seem squashed and insignificant, but

I got the impression her eyes were outlined heavily, Cleopatra fashion, her lips pale. This sounds grotesque but it was certainly the look admired at the time. All that reminded me of her child-self was the little humorous bump of her chin.

She—the bride, it said—had graduated from St. Hilda's College in Toronto.

So she must have been here in Toronto, going to St. Hilda's, while I was in the same city, going to University College. We had been walking around perhaps at the same time and on some of the same streets or paths on the campus. And never met. I did not think that she would have seen me and avoided speaking to me. I would not have avoided speaking to her. Of course I would have considered myself a more serious student, once I discovered she was going to St. Hilda's. My friends and I regarded St. Hilda's as a Ladies College.

Now I was a graduate student in anthropology. I had decided never to get married, though I did not rule out having lovers. I wore my hair long and straight—my friends and I were anticipating the style of the hippies. My memories of childhood were much more distant and faded and unimportant than they seem today.

I could have written to Charlene in care of her parents, whose Guelph address was in the paper. But I didn't do so. I would have thought it the height of hypocrisy to congratulate any woman on her marriage.

• • •

But she wrote to me, perhaps fifteen years later. She wrote in care of my publishers.

"My old pal Marlene," she wrote. "How excited and happy I was to see your name in *Maclean's* magazine. And how dazzled I am to think you have written a book. I have not picked it up yet because we had been away on holidays but I mean to do so—and read it too—as soon as I can. I was just going through the magazines that had accumulated in our absence and there I saw the striking picture of you and the interesting review. And I thought that I must write and congratulate you.

"Perhaps you are married but use your maiden name to write under? Perhaps you have a family? Do write and tell me all about yourself. Sadly, I am childless, but I keep busy with volunteer work, gardening, and sailing with Kit (my husband). There always seems to be plenty to do. I am presently serving on the Library Board and will twist their arms if they have not already ordered your book.

"Congratulations again. I must say I was surprised but not entirely because I always suspected you might do something special."

I did not get in touch with her at that time either. There seemed to be no point to it. At first I took no notice of the word "special" right at the end, but it gave me a small jolt when I thought of it later. However, I told myself, and still believe, that she meant nothing by it.

The book that she referred to was one that had grown out of a thesis I had been discouraged from writing. I went ahead and wrote another thesis but went back to the earlier one as a sort of hobby project when I had time. I have collaborated on a couple of books since then, as was duly expected of me, but that book I did on my own is the only one that got me a small flurry of attention in the outside world (and needless to say some disapproval from colleagues). It is out of print now. It was called *Idiots and Idols*—a title I would never get away with today and which even then made my publishers nervous, though it was admitted to be catchy.

What I was trying to explore was the attitude of people in various cultures—one does not dare say the word "primitive" to describe such cultures the attitude towards people who are mentally or physically unique. The words "deficient," "handicapped," "retarded" being of course also consigned to the dustbin and probably for good reason—not simply because such words may indicate a superior attitude and habitual unkindness but because they are not truly descriptive. Those words push aside a good deal that is remarkable, even awesome—or at any rate peculiarly powerful—in such people. And what was interesting was to discover a certain amount of veneration as well as persecution, and the ascribing—not entirely inaccurately—of quite a range of abilities, seen as sacred, magical, dangerous, or valuable. I did the best I could with historical as well as contemporary research and took into account poetry and fiction and of course religious custom. Naturally I was criticized in my profession for being too literary and for getting all my information out of books, but I could not run around the world then; I had not been able to get a grant.

Of course I could see a connection, a connection that I thought it just possible Charlene might get to see too. It's strange how distant and unimportant that seemed, only a starting point. As anything in childhood appeared to me then. Because of the journey I had made since, the achievement of adulthood. Safety.

"Maiden name," Charlene had written. That was an expression I had not heard for quite a while. It is next door to "maiden lady," which sounds so chaste and sad. And remarkably inappropriate in my case. Even when I looked at Charlene's wedding picture I was not a virgin—though I don't suppose she was either. Not that I have had a swarm of lovers—or would even want to call most of them lovers. Like most women in my age group who have not lived in monogamous marriage, I know the number. Sixteen. I'm sure that for many younger women that total would have been reached before they were out of their twenties or possibly out of their teens. (When I got Charlene's letter, of course, the total would have been less. I cannot—this is true—I cannot be bothered getting that straight now.) Three of them were important and all three of those in the chronological first half-dozen of the count. What I mean by "important" is that with those three— no, only two, the third meaning a great deal more to me than I to him—with those two, then, the time would come when you want to split open, surrender far more than your body, dump your whole life safely into one basket with his.

I kept myself from doing so, but just barely.

So it seems I was not entirely convinced of that safety.

Not long ago I got another letter. This was forwarded from the college where I taught before I retired. I found it waiting when I returned from a trip to Patagonia. (I have become a hardy traveller.) It was over a month old.

A typed letter—a fact for which the writer immediately apologized.

"My handwriting is lamentable," he wrote, and went on to introduce himself as the husband of "your old childhood buddy, Charlene." He said that he was sorry, very sorry, to send me bad news. Charlene was in Princess Margaret Hospital in Toronto. Her cancer had begun in the lungs and spread to the liver. She had, regrettably, been a lifelong smoker. She had only a short time left to live. She had not spoken of me very often, but when she did, over the years, it was always with delight in my remarkable accomplishments. He knew how much she valued me and now at the end of her life she seemed very keen to see me. She had asked him to get hold of me. It may be that childhood memories mean the most, he said. Childhood affections. Strength like no other.

Well, she is probably dead by now, I thought.

But if she was—this is how I worked things out—if she was, I would run no risk in going to the hospital and inquiring. Then my conscience or whatever you wanted to call it would be clear. I could write him a note saying that unfortunately I had been away, but had come as soon as I could.

No. Better not a note. He might show up in my life, thanking me. The word "buddy" made me uncomfortable. So in a different way did "remarkable accomplishments."

Princess Margaret Hospital is only a few blocks away from my apartment building. On a sunny spring day I walked over there. I don't know why I didn't just phone. Perhaps I wanted to think I'd made as much effort as I could.

At the main desk I discovered that Charlene was still alive. When asked if I wanted to see her I could hardly say no.

I went up in the elevator still thinking that I might be able to turn away before I found the nurses' station on her floor. Or that I might make a simple U-turn, taking the next elevator down. The receptionist at the main desk downstairs would never notice my leaving. As a matter of fact she would not have noticed my leaving the moment she had turned her attention to the next person in line, and even if she had noticed, what would it have mattered?

I would have been ashamed, I suppose. Not ashamed at my lack of feeling so much as my lack of fortitude.

I stopped at the nurses' station and was given the number of the room.

It was a private room, quite a small room, with no impressive apparatus or flowers or balloons. At first I could not see Charlene. A nurse was bending over the bed in which there seemed to be a mound of bedclothes but no visible person. The enlarged liver, I thought, and wished I had run while I could.

The nurse straightened up, turned, and smiled at me. She was a plump brown woman who spoke in a soft beguiling voice that might have meant she came from the West Indies.

"You are the Marlin," she said.

Something in the word seemed to delight her.

"She was so wanting for you to come. You can come closer."

I obeyed, and looked down at a bloated body and a sharp ruined face, a chicken's neck for which the hospital gown was a mile too wide. A frizz of hair—still brown—about a quarter of an inch long on her scalp. No sign of Charlene.

I had seen the faces of dying people before. The faces of my mother and father, even the face of the man I had been afraid to love. I was not surprised.

"She is sleeping now," said the nurse. "She was so hoping you would come."

"She's not unconscious?"

"No. But she sleeps."

Yes, I saw it now, there was a sign of Charlene. What was it? Maybe a twitch, that confident playful tucking away of a corner of her mouth.

The nurse was speaking to me in her soft happy voice. "I don't know if she would recognize you," she said. "But she hoped you would come. There is something for you."

"Will she wake up?"

A shrug. "We have to give her injections often for the pain."

She was opening the bedside table.

"Here. This. She told me to give it to you if it was too late for her. She did not want her husband to give it. Now you are here, she would be glad."

A sealed envelope with my name on it, printed in shaky capital letters.

"Not her husband," the nurse said, with a

twinkle, then a broadening smile. Did she scent something illicit, a women's secret, an old love?

"Come back tomorrow," she said. "Who knows? I will tell her if it is possible."

I read the note as soon as I got down to the lobby. Charlene had managed to write in an almost normal script, not wildly as in the sprawling letters on the envelope. Of course she might have written the note first and put it in the envelope, then sealed the envelope and put it by, thinking she would get to hand it to me herself. Only later would she see a need to put my name on it.

Marlene. I am writing this in case I get too far gone to speak. Please do what I ask you. Please go to Guelph and go to the cathedral and ask for Father Hofstrader. Our Lady of Perpetual Help Cathedral. It is so big you don't need the name. Father Hofstrader. He will know what to do. This I cannot ask C. and do not want him ever to know. Father H. knows and I have asked him and he says it is possible to help me. Marlene please do this bless you. Nothing about you.

C. That must be her husband. He doesn't know. Of course he doesn't.

Father Hofstrader.

Nothing about me.

I was free to crumple this up and throw it away once I got out into the street. And so I did, I threw the envelope away and let the wind sweep it into the gutter on University Avenue. Then I realized the note was not in the envelope; it was still in my pocket.

I would never go to the hospital again. And I would never go to Guelph.

Kit was her husband's name. Now I remembered. They went sailing. Christopher. Kit. Christopher. C.

When I got back to my apartment building I found myself taking the elevator down to the garage, not up to my apartment. Dressed just as I was I got into my car and drove out onto the street, and began to head towards the Gardiner Expressway.

The Gardiner Expressway, Highway 427, Highway 401. It was rush hour now, a bad time to get out of the city. I hate this sort of driving, I don't do it often enough to be confident. There was under half a tank of gas, and what was more, I had to go to the bathroom. Around Milton, I thought, I could pull off the highway and fill up on gas and use the toilet and reconsider. At present I could do nothing but what I was doing, heading north, then heading west.

I didn't get off. I passed the Mississauga exit, and the Milton exit. I saw a highway sign telling me how many kilometers to Guelph, and I translated that roughly into miles in my head, as I always have to do, and I figured the gas would hold out. The excuse I made to myself for not stopping was that the sun would be getting lower and more troublesome, now that we were leaving the haze that lies over the city even on the finest day.

At the first stop after I took the Guelph turnoff I got out and walked to the ladies' washroom with stiff trembling legs. Afterwards I filled the tank with gas and asked, when I paid, for directions to the cathedral. The directions were not very clear but I was told that it was on a big hill and I could find it from anywhere in the heart of town.

Of course that was not true, though I could see it from almost anywhere. A collection of delicate spires rising from four fine towers. A beautiful building where I had expected only a grand one. It was grand too, of course, a grand dominating cathedral for such a relatively small city (though someone told me later it was not actually a cathedral).

Could that have been where Charlene was married?

No. Of course not. She had been sent to a United Church camp, and there were no Catholic girls at that camp, though there was quite a variety of Protestants. And then there was the business about C. not knowing.

She might have converted secretly. Since.

I found my way in time to the cathedral parking lot, and sat there wondering what I should do. I was wearing slacks and a jacket. My idea of what was required in a Catholic church—a Catholic cathedral—was so antiquated that I was not even sure if my outfit would be all right. I tried to recall visits to great churches in Europe. Something about the arms being covered? Headscarves, skirts?

What a bright high silence there was up on this hill. April, not a leaf out yet on the trees, but the sun after all was still well up in the sky. There was one low bank of snow gray as the paving in the church lot.

The jacket I had on was too light for evening wear, or maybe it was colder here, the wind stronger, than in Toronto.

The building might well be locked at this time, locked and empty.

The grand front doors appeared to be so. I did not even bother to climb the steps to try them, because I decided to follow a couple of old women—old like me—who had just come up the long flight from the street and who bypassed those steps entirely, heading around to an easier entrance at the side of the building.

There were more people inside, maybe two or three dozen people, but there wasn't a sense that they were gathered for a service. They were scattered here and there in the pews, some kneeling and some chatting. The women ahead of me dipped their hands in a marble font without looking at what they were doing and said hello— hardly lowering their voices—to a man who was setting out baskets on a table.

"It looks a lot warmer out than it is," said one of them, and the man said the wind would bite your nose off.

I recognized the confessionals. Like separate small cottages or large playhouses in a Gothic style, with a lot of dark wooden carving, dark brown curtains. Elsewhere all was glowing, dazzling. The high curved ceiling most celestially blue, the lower curves of the ceiling—those that joined the upright walls—decorated with holy images on gold-painted medallions. Stained-glass windows hit by the sun at this time of day were turned into columns of jewels. I made my way discreetly down one aisle, trying to get a look at the altar, but the chancel being in the western wall was too bright for me to look into. Above the windows, though, I saw that there were painted angels. Flocks of angels, all fresh and gauzy and pure as light.

It was a most insistent place but nobody seemed to be overwhelmed by all the insistence. The chatting ladies kept chatting softly but not in whispers. And other people after some businesslike nodding and crossing knelt down and went about their routines.

As I ought to be going about mine. I looked around for a priest but there was not one in sight. Priests as well as other people must have a working day. They must drive home and go into their living rooms or offices or dens and turn on the television and loosen their collars. Fetch a drink and wonder if they were going to get anything decent for supper. When they did come into the church they would come officially. In their vestments, ready to perform some ceremony. Mass?

Or to hear confessions. But then you would never know when they were there. Didn't they enter and leave their grilled stalls by a private door?

I would have to ask somebody. The man who had distributed the baskets seemed to be here for reasons that were not purely private, though he was apparently not an usher. Nobody needed an usher. People chose where they wanted to sit—or kneel—and sometimes decided to get up and choose another spot, perhaps being bothered by the glare of the jewel-inflaming sun. When I spoke to him I whispered, out of old habit in a church—and he had to ask me to speak again. Puzzled or embarrassed, he nodded in a wobbly way towards one of the confessionals. I had to become very specific and convincing.

"No, no. I just want to talk to a priest. I've been sent to talk to a priest. A priest called Father Hofstrader."

The basket man disappeared down the more distant side aisle and came back in a little while with a briskly moving stout young priest in ordinary black costume.

He motioned me into a room I had not noticed—not a room, actually, we went through an archway, not a doorway—at the back of the church.

"Give us a chance to talk, in here," he said, and pulled out a chair for me.

"Father Hofstrader—"

"Oh no, I must tell you, I am not Father Hofstrader. Father Hofstrader is not here. He is on vacation."

For a moment I did not know how to proceed.

"I will do my best to help you."

"There is a woman," I said, "a woman who is dying in Princess Margaret Hospital in Toronto—"

"Yes, yes. We know of Princess Margaret Hospital."

"She asks me—I have a note from her here—she wants to see Father Hofstrader."

"Is she a member of this parish?"

"I don't know. I don't know if she is a Catholic or not. She is from here. From Guelph. She is a friend I have not seen for a long time."

"When did you talk with her?"

I had to explain that I hadn't talked with her, she had been asleep, but she had left the note for me.

"But you don't know if she is a Catholic?"

He had a cracked sore at the corner of his mouth. It must have been painful for him to talk.

"I think she is, but her husband isn't and he doesn't know she is. She doesn't want him to know."

I said this in the hope of making things clearer, even though I didn't know for sure if it was true. I had an idea that this priest might shortly lose interest altogether. "Father Hofstrader must have known all this," I said.

"You didn't speak with her?"

I said that she had been under medication but that this was not the case all the time and I was sure she would have periods of lucidity. This too I stressed because I thought it necessary.

"If she wishes to make a confession, you know, there are priests available at Princess Margaret's."

I could not think of what else to say. I got out the note, smoothed the paper, and handed it to him. I saw that the handwriting was not as good as I had thought. It was legible only in comparison with the letters on the envelope.

He made a troubled face.

"Who is this C.?"

"Her husband." I was worried that he might ask for the husband's name, to get in touch with him, but instead he asked for Charlene's. This woman's name, he said.

"Charlene Sullivan." It was a wonder that I even remembered the surname. And I was reassured for a moment, because it was a name that sounded

Catholic. Of course that meant that it was the husband who could be Catholic. But the priest might conclude that the husband had lapsed, and that would surely make Charlene's secrecy more understandable, her message more urgent.

"Why does she need Father Hofstrader?"

"I think perhaps it's something special."

"All confessions are special."

He made a move to get up, but I stayed where I was. He sat down again.

"Father Hofstrader is on vacation but he is not out of town. I could phone and ask him about this. If you insist."

"Yes. Please."

"I do not like to bother him. He has not been well."

I said that if he was not well enough to drive himself to Toronto I could drive him.

"We can take care of his transportation if necessary."

He looked around and did not see what he wanted, unclipped a pen from his pocket, and then decided that the blank side of the note would do to write on.

"If you'll just make sure I've got the name. Charlotte—"

"Charlene."

Was I not tempted, during all this palaver? Not once? You'd think that I might break open, be wise to break open, glimpsing that vast though tricky forgiveness. But no. It's not for me. What's done is done. Flocks of angels, tears of blood, notwithstanding.

I sat in the car without thinking to turn the motor on, though it was freezing cold by now. I didn't know what to do next. That is, I knew what I could do. Find my way to the highway and join the bright everlasting flow of cars towards Toronto. Or find a place to stay overnight, if I did not think I had the strength to drive. Most places would provide you with a toothbrush, or direct you to a machine where you could get one. I knew what was necessary and possible but it was beyond my strength, for the moment, to do it.

The motorboats on the lake were supposed to stay a good distance out from the shore. And especially from our camping area, so that the waves they raised would not disturb our swimming. But on that last morning, that Sunday morning, a couple of them started a race and circled close in—not as close as the raft, of course, but close enough to raise waves. The raft was tossed around and Pauline's voice was lifted in a cry of reproach and dismay. The boats made far too much noise for their drivers to hear her, and anyway they had set a big wave rolling towards the shore, causing most of us in the shallows either to jump with it or be tumbled off our feet.

Charlene and I both lost our footing. We had our backs to the raft, because we were watching Verna come towards us. We were standing in water about up to our armpits, and we seemed to be lifted and tossed at the same moment that we heard Pauline's cry. We may have cried out as many others did, first in fear and then in delight as we regained our footing and that wave washed on ahead of us. The waves that followed proved to be not as strong, so that we could hold ourselves against them.

At the moment we tumbled, Verna had pitched towards us. When we came up, with our faces streaming, arms flailing, she was spread out under the surface of the water. There was a tumult of screaming and shouting all around, and this increased as the lesser waves arrived and people who had somehow missed the first attack pretended to be knocked over by the second. Verna's head did not break the surface, though now she was not inert, but turning in a leisurely way, light as a jellyfish in the water. Charlene and I had our hands on her, on her rubber cap.

This could have been an accident. As if we, in trying to get our balance, grabbed on to this nearby large rubbery object, hardly realizing what it was or what we were doing. I have thought it all out. I think we would have been forgiven. Young children. Terrified.

Yes, yes. Hardly knew what they were doing.

Is this in any way true? It is true in the sense that we did not decide anything, in the beginning. We did not look at each other and decide to do what we subsequently and consciously did. Consciously, because our eyes did meet as the head of Verna tried to rise up to the surface of the water. Her head was determined to rise, like a dumpling in a stew. The rest of her was making misguided feeble movements down in the water, but the head knew what it should do.

We might have lost our grip on the rubber head, the rubber cap, were it not for the raised pattern that made it less slippery. I can recall the color perfectly, the pale insipid blue, but I never deciphered the pattern—a fish, a mermaid, a flower—whose ridges pushed into my palms.

Charlene and I kept our eyes on each other, rather than looking down at what our hands were doing. Her eyes were wide and gleeful, as I suppose mine were too. I don't think we felt wicked, triumphing in our wickedness. More as if we were doing just what was—amazingly—demanded of us, as if this was the absolute high point, the culmination, in our lives, of our being ourselves.

We had gone too far to turn back, you might say. We had no choice. But I swear that choice had not occurred, did not occur, to us.

The whole business probably took no more than two minutes. Three? Or a minute and a half?

It seems too much to say that the discouraging

clouds cleared up just at that time, but at some point—perhaps at the trespass of the motorboats, or when Pauline screamed, or when the first wave hit, or when the rubber object under our palms ceased to have a will of its own—the sun burst out, and more parents popped up on the beach, and there were calls to all of us to stop horsing around and come out of the water. Swimming was over. Over for the summer, for those who lived out of reach of the lake or municipal swimming pools. Private pools were only in the movie magazines.

As I've said, my memory fails when it comes to parting from Charlene, getting into my parents' car. Because it didn't matter. At that age, things ended. You expected things to end.

I am sure we never said anything as banal, as insulting or unnecessary, as *Don't tell.*

I can imagine the unease starting, but not spreading quite so fast as it might have if there had not been competing dramas. A child has lost a sandal, one of the youngest children is screaming that she got sand in her eye from the waves. Almost certainly a child is throwing up, because of the excitement in the water or the excitement of families arriving or the too-swift consumption of contraband candy.

And soon but not right away the anxiety running through this, that someone is missing.

"Who?"

"One of the Specials."

"Oh drat. Wouldn't you know."

The woman in charge of the Specials running around, still in her flowered bathing suit, with the custard flesh wobbling on her thick arms and legs. Her voice wild and weepy.

Somebody go check in the woods, run up the trail, call her name.

"What is her name?"

"Verna."

"Wait."

"What?"

"Is that not something out there in the water?"

But I believe we were gone by then.

Wood

Roy is an upholsterer and refinisher of furniture. He will also take on the job of rebuilding chairs and tables that have lost some rungs or a leg, or are otherwise in a dilapidated condition. There aren't many people doing that kind of work anymore, and he gets more business than he can handle. He doesn't know what to do about it. His excuse for not hiring somebody to help him is that the government will make him go through a lot of red tape, but the real reason may be that he's used to working alone—he's been doing this ever since he got out of the army—and it's hard for him to imagine having somebody else around all the time. If he and his wife, Lea, had had a boy, the boy might have grown up with an interest in the work and joined him in the shop when he was old enough. Or even if they'd had a daughter. Once he'd thought of training his wife's niece Diane. When she was a child she had hung around watching him and after she got married—suddenly, at the age of seventeen—she helped him with some jobs because she and her husband needed the money. But she was pregnant, and the smells of paint stripper, wood stain, linseed oil, polish, and wood smoke made her sick. Or that was what she told Roy. She told his wife the real reason—that her husband didn't think it was the right kind of work for a woman.

So now she has four children and works in the kitchen of an old people's home. Apparently her husband thinks that is all right.

Roy's workshop is in a shed behind the house. It is heated by a woodstove, and getting the fuel for the stove has led him to another interest, which is private but not secret. That is, everybody knows about it but nobody knows how much he thinks about it or how much it means to him.

Wood cutting.

He has a four-wheel-drive truck and a chain saw and an eight-pound splitting ax. He spends more and more time in the bush, cutting firewood. More than he needs for himself, as it turns out— so he has taken to selling it. Modern houses often have a fireplace in the living room and another in the dining room and a stove in the family room. And they want to have fires all the time—not just when they're having a party or at Christmas.

When he first started going to the bush Lea used to worry about him. She worried about whether he would have an accident out there by himself, but also about whether he was letting the business go slack. She didn't mean that his workmanship might suffer, but his timetable. "You don't want to let people down," she said. "If somebody says they want something for a certain time there's a reason."

She had the idea of his business being an obligation—something he did to help people out. She was embarrassed when he raised his prices—so in fact was he—and went out of her way to tell people what the materials were costing him nowadays.

While she had her job, it was not difficult for him to take off for the bush after she had gone to work and try to be back before she got home. She worked as a receptionist and bookkeeper for one of the dentists in town. It was a good job for her, because she enjoyed talking to people, and good for the dentist because she came from a large and loyal family who would never think of having their teeth tended to by anybody but the man who was her boss.

These relatives of hers, the Boles and the Jetters and the Pooles, used to be around the house a lot, or else Lea wanted to be at one of their houses. It was a clan that didn't always enjoy one another's company but who made sure they got plenty of it. Twenty or thirty would be crammed into one place for Christmas or Thanksgiving, and they could manage a dozen on an ordinary Sunday— watching television, talking, cooking, and eating. Roy likes to watch television and he likes to talk and he likes to eat, but not any two at the same time and certainly not all three. So when they chose to gather in his house on a Sunday, he got into the habit of getting up and going out to the shed and building up a fire of ironwood or applewood—either of those but particularly the apple has a sweet comforting smell. Right out in the open, on the shelf with the stains and oils, he always kept a bottle of rye. He had rye in the house as well, and he was not stingy about offering it to his company, but the drink he poured when he was alone in the shed tasted better, just as the smoke smelled better when there was nobody around to say, Oh, isn't that lovely? He never drank when he was working on the furniture, or going into the bush—just on these Sundays full of visitors.

His going off on his own like that didn't cause trouble. The relatives didn't feel slighted—they had a limited interest in people like Roy who had just married into the family, and not even contributed any children to it, and who were not like themselves. They were large, expansive, talkative. He was short, compact, quiet. His wife was an easygoing woman generally and she liked Roy the way he was, so she didn't reproach or apologize for him.

They both felt that they meant more to each other, somehow, than couples who were overrun with children.

Last winter Lea had been sick with almost steady flu and bronchitis. She thought that she was catching all the germs people brought into the dentist's office. So she quit her job—she said that she was getting a bit tired of it anyway and she wanted more time to do things she had always wanted to do.

But Roy never found out what those things were. Her strength had taken a slump that she could not recover from. And that seemed to bring about a profound change in her personality. Visitors made her nervous—her family more than anybody. She felt too tired for conversation. She didn't want to go out. She kept up the house adequately, but she rested between chores so that simple routines took her all day. She lost most of her interest in television, though she would watch it when Roy turned it on, and she lost also her rounded, jolly figure, becoming thin and shapeless. The warmth, the glow—whatever had made her nice looking—were drained out of her face and her brown eyes.

The doctor gave her some pills but she couldn't tell whether they did her any good or not. One of her sisters took her to a practitioner of holistic medicine, and the consultation cost three hundred dollars. She could not tell if that did her any good either.

Roy misses the wife he was used to, with her jokes and energy. He wants her back, but there's nothing he can do, except be patient with this grave, listless woman who sometimes waves her hand in front of her face as if she is bothered by cobwebs or has got stuck in a nest of brambles. Questioned about her eyesight, however, she claims that it is fine.

She no longer drives her car. She no longer says anything about Roy going to the bush.

She may snap out of it, Diane says. (Diane is about the only person who still comes to the house.) Or she may not.

That is pretty well what the doctor said, in a lot more careful words. He says that the pills he's got her on will keep her from sinking too low. How low is too low, Roy thinks, and when can you tell?

Sometimes he finds a bush that the sawmill people have logged out, leaving the tops on the ground. And sometimes he finds one where the forest management people have gone in and girdled the trees they think should come out because they are diseased or crooked or no good for lumber. Ironwood, for instance, is no good for lumber, and neither is hawthorn or blue beech. When he spots a bush like this he gets in touch with the farmer or whoever owns it, and they bargain, and if the payment is agreed on he goes in to get the wood. A lot of this activity happens in the late fall—now, in November, or early December—because that is the time for selling firewood and because it is the best time for getting his truck into the bush. Farmers nowadays don't always have a well-travelled lane going back there, as they did when they cut and hauled wood themselves. Often you have to drive in across the fields, and this is possible only at two times during the year—before the field is plowed and after the crop is off.

After the crop is off is the better time, when the ground is hardened by frost. And this fall the demand for wood is greater than ever, and Roy has been going out two or three times in one week.

Many people recognize trees by their leaves or by their general shape and size, but walking through the leafless deep bush Roy knows them by their bark. Ironwood, that heavy and reliable firewood, has a shaggy brown bark on its stocky trunk, but its limbs are smooth at their tips and decidedly reddish. Cherry is the blackest tree in the bush, and its bark lies in picturesque scales. Most people would be surprised at how high cherry trees grow here—they are nothing like the cherry trees in fruit orchards. Apple trees are more like their orchard representatives—not very tall, bark not so definitely scaled or dark as the cherry's. Ash is a soldierly tree with a corduroy-ribbed trunk. The maple's gray bark has an irregular surface, the shadows creating black streaks, which meet sometimes in rough rectangles, sometimes not. There is a comfortable carelessness about that bark, suitable to the maple tree, which is homely and familiar and what most people think of when they think of a tree.

Beech trees and oaks are another matter—there is something notable and dramatic about them, though neither has as lovely a shape as the big elm trees which are now nearly all gone. Beech has the smooth gray bark, the elephant skin, which is usually chosen for the carving of initials. These carvings widen with the years and decades, from the slim knife groove to the blotches that make the letters at last illegible, wider than they are long.

Beech will grow a hundred feet high in the bush. In the open they spread out and are as wide as high, but in the bush they shoot up, the limbs at the top will take radical turns and can look like stag horns. But this arrogant-looking tree may have a weakness of twisted grain, which can be detected by ripples in the bark. That's a sign that it may break, or go down in a high wind. As for oak trees, they are not so common in this country, not so common as beech but always easy to spot. Just as maple trees always look like the common necessary tree in the backyard, so oak trees always look like trees in storybooks, as if, in all the stories that begin, "Once upon a time in the woods," the woods were full of oak trees. Their dark, shiny, elaborately indented leaves contribute to this look, but they seem just as legendary when the leaves are off and you can see so well the thick corky bark with its gray-black color and intricate surface, and the devilish curling and curving of the branches.

Roy thinks that there is very little danger in

going tree cutting alone if you know what you are doing. When you are going to cut down a tree, the first thing is to assess its center of gravity, then cut a seventy-degree wedge, so that the center of gravity is just over it. The side the wedge is on, of course, determines the direction in which the tree will fall. You make a falling cut, from the opposite side, not to connect with the wedge cut but in line with its high point. The idea is to cut through the tree, leaving at the end a hinge of wood which is the very center of the tree's weight and from which it must fall. It is best to make it fall clear of all other branches, but sometimes there is no way this can happen. If a tree is leaning into the branches of other trees, and you can't get a truck into position to haul it out with a chain, you cut the trunk in sections from beneath, till the upper part drops free and falls. When you've dropped a tree and it's resting on its branches, you get the trunk to the ground by cutting through the limb wood until you come to the limbs that are holding it up. These limbs are under pressure—they may be bent like a bow—and the trick is to cut so that the tree will roll away from you and the limbs won't whack you. When it is safely down, you cut the trunk into stove lengths and split the stove lengths with the ax.

Sometimes there's a surprise. Some squirrelly wood blocks can't be split with the ax; they have to be laid on their sides and ripped with a chain saw; the sawdust cut this way, with the grain, is taken away in long shreds. Also, some beech or maple has to be side split, the great round chunk cut along the growth rings on all sides until it is almost square and can be more easily attacked. Sometimes there's dozy wood, in which a fungus has grown between the rings. But in general the toughness of the blocks is as you'd expect— greater in the body wood than in the limb wood, and greater in the broad trunks that have grown up partly in the open than in the tall slim ones that have pushed up in the middle of the bush.

Surprises. But you can be prepared for those. And if you're prepared, there's not the danger. He used to think of explaining all this to his wife. The procedures, the surprises, the identification. But he couldn't think of the way to go about it, so that she'd be interested. Sometimes he wished he had got around to passing on his knowledge to Diane when she was younger. She would never have the time to listen now.

And in a way his thoughts about wood are too private—they are covetous and nearly obsessive. He has never been a greedy man in any other way. But he can lie awake nights thinking of a splendid beech he wants to get at, wondering if it will prove as satisfactory as it looks or has some tricks up its sleeve. He thinks of all the woodlots in the county that he has never even seen, because they lie at the backs of farms, behind private fields. If he is driving along a road that goes through a bush, he swings his head from side to side, afraid of missing something. Even what is worthless for his purposes will interest him. A stand of blue beech, for instance, too delicate, too weedy, to bother with. He sees the dark vertical ribs slanting down the paler trunks—he will remember where these are. He would like to get a map in his mind of every bush he sees, and though he might justify this by citing practical purposes, that wouldn't be the whole truth.

A day or so after the first snow, he is out in a bush looking at some girdled trees. He has a right to be there—he has already been talking to the farmer, whose name is Suter.

At the edge of this bush there is an illegal dump. People have been throwing their trash in this hidden spot rather than taking it to the township dump, whose open hours may not have suited them, or whose location may not have been so handy. Roy sees something moving there. A dog?

But then the figure straightens up and he sees that it is a man in a filthy coat. In fact it is Percy Marshall, poking around the dump to see what he can find. Sometimes in these places you used to be able to find valuable old crocks or bottles or even a copper boiler, but that is not so likely anymore. And Percy is not a knowledgeable scavenger anyway. He will just be on the lookout for anything he can use—though it is hard to see what that could be in this heap of plastic containers and torn screens and mattresses with the stuffing popped out.

Percy lives alone in one room at the back of an otherwise empty and boarded-up house at a crossroads a few miles from here. He walks the roads, walks along the creeks and through the town, talking to himself, sometimes playing the part of a half-wit vagabond and sometimes presenting himself as a shrewd local character. His life of malnutrition, dirt, and discomfort is his own choice. He has tried the County Home, but he couldn't stand the routine and the company of so many other old people. Long ago he started out with a fairly good farm, but the life of a farmer was too monotonous—so he worked his way down through bootlegging, botched housebreaking, some spells in jail, and in the past decade or so he has worked his way up again, with the help of the old-age pension, to a certain protected status. He has even had his picture and a write-up in the local paper.

The Last of a Breed. Local Free Spirit Shares Stories and Insights.

He climbs out of the dump laboriously, as if he felt obliged to have a little conversation.

"You going to be taking them trees out?"

Roy says, "I might be." He thinks Percy may be after a donation of firewood.

"Then you better hurry up," Percy says.

"Why's that?"

"All of this here is going under contract."

Roy cannot but help gratifying him by asking what contract this might be. Percy is a gossip but not a liar. At least not about the things he is truly interested in, which are deals, inheritances, insurance, house break-ins, money matters of all sorts. It is a mistake to think that people who have never managed to get hold of money aren't busy thinking about it. A surprise, this would be, to people who expect him to be a philosophical tramp, all wrapped up in memories of olden times. Though he can shoot off a little of that too when required.

"Heard about this fellow," Percy says, drawing it out. "When I was in town. I don't know. Seems this fellow runs a sawmill and he's got a contract to the River Inn and he's going to supply them all the wood they want for the winter. Cord a day. That's what they burn. Cord a day."

Roy says, "Where did you hear that?"

"Beer parlor. All right, I go in there now and again. I never have no more than a pint. And these fellows I don't know who they were, but they weren't drunk neither. Talking about where the bush was and it was this one all right. Suter's bush."

Roy had talked to the farmer just last week, and he had thought he had the deal pretty well sewed up, just to do the usual clean out.

"That's a pile of wood," he says easily.

"It is so."

"If they mean to take it all they'd have to have a license."

"You bet. Unless there's something crooked," said Percy with intense pleasure.

"None of my business. I got all the work I can handle."

"I bet you do. All you can handle."

All the way home Roy can't keep himself from thinking about this story. He has sold some wood now and then to the River Inn. But now they must have decided to take on one steady supplier, and he is not the one.

He thinks about the problems of getting that much wood out now, when the snow has already started. The only thing you could do would be to pull the logs out into the open field, before the real winter got under way. You'd have to get them out as quickly as possible, make a big pile of them there, saw them, and chop them up later. And to get them out you'd need a bulldozer or at least a big tractor. You'd have to make a road in and pull them out with chains. You'd need a crew—there was no way this could be a one- or two-man operation. It would have to be done on a big scale.

So it wasn't sounding like a part-time enterprise, the kind he carried on himself. It could be a big outfit, somebody from out of the county altogether.

Eliot Suter had not given any hint of this offer when Roy was talking to him. But it is quite possible that an approach was made to him later and he decided to forget the casual sort of arrangement that had been put forward by Roy. Decided to let the bulldozer go in.

During the evening Roy thinks of phoning up and asking what is going on. But then he thinks that if the farmer has indeed changed his mind there is nothing to be done. A spoken agreement is nothing to hold to. The man could just tell him to clear off.

The best thing for Roy to do might be just to act as if he has never heard Percy's story, never heard about any other fellow—just go in and take what trees he can as quickly as he can, before the bulldozer gets there.

Of course there is always a possibility that Percy may have been mistaken about the whole thing. He isn't likely to have made it up just to bother Roy, but he could have got it twisted.

Yet the more Roy thinks about it the more he comes to discount this possibility. He just keeps seeing in his mind the bulldozer and the chained logs, the great log piles out in the field, the men with chain saws. That is the way they do things nowadays. Wholesale.

Part of the reason the story has made such an impact is that he has a dislike for the River Inn, which is a resort hotel on the Peregrine River. It is built on the remains of an old mill not far from the crossroads where Percy Marshall lives. In fact the inn owns the land Percy lives on and the house he lives in. There was a plan to tear the house down, but it turned out that the inn's guests, having nothing much to do, like to walk down the road and take pictures of this derelict building and the old harrow and upturned wagon beside it, and the useless pump, and Percy, when he allows himself to be photographed. Some guests do sketches. They come from as far away as Ottawa and Montreal and no doubt think of themselves as being in the backwoods.

Local people go to the inn for a special lunch or dinner. Lea went once, with the dentist and his wife and the hygienist and her husband. Roy would not go. He said that he didn't want to eat a meal that cost an arm and a leg, even when somebody else was paying. But he is not altogether sure what it is that he has against the inn. He is not exactly opposed to the idea of people spending money in the hope of enjoying themselves, or against the idea of other people making money out of the people who want to spend it. It is true that the antiques at the inn have been restored and reupholstered by craftsmen other than himself—people not from around here at all—but if he had been asked to do them he would probably have refused, saying he had more than enough work to do already. When Lea asked him what he thought was the matter with the inn, the only thing he could think of to say was that when Diane had applied for a job there, as a waitress, they had turned her down, saying that she was overweight.

"Well, she was," said Lea. "She is. She says so herself."

True. But Roy still thinks of those people as snobs. Grabbers and snobs. They are putting up new buildings supposed to be like an old-time store and an old-time opera house, just for show. They burn wood for show. A cord a day. So now some operator with a bulldozer will be levelling the bush as if it was a cornfield. This is just the sort of high-handed scheme you would expect, the kind of pillage you might know they would get up to.

He tells Lea the story he has heard. He still tells her things—it's a habit—but he is so used to her now not paying any real attention that he hardly notices whether there is an answer or not. This time she echoes what he himself has said.

"Never mind. You've got enough to do anyway."

That's what he would have expected, whether she was well or not. Missing the point. But isn't that what wives do—and husbands probably the same—around fifty percent of the time?

The next morning he works on a drop-leaf table for a while. He means to stay in the shed all day

335

and get a couple of past-due jobs finished. Near noon he hears Diane's noisy muffler and looks out the window. She'll be here to take Lea to the reflexologist—she thinks it does Lea good and Lea doesn't object.

But she is heading for the shed, not the house.

"Howdy," she says.

"Howdy."

"Hard at work?"

"Hard as ever," Roy says. "Offer you a job?"

This is their routine.

"I got one. Listen, what I came in here for, I want to ask you a favor. What I want is to borrow the truck. Tomorrow, to take Tiger to the vet. I can't handle him in the car. He's got too big for the car. I hate to have to ask you."

Roy says not to worry about it.

Tiger to the vet, he thinks, that's going to cost them.

"You weren't going to need the truck?" she says. "I mean, you can use the car?"

He has of course been meaning to go out to the bush tomorrow, providing he got his jobs done today. What he'll have to do, he decides now, is get out there this afternoon.

"I'll fill it up with gas for you," Diane says.

So another thing he'll have to do is remember to fill it up himself, to prevent her. He is just about to say, "You know the reason I want to get out there is something's come up that I can't help thinking about—" But she's out the door and going to get Lea.

As soon as they are out of sight and he has things cleaned up, he gets into the truck and drives out to where he was the day before. He thinks about stopping by and questioning Percy further but concludes that it would not be any use. Such a show of interest might just get Percy inventing things. He thinks again about talking to the farmer but decides against it for the same reasons as last night.

He parks the truck on the trail that leads into the bush. This trail soon peters out, and even before it does he has left it. He is walking around looking at the trees, which appear the same as they did yesterday and don't give a sign of being party to any hostile scheme. He has the chain saw and the ax with him, and he feels as if he has to hurry. If anybody else shows up here, if anybody challenges him, he will say that he has permission from the farmer and he knows nothing about any other deal. He will say that furthermore he intends to go on cutting unless the farmer comes and personally tells him to get out. If that really happens, of course he will have to go. But it's not likely it will happen because Suter is a hefty man with a bad hip, so he is not much taken to wandering around his property.

". . . no authority . . . ," Roy says, talking to himself like Percy Marshall, "I want to see it on paper."

He's talking to the stranger he's never even seen.

The floor of any bush is usually rougher than the surface of the surrounding land. Roy has always thought that this was caused by trees falling, pulling up the earth with their roots, then just lying there, rotting. Where they had lain and rotted there would be a mound—where their roots had torn out the earth there would be hollows. But he read somewhere—fairly recently, and he wishes he could remember where it was—that the cause was what happened long ago, just after the Ice Age, when ice formed between layers of earth and pushed it up into odd humps, just as it does today in the arctic regions. Where the land has not been cleared and worked the humps remain.

What happens to Roy now is the most ordinary and yet the most unbelievable thing. It is what might happen to any stupid daydreamer walking in the bush, to any holidayer gawking around at nature, to somebody who thought the bush was a kind of park to stroll in. Somebody who wore light shoes instead of boots and didn't bother to keep an eye on the ground. It has never happened to Roy before in hundreds of times of walking in the bush, it has never once come near to happening.

A light snow has been falling for some time, making the earth and dead leaves slippery. One of his feet skids and twists, and then the other foot plunges through a cover of snowy brush to the ground, which is farther down than he expected. That is, he steps carelessly—is thrown, almost—into the sort of spot where you should always step testingly, carefully, and not at all if you can see a nearby place that is better. Even so, what happens? He doesn't go down hard, it's not as if he has stumbled into a groundhog hole. He is thrown off balance, but he sways reluctantly, almost disbelievingly, then goes down with the skidding foot caught somehow under the other leg. He holds the saw out from himself as he falls, and flings the ax clear. But not clear enough—the ax handle hits him hard, against the knee of his twisted leg. The saw has pulled him over in its direction but at least he hasn't fallen against it.

He has felt himself go down almost in slow motion, thoughtfully and inevitably. He could have broken a rib, but he didn't. And the ax handle could have flown up and hit him in the face, but it didn't. He could have gashed his leg. He thinks of all these possibilities not with immediate relief, but as if he can't be sure yet that they have not happened. Because the way this started—the way he skidded and stepped onto the brush and fell—was so stupid and awkward, so hard to believe, that any preposterous outcome could follow.

He starts to pull himself up. Both knees hurt—

one from being hit by the handle and one from coming down hard on the ground. He gets hold of the trunk of a young cherry tree—where he could have bashed his head—and pulls himself up gradually. Tentatively he puts weight on one foot and just touches the ground with the other—the one that skidded and twisted underneath him. In a minute he'll try it. He bends to pick up the saw and nearly buckles again. A pain shoots up from the ground and doesn't stop till it reaches his skull. He forgets the saw, straightens up, not sure where the pain started. That foot—did he put weight on it as he bent over? The pain has drawn back into that ankle. He straightens the leg as much as he can, considering it, then very cautiously tries the foot on the ground, tries his weight. He can't believe the pain. He can't believe that it would continue so, could continue to defeat him. The ankle must be more than twisted—it must be sprained. Could it be broken? In his boot it doesn't look any different from his other, faithful, ankle.

He knows that he will have to bear it. He will have to get used to it to get out of here. And he keeps trying, but he does not make any progress. He can't set his weight on it. It must be broken. A broken ankle—even that is surely a minor injury, the sort of thing old ladies get when they slip on the ice. He has been lucky. A broken ankle, a minor injury. Nevertheless he can't take a step. He can't walk.

What he understands, finally, is that in order to get back to the truck he's going to have to abandon his ax and his chain saw and get down on his hands and knees and crawl. He lets himself down as easily as he can and hauls himself around into the track of his bootprints, which are now filling with snow. He thinks to check the pocket where his keys are, making sure it's zipped. He shakes off his cap and lets it lie—the peak interferes with his vision. Now the snow is falling on his bare head. But it's not so cold. Once he accepts crawling as a method of locomotion it's not bad—that is, it's not impossible, though it's hard on his hands and his good knee. He's careful enough now, dragging himself over the brush and through the saplings, over the hummocky ground. Even if he gets a little bit of a slope to roll himself down, he doesn't dare—he has to guard the bad leg. He's glad he didn't track through any boggy places and he's glad he didn't wait any longer before starting back; the snow is getting heavier and his prints are almost blotted out. Without that track to follow it would be hard to know, at ground level, whether he was going the right way.

The situation, which seemed at first so unreal to him, is getting to seem more natural. Going along on hands and elbows and the one knee, close to the ground, testing a log for rot, then pulling himself over it on his stomach, getting his hands full of rotten leaves and dirt and snow—he can't keep his gloves on, can't get the proper hold and feel of things on the bush floor except with his cold bare scratched hands—he is no longer surprised at himself. He doesn't think anymore about his ax and his saw back there, though at first he could hardly pull himself away from them. He scarcely thinks back as far as the accident itself. It happened, no matter how. The whole thing no longer seems in the least unbelievable or unnatural.

There is a fairly steep bank to get up, and when he reaches it he takes a breather, relieved to have come this far. He warms his hands inside his jacket, one at a time. For some reason he thinks of Diane in her unbecoming red ski jacket and decides that her life is her life, there is not much use worrying about it. And he thinks of his wife, pretending to laugh at the television. Her quietness. At least she's fed and warm, she isn't some refugee shuffling along the roads. Worse things happen, he thinks. Worse things.

He starts up the bank, digging in his elbows and his sore but serviceable knee where he can. He keeps going; he grits his teeth as if that will keep him from sliding back; he grabs at any exposed root or halfway-sturdy stem that he can see. Sometimes he slides, his hold breaks, but he gets himself stopped and inches upwards again. He never raises his head to judge how far he still has to go. If he pretends the incline goes on forever, it'll be a kind of bonus, a surprise, to get to the top.

It takes a long time. But he pulls himself onto level ground at last, and through the trees ahead and the falling snow he can see the truck. The truck, the old red Mazda, a faithful old friend, miraculously waiting. Being on the level raises his expectations of himself again and he gets onto his knees, going easy, easy on the bad leg, rises shakily onto his good leg, dragging the other, swaying like a drunk. He tries a sort of hop. No good—he'd lose his balance that way. He tries a little weight on the bad leg, just gently, and realizes that the pain could make him black out. He sinks back to the old position and crawls. But instead of crawling through the trees towards the truck he turns at right angles and makes for where he knows the track to be. When he gets there he begins to make better time, crawling over the hard ruts, the mud that has thawed in the daylight but is now starting to freeze again. It's cruel on the knee and his palms but otherwise so much easier than the route he had to take before that he feels almost light-headed. He can see the truck ahead. Looking at him, waiting for him.

He'll be able to drive. So lucky the damage is to the left leg. Now that the worst is over a lot of vexing questions come at him, along with his relief. Who will go and get the saw and the ax for him, how can he explain to anybody just where to find them? How soon will the snow cover them up? When will he be able to walk?

No use. He pushes all that away, raises his head to get another encouraging look at the truck. He stops again to rest and warm his hands. He could put his gloves on now, but why ruin them?

A large bird rises out of the bush to one side of him and he cranes his neck to see what it is. He thinks it's a hawk, but it could be a buzzard. If it's a buzzard will it have its eye on him, thinking it's in luck now, seeing he's hurt?

He waits to see it circle back, so he can tell what it is by the manner of its flight, and its wings.

And while he's doing that, while he's waiting, and taking note of the bird's wings—it is a buzzard—he is also getting a drastically new idea about the story that has preoccupied him for the last twenty-four hours.

The truck is moving. When did it start? When he was watching the bird? At first just a little movement, a wobble in the ruts—it could almost be a hallucination. But he can hear the engine. It's going. Did somebody just get into it while he was distracted, or was somebody waiting in it all the time? Surely he locked it, and he has the keys with him. He feels his zipped pocket again. Someone stealing the truck in front of his eyes and without the keys. He hollers and waves, from his crouched position—as if that would do any good. But the truck isn't backing into the turnaround to drive out; it's bumping along the track straight at him, and now the person driving it is honking the horn, not in a warning but a greeting way, and slowing down.

He sees who it is.

The only person who has the other set of keys. The only person it could be. Lea.

He struggles to get his weight onto the one leg. She jumps out of the truck and runs to him and supports him.

"I just went down," he tells her, panting. "It was the dumbest damn thing I ever did in my life." Then he thinks to ask how she got here.

"Well, I didn't fly," she says.

She came in the car, she says—she speaks just as if she'd never given up driving at all—she came in the car but she left it back at the road.

"It's way too light for this track," she says. "And I thought I might get stuck. But I wouldn't't've, the mud's froze hard.

"I could see the truck," she says. "So I just walked in and when I got to it I unlocked it and got in and sat there. I figured you'd be coming back soon, seeing it's snowing. But I never figured you'd be doing it on your hands and knees."

The walk, or maybe the cold, has brightened her face and sharpened her voice. She gets down and looks at his ankle, says she thinks it's swollen.

"Could have been worse," he says.

She says this was the one time she hadn't been worried. The one time she wasn't and she should have been. (He doesn't bother telling her that she hasn't shown worry about anything for a matter of months.) She didn't have a single premonition.

"I just came to meet you to tell you," she says, "because I couldn't wait to tell you. This idea I got when the woman was working on me. Then I saw you crawling. And I thought, *Oh my God.*"

What idea?

"Oh that," she says. "Oh—well, I don't know what you'll think. I could tell you later. We gotta get your ankle fixed."

What idea?

Her idea is that the outfit Percy heard about doesn't exist. Percy heard some talk but not about some strangers getting a license to log the bush. What he heard was all about Roy himself.

"Because that old Eliot Suter is all big talk. I know that family, his wife was Annie Poole's sister. He's going round blowing about the deal he got and added on to it quite a bit and first thing what have you? Ends up the River Inn for good measure and a hundred cords a day. Somebody drinking beer and listening in on somebody else drinking beer and there you are. And you have got a kind of a contract—I mean you've got an agreement—"

"It may be stupid all right—" Roy says.

"I knew you'd say that but you think about it—"

"It may be stupid but it's the same idea I had myself about five minutes ago."

And this is so. This is what came to him when he was looking up at the buzzard.

"So there you are," Lea says, with a satisfied laugh. "Everything remotely connected with the inn, it just turns into some big story. Some big-money kind of a story."

That was it, he thinks. He was hearing about himself. All the ruction comes back to himself.

The bulldozer isn't coming, the men with the chain saws are not converging. The ash, the maple, the beech, the ironwood, the cherry, are all safe for him. For the time being, all safe.

Lea is out of breath with the effort of supporting him, but able to say, "Great minds think alike."

This is not the moment to mention the change in her. No more than you'd call your congratulations to somebody up on a ladder.

He has knocked his foot hoisting himself—and partly being hoisted—into the passenger seat of the truck. He groans, and it's a different kind of groan than would come out of him if he was alone. It's not that he means to dramatize the pain, just that he takes this way of describing it to his wife.

Or even offering it to his wife. Because he knows that he isn't feeling quite the way he thought he would if her vitality came back to her. And the noise he makes could be to cover that lack, or excuse it. Of course it's natural that he'd feel a bit cautious, not knowing if this is for good, or just a flash in the pan.

But even if it is for good, even if it's all good there's something more. Some loss fogging up this gain. Some loss he'd be ashamed to admit to, if he had the energy.

The dark and the snow are too thick for him to see beyond the first trees. He's been in there before at this time, when the dark shuts down in early winter. But now he pays attention, he notices something about the bush that he thinks he has missed those other times. How tangled up in itself it is, how dense and secret. It's not a matter of one tree after another, it's all the trees together, aiding and abetting one another and weaving into one thing. A transformation, behind your back.

There's another name for the bush, and this name is stalking around in his mind, in and out of where he can almost grasp it. But not quite. It's a tall word that seems ominous but indifferent.

"I left the ax," he says mechanically. "I left the saw."

"So what if you did. We'll find somebody to go and get them."

"And there's the car too. Are you going to get out and drive that and let me take the truck?"

"Are you insane?"

Her voice is absentminded, because she is in the process of backing the truck into the turnaround. Slowly but not too slowly, bouncing in the ruts but keeping on the track. He is not used to the rearview mirrors from this angle, so he lowers the window and cranes around, getting the snow in his face. This is not just to see how she's doing but to clear to a certain extent the warm wooziness coming on him.

"Easy," he says. "That's it. Easy. Okay now. You're okay. You're okay."

While he is saying this she is saying something about the hospital.

". . . get them to take a look at you. First things first."

To his knowledge, she has never driven the truck before.

It's remarkable the way she manages it.

Forest. That's the word. Not a strange word at all but one he has possibly never used. A formality about it that he would usually back away from.

"The Deserted Forest," he says, as if that put the cap on something.

Too Much Happiness

*Many persons who have not studied math-
ematics confuse it with arithmetic and
consider it a dry and arid science.
Actually, however, this science requires
great fantasy.*
—Sophia Kovalevsky

I

On the first day of January, in the year 1891, a
small woman and a large man are walking in the
Old Cemetery, in Genoa. Both of them are
around forty years old. The woman has a child-
ishly large head, with a thicket of dark curls, and
her expression is eager, faintly pleading. Her face
has begun to look worn. The man is immense. He
weighs 285 pounds, distributed over a large
frame, and being Russian, he is often referred to
as a bear, also as a Cossack. At present he is
crouching over tombstones and writing in his
notebook, collecting inscriptions and puzzling
over abbreviations not immediately clear to him,
though he speaks Russian, French, English,
Italian and has an understanding of classical and
medieval Latin. His knowledge is as expansive as
his physique, and though his speciality is govern-

mental law, he is capable of lecturing on the growth of contemporary political institutions in America, the peculiarities of society in Russia and the West, and the laws and practices of ancient empires. But he is not a pedant. He is witty and popular, at ease on various levels, and able to live a most comfortable life, due to his properties near Kharkov. He has, however, been forbidden to hold an academic post in Russia, because of being a Liberal.

His name suits him. Maksim. Maksim Maksimovich Kovalevsky.

The woman with him is also a Kovalevsky. She was married to a distant cousin of his, but is now a widow.

She speaks to him teasingly.

"You know that one of us will die," she says. "One of us will die this year."

Only half listening, he asks her, Why is that?

"Because we have gone walking in a graveyard on the first day of the New Year."

"Indeed."

"There are still a few things you don't know," she says in her pert but anxious way. "I knew that before I was eight years old."

"Girls spend more time with kitchen maids and boys in the stables—I suppose that is why."

"Boys in the stables do not hear about death?"

"Not so much. Concentration is on other things."

There is snow that day but it is soft. They leave melted, black footprints where they've walked.

She met him for the first time in 1888. He had come to Stockholm to advise on the foundation of a school of social sciences. Their shared nationality, going so far as a shared family name, would have thrown them together even if there was no particular attraction. She would have had a responsibility to entertain and generally take care of a fellow Liberal, unwelcome at home.

But that turned out to be no duty at all. They flew at each other as if they had indeed been long-lost relatives. A torrent of jokes and questions followed, an immediate understanding, a rich gabble of Russian, as if the languages of Western Europe had been flimsy formal cages in which they had been too long confined, or paltry substitutes for true human speech. Their behavior, as well, soon overflowed the proprieties of Stockholm. He stayed late at her apartment. She went alone to lunch with him at his hotel. When he hurt his leg in a mishap on the ice, she helped him with the soaking and dressing and, what was more, she told people about it. She was so sure of herself then, and especially sure of him. She wrote a description of him to a friend, borrowing from De Musset.

*He is very joyful, and at the same time very
gloomy—*
Disagreeable neighbor, excellent comrade—
*Extremely light-minded, and yet very
affected—*
Indignantly naïve, nevertheless very blasé—
*Terribly sincere, and at the same time very
sly.*

And at the end she wrote, "A real Russian, he is, into the bargain."

Fat Maksim, she called him then.

"I have never been so tempted to write romances, as when with Fat Maksim."

And "He takes up too much room, on the divan and in one's mind. It is simply impossible for me, in his presence, to think of anything but him."

This was at the very time when she should have been working day and night, preparing her submission for the Bordin Prize. "I am neglecting not only my Functions but my Elliptic Integrals and my Rigid Body," she joked to her fellow mathematician, Mittag-Leffler, who persuaded Maksim that it was time to go and deliver lectures in Uppsala for a while. She tore herself from thoughts of him, from daydreams, back to the movement of rigid bodies and the solution of the so-called mermaid problem by the use of theta functions with two independent variables. She worked desperately but happily, because he was still in the back of her mind. When he returned she was worn out but triumphant. Two triumphs—her paper ready for its last polishing and anonymous submission; her lover growling but cheerful, eagerly returned from his banishment and giving every indication, as she thought, that he intended to make her the woman of his life.

The Bordin Prize was what spoiled them. So Sophia believed. She herself was taken in by it at first, dazzled by all the chandeliers and champagne. The compliments quite dizzying, the marvelling and the hand kissing spread thick on top of certain inconvenient but immutable facts. The fact that they would never grant her a job worthy of her gift, that she would be lucky indeed to find herself teaching in a provincial girls' high school. While she was basking Maksim decamped. Never a word about the real reason, of course—just the papers he had to write, his need for the peace and quiet of Beaulieu.

He had felt himself ignored. A man who was not used to being ignored, who had probably never been in any salon, at any reception, since he was a grown man, where that had been the case. And it wasn't so much the case in Paris either. It wasn't that he was invisible there, in Sonya's limelight, as that he was the usual. A man of solid worth and negotiable reputation, with a certain

bulk of frame and intellect, together with a lightness of wit, an adroit masculine charm. While she
was an utter novelty, a delightful freak, the
woman of mathematical gifts and female timidity,
quite charming, yet with a mind most unconven-
tionally furnished, under her curls.

He wrote his cold and sulky apologies from
Beaulieu, refusing her offer to visit once her
flurry was over. He had a lady staying with him,
he said, whom he could not possibly present to
her. This lady was in distress and needed his
attention at the moment. Sonya should make her
way back to Sweden, he said; she should be happy
where her friends were waiting for her. Her students would have need of her and so would her
little daughter. (A jab there, a suggestion familiar
to her, of faulty motherhood?)

And at the end of his letter one terrible sentence.
"If I loved you I would have written differently."

The end of everything. Back from Paris with her
prize and her freaky glittery fame, back to her
friends who suddenly meant no more than a snap
of her fingers to her. Back to the students who
meant something more, but only when she stood
before them transformed into her mathematical
self, which was oddly still accessible. And back to
her supposedly neglected but devastatingly merry
little Fufu.

Everything in Stockholm reminded her.

She sat in the same room, with the furniture brought at such foolish expense across the Baltic Sea. The same divan in front of her that had recently, gallantly, supported his bulk. And hers in addition when he skillfully gathered her into his arms. In spite of his size he was never clumsy in lovemaking.

This same red damask, on which distinguished and undistinguished guests had sat in her old lost home. Maybe Fyodor Dostoyevsky had sat there in his lamentable nervous state, dazzled by Sophia's sister Aniuta. And certainly Sophia herself as her mother's unsatisfactory child, displeasing as usual.

The same old cabinet brought also from her home at Palibino, with the portraits of her grandparents set into it, painted on porcelain.

The Shubert grandparents. No comfort there. He in uniform, she in a ball gown, displaying absurd self-satisfaction. They had got what they wanted, Sophia supposed, and had only contempt for those not so conniving or so lucky.

"Did you know I'm part German?" she had said to Maksim.

"Of course. How else could you be such a prodigy of industry? And have your head filled with mythical numbers?"

If I loved you.

Fufu brought her jam on a plate, asked her to play a child's card game.

357

"Leave me alone. Can't you leave me alone?"

Later she wiped the tears out of her eyes and begged the child's pardon.

But Sophia was, after all, not one to mope forever. She swallowed her pride and gathered her resources, wrote lighthearted letters which by their easy mention of frivolous pleasures—her skating, her horseback riding—and by their attention to Russian and French politics might be enough to put him at his ease, and perhaps even enough to make him feel that his warning had been brutal and unnecessary. She managed to pry out another invitation, and was off to Beaulieu as soon as her lectures were over, in the summer.

Pleasant times. Also misunderstandings, as she called them. (She changed this, in time, to "conversations.") Chilly spells, breakups, near breakups, sudden geniality. A bumpy trip around Europe, presenting themselves, openly and scandalously, as lovers.

She sometimes wondered whether he had other women. She herself toyed with the idea of marrying a German who paid court to her. But the German was far too punctilious, and she suspected him of wanting a hausfrau. Also, she was not in love with him. Her blood ran cooler and cooler as he spoke the scrupulous German words of love.

Maksim, once he had heard of this honorable

courtship, said that she had better marry himself. Provided, he said, that she could be comfortable with what he had to offer. He pretended to be talking about money, when he said this. To be comfortable with his wealth was of course a joke. To be comfortable with a tepid, courteous offering of feeling, ruling out the disappointments and scenes which had mostly originated with her— that was another matter altogether.

She took refuge in teasing, letting him think she believed him not to be in earnest, and no more was decided. But when she was back in Stockholm she thought herself a fool. And so she had written to Julia, before she went south at Christmas, that she did not know whether she was going to happiness or sorrow. She meant that she would declare herself in earnest and find out if he was. She had prepared herself for the most humiliating disappointment.

She had been spared that. Maksim was after all a gentleman and he kept to his word. They would be married in the spring. That decided, they became more comfortable with each other than since the very beginning. Sophia behaved well, with no sulks or outbursts. He expected some decorum, but not the decorum of the hausfrau. He would never object, as a Swedish husband might, to her cigarettes and endless tea drinking and political outbursts. And she was not displeased to see that when his gout bothered him he could be as unreasonable, as irritating and self-pitying, as herself. They were countryfellows, after all. And she was guiltily bored with the reasonable Swedes who had been the only people in Europe willing to hire a female mathematician for their new university. Their city was too clean and tidy, their habits too regular, their parties too polite. Once they decided that some course was correct they just went ahead and followed it, with none of those exhilarating and probably dangerous nights of argument that would go on forever in Petersburg or Paris.

Maksim would not interfere with her real work, which was research, not teaching. He would be glad she had something to absorb her, though she suspected that he found mathematics not trivial, but somehow beside the point. How could a professor of law and sociology think otherwise?

The weather is warmer at Nice, a few days later, when he takes her to board her train.

"How can I go, how can I leave this soft air?"

"Ah, but your desk and your differential equations will be waiting. In the spring you won't be able to tear yourself away."

"Do you think not?"

She must not think—she must not think that is a roundabout way of saying he wished they would not marry in the spring.

She has already written to Julia, saying it is to be happiness after all. Happiness after all. Happiness.

● ● ●

On the station platform a black cat obliquely crosses their path. She detests cats, particularly black ones. But she says nothing and contains her shudder. And as if to reward her for this self-control he announces that he will ride with her as far as Cannes, if she is agreeable. She can barely answer, she feels such gratitude. Also a disastrous pressure of tears. Weeping in public is something he finds despicable. (He does not think he should have to put up with it in private either.)

She manages to reabsorb her tears, and when they reach Cannes, he folds her into his capacious well-cut garments with their smell of manliness— some mixture of fur-bearing animals and expensive tobacco. He kisses her with decorum but with a small flick of his tongue along her lips, a reminder of private appetites.

She has not, of course, reminded him that her work was on the Theory of *Partial* Differential Equations, and that it was completed some time ago. She spends the first hour or so of her solitary journey as she usually spends some time after a parting from him—balancing signs of affection against those of impatience, and indifference against a certain qualified passion.

"Always remember that when a man goes out of the room, he leaves everything in it behind," her friend Marie Mendelson has told her. "When a woman goes out she carries everything that happened in the room along with her."

At least she has time now to discover that she has a sore throat. If he has caught it she hopes he won't suspect her. Being a bachelor in robust health he regards any slight contagion as an insult, bad ventilation or tainted breath as personal attacks. In certain ways he is really quite spoiled.

Spoiled and envious, actually. A while ago he wrote to her that certain writings of his own had begun to be attributed to her, because of the accident of the names. He had received a letter from a literary agent in Paris, starting off by addressing him as Dear Madam.

Alas he had forgotten, he said, that she was a novelist as well as a mathematician. What a disappointment for the Parisian that he was neither. Merely a scholar, and a man.

Indeed a great joke.

II

She falls asleep before the lamps are lit in the train. Her last waking thoughts—unpleasant thoughts—are of Victor Jaclard, her dead sister's husband, whom she plans to see in Paris. It is really her young nephew, Urey, her sister's child, that she is anxious to see, but the boy lives with his father. She always sees Urey in her mind as he

362

was at about the age of five or six, angelically blond, trusting and sweet natured, but not in temperament so much like his mother, Aniuta.

She finds herself in a confused dream of Aniuta, but of an Aniuta long before Urey and Jaclard were on the scene. Aniuta unmarried, golden haired, beautiful, and bad tempered, back at the family estate of Palibino, where she is decorating her tower room with Orthodox icons and complaining that these are not the proper religious artifacts for medieval Europe. She has been reading a novel by Bulwer-Lytton and has draped herself in veils, the better to impersonate Edith Swan-neck, the mistress of Harold of Hastings. She plans to write her own novel about Edith, and has already written a few pages describing the scene where the heroine must identify her butchered lover's body by certain marks known only to herself.

Having somehow arrived on this train she reads these pages to Sophia who cannot bring herself to explain to her how things have changed and what has come about since those days in the tower room.

When she wakes Sophia thinks how all that was true—Aniuta's obsession with medieval and particularly English history—and how one day that vanished, veils and all, as if none of it had ever been, and instead a serious and contemporary Aniuta was writing about a young girl who at her parents' urging and for conventional reasons rejects a young scholar who dies. After his death she realizes that she loves him, so has no choice but to follow him in death.

She secretly submitted this story to a magazine edited by Fyodor Dostoyevsky, and it was printed.

Her father was outraged.

"Now you sell your stories, how soon before you will sell yourself?"

In this turmoil Fyodor himself appeared on the scene, behaving badly at a party but mollifying Aniuta's mother by a private call, and ending up by proposing marriage. Her father's being so decidedly against this did almost persuade Aniuta to accept, to elope. But she had after all a fondness for her own limelight, and perhaps a premonition of how that might have to be sacrificed, with Fyodor, so she refused him. He put her into his novel *The Idiot* as Aglia, and married a young stenographer.

Sophia dozes again, slips into another dream in which she and Aniuta are both young but not so young as when at Palibino, and they are together in Paris, and Aniuta's lover Jaclard—not yet her husband—has supplanted Harold of Hastings and Fyodor the novelist as her hero, and Jaclard is a genuine hero, though bad mannered (he glories in his peasant background) and, from the first, unfaithful. He is fighting somewhere outside of Paris, and Aniuta is afraid he will be killed, because he is so brave. Now in Sophia's dream Aniuta has gone looking for him, but the streets where she wanders weeping and calling his name are in Petersburg, not Paris, and Sophia is left behind in a huge Parisian hospital full of dead soldiers and bloodied citizens, and one of the dead is her own husband, Vladimir. She runs away from all these casualties, she is looking for Maksim, who is safe from the fighting in the Hotel Splendide. Maksim will get her out of this.

She wakes. It's raining outside and dark, and she is not alone in the compartment. An untidy-looking young woman sits next to the door, holding a drawing portfolio. Sophia is afraid she might have cried out in her dream, but she probably didn't, because the girl is sleeping undisturbed.

Suppose this girl had been awake and Sophia had said to her, "Forgive me, I was dreaming of 1871. I was there, in Paris, my sister was in love with a Communard. He was captured and he might have been shot or sent to New Caledonia but we were able to get him away. My husband did it. My husband Vladimir who was not a Communard at all but only wanted to look at the fossils in the Jardin des Plantes."

The girl would have been bored. She might have been polite but would still have conveyed the feeling that all this, in her opinion, might have happened before the banishment of Adam and

Eve. She was probably not even French. French girls who could afford to travel second class did not usually travel alone. American?

It was strangely true that Vladimir had been able to spend some of those days in the Jardin des Plantes. And untrue that he had been killed. In the midst of the turmoil he was laying the foundations of his only real career, as a paleontologist. And true too that Aniuta took Sophia along to a hospital from which all the professional nurses had been fired. They were considered counterrevolutionary, and were to be replaced by the wives and comrades from the Commune. The common women cursed the replacements because they did not even know how to make bandages, and the wounded died, but most of them might have died anyway. There was disease as well as the wounds of battle to be dealt with. The common people were said to be eating dogs and rats.

Jaclard and his revolutionaries fought for ten weeks. After the defeat he was imprisoned at Versailles, in an underground cell. Several men had been shot because they were mistaken for him. Or so it was reported.

By that time Aniuta and Sophia's father, the General, had arrived from Russia. Aniuta had been taken off to Heidelberg, where she collapsed in bed. Sophia went back to Berlin and her study of mathematics, but Vladimir remained, abandoning his tertiary mammifers to connive with the

General to get Jaclard free. This was managed by bribery and daring. Jaclard was to be transferred under guard of one soldier to a jail in Paris, and taken along a certain street where there would be a crowd of people, because of an exhibition. Vladimir would snatch him away while the guard looked aside, as he was being paid to do. And still under Vladimir's guidance Jaclard would be hustled through the crowd to a room where a civilian suit of clothes was waiting, then taken to the railway station and supplied with Vladimir's own passport, so that he could escape to Switzerland.

All this was accomplished.

Jaclard did not bother to mail back the passport until Aniuta joined him, and then she returned it. No money was ever repaid.

Sophia sent notes from her hotel in Paris to Marie Mendelson and Jules Poincaré. Marie's maid responded that her mistress was in Poland. Sophia sent a further note to say that she might ask her friend's assistance, come spring, in "selecting whatever costume would suit that event which the world might consider the most important in a woman's life." In brackets she added that she herself and the fashionable world were "still on fairly confused terms."

Poincaré arrived at an exceptionally early hour of the morning, complaining at once about the behavior of the mathematician Weierstrass,

Sophia's old mentor, who had been one of the judges for the king of Sweden's recent mathematical prize. Poincaré had indeed been awarded the prize, but Weierstrass had seen fit to announce that there were possible errors in his—Poincaré's—work which he, Weierstrass, had not been given time to investigate. He had sent a letter submitting his annotated queries to the king of Sweden—as if such a personage would know what he was talking about. And he had made some statement about Poincaré being valued in future more for the negative than the positive aspects of his work.

Sophia soothed him, telling him she was on her way to see Weierstrass and would take the matter up with him. She pretended not to have heard anything about it, though she had actually written a teasing letter to her old teacher.

"I am sure the king has had much of his royal sleep disturbed since your information arrived. Just think of how you have upset the royal mind hitherto so happily ignorant of mathematics. Take care you don't make him repent of his generosity . . ."

"And after all," she said to Jules, "after all you do have the prize and will have it forever."

Jules agreed, adding that his own name would shine when Weierstrass would be forgotten.

Every one of us will be forgotten, Sophia thought but did not say, because of the tender sen-

sibilities of men—particularly of a young man—
on this point.

She said good-bye to him at noon and went to
see Jaclard and Urey. They lived in a poor part of
the city. She had to cross a courtyard where
laundry was hung—the rain had stopped but the
day was still dark—and mount a long, somewhat
slippery outdoor staircase. Jaclard called out that
the door was unbolted, and she entered to find him
sitting on an overturned box, blacking a pair of
boots. He did not stand up to greet her, and when
she started to remove her cloak he said, "Better
not. The stove isn't lit till evening." He motioned
her to the only armchair, which was tattered and
greasy. This was worse than she had expected.
Urey was not here, had not waited to see her.

There were two things she had wanted to find
out about Urey. Was he getting more like Aniuta
and the Russian side of his family? And was he
getting any taller? At fifteen, last year in Odessa,
he had not looked more than twelve.

Soon she discovered that things had taken a turn
that made such concerns less important.

"Urey?" she said.

"He's out."

"He's at school?"

"He may be. I know little about him. And the
more I do know the less I care."

She thought to soothe him and take up the
matter later. She inquired about his—Jaclard's—

health, and he said his lungs were bad. He said he had never got over the winter of '71, the starvation and the nights in the open. Sophia did not remember that the fighters had starved—it was their duty to eat, so that they could fight—but she said agreeably that she had just been thinking about those times, on the train. She had been thinking, she said, about Vladimir and the rescue that was like something out of a comic opera.

It was no comedy, he said, and no opera. But he grew animated, talking about it. He spoke of the men shot because they were taken for him, and of the desperate fighting between the twentieth and the thirtieth of May. When he was captured at last, the time of summary executions was over, but he still expected to die after their farcical trial. How he had managed to escape God only knew. Not that he believed in God, he added, as he did every time.

Every time. And every time he told the story, Vladimir's part—and the General's money's part—grew smaller. No mention of the passport either. It was Jaclard's own bravery, his own agility, that counted. But he did seem to be better disposed to his audience, as he talked.

His name was still remembered. His story still was told.

And more stories followed, also familiar. He rose and fetched a strongbox from under the bed. Here was the precious paper, the paper that had ordered him out of Russia, when he was in Petersburg with Aniuta some time after the days of the Commune. He must read it all.

"Gracious sir, Konstantin Petrovich, I hasten to bring to your attention that the Frenchman Jaclard, a member of the former Commune, when living in Paris was in constant contact with representatives of the Polish Revolutionary Proletariat Party, the Jew Karl Mendelson, and thanks to the Russian connection through his wife was involved in the transfer of Mendelson's letters to Warsaw. He is a friend of many outstanding French radicals. From Petersburg Jaclard sent most false and harmful news into Paris about Russian political affairs and after the first of March and the attempt against the czar this information passed all bounds of patience. That is why at my insistence the minister decided to send him beyond the borders of our empire."

Delight had come back to him as he read, and Sophia remembered how he used to tease and caper, and how she, and even Vladimir, felt somehow honored to be noticed by him, even if it was only as an audience.

"Ah, too bad," he said. "Too bad the information is not complete. He never mentions that I was chosen by the Marxists of the International in Lyon to represent them in Paris."

At this moment Urey came in. His father went on talking.

"That was secret, of course. Officially they put me on the Lyon Committee for Public Safety." He was walking back and forth now, in joyful rampaging earnest. "It was in Lyon that we heard that Napoleon le Neveu had been captured. Painted like a whore."

Urey nodded to his aunt, removed his jacket—evidently he did not feel the cold—and sat down on the box to take up his father's task with the boots.

Yes. He did look like Aniuta. But it was the Aniuta of later days to whom he bore a resemblance. The tired sullen droop to the eyelids, the skeptical—in him scornful—curl to the full lips. There was not a sign of the golden-haired girl with her hunger for danger, for righteous glory, her bursts of wild invective. Of that creature Urey would have no memory, only of a sick woman, shapeless, asthmatic, cancerous, declaring herself eager for death.

Jaclard had loved her at first, perhaps, as much as he could love anybody. He noted her love for him. In his naïve or perhaps simply braggartly letter to her father, explaining his decision to marry her, he had written that it seemed unfair to desert a woman who had so much attachment to himself. He had never given up other women, not even at the beginning of the liaison when Aniuta was delirious with her discovery of him. And certainly not throughout the marriage. Sophia supposed that he might still be attractive to women, though his beard was untidy and gray and when he talked he sometimes got so excited that his words came in a splutter. A hero worn out by his struggle, one who had sacrificed his youth—that was how he might present himself, not without effect. And it was true, in a way. He was physically brave, he had ideals, he was born a peasant and knew what it was to be despised.

And she too, just now, had been despising him.

The room was shabby, but when you looked at it closely you saw that it had been cleaned as well as possible. A few cooking pots hung from nails on the wall. The cold stove had been polished, and so had the bottoms of those pots. It occurred to her that there might be a woman with him, even now.

He was talking about Clemenceau, saying they were on good terms. He was ready now to brag about a friendship with a man she would have expected him to accuse of being in the pay of the British Foreign Office (though she herself believed this false).

She deflected him by praising the apartment's tidiness.

He looked around, surprised at the change of subject, then slowly smiled, and with a new vindictiveness.

"There is a person I am married to, she takes care of my welfare. A French lady, I am glad to say, she is not so garrulous and lazy as the Russians. She is educated, she was a governess but was dismissed for her political sympathies. I am afraid I cannot introduce you to her. She is poor but decent and she still values her reputation."

"Ah," said Sophia, rising. "I meant to tell you that I too am marrying again. A Russian gentleman."

"I had heard that you went about with Maksim Maksimovich. I did not hear anything about a marriage."

Sophia was trembling from sitting so long in the cold. She spoke to Urey, as cheerfully as she could.

"Will you walk with your old aunt to the station? I have not had a chance to talk to you."

"I hope I have not offended you," said Jaclard quite poisonously. "I always believe in speaking the truth."

"Not at all."

Urey put on his jacket, which she now saw was too big for him. It had probably been bought in a rag market. He had grown, but he was no taller than Sophia herself. He might not have had the right food at an important time in his life. His mother had been tall, and Jaclard was tall still.

Though he had not seemed eager to accompany her, Urey began to talk before they had reached the bottom of the stairs. And he had picked up her bag immediately, without being asked.

"He is too stingy to even light a fire for you. There is firewood in the box, she brought some up this morning. She is as ugly as a sewer rat, that's why he didn't want you to meet her."

"You shouldn't talk that way about women."

"Why not, if they want to be equal?"

"I suppose I should say 'about people.' But I don't want to talk about her or your father. I want to talk about you. How are you doing with your studies?"

"I hate them."

"You cannot hate all of them."

"Why can't I? It isn't at all difficult to hate all of them."

"Can you speak Russian to me?"

"It's a barbaric language. Why can't you speak better French? He says your accent is barbaric. He says my mother's accent was barbaric too. Russians are barbaric."

"Does he say that too?"

"I make up my own mind."

They walked for a time in silence.

"It's a bit dreary in Paris this time of year," Sophia said. "Do you remember what a good time we had that summer at Sèvres? We talked about all kinds of things. Fufu remembers you still and talks about you. She remembers how much you wanted to come and live with us."

"That was childish. I didn't think realistically at that time."

"So have you now? Have you thought of a life-work for yourself?"

"Yes."

Because of a taunting satisfaction in his voice she did not ask what this might be. He told her anyway.

"I'm going to be an omnibus boy and call out the stations. I got a job doing that when I ran away at Christmastime, but he came and got me back. When I am one year older he won't be able to do that."

"Perhaps you would not always be happy calling out the stations."

"Why not? It's very useful. It's always necessary. Being a mathematician isn't necessary, as I see it."

She kept silent.

"I could not respect myself," he said. "Being a professor of mathematics."

They were climbing to the station platform.

"Just getting prizes and a lot of money for things nobody understands or cares about and that are no use to anybody."

"Thank you for carrying my bag."

She handed him some money, though not so much as she had intended. He took it with an unpleasant grin, as if to say, You thought I'd be too proud, didn't you? Then he thanked her, hurriedly, as if this was against his will.

She watched him go and thought it was quite

376

likely she would never see him again. Aniuta's child. And how like Aniuta he was, after all. Aniuta disrupting almost every family meal at Palibino with her lofty tirades. Aniuta pacing the garden paths, full of scorn for her present life and faith in her destiny which would take her into some entirely new and just and ruthless world.

Urey might change his course; there was no telling. He might even come to have some fondness for his aunt Sophia, though probably not till he was as old as she was now, and she long dead.

III

Sophia was half an hour early for her train. She wanted some tea, and lozenges for her throat, but she could not face the waiting in line or the speaking French. No matter how well you can manage when you are in good health, it does not take much of a droop of spirits or a premonition of sickness to send you back to the shelter of your nursery language. She sat on a bench and let her head drop. She could sleep for a moment.

More than a moment. Fifteen minutes had passed by the station clock. There was a crowd gathered now, a great deal of bustle around her, baggage carts on the move.

As she hurried towards her train she saw a man wearing a fur hat like Maksim's. A big man, in a dark overcoat. She could not see his face. He was

377

moving away from her. But his wide shoulders, his courteous but determined manner of making way for himself, strongly reminded her of Maksim.

A cart piled high with freight passed between them, and the man was gone.

Of course it could not be Maksim. What could he be doing in Paris? What train or appointment could he be hurrying towards? Her heart had begun to beat unpleasantly as she climbed aboard her train and found her seat by a window. It stood to reason that there should have been other women in Maksim's life. There had been, for instance, the woman he could not introduce Sophia to, when he refused to invite her to Beaulieu. But she believed that he was not a man for tawdry complications. Much less for jealous fits, for female tears and scoldings. He had pointed out on that earlier occasion that she had no rights, no hold on him.

Which surely meant that he would consider she had some hold now, and would have felt it beneath his dignity to deceive her.

And when she thought she saw him she had just wakened out of an unnatural unhealthy sleep. She had been hallucinating.

The train got itself together with the usual groans and clatter and slowly passed beyond the station roof.

How she used to love Paris. Not the Paris of the Commune where she had been under Aniuta's excited and sometimes incomprehensible orders, but the Paris she had visited later, in the fullness of her adult life, with introductions to mathematicians and political thinkers. In Paris, she had proclaimed, there is no such thing as boredom or snobbishness or deception.

Then they had given her the Bordin Prize, they had kissed her hand and presented her with speeches and flowers in the most elegant lavishly lit rooms. But they had closed their doors when it came to giving her a job. They would no more think of that than of employing a learned chimpanzee. The wives of the great scientists preferred not to meet her, or invite her into their homes.

Wives were the watchers on the barricade, the invisible implacable army. Husbands shrugged sadly at their prohibitions but gave them their due. Men whose brains were blowing old notions apart were still in thrall to women whose heads were full of nothing but the necessity of tight corsets, calling cards, and conversations that filled your throat with a kind of perfumed fog.

She must stop this litany of resentment. The wives of Stockholm invited her into their houses, to the most important parties and intimate dinners. They praised her and showed her off. They welcomed her child. She might have been an oddity there, but she was an oddity that they approved of. Something like a multilingual parrot

379

or those prodigies who could tell you without hesitation or apparent reflection that a certain date in the fourteenth century fell on a Tuesday.

No, that was not fair. They had respect for what she did, and many of them believed that more women should do such things and someday they would. So why was she a little bored by them, longing for late nights and extravagant talk. Why did it bother her that they dressed either like parsons' wives or like Gypsies?

She was in a shocking mood, and that was on account of Jaclard and Urey and the respectable woman she could not be introduced to. And her sore throat and slight shivers, surely a full-fledged cold coming on her.

At any rate she would soon be a wife herself, and the wife of a rich and clever and accomplished man into the bargain.

The tea wagon has come. That will help her throat, though she wishes it was Russian tea. Rain started soon after they left Paris, and now that rain has turned to snow. She prefers snow to rain, white fields to land dark and sodden, as every Russian does. And where there is snow most people recognize the fact of winter and take more than halfhearted measures to keep their houses warm. She thinks of the Weierstrass house, where she will sleep tonight. The professor and his sisters would not hear of a hotel.

Their house is always comfortable, with its dark rugs and heavy fringed curtains and deep armchairs. Life there follows a ritual—it is dedicated to study, particularly to the study of mathematics. Shy, generally ill-dressed male students pass through the sitting room to the study, one after the other. The professor's two unmarried sisters greet them kindly as they pass, but scarcely expect a reply. They are busy with their knitting or their mending or rug hooking. They know that their brother has a wonderful brain, that he is a great man, but they know also that he must have a dose of prunes every day, because of his sedentary occupation, that he cannot wear even the finest wool next to his skin, because it gives him a rash, that his feelings are hurt when a colleague has failed to give credit to him in a published article (though he pretends to take no notice, both in conversation and in his writing, praising punctiliously the very person who has slighted him).

Those sisters—Clara and Elisa had been startled the first day Sophia entered their sitting room on her way to the study. The servant who admitted her had not been trained to be selective, because those in the house lived such a retired life, also because the students who came were often shabby and unmannerly, so that the standards of most respectable houses did not apply. Even so, there had been some hesitation in the maid's voice before she admitted this small woman whose face was mostly hidden by a dark bonnet and who moved in a frightened way, like a shy mendicant. The sisters could get no idea of her real age but concluded—after she was admitted to the study— that she might be some student's mother, come to haggle or beg about the fees.

"My goodness," said Clara, whose speculations were the more lively, "my goodness, we thought, what have we here, is it a Charlotte Corday?"

This was all told to Sophia later, when she had become their friend. And Elisa added drily, "Fortunately our brother was not in his bath. And we could not get up to protect him because we were all wrapped up in those endless mufflers."

They had been knitting mufflers for the soldiers at the front. It was 1870, before Sophia and Vladimir took what they meant to be their study trip to Paris. So deep they were then in other dimensions, past centuries, so scant their attention to the world they lived in, that they had scarcely heard of a contemporary war.

Weierstrass had no more idea than his sisters of Sophia's age or mission. He told her afterwards that he had thought her some misguided governess who wanted to use his name, claiming mathematics among her credentials. He was thinking he must scold the maid, and his sisters, for letting her break in on him. But he was a courteous and kindly man, so instead of sending her away at once, he explained that he took only advanced students, with recognized degrees, and that he had at the moment as many of those as he could handle. Then, as she remained standing—and trembling—in front of him, with that ridiculous hat shading her face and her hands clutching her shawl, he remembered the method, or trick, he had used once or twice before, to discourage an inadequate student.

"What I am able to do in your case," he said, "is to set you a series of problems, and ask you to solve them and bring them back to me one week from today. If they are done to my satisfaction, we will talk again."

A week from that day he had forgotten all about her. He had expected, of course, never to see her again. When she came into his study he did not recognize her, perhaps because she had cast off the cloak that had disguised her slender figure. She must have felt bolder, or perhaps the weather had changed. He had not remembered the hat—his sisters had—but he had not much of an eye for female accessories. But when she pulled the papers out of her bag and set them down on his desk, he remembered, and sighed, and put on his spectacles.

Great was his surprise—he told her this too at a later time—to see that every one of the problems had been solved, and sometimes in an entirely original way. But he suspected her still, thinking now that she must be presenting the work of someone else, perhaps a brother or lover who was in hiding for political reasons.

"Sit down," he said. "And now explain to me each of these solutions, every step taken."

She began to talk, leaning forward, and the floppy hat fell over her eyes, so she pulled it off and let it lie on the floor. Her curls were revealed, her bright eyes, her youth, and her shivering excitement.

"Yes," he said. "Yes. Yes. Yes." He spoke with ponderous consideration, hiding as well as he could his astonishment, especially at the solutions whose method diverged most brilliantly from his own.

She was a shock to him in many ways. She was so slight and young and eager. He felt that he must soothe her, hold her carefully, letting her learn how to manage the fireworks in her own brain.

All his life—he had difficulty saying this, as he admitted, being always wary of too much enthusiasm—all his life he had been waiting for such a student to come into this room. A student who would challenge him completely, who was not only capable of following the strivings of his own mind but perhaps of flying beyond them. He had to be careful about saying what he really believed—that there must be something like intuition in a first-rate mathematician's mind, some lightning flare to uncover what has been there all along. Rigorous, meticulous, one must be, but so must the great poet.

When he finally brought himself to say all this to Sophia, he also said that there were those who would bridle at the very word, "poet," in connection with mathematical science. And others, he said, who would leap at the notion all too readily, to defend a muddle and laxity in their own thinking.

As she had expected, there was deeper and deeper snow outside the train windows as they travelled east. This was a second-class train, quite spartan in comparison with the train she had taken from Cannes. There was no dining car, but cold buns—some filled with various spicy sausages—were available from the tea wagon. She bought a cheese-filled bun half the size of a boot and thought she would never finish it, but in time she did. Then she got out her little volume of Heine, to assist in bringing the German language to the surface of her mind.

Every time she lifted her eyes to the window it seemed that the snow fell more thickly, and sometimes the train slowed, almost stopping. They would be lucky at this rate to reach Berlin by midnight. She wished that she had not let herself be talked out of going to a hotel, instead of to the house on Potsdam Street.

"It will do poor Karl so much good just to have you for one night under the same roof. He still thinks of you as the little girl on our doorstep, even though he gives great credit to your achievements and takes pride in your great success."

It was in fact after midnight when she rang the bell. Clara came, in her wrapper, having sent the servant to bed. Her brother—she said this in a half whisper—had been wakened by the noise of the cab and Elisa had gone to settle him down and to assure him that he would see Sophia in the morning.

The word "settle" sounded ominous to Sophia. The sisters' letters had mentioned nothing but a certain fatigue. And Weierstrass's own letters had held no personal news, being full of Poincaré and his—Weierstrass's—duty to mathematics in making matters clear to the king of Sweden.

Now hearing the old woman's voice take that little pious or fearful drop as she mentioned her brother, now smelling the once-familiar and reassuring but tonight faintly stale and dreary odors of that house, Sophia felt that teasing was not perhaps so much in order as it used to be, that she herself had brought not only the cold fresh air, but some bustle of success, an edge of energy, of which she had been quite unaware, and which might be a little daunting and disturbing. She who used to be welcomed with hugs and robust pleasure (one of the surprises about the sisters was how jolly they could be yet how conventional) was still hugged, but with tears standing in faded eyes, with old arms trembling.

But there was warm water in the jug in her room, there was bread and butter on her night table.

As she undressed she could hear faintly agitated whispering out in the upper hall. It might have been about their brother's state or about herself or about the absence of a cover on the bread and butter, which maybe had not been noticed until Clara ushered her into her room.

When she worked with Weierstrass, Sophia had lived in a small dark apartment, most of the time with her friend Julia, who was studying chemistry. They did not go to concerts or plays—they had limited funds and were absorbed by their work. Julia did go out to a private laboratory where she had obtained privileges hard for a woman to get. Sophia spent day after day at her writing table, not rising from her chair sometimes till the lamp had to be lit. Then she would stretch and walk, quickly, quickly, from one end of the apartment to the other—a short enough distance—sometimes breaking into a run and talking aloud, bursting into nonsense, so that anybody who did not know her as well as Julia did would wonder if she was sane.

Weierstrass's thoughts, and now hers, were concerned with elliptic and Abelian functions, and the theory of analytic functions based on their representation as an infinite series. The theory named for him contended that every bounded infinite sequence of real numbers has a convergent subsequence. In this she followed him and later challenged him and even for a time jumped ahead of him, so that they progressed from being teacher and pupil to being fellow mathematicians, she being often the catalyst to his investigations. But this relationship took time to develop, and at the Sunday suppers—to which she was invited readily because he had given up his Sunday afternoons to her—she was like a young relation, an eager protégée.

When Julia came she was invited as well, and the two girls were fed roast meat and creamed potatoes and light delectable puddings that upset all the ideas that they had about German cooking. After the meal they sat by the fire and heard Elisa read aloud. She read with great spirit and expression from the stories of the Swiss writer Conrad Ferdinand Meyer. Literature was the weekly treat, after all the knitting and mending.

At Christmas there was a tree for Sophia and Julia, though the Weierstrasses themselves had not bothered about one for years. There were bonbons wrapped in glittery paper, and fruitcake and roast apples. As they said, for the children.

But there came before long a disturbing surprise.

The surprise was that Sophia, who seemed the very image of a shy and inexperienced young girl, should have a husband. In the first few weeks of her lessons, before Julia arrived, she had been picked up at their door, on Sunday nights, by a young man who was not introduced to the Weierstrass family and was taken to be a servant. He was tall and unattractive, with a thin red beard, a large nose, untidy clothes. In fact, if the Weierstrasses had been more worldly, they would have realized that no self-respecting noble family—which they knew Sophia's to be—would have such an unkempt servant, and that therefore he must be a friend.

Then Julia came, and the young man disappeared.

It was some time later that Sophia released the information that he was named Vladimir Kovalevsky and that she was married to him. He was studying in Vienna and Paris though he already had a law degree and had been trying to make his way in Russia as a publisher of textbooks. He was several years older than Sophia.

Almost as surprising as this news was the fact that Sophia gave it out to Weierstrass and not to the sisters. In the household they were the ones who had some dealings with life—if only in the lives of their servants and the reading of fairly up-to-date fiction. But Sophia had not been a favorite with her mother or her governess. Her negotiations with the General had not always been successful but she respected him and thought that perhaps he respected her. So it was to the man of the house that she turned with an important confidence.

She realized that Weierstrass must have been embarrassed—not when she was talking to him but when he had to tell his sisters. For there was more to it than the fact that Sophia was married. She was well and legally married, but it was a White Marriage—a thing he had never heard of, nor the sisters either. Husband and wife not only did not live in the same place, they did not live together at all. They did not marry for the universally accepted reasons but were bound by their secret vow never to live in that way, never to—

"Consummate?" Perhaps it would be Clara who said this. Briskly, even impatiently, to get the moment over with.

Yes. And young people—young women—who wanted to study abroad were compelled to go through with this deception because no Russian woman who was unmarried could leave the country without her parents' consent. Julia's parents were enlightened enough to let her go, but not Sophia's.

What a barbarous law.

Yes. Russian. But some young women found their way around this with the help of young men who were very idealistic and sympathetic. Perhaps they were anarchists as well. Who knows?

It was Sophia's older sister who had located one of these young men, and she and a friend of hers set up a meeting with him. Their reasons were perhaps political, rather than intellectual. God knows why they took Sophia along—she had no passion for politics and did not think herself ready for any such venture. But the young man looked over the two older girls—the sister named Aniuta however businesslike could not disguise her beauty—and he said no. No, I do not wish to go through with this contract with either of you estimable young ladies, but I would agree to do so with your younger sister.

"Possibly he thought the older ones would be troublesome"—it might be Elisa who said this, with her experience of novels—"particularly the beauty. He fell in love with our little Sophia."

Love is not supposed to enter into it, Clara may have reminded her.

Sophia accepts the proposal. Vladimir calls upon the General, to ask the hand of his younger daughter in marriage. The General is polite, aware the young man comes from a good family, though he has not so far made much of a mark in the world. But Sophia is too young, he says. Does she even know of these intentions?

Yes, said Sophia, and she was in love with him.

The General said that they could not act on their feelings immediately but must spend some time, some very considerable time, getting to know each other at Palibino. (They were at present in Petersburg.)

Things were at a standstill. Vladimir would never make a good impression. He did not try hard enough to disguise his radical views and he dressed badly, as if on purpose. The General was confident that the more Sophia saw of this suitor, the less she would want to marry him.

Sophia, however, was making plans of her own.

There came a day on which her parents were giving an important dinner party. They had invited a diplomat, professors, military comrades of the General's from the School of Artillery. Amidst all the bustle Sophia was able to slip away.

She went out alone into the streets of Petersburg, where she had never walked before without a servant or a sister. She went to Vladimir's lodgings in a part of the city where poor students lived. The door was opened to her at once, and as soon as she was inside she sat down and wrote a letter to her father.

"My dear father, I have gone to Vladimir and will remain here. I beg you that you will no longer oppose our marriage."

All were seated at the table before Sophia's absence was noticed. A servant found her room empty. Aniuta was asked about her sister and flushed as she answered that she knew nothing. To hide her face she dropped her napkin.

The General was handed a note. He excused himself and left the room. Sophia and Vladimir were soon to hear his angry footsteps outside their door. He told his compromised daughter and the man for whom she was willing to forfeit her reputation to come with him at once. They rode home, all three without a word, and at the dinner table he said, "Allow me to introduce to you my future son-in-law, Vladimir Kovalevsky."

So it was done. Sophia was overjoyed, not indeed to be marrying Vladimir but to be pleasing Aniuta by striking a blow for the emancipation of Russian women. There was a conventional and splendid wedding in Palibino, and the bride and groom went off to live under one roof in Petersburg.

And once their way was clear they went abroad and did not continue to live under one roof anymore. Heidelberg, then Berlin for Sophia, Munich for Vladimir. He visited Heidelberg when he could, but after Aniuta and her friend Zhanna arrived there, and Julia—all four women theoretically under his protection—there was not enough room for him any longer.

Weierstrass did not reveal to the women that he had been in correspondence with the General's wife. He had written to her when Sophia returned from Switzerland (really from Paris) looking so worn and frail that he was concerned for her health. The mother had replied, informing him

393

that it was Paris, in these most dangerous times, that was responsible for her daughter's state. But she seemed less upset by the political upheaval her daughters had lived through than by the revelations that one of them, while unmarried, lived openly with a man, and the other, properly wed, did not truly live with her husband at all. So he was made rather against his will to be the mother's confidant even before he was the daughter's. And indeed he told Sophia nothing about this until her mother was dead.

But when he did tell her at last, he told her also that Clara and Elisa had asked immediately what was to be done.

This seemed to be the way of women, he had said, to assume that something should be done.

He had replied, quite severely, "Nothing."

In the morning Sophia took a clean though crumpled frock out of her bag—she had never learned how to pack tidily—fixed her curly hair as well as she could to hide some little patches of gray, and came downstairs to the sounds of a household already astir. Her place was the only one still set in the dining room. Elisa brought in the coffee and the first German breakfast that Sophia had ever eaten in this house—cold sliced meat and cheese and thickly buttered bread. She said that Clara was upstairs preparing their brother for his meeting with Sophia.

"At first we had the barber come in," she said. "But then Clara learned to do it quite well. She turned out to be the one who has the skills of a nurse, it is fortunate one of us has them."

Even before she said this Sophia had sensed that they were short of money. The damask and net curtains had a dingy look, the silver knife and fork she used had not recently been polished. Through the open door to the sitting room a rough-looking young girl, their present servant, was visible cleaning out the grate and raising clouds of dust. Elisa looked her way, as if to ask her to shut the door, then got up and did it herself. She came back to the table with a flushed, downcast face, and Sophia asked hastily, if rather impolitely, what was the illness of Herr Weierstrass?

"It is a weakness of his heart for one thing, and the pneumonia he had in the autumn that he cannot seem to get over. Also he has a growth in the generative organs," said Elisa, lowering her voice but speaking frankly as German women did.

Clara appeared in the doorway.

"He is waiting for you now."

Sophia climbed the stairs thinking not of the professor but of these two women who had made him the center of their lives. Knitting mufflers, mending the linen, making the puddings and preserves that could never be trusted to a servant. Honoring the Roman Catholic Church as their brother did—a cold undiverting religion in

Sophia's opinion—and all without a moment of mutiny as far as you could see, or any flicker of dissatisfaction.

I would go mad, she thought.

Even to be a professor, she thought, I would go mad. Students have mediocre minds, generally speaking. Only the most obvious, regular patterns can be impressed on them.

She would not have dared admit this to herself before she had Maksim.

She entered the bedroom smiling at her luck, her coming freedom, her soon-to-be husband.

"Ah, here you are at last," said Weierstrass, speaking somewhat weakly and laboriously. "The naughty child, we thought she had deserted us. Are you on your way to Paris again, off to amuse yourself?"

"I am on my way back from Paris," said Sophia. "I am going back to Stockholm. Paris was not at all amusing, it was dreary as can be." She gave him her hands to kiss, one after the other.

"Is your Aniuta ill, then?"

"She is dead, *mein liebe* professor."

"She died in prison?"

"No, no. That was long ago. She was not in prison that time. Her husband was. She died of pneumonia, but she had been suffering in many ways for a long time."

"Oh, pneumonia, I have had it too. Still, that was sad for you."

"My heart will never heal. But I have something good to tell you, something happy. I am to be married in the spring."

"Are you divorcing the geologist? I do not wonder, you should have done that long ago. Still, a divorce is always unpleasant."

"He is dead too. And he was a paleontologist. It is a new study, very interesting. They learn things from fossils."

"Yes. I remember now. I have heard of the study. He died young then. I did not wish him to stand in your way, but truly I did not wish him dead. Was he ill long?"

"You might say that he was. You surely remember how I left him and you recommended me to Mittag-Leffler?"

"In Stockholm. Yes? You left him. Well. It had to be done."

"Yes. But it is over now and I am going to marry a man of the same name but not closely related and a different sort of man entirely."

"A Russian, then? Does he read fossils also?"

"Not at all. He is a professor of law. He is very energetic and very good-humored except when he is very gloomy. I will bring him to meet you and you shall see."

"We will be pleased to entertain him," said Weierstrass sadly. "It will put an end to your work."

"Not at all, not at all. He does not wish it. But I

will not teach anymore, I will be free. And I will live in a delightful climate in the south of France and I shall be healthy there all the time and do all the more work."

"We shall see."

"Mein Liebe," she said. "I order you, order you to be happy for me."

"I must seem very old," he said. "And I have led a sedate life. I have not as many sides to my nature as you have. It was such a surprise to me that you would write novels."

"You did not like the idea."

"You are wrong. I did like your recollections. Very pleasant to read."

"That book is not really a novel. You would not like the one I have written now. Sometimes I don't even like it myself. It is all about a girl who is more interested in politics than in love. Never mind, you will not have to read it. The Russian censors will not let it be published and the world outside will not want it because it is so Russian."

"I am not generally fond of novels."

"They are for women?"

"Truly I sometimes forget that you are a woman. I think of you as—as a—"

"As a what?"

"As a gift to me and to me alone."

Sophia bent and kissed his white forehead. She held back her tears till she had said good-bye to his sisters and left the house.

I will never see him again, she thought.

She thought of his face as white as the fresh starched pillows that Clara must have placed behind his head just that morning. Perhaps she had already taken them away, letting him slump down into the softer shabbier ones beneath. Perhaps he had fallen asleep at once, tired out from their exchange. He would have thought that they were meeting for the last time and he would have known that the thought was in her mind as well, but he would not know—this was her shame, her secret—how lightened, how free, she felt now, in spite of her tears, freer with every step away from that house.

Was his life, she thought, so much more satisfactory to contemplate than his sisters'?

His name would last awhile, in textbooks. And among mathematicians. Not so long as it might have done if he had been more zealous about establishing his reputation, keeping himself to the fore in his select and striving circle. He cared more for the work than for his name, when so many of his colleagues cared equally for both.

She should not have mentioned her writing. Frivolity to him. She had written the recollections of her life at Palibino in a glow of love for everything lost, things once despaired of as well as things once treasured. She had written it far from home when that home and her sister were gone.

And *Nihilist Girl* came out of pain for her country, a burst of patriotism and perhaps a feeling that she had not been paying enough attention, with her mathematics and the tumults of her life.

Pain for her country, yes. But in some sense she had written that story in tribute to Aniuta. It was the story of a young woman who gives up the prospect of any normal life in order to marry a political prisoner exiled to Siberia. In this way she ensured that his life, his punishment, should be somewhat alleviated—southern instead of northern Siberia—as was the rule for men accompanied by their wives. The story would be praised by those banished Russians who might manage to read it in manuscript. A book had only to be refused publication in Russia to engender such praises among political exiles, as Sophia well knew. *The Raevsky Sisters*—the recollections—pleased her more, though the censor had passed it, and some critics dismissed it as nostalgia.

IV

She had failed Weierstrass once before. She failed him when she had achieved her early success. It was true, though he never mentioned it. She had turned her back on him and on mathematics altogether; she had not even answered his letters. She went home to Palibino in the summer of 1874, with her degree won, stored in a velvet case, and then put away in a trunk, to be forgotten for months—years—at a time.

The smell of the hay fields and the pine woods, the golden hot summer days, and the long bright evenings of northern Russia intoxicated her. There were picnics and amateur plays, balls, birthdays, the welcome of old friends, and the presence of Aniuta, happy with her year-old son. Vladimir was there as well, and in the easy summer atmosphere, with the warmth and wine and long merry suppers, the dances and the singing, it was natural to give in to him, to establish him after all this time as not just her husband but her lover.

This was not done because she had fallen in love with him. She had been grateful to him, and had convinced herself that such a feeling as love did not exist in real life. It would make them both happier, she thought, to agree with what he wanted, and for a while it did.

In the autumn they went to Petersburg, and the life of important amusement continued. Dinners, plays, receptions, and all the papers and periodicals to read, both frivolous and serious. Weierstrass begged Sophia, by letter, not to desert the world of mathematics. He saw to it that her dissertation was published in *Crelle's Journal* for mathematicians. She barely looked at it. He asked her to spend a week—just a week—polishing up her work on the rings of Saturn, so that it too might be published. She could not be bothered. She was too busy, wrapped up in more or less constant celebration. A celebration of name days and court honors and new operas and ballets, but really, it seemed to be, a celebration of life itself.

She was learning, quite late, what many people around her appeared to have known since child-hood—that life can be perfectly satisfying without major achievements. It could be brimful of occupations which did not weary you to the bone. Acquiring what you needed for a comfort-ably furnished life, and then to take on a social and public life of entertainment, would keep you from even being bored or idle, and would make you feel at the end of the day that you had done exactly what pleased everybody. There need be no agonizing.

Except in the matter of how to get money.

Vladimir revived his publishing business. They borrowed where they could. Both of Sophia's par-ents died before long, and her inheritance was invested in public baths attached to a greenhouse, a bakery, and a steam laundry. They had grand projects. But the weather in Petersburg happened to have turned colder than usual, and people were not tempted even by steam baths. The builders and other people cheated them, the market became unstable, and instead of managing to make a reliable foundation for their lives they went deeper and deeper into debt.

And behaving like other married couples had the usual expensive result. Sophia had a baby girl. The infant was given her mother's name but they called her Fufu. Fufu had a nurse and a wet nurse and her own suite of rooms. The family employed also a cook and a maid. Vladimir bought fashionable new clothes for Sophia and wonderful presents for his daughter. He had his degree from Jena and he had managed to become a subprofessor in Petersburg, but this was not enough. The publishing business was more or less in ruins.

Then the czar was assassinated and the political climate became disturbing and Vladimir entered a period of such deep melancholy that he could not work or think.

Weierstrass had heard of the death of Sophia's parents, and to allay her grief a little, as he said, he sent her information on his own new and excellent system of integrals. But instead of being drawn back to mathematics she took to writing theater reviews and popular science pieces for the papers. That was using a talent more marketable and not so disturbing to other people or so exhausting to herself, as mathematics.

The Kovalevsky family moved to Moscow, hoping that their luck would change.

Vladimir recovered, but he did not feel able to go back to teaching. He found a new opportunity for speculation, being offered a job in a company that produced naphtha from a petroleum spring. The company was owned by the brothers Ragozin, who had a refinery and a modern castle on the Volga. The job was contingent on Vladimir's investing a sum of money, which he managed to borrow.

But this time Sophia sensed trouble ahead. The Ragozins did not like her and she did not like them. Vladimir was now more and more in their power. These are the new men, he said, they have no nonsense in them. He became aloof, he took on rough and superior airs. Name me one truly important woman, he said. One who has made any real difference in the world, except by seducing and murdering men. They are congenitally backwards and self-centered and if they get hold of any idea, any decent idea to devote themselves to, they become hysterical and ruin it with their self-importance.

That is the Ragozins talking, said Sophia.

Now she picked up her correspondence with Weierstrass. She left Fufu with her old friend Julia and set out for Germany. She wrote to Vladimir's brother Alexander that Vladimir had bitten at the Ragozins' bait so readily that it was really as if he were tempting fate to send him another blow. Nevertheless she wrote to her husband offering to come back. He did not reply favorably.

They met once more, in Paris. She was living there cheaply while Weierstrass tried to get her a job. She was again submerged in mathematical problems and so were the people she knew. Vladimir had become suspicious of the Ragozins but he had involved himself to the point where he could not pull out. Yet he talked of going to the United States. And did go, but came back.

In the fall of 1882 he wrote to his brother that he realized now that he was a completely worthless person. In November he reported the bankruptcy of the Ragozins. He was afraid that they might try to implicate him in certain criminal procedures. At Christmas he saw Fufu, who was now in Odessa with his brother's family. He was happy that she remembered him, and that she was healthy and clever. After that he prepared farewell letters for Julia, his brother, certain other friends, but not Sophia. Also a letter for the court explaining some actions of his in the Ragozin matter.

He delayed a while longer. It was not until April that he tied a bag over his head and inhaled chloroform.

Sophia, in Paris, refused food and wouldn't come out of her room. She concentrated all her thought on the refusal of food, so she would not have to feel what she was feeling.

She was force-fed, at last, and fell asleep. When she woke she was deeply ashamed of this performance. She asked for a pencil and paper, that she might continue working on a problem.

•••

There was no money left. Weierstrass wrote and asked her to live with him as another sister. But he continued to pull strings wherever he could and was successful, finally, with his past student and friend Mittag-Leffler, in Sweden. The new University of Stockholm agreed to be the first university in Europe to take on a female mathematics professor.

At Odessa Sophia collected her daughter, taking her to live for the present with Julia. She was furious with the Ragozins. She wrote to Vladimir's brother calling them "subtle, poisonous villains." She persuaded the magistrate hearing the case to proclaim that all the evidence showed Vladimir to have been gullible but honest.

Then she took a train once more from Moscow to Petersburg to travel to her new and much publicized—and no doubt deplored—job in Sweden. She made the trip from Petersburg by sea. The boat rode into an overwhelming sunset. No more foolishness, she thought. I am now going to make a proper life.

She had not then met Maksim. Or won the Bordin Prize.

V

She left Berlin in the early afternoon, shortly after having said that last sad but relieved good-bye to Weierstrass. The train was old and slow, but clean and well heated, as you would expect any German train to be.

About halfway in the journey the man across from her opened up his newspaper, offering her any section she might like to read.

She thanked him, and refused.

He nodded towards the window, at the fine driving snow.

"Ah well," he said. "What can one expect?"

"What indeed," said Sophia.

"You are going beyond Rostock?"

He might have noted an accent that was not German. She did not mind his speaking to her or coming to such a conclusion about her. He was a good deal younger than she, decently dressed, slightly deferential. She had a feeling that he was someone she had met or seen before. But this did happen when you were travelling.

"To Copenhagen," she said. "And then to Stockholm. For me the snow will only get thicker."

"I will be leaving you at Rostock," he said, perhaps to reassure her that she was not letting herself in for a long conversation. "Are you satisfied with Stockholm?"

407

"I detest Stockholm at this time of year. I hate it."

She was surprised at herself. But he smiled delightedly and began to speak in Russian.

"Excuse me," he said. "I was right. Now it is I who speak like a foreigner to you. But I studied in Russia at one time. In Petersburg."

"You recognized my accent as Russian?"

"Not surely. Until you said what you did about Stockholm."

"Do all Russians hate Stockholm?"

"No. No. But they say they hate. They hate. They love."

"I should not have said it. The Swedes have been very good to me. They teach you things—"

At this point he shook his head, laughing.

"Really," she said. "They have taught me to skate—"

"Assuredly. You did not learn to skate in Russia?"

"They are not so—so insistent about teaching you things as the Swedes are."

"Nor on Bornholm," he said. "I live now on Bornholm. The Danes are not so—insistent, that is the word. But of course on Bornholm we are not even Danes. We say we are not."

He was a doctor, on the island of Bornholm. She wondered if it would be entirely out of line to ask him to look at her throat, which was now very sore. She decided that it would be.

He said that he had a long and probably a rough ferry ride ahead of him, after they had crossed the Danish border.

People on Bornholm did not think of themselves as Danes, he said, because they thought of themselves as Vikings taken over by the Hanseatic League in the sixteenth century. They had a fierce history, they took captives. Had she ever heard of the wicked Earl of Bothwell? Some people say he died on Bornholm, though the people of Zealand say he died there.

"He murdered the husband of the queen of Scotland and married her himself. But he died in chains. He died insane."

"Mary Queen of Scots," she said. "So I have heard." And indeed she had, for the Scottish queen had been one of Aniuta's early heroines.

"Oh, forgive me. I am chattering."

"Forgive you?" said Sophia. "What have I to forgive you for?"

He flushed. He said, "I know who you are."

He had not known in the beginning, he said. But when she spoke in Russian, he was sure.

"You are the female professor. I have read about you in a journal. There was a photograph as well, but you looked much older in it than you do. I am sorry to intrude on you but I could not help myself."

"I looked quite stern in the photograph because I think people will not trust me if I smile," said

Sophia. "Is it not something the same for physicians?"

"It may be. I am not accustomed to being photographed."

Now there was a slight constraint between them; it was up to her to put him at ease. It had been better before he told her. She returned to the subject of Bornholm. It was bold and rugged, he said, not gentle and rolling like Denmark. People came there for the scenery and the clear air. If she should ever wish to come he would be honored to show her around.

"There is the most rare blue rock there," he said. "It is called blue marble. It is broken up and polished for ladies to wear around the neck. If you would ever like to have one—"

He was talking foolishly because there was something he wanted to say but couldn't. She could see that.

They were approaching Rostock. He was becoming more and more agitated. She was afraid he would ask her to sign her name on a piece of paper or a book he had with him. It was very seldom that anybody did that, but it always made her feel sad; there was no telling why.

"Please listen to me," he said. "Something I must say to you. It is not supposed to be spoken of. Please. On your way to Sweden, please do not go to Copenhagen. Do not look frightened, I am completely in my right mind."

"I am not frightened," she said. Though she was, a little.

"You must go the other way, by the Danish Islands. Change your ticket in the station."

"May I ask why? Is there a spell on Copenhagen?"

She was suddenly sure he was going to tell her about a plot, a bomb.

So he was an anarchist?

"There is smallpox in Copenhagen. There is an epidemic. Many people have left the city, but the authorities are trying to keep it quiet. They are afraid of a panic or that some people will burn down the government buildings. The problem is the Finns. People say the Finns brought it. They don't want the people to rise up against the Finnish refugees. Or against the government for letting them in."

The train stopped and Sophia stood up, checking her bags.

"Promise me. Do not leave me here without promising me."

"Very well," said Sophia. "I promise."

"You will be taking the ferry to Gedser. I would go with you to change the ticket but I must go on to Rutgen."

"I promise."

Was it Vladimir he reminded her of? Vladimir in the early days. Not his features, but his beseeching care for her. His constant humble and stubborn and beseeching care.

He held out his hand and she gave him hers to shake, but that was not his only intention. He placed in her palm a small tablet, saying, "This will give you a little rest if you find the journey tedious."

I will have to talk to some responsible person about this epidemic of smallpox, she decided.

But that she did not do. The man who changed her ticket was annoyed at having to do anything so complicated and would be even angrier if she changed her mind. He seemed at first to answer to no language except Danish, as spoken by her fellow passengers, but when he finished the transaction with her he said in German that the trip would take a good deal longer now, did she understand that? Then she realized that they were still in Germany and he might know nothing about Copenhagen—what had she been thinking of?

He added gloomily that it was snowing on the islands.

The small German ferry to Gedser was well heated, though you had to sit on wooden slat seats. She was about to swallow the tablet, thinking that seats like these might be what he meant when he spoke of the journey being tedious. Then she decided to save it, in case of seasickness.

The local train she got into had regular though threadbare second-class seats. It was chilly, however, with a smoky almost useless stove at one end of the car.

This conductor was friendlier than the ticket master, and not in so much of a hurry. Understanding that they really were in Danish territory, she asked him in Swedish—which she thought might be closer than German to Danish—whether it was true that there was sickness in Copenhagen. He replied that no, the train she was on did not go to Copenhagen.

The words "train" and "Copenhagen" seemed to be all he knew of Swedish.

In this train there were of course no compartments, only the two coaches with their wooden benches. Some of the passengers had brought their own cushions and their blankets and cloaks to wrap around themselves. They did not look at Sophia, much less try to speak to her. What use would it be if they did? She would not be able to understand or reply.

No tea wagon either. Packages wrapped in oiled paper were being opened, cold sandwiches taken out. Thick slices of bread, sharp-smelling cheese, slabs of cold cooked bacon, somewhere a herring. One woman took a fork out from a pocket in the folds of her clothing and ate pickled cabbage from a jar. That made Sophia think of home, of Russia.

But these are not Russian peasants. None of them are drunk, or garrulous, or laughing. They are stiff as boards. Even the fat that blankets the bones of some of them is stiff fat, self-respecting, Lutheran fat. She knows nothing about them.

But what does she really know about Russian peasants, the peasants at Palibino, when it comes to that? They were always putting on a show for their betters.

Except perhaps the one time, the Sunday when all the serfs and their owners had to go to church to hear the Proclamation read. Afterwards Sophia's mother was completely broken in spirit and moaned and cried, "Now what will become of us? What will become of my poor children?" The General took her into his study to comfort her. Aniuta sat down to read one of her books, and their little brother Feodor played with his blocks. Sophia wandered about, making her way to the kitchen where house serfs and even many field serfs were eating pancakes and celebrating—but in a rather dignified way, as if it was a saint's day. An old man whose only job was to sweep the yard laughed and called her Little Missus. "Here's the Little Missus come to wish us well." Then some cheered for her. How nice they were, she thought, though she understood that the cheering was some kind of joke.

Soon the governess appeared with a face like a black cloud and took her away.

Afterwards things went on pretty much as usual.

Jaclard had told Aniuta she could never be a true revolutionary, she was only good for getting money out of her criminal parents. As for Sophia and Vladimir (Vladimir who had snatched him away from the police), they were preening parasites, soaking up their worthless studies.

The smell of the cabbage and the herring is making her slightly sick.

At some farther point the train stops and they are all told to get out. At least that is what she assumes, from the conductor's bark and the heaving up of reluctant but obedient bodies. They find themselves in knee-deep snow, with no town or platform in sight and smooth white hills around them, looming up through what is now lightly falling snow. Ahead of the train men are shovelling away the snow that has collected in a railway cut. Sophia moves around to keep her feet from freezing in their light boots, sufficient for city streets but not here. The other passengers stand still, and pass no comment on the state of affairs.

After half an hour, or perhaps only fifteen minutes, the track is clear and the passengers clamber back onto the train. It must be a mystery to all of them, as to Sophia, why they had to get out in the first place, instead of waiting in their seats, but of course nobody complains. On and on they go, through the dark, and there is something other than snow driving against the windows. A scratching malevolent sound. Sleet.

Then the dim lamps of a village, and some passengers are getting up, methodically bundling themselves and collecting their bags and packages and clambering down from the train, disappearing. The journey resumes, but in a short time everybody is ordered off again. Not because of snowdrifts this time. They are herded onto a boat, another small ferry, which takes them out onto black water. Sophia's throat is so sore now that she is sure she could not speak if she had to.

She has no idea how long this crossing is. When they dock everybody has to enter a three-sided shed, where there is little shelter and no benches. A train arrives after a wait she cannot measure. And when this train comes, what gratitude Sophia feels, though it is no warmer and has the same wooden benches as the first train. One's appreciation of meager comforts, it seems, depends on what misery one has gone through before getting them. And is not that, she wants to say to somebody, a dreary homily?

In a while they stop in a larger town where there is a station buffet. She is too tired to get off and make her way to it as some passengers do, coming back with steaming cups of coffee. The woman who ate the cabbage is, however, carrying two cups, and it turns out that one is for Sophia. Sophia smiles and does her best to express gratitude. The woman nods as if this fuss is unnecessary, even unseemly. But she keeps standing there till Sophia takes out the Danish coins she received from the ticket agent. Now the woman, grunting, picks out two of them with her damp mittened fingers. The cost of the coffee, very likely. For the thought, and for carrying it, no charge. This is the way of things. Without a word the woman then returns to her seat.

Some new passengers have got on. A woman with a child about four years old, one side of its face bandaged and one arm in a sling. An accident, a visit to a country hospital. A hole in the bandage shows a sad dark eye. The child puts its good cheek down in its mother's lap and she spreads part of her shawl over its body. She does this in a way that is not particularly tender or concerned, but somewhat automatic. Something bad has happened, more care has been added on to her, that is all. And the children waiting at home, and perhaps one in her belly.

How terrible it is, Sophia thinks. How terrible is the lot of women. And what might this woman say if Sophia told her about the new struggles, women's battle for votes and places at the universities? She might say, But that is not as God wills. And if Sophia urged her to get rid of this God and sharpen her mind, would she not look at her—Sophia—with a certain stubborn pity, and exhaustion, and say, How then, without God, are we to get through this life?

They cross the black water again, this time on a long bridge, and stop in another village where the woman and child get off. Sophia has lost interest, does not look to see if there is somebody waiting for them, she is trying to see the clock outside the station, lit up by the train. She expects the time to be near midnight, but it is just past ten o'clock.

She is thinking of Maksim. Would Maksim ever in his life board such a train as this? She imagines her head lying comfortably on his broad shoulder—though the truth is he would not care for that, in public. His coat of rich expensive cloth, its smell of money and comfort. Good things he believes he has a right to expect and a duty to maintain, even though he is a Liberal unwelcome in his own country. That marvellous assurance he has, that her father had, you can feel it when you are a little girl snuggled up in their arms and you want it all your life. More delightful of course if they love you, but comforting even if it is only a kind of ancient noble pact that they have made, a bond that has been signed, necessarily even if not enthusiastically, for your protection.

They would be displeased to have anybody call them docile, yet in a way they are. They submit themselves to manly behavior. They submit themselves to manly behavior with all its risks and cruelties, its complicated burdens and deliberate frauds. Its rules, which in some cases you benefited from, as a woman, and then some that you didn't.

Now she had an image of him—Maksim, not sheltering her at all but striding through the station in Paris as befitted a man who had a private life.

His commanding headgear, his courtly assurance.

That had not happened. It was not Maksim. Assuredly it was not.

Vladimir had not been a coward—look how he had rescued Jaclard—but he did not have the manly certainties. That was why he could grant her some equality those others couldn't and why he could never grant her that enveloping warmth and safety. Then near the end when he came under the Ragozin influence and changed his tune—desperate as he was and thinking that he might save himself by aping others—he turned to treating her in an unconvincing, even ridiculous, lordly style. He had given her then an excuse for despising him, but maybe she had despised him all along. Whether he worshipped or insulted her it was impossible for her to love him.

As Aniuta loved Jaclard. Jaclard was selfish and cruel and unfaithful and even while she hated him she was in love with him.

What ugly and irksome thoughts could surface, if you didn't keep a lid on them.

When she closed her eyes she thought she saw him—Vladimir—sitting on the bench across from her, but it is not Vladimir, it is the doctor from Bornholm, it is only her memory of the doctor from Bornholm, insistent and alarmed, pushing himself in that queer humble way into her life.

There came a time—surely it was near midnight—when they had to leave this train for good. They had reached the border of Denmark. Helsingor. The land border, at least—she supposed the true border was somewhere out in the Kattegat.

And there was the last ferry, waiting for them, looking large and pleasant, with its many bright lights. And here came a porter to carry her bags on board, and thank her for her Danish coins and hasten away. Then she showed her ticket to the officer on board and he spoke to her in Swedish. He assured her that they would make connections on the other side with the train for Stockholm. She would not have to spend the rest of the night in a waiting room.

"I feel as if I have come back to civilization," she said to him. He looked at her with slight misgiving. Her voice was a croak, though the coffee had helped her throat. It is just because he is a Swede, she thought. It is not necessary to smile or pass remarks among the Swedes. Civility can be maintained without that.

The crossing was a little rough, but she was not seasick. She remembered the tablet but she did not need it. And the boat must have been heated, because some people had taken off the upper layer of their winter clothing. But she still shivered. Perhaps it was necessary to shiver, she had collected so much cold in her body in her journey through Denmark. It had been stored inside her, the cold, and now she could shiver it out.

The train for Stockholm was waiting, as promised, in the busy port of Helsingborg, so much livelier and larger than its similarly named cousin across the water. The Swedes might not smile at you, but the information they gave out would be correct. A porter reached for her bags and held them while she searched in her purse for some coins. She took a generous number out and put them in his hand, thinking they were Danish; she would not need them anymore.

They were Danish. He gave them back to her, saying in Swedish, "These will not do."

"They are all I have," she cried, realizing two things. Her throat felt better and indeed she had no Swedish money.

He put down her bags and walked away.

French money, German money, Danish money. She had forgotten Swedish.

The train was getting up steam, the passengers boarding, while she still stood there in her quandary. She could not carry her bags. But if she could not, they would be left behind.

She grasped the various straps and started to run. She ran lurching and panting with a pain in her chest and around under her arms and the bags bumping against her legs. There were steps to climb. If she stopped for a breath she would be too late. She climbed. With tears of self-pity filling her eyes she beseeched the train not to move.

And it did not. Not till the conductor, leaning out to fasten the door, caught her arm, then somehow managed to catch her bags and pulled all aboard.

Once saved, she began to cough. She was trying to cough something out of her chest. The pain, out of her chest. The pain and tightness out of her throat. But she had to follow the conductor to her compartment, and she was laughing with triumph in between spells of coughing. The conductor looked into a compartment where there were already some people sitting, then took her along to one that was empty.

"You were right. To put me where I cannot. Be a nuisance," she said, beaming. "I didn't have money. Swedish money. All other kinds but Swedish. I had to run. I never thought I could—"

He told her to sit down and save her breath. He went away and came back soon with a glass of water. As she drank she thought of the tablet that had been given her, and took it with the last gulp of water. The coughing subsided.

"You must not do that again," he said. "Your chest is heaving. Up and down."

Swedes were very frank, as well as being reserved and punctual.

"Wait," she said.

For there was something else to be established, almost as if the train could not get her to the right place otherwise.

"Wait a moment. Did you hear about—? Did you hear there is smallpox? In Copenhagen?"

"I shouldn't think so," he said. He gave a severe though courteous nod and left her.

"Thank you. Thank you," she called after him.

Sophia has never been drunk in her life. Any medicine she has taken, that might addle her brain, has put her to sleep before any such disturbance could happen. So she has nothing with which to compare the extraordinary feeling—the change of perception—which is rippling through her now. At first it might have been just relief, a grand though silly sense of being favored, because she had managed to carry her bags and run up the steps and reach her train. And then she had survived the fit of coughing and the squeezing of her heart and been able somehow to disregard her throat.

But there is more, as if her heart could go on expanding, regaining its normal condition, and continuing after that to grow lighter and fresher and puff things almost humorously out of her way. Even the epidemic in Copenhagen could now become something like a plague in a ballad, part of an old story. As her own life could be, its bumps and sorrows turning into illusions. Events and ideas now taking on a new shape, seen through sheets of clear intelligence, a transforming glass.

There was one experience that this reminded her of. That was her first stumbling on trigonometry, when she was twelve years old. Professor Tyrtov, a neighbor at Palibino, had dropped off the new text he had written. He thought it might interest her father the General, with his knowledge of artillery. She came upon it in the study and opened it by chance at the chapter on optics. She began to read it and to study the diagrams and she was convinced that shortly she would be able to understand it. She had never heard of sines or cosines, but by substituting the chord of an arc for the sine, and by the lucky chance that in small angles these almost coincide, she was able to break into this new and delightful language.

She was not very surprised then, though intensely happy.

Such discoveries would happen. Mathematics was a natural gift, like the northern lights. It was not mixed up with anything else in the world, not with papers, prizes, colleagues, and diplomas.

The conductor woke her a little while before the train reached Stockholm. She said, "What day is this?"

"It is Friday."

"Good. Good, I will be able to give my lecture."

"Take care of your health, madam."

At two o'clock she was behind her lectern, and she lectured ably and coherently, without any pain or coughing. The delicate hum that had been travelling through her body, as on a wire, did not affect her voice. And her throat seemed to have healed itself. When she was finished she went home and changed her dress and took a cab to the reception she had been invited to, at the Guldens' house. She was in good spirits, talking brightly about her impressions of Italy and the south of France, though not about her trip back to Sweden. Then she left the room without excusing herself and went outside. She was too full of glowing and exceptional ideas to speak to people any longer.

Darkness already, snow falling, without any wind, the streetlamps enlarged like Christmas globes. She looked around for a cab but did not see one. An omnibus was passing and she waved it down. The driver informed her that this was not a scheduled stop.

"But you stopped," she said without concern.

She did not know the streets of Stockholm at all well, so it was some time later that she realized she had been travelling into the wrong part of town. She laughed as she explained this to the driver, and he let her off to walk home through the snow in her party dress and her light cloak and slippers. The pavements were wonderfully silent and white. She had to walk about a mile, but was pleased to discover that she knew the way, after all. Her feet were soaked but she was not cold. She thought this was because of the lack of wind, and the enchantment in her mind and body that she had never been aware of before, but could certainly count on from now on. It might be quite unoriginal to say so, but the city was like a city in a fairy tale.

The next day she stayed in bed, and sent a note to her colleague Mittag-Leffler asking him to get her his doctor, as she had none. He came himself as well, and during a long visit she talked to him with great excitement about a new mathematical work she was planning. It was more ambitious, more important, more beautiful, than anything that had occurred to her up until this time.

The doctor thought that the problem was with her kidneys, and left her some medicine.

"I forgot to ask him," Sophia said when he had gone.

"Ask him what?" said Mittag-Leffler.

"Is there plague? In Copenhagen?"

"You're dreaming," said Mittag-Leffler gently. "Who told you that?"

"A blind man," she said. Then she said, "No, I meant kind. Kind man." She waved her hands about, as if trying to make some shape that would fit better than words. "My Swedish," she said.

"Wait to speak until you are better."

She smiled and then looked sad. She said with emphasis, "My husband."

"Your betrothed? Ah, he is not your husband yet. I am teasing you. Would you like him to come?"

But she shook her head. She said, "Not him. Bothwell.

"No. No. No," she said rapidly. "The other."

"You must rest."

Teresa Gulden and her daughter Elsa had come, also Ellen Key. They were to take turns nursing her. After Mittag-Leffler had gone she slept awhile. When she woke she was talkative again but did not mention a husband. She talked about her novel, and about the book of recollections of her youth at Palibino. She said she could do something much better now and started to describe her idea for a new story. She became confused and laughed because she was not doing this more clearly. There was a movement back and forth, she said, there was a pulse in life. Her hope was that in this piece of writing she would discover what went on. Something underlying. Invented, but not.

What could she mean by this? She laughed.

She was overflowing with ideas, she said, of a whole new breadth and importance and yet so natural and self-evident that she couldn't help laughing.

She was worse on Sunday. She could barely speak, but insisted on seeing Fufu in the costume that she was going to wear to a children's party.

It was a Gypsy costume, and Fufu danced in it, around her mother's bed.

On Monday Sophia asked Teresa Gulden to look after Fufu.

That evening she felt better, and a nurse came in to give Teresa and Ellen a rest.

In the early hours of the morning Sophia woke. Teresa and Ellen were wakened from sleep and they roused Fufu that the child might see her mother alive one more time. Sophia could speak just a little.

Teresa thought she heard her say, "Too much happiness."

She died around four o'clock. The autopsy would show her lungs completely ravaged by pneumonia and her heart displaying trouble which went back several years. Her brain, as everybody expected, was large.

. . .

The doctor from Bornholm read of her death in the newspaper, without surprise. He had occasional presentiments, disturbing to one in his profession, and not necessarily reliable. He had thought that avoiding Copenhagen might preserve her. He wondered if she had taken the drug he had given her, and if it had brought her solace, as it did, when necessary, to him.

Sophia Kovalevsky was buried in what was then called the New Cemetery, in Stockholm, at three o'clock in the afternoon of a still cold day when the breath of mourners and onlookers hung in clouds on the frosty air.

A wreath of laurel came from Weierstrass. He had said to his sisters that he knew he would never see her again.
He lived for six more years.

Maksim came from Beaulieu, summoned by Mittag-Leffler's telegram before her death. He arrived in time to speak at the funeral, in French, referring to Sophia rather as if she had been a professor of his acquaintance, and thanking the Swedish nation on behalf of the Russian nation for giving her a chance to earn her living (to use her knowledge in a worthy manner, he said) as a mathematician.

• • •

Maksim did not marry. He was allowed after some time to return to his homeland, to lecture in Petersburg. He founded the Party for Democratic Reform in Russia, taking a stand for constitutional monarchy. The czarists found him much too liberal. Lenin, however, denounced him as a reactionary.

Fufu practiced medicine in the Soviet Union, dying there in the mid-fifties of the twentieth century. She had no interest in mathematics, so she said.

Sophia's name has been given to a crater on the moon.

Acknowledgments

I discovered Sophia Kovalevsky ("Too Much Happiness") while searching for something else in the *Britannica* one day. The combination of novelist and mathematician immediately caught my interest, and I began to read everything about her I could find. One book enthralled me beyond all others, and so I must record my indebtedness, my immense gratitude, to the author of *Little Sparrow: A Portrait of Sophia Kovalevsky* (Ohio University Press, Athens, Ohio, 1983), Don H. Kennedy, and his wife, Nina, a collateral descendent of Sophia's, who provided quantities of texts translated from the Russian, including portions of Sophia's diaries, letters and numerous other writings.

I have limited my story to the days leading up to Sophia's death, with flashbacks to her earlier life. But I do urge anybody interested to read the Kennedys' book, which presents such historical and mathematical riches.

June 2009

Alice Munro
Clinton, Ontario
Canada

Center Point Publishing
600 Brooks Road ● PO Box 1
Thorndike ME 04986-0001 USA

(207) 568-3717

US & Canada:
1 800 929-9108
www.centerpointlargeprint.com